A PUB IN
THE
UNDERWORLD

A PUB IN THE UNDERWORLD

THE COZY ABYSS BOOK 1

HARMON COOPER

Podium

For every reader who has touched the abyss and dared to dream of a cozy haven beyond it. This journey is as much yours as it is mine.

All rights reserved. No part of this publication may be reproduced, stored in a retrieval system, or transmitted in any form or by any means electronic, mechanical, photocopying, recording, or otherwise without prior written permission from Podium Publishing.

This is a work of fiction. Names, characters, places, and incidents are either products of the author's imagination or used fictitiously. Any resemblance to actual events, locales, or persons, living, dead, or undead, is entirely coincidental.

Copyright © 2024 by Harmon Cooper

Cover design by Daniel Kamarudin

ISBN: 978-1-0394-4839-1

Published in 2024 by Podium Publishing
www.podiumaudio.com

A PUB IN THE UNDERWORLD

CHAPTER ONE

WELCOME TO THE UNDERWORLD

The last thing Sylas Runewulf remembered was the sharp sting of an iron blade followed by a flash of darkness.

He came to consciousness some time later with a gasp, one that brought with it the acrid smell of a war that had raged endlessly. Scattered around Sylas were discarded shields, swords, pikes, great battleaxes, and bodies. So many bodies.

The moans of the injured were what ultimately stirred Sylas into action.

He winced as he discovered a wound from his lower back up to the side of his ribcage, a throbbing reminder of how close he had just come to death.

But Sylas still had some fight left in him.

He placed his hand on his muddied helmet as a spark of defiance in the pit of his belly kindled something deep within. Sylas could hear the fight, from clashing blades to desperate shouts.

He had to get there.

He had to join the others.

With all his might, everything he could muster, Sylas pushed himself to his feet. He took a shaky step forward, sucked in a deep breath, and ignored the blooming pain across his side.

Ahead, something gleamed in the thick gray fog that had covered the battlefield. His sword. Sylas staggered toward it and gingerly pulled the blade from beneath the body of a sworn enemy, a knight of the Shadowthorne Empire.

Both hands gripping his blade, Sylas turned in the direction of the battle.

A relic of his past flashed before him as he stood there dazed, Sylas mere moments away from seizing whatever destiny he had left. It was one of the stranger visions Sylas had experienced in a long time.

The jovial crowds at The Old Lamplighter, the smell of the stews, the pervasive aroma of aged oak, the ale sloshing in the casks as he hoisted them up the stairs to help his father, the malty sweetness that seemed to be baked into the walls, and the laughter. So much laughter and merriment. The memory was real, almost as if he had somehow been transported back to the pub, away from this wretched battlefield.

It felt like a lifetime ago, and it was.

Sylas had been part of this war for ten years now. The only ales he'd had since his days at The Old Lamplighter were given to him in leather flasks, part of his rations. Yet even this simple memory of his youth spent working in his father's pub was enough to push him forward.

There had to be a better life waiting for Sylas somewhere.

He merely needed to get there.

Sylas dragged his sword over a ridge, the battle-hardened warrior finally getting his second wind once he saw the fight below. The ominous red Shadowthorne flags on the horizon overpowered the gold of the Aurum Kingdom.

His side was losing.

Sylas brought his sword to the ready.

He shouted at the tops of his lungs and took off toward the battle. What followed was a mix of crimson and battlefield grime as Sylas cut down two of the Shadowthorne knights. He rallied the soldiers that were left, the Royal Guard joining him in his epic push forward.

Ignoring the burning pain in his side, Sylas fought harder than he ever had before, his focus so intense, his strikes so powerful, that to many that day it would seem as if he had been possessed by one of the gods.

The rally was working. Hope was on the horizon until it was suddenly stripped away.

"The enemy approaches!" one of Sylas's fellow soldiers shouted.

"Hold steady!" yelled another.

The ground rumbled as a cavalry of mounted Shadowthorne knights charged into the fray: the Vanguard, as they were known. They made quick work of Sylas's men, and soon, Sylas found himself all alone, surrounded by a menacing tide of foes.

"He's the last one," said one of the Vanguard knights as he pointed his sword at Sylas.

After conferring with the mounted knight next to him, the man returned his focus to Sylas, who stood before him hunched over, covered in mud, and bleeding profusely from his side.

The Vanguard knight spoke again, "Lay down your weapon, Aurumite. You will be taken prisoner. The Shadowthorne Empire will—"

Sylas lifted his blade and glared at the man through the slit on his helmet. He knew all too well what the Shadowthorne Empire did to their prisoners.

He spat blood onto the ground in defiance.

In the end, it wasn't the mounted Vanguard knight that brought Sylas Runewulf down. It wasn't a stray arrow, a pikeman, nor was it a battleaxe.

It was Sylas's injury from earlier, the one he could barely remember getting.

A newfound sense of weakness sent Sylas to his knees. His surroundings swirled into an array of blinding lights. A distant roar like that of the ocean brought a cold sensation that spread through his body, signaling death.

His time had come, but Sylas's story wasn't over yet.

A stark silence gave way to a sense of weightlessness that Sylas hadn't felt in years. It was the weightlessness of youth, of good health, of warm summers spent at The Old Lamplighter.

A pull at the center of his chest interrupted this weightlessness and a blinding flash drew Sylas forward.

The tapestry of his life unspooled as Sylas flew toward the light, the good and the bad, the triumphant and the tragic all behind him. His victories, the honors, and the camaraderie of his fellow soldiers were lumped into the same moving images as his failures, the betrayals, the violence, the life Sylas had wasted fighting, and the constant wish at the back of his mind to finally go home, for the war to end.

Sylas collided with the light and abruptly found himself dwarfed by a giant gate made of purple metal, one that loomed overhead. The gate was flanked by the statues of beasts Sylas had never seen before, demonic in nature, with long snouts, barbed tails, and sharp teeth.

A strange compulsion called him forward.

As the gate began to open, a prompt appeared before Sylas rimmed in blue:

[Welcome to the Underworld.]

CHAPTER TWO

THE PERFECT ASSIGNMENT

The purple gate fizzled away and was replaced by a darkened forest. Sylas looked down at his hands and noticed that there was something different about them. Gone were his gauntlets, the blood, and the battlefield muck. They were now coated in the slight glow of magic, golden in nature.

A new prompt appeared:

[Continue to Ember Hollow to receive your assignment.]

"Ember Hollow? Did it say I was in the Underworld?" Sylas looked ahead, where he found a wooden sign with arrows pointed to several locations. Like his hands, it too had a soft golden glow to it.

Sylas read some of the names: *Duskhaven, Cinderpeak, Battersea, The Hexveil*. There were more. He found Ember Hollow and started in that direction.

Sylas had only taken a few steps when he started to feel as if something was missing. He placed his hand where the hilt of his sword should have been and felt a pang of apprehension.

He no longer had a weapon, nor did he wear any of his battlefield armor. Instead, he wore a tunic, a pair of trousers, and leather boots that seemed to be aged perfectly.

He lowered his hand.

Sylas wasn't as scared as he should have been, but he did feel the need for some security. He found a fallen limb and used his foot to break it into a piece that would work as a club.

He rested his makeshift weapon over his shoulder and continued on. "Better."

As he stepped past an old campfire, one that hadn't been used in weeks,

Sylas stopped to examine a slight orange glow that hadn't existed just moments ago. He crouched in front of the ash and reached his hand out to it. The golden energy stretched from his fingers to the fire, igniting it.

Sylas pulled his hand away and examined his fingertips, which were now warm.

Not certain of what had just happened, Sylas turned away from the fire, club over his shoulder. Aside from the campsite, he saw no signs of human activity, yet the path ahead seemed well maintained.

"To Ember Hollow," Sylas said as he continued on. "Whatever that is."

He came to a hill. Once Sylas reached the top, he saw the first signs of civilization in a valley below. An array of stone and timber structures were huddled around a plaza covered in weeds. There was a large tree in the center of the village, one that seemed on the verge of death. Cobblestone pathways extended outward from the center, the streets around them narrow, empty, and partially covered in moss.

"Is this Ember Hollow?"

If so, it didn't seem like there was anyone out for Sylas to ask. He noticed a couple of lights on in a few of the buildings. Maybe he could knock on a door and ask some questions.

As Sylas started off toward the village, a new prompt came to him:

[**You have reached Ember Hollow. You have been given the deed to the local pub. Reach the pub and claim your ownership.**]

"A pub . . . in the Underworld?" Sylas read the text again, just to be certain.

A rare smile took shape on his face, one at odds with the trauma he had just experienced on the battlefield. This brought another thought. Sylas noticed then that he didn't feel anything about his recent death. No remorse, no shock, no anxiety for what was to come.

It almost felt like Sylas wasn't dead, but merely dreaming.

Was any of this true? Was he supposed to believe the prompt? Was he really in the Underworld?

"Mister," came an old, haggard voice.

Sylas looked to his left to see a man seated with his back to a wheelbarrow, one that he hadn't noticed while reading the text. The man had a flimsy hat on his head, one that obscured his eyes. He reached a shaky hand to Sylas. "Spare some Mana Lumens?"

"Mana Lumens?"

"Just a little," the man coughed. "Getting low myself. I don't want to get sent to the Chasm on the account of MLus."

Sylas shook his head. "M-L-yous?"

"Mana Lumens. MLus. You call them something else?"

"You want mana, magic?" Sylas remembered what it had been like to hold his hand over the ashes earlier, how he had reignited the flames. He took a step closer to the man.

Could the stranger be referring to that?

Sylas reached his hand down and the older man grabbed it. The hat on his head fell back revealing a pair of yellow eyes, a burnt face, and a sinister set of teeth.

Sylas tried to pull away, but the older man held tight. He began to feel lightheaded. His heart pounding in his chest, Sylas's legs buckled as he fought to keep consciousness.

"Hey!" came a female voice off to his right.

A bolt of golden mana struck the wheelbarrow, causing the stranger to fall backward and lose his grip on Sylas's hand. The older man morphed into a hideous creature and took off into the woods, leaving Sylas alone with the woman.

Sylas took one look at her, and his vision started to fade.

This wasn't the first time that Mira had seen a newcomer fall prey to a trickster demon, the kind that her uncle actively hunted. These creatures hailed from the Chasm, and they came to the Underworld by breaking through the Hexveil, which wasn't very far from Ember Hollow.

Mira propped the newcomer she had just saved up against the wheelbarrow. "You can't trust anyone here."

The newcomer's calloused hands and his arms covered in deep scars told Mira all she needed to know about who he had been before he died. He had a medium-length beard that was a mix of dark and light hairs that did little to obscure a handsome face. What was left of his soul was held in his eyes, which were a piercing blue that glowed as bright as mana.

His eyes were the first thing Mira noticed once she started healing him using a balm she had created, the way they drew her in and pushed her away with their coldness.

Sylas blinked a few times as he took the woman in, his vision steadying. "Who are you?"

The woman before him wore a purple dress with a high-waisted belt, the buckle made of silver. Her long hair, dark as a starless night, contrasted heavily with her silver eyes.

He wasn't certain of who she was, but he was certain she had just saved him.

"What's your name?" she asked, her voice soft and instantly soothing.

"I could ask you the same question," Sylas told her as he got to his feet. He turned away from the woman, not ready to accept how enchanted he had just been by her beauty.

It could be another trap.

She placed her hands on her waist. "If you were to ask me the same question, I would tell you my name is Mira Ravenbane. I am Ember Hollow's apothecary."

"Ember Hollow, huh?" Sylas looked ahead toward the village. "Good. This is where I need to be."

"Is it?" she asked.

"'Continue to Ember Hollow to get your assignment.' That's what I was told." Thinking of the prompt caused it to appear before Sylas again, the words glowing. "Well, here I am."

"Yes, here you are," Mira told him. "You still haven't told me your name, nor have you thanked me for saving you."

"Thanks for that." Sylas took another step forward and felt a rush of pain. He brought his hand to his chest.

"Easy. You're still weak from having your MLus stolen. I only provided a little when I healed you."

"MLus?" Sylas asked. "There's that word again."

"Mana Lumens. We call them MLus."

"The man mentioned something about that, MLus."

"That was no man."

Sylas looked down at the faint glow around his arms. "So it is mana. Huh. Is this really the Underworld?"

"It is. I'm sure you're confused."

"I am not as confused as I should be considering I just died." He ran his hand over his beard. "I can't believe I'm able to say something like that."

"I know that feeling. We all do. Do you remember what you were told when you reached Ember Hollow? Try to remember."

Sylas recalled the prompt that had come to him right before his Mana Lumens had been stolen from him. Thinking about it produced the prompt again:

[You have been given the deed to the local pub. Reach the pub and claim your ownership.]

"A pub," he said. "I have been given the deed to a pub."

Sylas's eyes lit up, which was something that Mira certainly noticed. They'd been so cold just moments ago, but now they shone like he was reliving a fond memory. Mira had a feeling this would change when he saw the pub itself, which was in utter disarray. It had been like this since before she arrived a few years ago.

According to her uncle, the pub's closing was one that led to the mass exodus of people that used to live in Ember Hollow. The pub had been a meeting place, a third space where people could gather and discuss their past and current lives. Once it closed, the people of Ember Hollow moved on to the bigger cities of the Underworld.

Mira looked the rugged man over again. To find out that he'd been assigned the vacant pub in Ember Hollow was quite the development.

"I can show you to the pub," she finally told him. "If you tell me your name."

"I'm Sylas Runewulf. Or at least I was."

"You still are. That part doesn't change."

"Good to know."

Mira mulled the name over and found its coarse, enigmatic ring oddly fitting. Sylas was, after all, the stranger who had just shown up to Ember Hollow with a deed to the pub and had cheated a second death in the process.

Instead of saying anything else to her, Sylas found the club he'd been carrying. He picked it up and rested it on his shoulder. "Some good this thing did me." He turned back to Mira to find that she was still looking at him curiously. "What?"

"Nothing," she finally said. "It's just been a while since we've had a newcomer. Come. I'll show you to the pub."

"Thanks. Before you do, can you tell me more about these Mana Lumens? I just want to be prepared next time."

"Yes. MLus. First, you must learn how to access them."

Sylas cocked an eyebrow at her. "Access them?"

"What were you in the mortal realm?"

"Me?" Sylas shook his head. Of course she was talking to him. "I was a soldier in the Aurum Kingdom's Royal Guard."

"I see." Mira nearly placed a hand over her mouth, her suspicions confirmed. She'd heard all about the Royal Guard from her uncle, a former lord commander in the Shadowthorne Vanguard, the Aurum Kingdom's sworn enemies. After all, she had grown up on the border of the two kingdoms.

"Did I say something?" Sylas asked as he registered the concern on her face.

"Let's sidestep that for now," she said, not wanting to talk about her uncle. "I am curious about your life in the mortal realm. Archmages. Heard of them? They have a rudimentary knowledge of Mana Lumens, MLus, but nothing like we have here in the Underworld."

"I know archmages," Sylas told her.

What he didn't say was that he'd killed a good many of the Shadowthorne variety in one of the trickier fights of his life. Swords and shields did little against bolts of searing mana, but an ambush was an ambush, and Sylas had survived that encounter.

"MLus, mana, are what keep you alive here."

"But I thought I was dead?" Sylas tried to make this sound funny, but it only made him feel sad. His sadness wasn't for his own sake, it was for the sake of the brothers of the Royal Guard. He was particularly fond of a few of them, some of whom had died over the years. This brought another question to the forefront of his mind. Were some of them here in the Underworld as well? Kael, Quinlan, and Raelis? Would he be able to find them?

Sylas would need to ask the apothecary later, once he knew the world better.

"There are worse things than being dead, namely ending up in the Chasm. There are better things as well." Mira tilted her head back. "Do you see the clouds?"

"Yeah, I see them." Sylas glanced to the sky, where the gold-rimmed clouds were at odds with the gloom he sensed of the Underworld. "Never seen a sky like this."

"There are three realms for those that pass on. The Chasm is the worst of the three. The Celestial Plains, above, are the best."

"Those are the Celestial Plains?" Sylas had heard of the Celestial Plains. Battlefield prayers often mentioned them. They also mentioned the Chasm, the pits of hell itself. But to his knowledge, they never mentioned the Underworld. "So we're between the two."

She nodded. "That's one way to look at it. And if you run out of MLus, you will pass on to the Chasm. You will die again."

"Again?"

"The trickster demon you just encountered was most certainly someone who lived here in the Underworld and moved on to the Chasm. My point? Lose all your MLus, and you will move on as well."

"And you said I could access this information somehow?"

"The same way you produced the prompt earlier. Simply think of your MLus, and they'll appear. You'll see your class as well, but given the fact you have the deed to a pub, I'm guessing it will be something to do with that."

Sylas bit his lip and tried to think of Mana Lumens, which turned out to be an exercise in something quite abstract. He was just about to give up when they appeared along with his name and class.

Name: Sylas Runewulf
Mana Lumens: 23/100
Class: Brewer

"I only have a hundred total?"

"You just arrived. Did you expect to have a thousand?"

He laughed at Mira's playful, yet derisive tone. "I don't really know what to expect."

"MLus are life force. When you expend too much energy, you *lose* MLus. When you purchase things, you *use* MLus. When you sleep, you *gain* MLus. If you reach zero, you pass on."

"And the pub? What does my assignment at the pub have to do with any of this aside from my class?"

Mira turned to the center of the village and motioned for him to follow. "Good question. Once you get the pub up and running, you'll gain MLus for every ale that you sell. You can also gain MLus through other things, like forming quest contracts with—you know what? I'd rather not confuse you with this early on. I'll show you to the pub, I'll explain some things, and I'll top off your MLus before I leave. How's that?"

"Won't that take away from your power?" Sylas asked as he caught up with her. While graceful, Mira moved swiftly, almost as if she was floating.

"I'm the apothecary. I gain power overnight when I help those in need."

"And you think I'm in need?" Sylas smirked at his own question. "I guess that checks out."

"It does. I hope you know something about running a pub."

The grin on Sylas's face widened considerably.

Sylas Runewulf knew two things in life: one was waging war, and the other was running a pub. While he didn't like the fact that he was dead—who would?—he was interested in seeing the pub.

"And be thinking of a name for the pub as well," Mira told him.

"I've already got one in mind."

CHAPTER THREE

FOUR INGREDIENTS

The pub was certainly in need of repair. The paint was badly chipped and fading, and upon quick glance, Sylas saw that the gutter was clogged with leaves and grime. The roof had shingles that needed replacing, and its once sturdy timber structure now sagged, much of the building reclaimed by ivy and moss. While the door was locked tight, Sylas got the feeling that he'd be able to shoulder through it if he wanted.

A glowing prompt flashed in front of Sylas as he examined the roof again.

[You have reached the pub. Claim your ownership.]

"How do I claim my ownership?" Sylas asked Mira the apothecary, even though he really wanted to ask her *why* he would claim ownership of such a rundown place.

Mira smoothed her hands over her purple dress. This wasn't the first time she'd seen someone unenthused about the assignment that the Underworld system had given them.

But Sylas was lucky to have an assignment.

Many didn't actually get assignments, and were forced to fend for themselves and figure out ways to survive in an environment that could be quite unforgiving. There was always the option of having an archlumen give someone a new class, but that cost a lot of Mana Lumens.

"You claim ownership by forming a bond with the structure. You can't form this with any structure you come across unless you change your class or purchase it with fixed MLus. You're classed as a brewer, hence the deed to the pub."

"Indeed I am." Sylas gave her a skeptical look. "So you want me to touch it?"

"That or cast your hand out at the pub with the intent of ownership."

"With the intent of ownership," Sylas said under his breath as he stepped up to the old door. He put his hand out as if he were casting a spell and knocked on the door instead.

It shone with a golden hue before settling.

[The pub is now yours. What would you like to name it?]

"The Old Lamplighter," Sylas told the prompt without hesitation.

The door popped open in response.

Sylas looked back to Mira, who crossed her arms over her chest. "I hope it's not too bad in there," she said.

Sylas, who still had his wooden club resting on one shoulder, shrugged her statement away. He had encountered buildings in far graver disrepair than the pub. Compared to the sights he'd seen over the years—thriving communities turned to ash, abandoned villages overrun by rats and ruled by ravenous packs of wolves—the pub was practically a sanctuary of order and maintenance.

With this in mind, Sylas stepped in, where he waited for Mira to join him. He scanned the space from the bar to the back door. "Not bad, huh?" he asked, ignoring the dust.

Mira pinched her nose. "This place reeks."

"It is definitely fragrant," Sylas told her as he took a short inhale in through his nostrils. The musty odor of age and damp wood was brightened by a yeasty scent. As he approached the bar—which was covered in dust and discarded bottles, the stools all broken—this smell mixed with the faint metallic tang of rust permeating from the old taps that were no longer usable.

Sylas took another step forward and the floorboard creaked.

As he started to explore, Mira watched Sylas with hesitation. He seemed to be both in over his head and yet entirely comfortable in this environment. He certainly was a peculiar man.

Mira followed behind him as Sylas ran his hand through the dust on one of the tables. She was exceedingly careful of where she stepped. She'd seen people fall through floorboards before, yet this thought didn't seem to even cross the newcomer's mind as he explored the place.

After shuffling around some of the broken furniture, Sylas reached a trapdoor that he immediately propped open to reveal a set of stairs. "Ah, the cellar," he told her. "We'd better take a look." He glanced across from the cellar to another set of stairs leading to a second floor. "Or do you want to take the stairs first?"

Mira took another look around the dim and stuffy space, to the thick cobwebs in the corners and holes in the walls that were large enough for rats to fit through. She'd seen no signs of rodents, not even their droppings, which made her curious.

Rather than answer Sylas, she turned back toward the center of the pub and closed her eyes. As much as she didn't want to, Mira took a deep breath in through her nostrils and closed her eyes as she used one of her powers to examine the active Mana Lumens in the space.

A subtle outline took shape, one that led up the stairs. "That makes sense."

"What makes sense?"

Mira tensed up, the woman clearly in some sort of trance. Sylas watched her for a moment, not certain of what she was doing.

One thing he'd learned as a soldier in the Royal Guard was to read people's quirks. While Mira had undeniable charm, there was something distant in her silvery eyes, something entirely odd about her gait and the way she held herself. Mira seemed like the type to get lost in her own thoughts. Considering she had figured out how to survive in the Underworld, Sylas couldn't blame her.

The apothecary finally lowered her shoulders. "Let's check the cellar first."

"Follow me." Sylas took the steps down to find an even damper space below, one that was a few degrees colder and smelled of wet stone. He was about to comment that it was too dark to see when a lamp came on above him.

"Good. It still works," Mira told him.

"What does?"

"The lumen lamps down here. The ones in the main space are all broken."

The golden glow cast by a single hanging rusty lamp showed Sylas all he needed to know about the pub's capabilities.

Small casks were stacked on a shelf against the stone wall, twelve in total. Straw had been used to prevent the small casks from rolling away, bits of which were scattered across an uneven floor. Whole portions of the cobblestone were sunk into the ground, but this didn't bother Sylas as he approached a table with dried herbs on it, most of them practically dust.

He spotted a large chopping block in the corner near a kiln, a grinder, an oven, and a stove. There was also a rack of empty growlers, the glass dark and murky, and plenty of pints, all of which needed to be thoroughly scrubbed. He also saw cleaning and kitchen supplies next to a storeroom for grains. Sylas checked this room and found that there was a large barrel here, likely for barley, and a few smaller ones, all bigger than the casks.

"Grains, water, hops, and yeast. Four ingredients to make ale," he said as he showed Mira the number four with his fingers. Sylas finally removed the club from his shoulder and set it on the wooden table in the center of the cellar.

"Where do I get them? I'm going to need an oast as well. Didn't see one out back, but maybe I missed it. I suppose I can soak and germinate the grains here, but that's not ideal. There's a kiln here and a grinder, that'll help. It'll take at least a week if not longer to get started."

"To make ale?" Mira asked, feeling foolish as soon as this question left her lips. She turned, prepared to blush, but ultimately didn't have to as Sylas sent his fingers through the dust on the table. She quickly corrected herself, "You will brew ale with MLus, not the way you have done it in the past."

"Really?"

"Well, you would still need the ingredients first, but after you had them, you'd continue the operation with MLus."

She watched as Sylas placed his hand on his chin, the same hand that he had just run through the dust on the table. Mira frowned, but ultimately didn't say anything as she continued her explanation, "Remember what I told you earlier about MLus being your life force and at the same time being the currency of our world?"

Sylas grunted a positive response.

"It is also how you create things. Once you have the ingredients, you will use MLus to create ale."

"So mana to make ale. And what's with the tiny casks?" Sylas gestured to the casks arranged by the wall. "They're more like portable kegs. Not the kind of casks I'm used to."

"I don't know the answer to that question, but yes, you will use mana to make ale, then you will sell this ale for MLus. You will have to pay some attention not to overextend yourself."

"Overextend myself? What do you mean?"

"If you sell too much, if you run out of MLus, you'll move on to the Chasm. If you sell just the right amount, and orchestrate it in a way that allows you to continually increase the amount of MLus you can keep on reserve, you'll grow . . ." Mira offered him an uncertain smile. How newcomers took this next part was a sign of their character. She was starting to feel a fondness for Sylas, and hoped he didn't take her next statement in the wrong way. "You'll grow stronger than you can possibly imagine."

Her words had little to no effect on the man, which was a relief to Mira. "And the max amount of MLus I can have is a hundred?"

Mira shook her head. "There is no max, but the more you have, the stronger you become and the more you're able to do with Mana Lumens. Right now, you have how much?"

Sylas accessed his status.

Name: Sylas Runewulf
Mana Lumens: 23/100
Class: Brewer

"Twenty-three."

"When you rest, you'll gain more. But you'll also spend more doing things like rebuilding the pub—if that's what you want to do, I'm going to assume it is—and venturing outside of town, which you'll need to do to get the initial ingredients."

Sylas sent his slightly dusty hand through his beard again. It amused him to some degree the way Mira both noticed this and tried not to notice it at the same time. "I think I get it. And I'm guessing I'll probably need some help along the way."

The apothecary turned away from him. "I'm sure you will. Now come, let's head upstairs. I believe there's a surprise waiting for us. But you should grab your club just in case. Always be prepared here in the Underworld."

CHAPTER FOUR

PATCHES, GUARDIAN OF THE TAVERNLY REALM

The stairs that weren't missing were creaky and Sylas was careful not to fall through. It was certainly something he would need to fix over the coming days.

"Easy enough," Sylas said as he reached the top floor of the pub, where he found a long hallway with four rooms, one of which was at the end. Sylas loved a good wood floor, and was glad to find the upstairs had the same sturdy wood as the pub below, worn smooth by years of foot traffic. He also liked the emerald-green wallpaper, hand-decorated with scenes of gardens, which was in decent shape. The smell, however, was no better than it had been downstairs, the yeasty scent replaced by the overpowering pungence of mildew.

Someone needed to open a window or three.

"Whatever you do first, please air this place out," Mira said.

"Doable. No light in here either." Sylas pointed at a few empty sconces.

"You can pick up some lumen lamps and install them, like the one you have in the basement."

"Good point." Sylas tried to open the first door he came to and found it to be locked. He thought about forcing his way through but decided against this when Mira moved on.

"You can check the rooms later. Just remember that any door you force open will have to be repaired. Is that something you're actually able to do?" Mira turned to him, a scrutinizing look on her face. "Well?"

"Repair stuff? Sure." Sylas stepped past the locked door. "I used to do all sorts of things when I was younger, before I was drafted into the war." He didn't elaborate, and he was glad Mira didn't press him to. "What's this surprise you were going on about down there?"

"Yes, the surprise. Let's keep checking the rooms." Mira opened the next door to reveal a space with a single bed. Aside from the threadbare linens on the bed, there was a small nightstand and a desk that sat in front of a murky window. "For one of your future guests. Also, it looks like you can open this window."

Sylas popped the window open and nodded. "Good. That's a start."

While it didn't happen often at the pub in his youth, there were several occasions where someone was too drunk to make it home. In this case, they usually stayed the night in a room that later went on their tab.

"What do we have here?" Mira asked after she opened the door across from the guest room. "Nice, a washroom. And it's clean."

Sylas peeked his head in to find that the washroom was indeed clean, aside from a layer of dust on everything. "Is this the surprise?"

"Not yet," Mira said as they came to the final room at the end of the hallway, the door slightly ajar. "After you," she told Sylas.

"Is this what I need to be ready for?"

"You need to be ready for anything in the Underworld, but yes." Mira watched Sylas use the end of his wooden club to carefully push the door open. He did so cautiously, and by the way he stood, it was clear that he felt like he needed to protect her to some degree.

This amused Mira. If anyone needed protection, it was a newcomer. She'd already proven that point earlier when she'd saved him from the shape-shifting demon.

"Anyone home?" Sylas asked as he peeked inside the darkened room. He gave Mira an unconvincing look. "You're just trying to scare me, aren't you?"

"Not at all. Aren't you going to go inside?"

"How do I know you aren't a demon like the one from earlier?" Sylas asked her.

"Ha! If I was a demon, would I have led you to your cozy little pub?"

"It's not cozy yet." Sylas stepped into the final room, Mira doing the same.

As soon as she was in, she cast her hand out at the lumen lamp, which brightened the room to some degree.

"Not bad, not bad at all," Sylas said as he looked around the lofty space. "I'm guessing this is the owner's suite."

"Or you could sleep in the smaller bedroom."

"I think this will do just fine," he said as he examined the ceiling. The slanted roof followed the roofline, yet it was quite high. The bed was larger than the one in the other room, and there was a desk with some old books on it, the pages brittle and yellow with age.

Sylas was just approaching the desk when an overweight black-and-white cat burst out of the closet. The piebald cat collided with Sylas's leg, scratched him, and tried to bolt away only to lose his footing and slide toward the open door.

Mira started laughing. "Surprise!"

"The surprise was a fat pub cat? Look how big he is." Sylas grinned at the heavy cat, who now sat by the door, examining the two of them.

"He's the reason there are no rats here. You should be thanking him."

"He's done a damn good job, I'll give him that. Scratched me too." Sylas chuckled. "I thought that was a wild boar for a second, especially the way he collided with me. We had to deal with those sometimes in Old Tucker's Thicket. Nasty critters."

The cat's eyebrows narrowed on Sylas.

"Do you think he understand me?"

Mira crouched in front of the black-and-white cat. She calmly reached her hand out to it. The cat looked from Sylas to Mira, gave Sylas a proud huff, and strutted over to Mira to get his ears scratched. "The animals you encounter here aren't like the ones from our previous world."

"What do you mean?"

"Sometimes, they have powers. I haven't met ones that can understand humans, but I have seen some with powers."

"Powers?" Sylas looked the piebald pub cat over.

"Yes, abilities."

"Abilities? He doesn't look like he has any of those to me."

Mira shrugged. "You never know."

"Eh, I guess he'll need a name too if he's sticking around." Sylas scratched the back of his head. He plopped down onto the bed and watched as Mira continued to pet the overweight black-and-white cat. "How about Patches?" he asked.

"That's a cute name."

"Patches." Sylas reached his hand out the cat. The cat gave him a defiant look. "Come on, buddy," he said. "Come on, Patches."

"Just offer him a little love." Mira approached. She looked down at Sylas, and was just about to sit on the bed next to him when she thought otherwise. "Watch."

Mira turned her palm toward the cat. A bit of golden mana took shape, the energy pulsing. Patches rushed over to her. To better reach her palm, the cat hopped up onto the bed and nearly jumped off.

"He's attracted to mana. This is the same thing patrons will use to pay for their ales here at the . . ." Mira looked up at Sylas. "What was the name again?"

"The Old Lamplighter."

"Yes, The Old Lamplighter." She placed her glowing hand on Patches's head. The cat purred so loudly that the bed shook.

Sylas turned his hand around and focused on his calloused palm. The glow that followed was much dimmer than what Mira could produce, but it was enough to draw the cat's attention.

Patches came forward, cautious as ever.

His whiskers twitched, his nostrils flared, and then he relaxed. The piebald pub cat gave into Sylas's influence and pressed his head into his open hand. Patches looked up at Sylas with a set of big green eyes.

"Well, I think I'll be on my way," Mira said. "You should make plans for tomorrow and rest. There's a lot to do around here. Maybe I'll stop by?"

"Sure," Sylas told her. "What about ingredients?"

"Yes, those. You'll need those. See how many MLus you can recharge overnight. I'll be back in the morning to help you gather some ingredients."

"You'd do that?" Sylas asked as he continued to pet the cat.

"Sure. We were all newcomers at one point, from here to Battersea."

"Which is?"

Mira smiled at Sylas. "We'll save a geography lesson for later. Bye, for now, and try not to get restless and go out. You should sleep. You might feel strong, but the shift from being alive to being in the Underworld will sneak up on you."

Sylas yawned.

"See?"

"Maybe you're right," he said as he relaxed a bit. "See you tomorrow."

Mira left The Old Lamplighter. She stopped outside of the entrance and looked up at the light that was on upstairs. She'd never seen the light on in the pub before. She knew that others in the village would see it too.

This would prove both good and bad. Things would get more complicated once Mira's uncle, a respected former Shadowthorne lord commander, and current head of the Ember Hollow militia, got wind of the newcomer.

Mira's uncle was naturally suspicious, and his suspicion would only intensify upon discovering the pub's new owner was from the Aurum Kingdom.

It was too early to tell, but she suspected there would be trouble.

Rats.

It was almost morning when Patches pushed himself to his feet. He listened intently to a noise downstairs, his ears twitching.

The sound came from the basement.

Patches licked his lips, stretched, and quietly hopped off the bed. The piebald pub cat looked over his shoulder at the big sleeping man. Patches didn't know exactly how to feel about the snoring newcomer yet, but he had a feeling that he would be sticking around.

As the self-appointed Guardian of the Tavernly Realm, Patches welcomed the company, especially if the man brought the place back to its former glory.

Happy patrons were a much easier Mana Lumen fuel source than hunting rats, even if hunting rats kept Patches nice and fit.

He shook his rump. *Well, fit enough,* he thought as he reached the door.

Patches was glad that the medicine woman who had been there earlier hadn't shut the door completely. After taking another look at the big man and confirming he was still asleep, Patches pawed open the door and squeezed his head through the opening. This caused the door to creak loudly, which drew the big man's attention. He stirred, and in doing so, whipped the tattered blanket off him and fell back asleep in a different position.

Patches simply turned himself invisible and moved on.

Easy enough.

Now invisible, Patches took the stairs down to the pub and ignored the sweetsick smell that he'd grown used to over the years. The man had opened several windows upstairs to air the place out. But the realm needed more than that, it also needed a good mopping. Patches had even tried doing this a couple of times using a discarded curtain, but he just couldn't clean as well as a human could.

No matter, now that Patches had an employee, a loyal subject, things in the Tavernly Realm would be looking up soon enough.

Yet there was still the problem of the rats.

Patches knew every nook and cranny of the pub, every entrance big enough for a rat to crawl through, and the best ways to trap them. He wasn't as fast as he'd been in his youth, when he'd first taken ownership of the pub. But being able to turn invisible helped to some degree.

It burned Mana Lumens, but Patches had saved up more of this strange magical power than he knew what to do with. Thinking about his power caused a set of glowing words and numbers to appear before him. Patches couldn't quite read the information, and he certainly didn't know the power was called Mana Lumens, but he could tell that the number was pretty high.

Mana Lumens: 1093/1200
Class: Pub Cat

Patches paused at the steps that led down to the cellar. He focused again on the sound he'd heard. Now concentrating, Patches felt a shift in the Mana Lumens present in the air. It was subtle, but he could feel the change in temperature.

He hesitated. There were rats, and then there were demonic rats, those that had also learned to cultivate and utilize Mana Lumens to some degree. What he was sensing was certainly the latter.

Yet even if he knew that the rat would put up a good fight, Patches needed to deal with it. This was his territory, his pub, his Tavernly Realm. Regardless of if he had a new employee, a loyal subject, it was Patches's job to take care of the place.

He considered his options.

There was a chance he could sneak up on the rat. That would give him some advantage. But he'd encountered these kinds of rats in the past, ones that could actually see him when he was invisible.

In that case, a distraction was in order.

I hate doing this.

Patches crept to the other side of the pub where the rat below wouldn't hear him. He began licking himself, gathering up any loose hairs that he could. This took him a while, but eventually, he was able to hack up a hairball, one consisting of black-and-white fur.

Patches examined it for a moment, his whiskers glowing as the hairball came alive. His hairball slopped forward, leaving a trail behind it. It stopped at the entrance to the cellar.

Patches approached. Yet again, he felt the dark pull of demonic Mana Lumens below. He heard more scurrying. In listening to the rat, Patches came to the conclusion that it was probably close to half his size.

He needed to act fast.

To better his odds, Patches enhanced the size of his teeth until they rivaled that of the wolves that lived in the woods beyond Ember Hollow. He focused on his claws, watching them grow until they were each about an inch long, bathed in golden power, and razor sharp.

Patches couldn't see himself in a mirror, but he knew by the time he'd finished his transformation that he was more than double his size. He checked his power levels.

Mana Lumens: 890/1200

Patches intuited that he still had plenty, and he'd be able to recover the rest after his battle through what he liked to call Dream Napping. Plus, there was the rat, which he could eat. Then again, the big man upstairs might be hungry, and the rat would be a good welcoming gift.

I'll figure that out later. Dead rat first.

Patches sent the animated hairball forward.

It hopped down the stairs to the cellar, providing the perfect distraction. Invisible again, Patches crouched and focused on the action below. His vision and hearing synced to the point that he had an almost spatial awareness of the cellar, Patches was now able to see the large rat even if the demonic rodent had yet to approach the hairball.

The rat turned to the hairball, curious as to what had just arrived.

It hesitated.

Come on...

The hairball came alive. It latched onto the rat, which shrieked as it tried to run back toward the wall.

Patches came bounding down the stairs of the cellar. Once he was at the halfway point he launched himself into the air using a burst of Mana Lumens, his belly shifting in front of his body as he landed on the rat.

Patches drove his claws into the rat's sides as the fight quickly became a blur of fangs, fur, claws, and menacing yowls. The demonic rat overpowered Patches, only to be blindsided by the furball, which wrapped around the rodent's head.

Patches used this opportunity to bite into its neck, yet the rat managed to pull away in time to avoid a fatal bite. The rat fled toward a hole in the wall, one that Patches wouldn't be able to fit through. Back on his feet, and hissing with anger now, Patches chased after the rat.

He reached it before the rat could slip into the hole.

Patches bit down onto its tail and yanked the rat to the side. With his sharpened teeth and the strength of his jaws, Patches was able to pull the rat's tail off.

The rodent may have gotten away had it not been for the hairball, which had rushed over to the opening and temporarily blocked it. Patches let out a guttural growl, one that he amplified with Mana Lumens. The bewildering noise created a new opportunity for Patches, who landed a lethal blow, ending the demonic rat's existence.

The rat was dead, and Patches was suddenly tired. But before he rested, it was important that he deliver the rat to the big man upstairs.

The pub was his kingdom, and as the self-appointed Guardian of the Tavernly Realm, Patches wanted his loyal subjects to be happy.

CHAPTER FIVE

GRAINS, WATER, HOPS, AND YEAST

Sylas couldn't tell if it was morning. The window in the roomy loft was too stained with age for him to really make out what time of day it was. Either way, he felt rested enough, and was just sitting up when a new prompt came to him, one with an ominous message.

[You have 89 days until the invasion.]

"Eighty-nine days?" As he rubbed the sleep out of his eyes, Sylas tried to make sense of the new message. "Eighty-nine days until what invasion?"

Rather than dwell on the message, Sylas got out of bed and slipped into his boots. He glanced over to Patches, who now lay on his side in a corner of the room, snoring lightly. "You lazy old thing," he said, a smile forming on his face.

His voice woke the pub cat, who looked over at him, yawned, flipped sides, and went back to sleep.

Once Sylas was ready, he opened the bedroom door to find a dead rat, bigger than any he'd seen before. Patches had apparently ripped its tail off, and the cat had lined it up next to the rat's body.

"Maybe you aren't so lazy after all," Sylas called back into the room.

There was no way around it. Sylas would need to remove the rat from the premises. Sylas headed down to the cellar to fetch the broom and dustpan he'd seen last night. He returned, swept the rat and its tail into the dustpan, and took the rat out behind the pub.

The strange sky of the Underworld greeted Sylas, one illuminated by the clouds of the Celestial Plains above. Only it was brighter now. Was this what morning looked like? Sylas couldn't be sure.

"Now to deal with you," Sylas told the dead rat.

There was a bit of space behind the pub and what looked to be an abandoned building beyond, but certainly nothing large enough to call a yard. Aside from a few mossy stones that led from the back door to a well, the space was empty.

Sylas considered dumping the rat and letting whatever varmint lived in the vicinity take it away. But he didn't want to start a habit like this, and figured he'd bury the rodent instead.

"Which would be easier if there was a shovel," he muttered. In the end, he used one of the flat stepping stones to break into the loose soil, and was able to dig a hole with his boot from there.

He dropped the rat and its tail into the hole. Sylas covered this with dirt, using his boot again, and then put the stepping stone on top of it.

"Sylas?" Mira, who had been watching him kick at the dirt, gave the newcomer a skeptical look. Had he really just dug a hole and buried a rat with his bare hands? He'd also forgotten to lock the front door of the pub, which was dangerous in this part of the Underworld, especially so close to the Hexveil.

"Hey." Sylas looked from Mira to the picnic basket she was holding and back to the hole he'd dug. "Sorry, already ate. Patches left me a treat."

"I saw that. How sweet of him."

Sylas offered her an uncertain grin as he considered mentioning the strange invasion prompt he'd received that morning. He decided against it. "I don't know how he killed the rat. Biggest rat I've ever seen, and I've seen some fairly large ones." He shuddered. "Anyway, to town."

"Yes, to Cinderpeak. I have some things I need to pick up there anyway and I figured I'd show you around. Have you checked your MLus?"

"I have not." Sylas accessed his status and saw he had just over forty Mana Lumens. "At just below the halfway point."

"I figured as much. Eat this." She produced a bread roll from her picnic basket. The crust was flawless, baked to a rich amber shade. Much to her dismay, he took the roll with his dirty right hand and popped it in his mouth.

"Not bad," he said, smacking his lips.

Mira figured he'd at least want to wash his hands, but this didn't seem to be the case. "Right," she said with a grim smile. "Check your MLus now."

She watched his eyes flash as he did so. Sylas looked up at her. "It's back to a hundred. How did you do that?"

"I'm an apothecary. It's what I do. I should say, though, I can't just make these kinds of MLu-powered bread rolls all the time. It takes time and drains me of my ability to make something like that for several days. But it is within the wheelhouse of what I can do. I can heal small amounts, certain injuries, and other medical peccadilloes."

"So you're saying I shouldn't have eaten it so fast?"

"Something like that. Anyway, come on. I have horses waiting for us out front. I wanted to show you what it's like traveling here in the Underworld. You are also able to fast travel using portals, which can be helpful. But you have to activate the portals first."

"Portals?"

"I'll show you what I mean on the way. But we'll want to take horses there, and luckily, my uncle has a pair that we can use."

"Your uncle, huh? You didn't mention you had an uncle. Will we meet him today?" Sylas asked as he followed Mira around to the front of the pub.

"Not today." She stopped at the entrance and handed him the basket. "There is more food in the picnic basket to get you going. I won't be delivering groceries every day, I'm afraid."

"Too bad," he said, a bit of charm behind the smile he was giving her.

Flustered, Mira turned away from Sylas. She entered the pub, placed the picnic basket on the bar, and returned. "And lock the door. It's not safe to leave the doors unlocked here unless you have someone looking after the place."

"I was airing out the place."

"With the doors shut?"

"The windows were open."

"Did you at least close them?"

"Of course I did."

"That's a start."

"What's there to worry about? Patches can watch the place, can't he?" He glanced up the stairs.

"Ha. Lock the door. And definitely air out the place when you get back. It's still pretty musty in there."

"I don't exactly have a key."

"You don't need one. You own the pub. Just wave your hand over the handle."

Sylas did as instructed and the door locked tight. He waved his hand again and it opened. "Now that's useful. Let me lock the back as well."

Once the doors were locked, Sylas got onto a black horse and joined Mira, who rode another black steed, one with red beads braided into its mane.

"How many people live here in Ember Hollow?" he asked.

"Not many, but there are some. Most people keep to themselves, though. We trade, and there's a farmer's market near the Cinderpeak portal."

"Seems pretty sleepy to me."

"Ember Hollow? That would be a polite way to describe it. Try to keep up." She rode ahead, Sylas matching her pace.

"Is that the portal?" Sylas asked after they reached a peculiar-looking structure at the edge of the woods. There were three spires around it and a large rune carved into a platform.

She nodded. "That's it. Go ahead and activate it."

"How exactly?"

"Just go near it."

Sylas led his horse over to the portal. He examined the three stone spires, which had strange characters carved into them. The rune at the base began to glow. "I think that does it."

"Yes, it's activated now. I'll show you how to use it in Cinderpeak."

"And I can use it with the horse?"

Mira laughed. "Certainly not. I'll lead the horses back myself. After all, you want to get started on the pub, right?"

"Right. And I'm going to need some tools to do so. And ingredients."

"Four ingredients, right?"

"Grains, hops, and yeast. The water I can get from the well."

"Did you check the well this morning?" Mira wanted to say something about him failing to wash his hands, but she didn't.

"I did not, why?"

"How do you know it has water?"

"Don't all wells have water?" Sylas smirked at his own question. "I suppose you're right, I should have checked. If it doesn't have water, maybe I can ask the neighbors for some. Maybe if I'm lucky, someone will show up at my doorstep with a picnic basket full of water."

Something in the woods caught Sylas's attention. He pulled the reins, the expression on his face going from happy to incredibly serious.

"What is it?" Mira asked.

"Something moved."

"I didn't see anything."

"I can almost feel it," Sylas said, wishing he'd brought his club along. He hopped down from the horse. "I don't know how to use magic yet, so if something jumps out at us—"

"You want me to do something about it. Got it."

Sylas approached the edge of the trail. He inhaled deeply, and felt something change in the air around him. Sylas still wasn't familiar enough with Mana Lumens to notice the dark side of them, the side that indicated something sinister was in the air, but he could definitely feel something.

Whatever it was, it moved on.

Mira felt it too, but she never told Sylas this. There was a lot he had to learn as a newcomer, and it was best for him to gradually come to understand the

Underworld. She'd seen newcomers rush off into the forest chasing demons, never to return.

He needed to be much stronger before he did something stupid like that.

Sylas mounted up again and they continued on. "I've been wondering something," he told her as they took a small bridge over a bubbling brook of purple-hued water.

"Yes?"

"People from my past. My father, a couple of soldiers I know who died. How would I go about finding them? I mean, I don't know if they're here, but if they were here, how have people done that in the past?"

"Did you make a list?"

"A list?"

"A list of people you hope to find. You should make a list soon. From what I've seen, people tend to forget their loved ones after enough time here."

"I know who they are, and I won't forget them," Sylas said, thinking of his father and three of his closest friends—Raelis Sund, Kael Ashdown, and Kael's brother, Quinlan.

"You might be able to find some of them, but don't forget they could be above, in the Celestial Plains, or beyond, in the Chasm. To do so, you'd have to head to Battersea and speak to an archlumen who has access to the Book of Shadows."

"Book of Shadows. Got it. Another question: How do I know that it's morning?"

"The clouds shine brighter during the day. Stay up tonight and you'll see what I mean. That's how you know. If the clouds are bright, it is day. If they are not, it is night. There really isn't a morning like there was in our world. No sunrise and sunset."

"Yeah? Too bad." Sylas looked back to the forest. He was certain that something had been watching them, and didn't like the fact that he hadn't been able to sniff it out.

Cinderpeak lived up to its namesake. The bustling town was cast in the shadow of a volcano, one with smoke billowing out the top thick enough to blot out the golden clouds of the Celestial Plains. From afar, the village blended in seamlessly with the mountain's blackened terrain, the scattering of homes and businesses built with an artistic harmony that seemed natural once they approached.

Up close, their unique structures became more apparent. With thick stone roofs, the gray buildings of Cinderpeak seemed much stronger than the wooden houses Sylas had seen in Ember Hollow. It was no wonder with the active volcano so near. Yet the soil was clearly fertile, leading to large fields that pressed right up to the woods they had just passed through.

"It's the closest town," Mira told Sylas as they passed through the town gates. "Not the largest in the area, but we end up coming here quite often."

"Because most people have moved away from Ember Hollow."

"That's right," she told him as they passed one of the farms. "For tools, your best bet will be a shop I know in the town center. But for the grains you need, there's a place closer to here."

The two arrived at the Cinderpeak Market, one with a variety of vendors all set up around a huge black stone that looked as if it had been spit out of the volcano. After circling around to the back, they tied their horses off.

"Grains, hops, and yeast," Sylas said as he scanned the market. The sellers here had a variety of fruits and vegetables, many of which Sylas had never seen before. There were luminous mushrooms, berries, and glowing greens, all of which were fresher than anything he'd come across before.

This was also the first time he'd come upon a large crowd of people in the Underworld, Sylas noticing that many were dressed in the type of clothing people wore back when he was alive.

There were tunics and high-waisted trousers, embroidered vests and collared capes. Yet there were also robes and dresses, flowing capes, leather armor, and knee-high boots and sandals. Most of the color schemes fit the Underworld itself—dark, with undertones of purple and hints of a mossy gray green, some of the nicer pieces with gold threading.

They came to a man sharpening knives. Near his shop, a woman sold herbs and spices.

"I need yeast," Sylas told the herbalist, a short woman in a tattered dress and a stained apron. "What are my options?"

The herbalist cocked an eyebrow at him. "You planning on baking something?"

"I'm planning on making ale," he told her.

The herbalist puffed her cheeks out as she looked from Sylas to Mira. She was pretty sure that she recognized the woman—an apothecary out of Ember Hollow?—but she certainly hadn't seen the man before. Maybe he was a newcomer, which would have allowed her to make quite the profit had he not shown up with the woman.

She grumbled at this fact and motioned the two into her shop. "Careful of the hanging garlic."

Sylas ducked under the garlic to find the woman already climbing onto a stool to reach for a high shelf. She hopped down and handed him a glass bottle with a silvery powder inside. He examined it. "I've never seen yeast like this before."

"That's because it's spirit yeast."

"Imbued with MLus," Mira told Sylas. "And usually, it goes for a premium. Just regular yeast will do."

The seller swiped the glass bottle of yeast out of Sylas's hand and returned with another bottle, this one bigger.

"Wait," Sylas said. "How much for the spirit yeast?"

Mira wanted to elbow him. She could make "spirit yeast" herself by simply imbuing the generic stuff with Mana Lumens. She would have told him this too had the seller not launched into a litany of ways the spirit yeast was better, the woman cutting Mira off every time she tried to interject.

"Then that's what we need—"

"No," Mira told Sylas. "Just the regular yeast. How much?"

The seller gave her a scornful look. "Fifty MLus."

Mira grabbed Sylas's arm. "We'll head into the town. There are plenty of bakeries there and a grocer. We can find yeast there—"

"Twenty MLus," the woman said, quickly changing her tune. "It's a bargain, and much cheaper than it is in the city."

Mira offered the woman a short nod. "Pay her."

"Do what?" Sylas asked.

The seller turned her palm toward Sylas, who made a gesture like he was going to put money into it.

[Transfer 20 Mana Lumens to shopkeep? Y/N?]

"Yes," Sylas said, not sure if he was answering the strange prompt or the woman. The seller handed him the yeast and they stepped out of her stall.

"Don't buy anything that has been augmented with MLus," Mira said. "People will call it all sorts of things: spirit, lumened, mana-enhanced. Not until you know more about what you can do. There are certain things that are worth it, items produced by powerful people who have been working with Mana Lumens for a while, like an archlumen or a lumengineer."

"How do I notice the difference?" Sylas asked.

"You'll know. Let's get the grains you need. We'll head to town after, get some supplies, and you can portal back to the pub."

Sylas couldn't help but grin at the apothecary as she charged ahead. Mira was bossy, but sometimes that was necessary. "You would have made a good sergeant, you know that?"

She turned back to him, the stern look on Mira's face instantly softening when she saw Sylas standing there like a big dummy with his bottle of yeast. "A what?" she asked.

"A commander. It's a compliment. I'm saying you run a tight ship."

This wasn't the first time that Mira had been told this. Her uncle said it from time to time. Yet she didn't reveal this to Sylas as they located a stall that sold grains, most notably barley, rye, and hops.

The man that ran the shop had a weathered face and he wore a cap that tied off under his neck. He squinted at the pair as they approached.

Sylas instantly moved to one of the open barrels filled with barley. He recognized the plump grain with its distinctive crease that ran down the middle. He turned to the rye, the uniform grains with a deep reddish brown. "Do you mind?" he asked the seller.

"By all means."

Sylas scooped up a few of the hardened grains and smelled them. They would make a perfect lighter ale, something with a distinct flavor profile that was slightly tangy. He returned to the barley and gave them a big whiff. This would be for his stronger ale. Perhaps he'd also do a combination of both, or a weaker version of one of them to sell cheaply. But to begin with, he'd have an ale made from rye, and one made from barley.

Sylas moved on to the hops, which were vibrant green with cone-shaped flowers. He knew from experience that the flavor came from these yellowish cones, the hops with herbal and citrusy notes. Rather than start asking prices, Sylas approached Mira.

"I'm going to need at least a barrel of the barley to get started and a few pounds of rye. Less of the hops. You said I can do this magically, right?"

"Yes, using MLus. This is because of your class. Once you get your recipes set—"

"—I'll need to malt the grains too. But I can figure that out tonight."

"Once you get your recipes set," Mira said, surprised at the excitement in his eyes, "things should move pretty easily from there. You'll sell the ale, get MLus from doing so, which you'll use to brew. It may take some trial and error, but you'll eventually get a system going that works for you. At least if your class is like any of the other classes. I can't really describe it. The process is very instinctual, personal, even. Like you've been doing it all your life."

Sylas grinned at the seller. "A barrel of barley, six pounds of rye, and two pounds of the hops. I'll set up a delivery at some point."

The seller nodded. "Fifty MLus."

Sylas exchanged glances with Mira, shocked at how cheap it was.

"That's fine," she said. "That still leaves you enough to get a few tools." Mira turned to the seller. "Can you have the grains delivered to the nearest portal?"

"I can do you one better. Where are you coming from, Milady?"

"Ember Hollow. The pub."

The old man squinted at her again from beneath his bushy eyebrows. "The pub, huh? It's been years since that place was open. Or at least it has felt like years."

"It'll be open again soon," Sylas told him. "Under the name The Old Lamplighter. Give me a few weeks."

The man offered him a toothy grin. "Good to know. Can't wait to taste whatever you brew up."

The next stop was Cinderpeak itself. The small town seemed peaceful enough, and several people even greeted Mira as they wound their way through a complex tangle of cobblestone streets and stone buildings. Cinderpeak was dense, yet this also gave it a sense of security that Sylas appreciated.

They found a man selling tools in a shop with a wide-open door. "Greetings," he told them as the man looked up from a desk. His wife came out of the back room, saw Sylas and Mira, smiled at them, and stepped away. Both were dressed in a dapper way, as if they did this job part-time and they were on their way to a café afterward.

"He's repairing the old pub in Ember Hollow," Mira said in lieu of a greeting. "What do you think we'll need?"

"What kind of repairs?" the man asked as he looked Sylas over.

"Basics. I'll also need a shovel too."

"In, that case, I have a newcomer's kit that should suit your needs. Includes a hammer, nails, a handsaw, a chisel, a pry bar, and a wrench. I've got a shovel for it too. But it isn't cheap. None of my stuff is cheap. That's because it is good. And in this world, good is never cheap."

"Yeah?" Sylas checked his MLus and saw that he only had thirty now.

The shop owner stroked his chin. "But a big fella like you could be helpful to me."

"Mr. Brassmere?" Mira asked.

"What? I might have a job for your friend here, that's all I'm saying."

"His name is Sylas."

"I might have a job for Sylas, then."

Sylas glanced back at Mira, half expecting her to intervene. She didn't.

The man continued, "So how about this: You keep your MLus and take care of something for me?"

"What kind of something?" Sylas asked.

Mr. Brassmere looked the newcomer over one last time. He was certainly a large man, and while he didn't ask, he got this feeling that Sylas might be ex-military. He just carried himself that way. "I let someone borrow some tools a while back. He took off with them and hasn't returned them. Now, most of these tools aren't that special to me, but that hammer is. A friend of mine in Duskhaven made it for me. I'm not going to say it has magical properties but…"

"You want me to get this hammer?" Sylas asked.

"I do. How's this? Take the newcomer kit, and once you've got your pub—what's the name again?"

"The Old Lamplighter."

"Nice. I like that name. Once you have The Old Lamplighter up and running, see if you can't get this hammer for me."

Sylas nodded. "Just give me the details and I'll take care of it."

"Good, but don't kill him or anything, nothing like that."

"I wasn't planning on it," Sylas assured him.

"Good, I guess I should properly introduce myself. My name is Halden Brassmere, by the way. But people just call me Mr. Brassmere on account of the missus, who cares about titles like that. And you are?"

"Sylas Runewulf."

"Here you go," he said as he waved his hand at Sylas. "Is this your first quest contract? I'm guessing it is by the look on your face."

The words, rimmed in blue, glowed in front of Sylas and faded. He tried to reach out and touch them as they did, which brought an amused look from both Mira and Mr. Brassmere.

[New Quest Contract - Retrieve Halden Brassmere's hammer. Accept? Y/N?]

"Pleasure doing business, Sylas. And don't let my wife know about the quest contract." Mr. Brassmere leaned forward and winked. "She hates it when I make these things."

Mira and Sylas left the shop with a leather bag full of tools. Once they were outside, Mira stopped him. "And now you know about quest contracts."

"Personally, I'm surprised you didn't hop in and start bargaining. You've got a knack for that."

"I basically paid for your grains and the yeast," she reminded him.

"Through that bread roll you made me, right?"

"Quest contracts are ways to avoid paying MLus for certain services. Just be sure not to take too many, they can be overwhelming."

"Yeah?" Sylas asked as they continued down the cobblestone road. "Is there an easy way to keep track of them?"

"Check your status."

Name: Sylas Runewulf
Mana Lumens: 30/100
Class: Brewer
[Active Quest Contracts:]
Retrieve Halden Brassmere's hammer

"Easy enough," Sylas told her.

Mira stopped and turned to him. "And when do you think the ale will be ready?"

"I don't know, I've never magically brewed ale before. In the real world, it would take a few weeks."

She offered Sylas a playful smirk. "First of all, this *is* the real world now. Your real world, and mine. And it shouldn't take that long. I'd be surprised if you didn't have your first ale available by this time tomorrow. But try not to overdo it. Remember, if you spend too many MLus, you'll pass on to Chasm."

"I'll die again."

"Yes, and from what I've heard, the second time is much worse than the first."

CHAPTER SIX

THE FIRST BATCH

P atches sat in front of the grimy window of the pub looking out at the street, surveying the borders of his Tavernly Realm. He had a way to get out of the pub itself, but it was getting harder and harder to squeeze through. No matter. From his vantage point, Patches could see what mattered most to him at that very moment.

Someone had delivered a barrel of supplies, a world of scent to the piebald cat that called the pub home. Patches didn't know what the grains were, but he certainly recognized their almost intoxicating smell, with tangy overtones and an undercurrent of citrus on top of a nutty, comforting aroma.

It's exactly what this place needs to get running again, he thought.

While the grains would make the perfect ale, as long as Patches's newest subject was a good brewer, they could also attract unwanted company in the form of rats or mice, which were harder for him to catch. Mice were small, nimble, and where there was one, there were many.

Yet it was a necessary evil.

With good ale came more loyal subjects, who would provide Patches with enough Mana Lumens to keep him powered and energized.

Aside from being able to turn invisible, he was able to amplify his speed to some degree and turn his purrs into a sonic attack, on top of weaponizing his hairballs. There was another thing he was able to do with his Mana Lumens, something Patches intended to try that night once the big man went to sleep.

I don't know what will happen with more of this magic, but I'm certain it's good.

Thinking of Mana Lumens, even if Patches didn't quite know or fully understand how this worked, produced his status:

Mana Lumens: 1100/1200

His Dream Napping had helped. It had been a good dream too, one in which Patches twisted through the legs of happy subjects in the pub, getting belly scratches and plenty of Mana Lumens.

He liked those kinds of dreams.

New activity outside the pub drew Patches's attention. He heard the increasingly familiar footsteps of the big man, which meant that things were looking up.

It was only a matter of time now.

———

Sylas approached the door of The Old Lamplighter to find the supplies he'd ordered, just as he had been promised. Mira was no longer with him. She had insisted he portal to Ember Hollow, even though Sylas had pressed her to let him take the horses back with her.

The apothecary had also left another MLu-powered bread roll in the picnic basket she'd given him that morning. According to her, this was so he had plenty to work with for his first batch of ale. After that, he was cut off.

"Heh." Sylas opened the door. Patches bolted over to him to investigate the new tools as Sylas ate the second bread roll. He brought the grains in. "Come on, then," he told the mewing pub cat as he took the supplies down to the cellar. "Smells good, right?" Sylas asked once Patches had joined him in the cellar.

He bent over and scratched the cat behind the ear. "I know, I know, you're wondering what I'm up to. If you couldn't tell, I know what I'm doing, but I also don't know what I'm doing at the same time." Sylas stood and rubbed his hands together. "Funny, right? Hopefully this works." He found a bucket in the storeroom and grabbed it. "Water. Let's get some water."

Sylas went to the well behind the pub and sent a bucket down. He pulled the bucket up and smelled the water. It was fine. He brought it to his lips and took a drink. The water was pure, yet there was the hint of something he'd never tasted before. It left his tongue tingling in a good way, and the aftereffects sort of reminded him of the bread roll that Mira had given him. Did all the food taste like this in the Underworld?

Sylas returned to the cellar and filled a pot with water. He placed some of the barley in the large pot.

"Normally, it would take a while for these to soak and germinate," he explained to Patches, who listened intently. "We need more water." After a few more trips, Sylas stood over the soaking grains as Patches mewed at him.

"What I'm about to attempt would bring joy to a brewer's life back in my world. Or, I guess, this is my world now. You know what I mean." Sylas cleared his throat. "'Malting, Milling, and Mashing.' Ever heard that song?"

Patches weaved through Sylas's legs.

"Of course you haven't." Sylas focused on the pot in the same way he'd seen Mira do. It was subtle, but he could sort of recognize when she was using Mana Lumens. He willed the barley to soak long enough for it to germinate. "It worked."

Excitement grew in his chest as Sylas saw the swollen, golden grains each of which had sprouted a tiny hair-thin rootlet.

He drained the water into another pot, and dried the barley with a heat that he couldn't quite understand. The power came from the palm of his hand, hot enough that Patches moved away from him. It was all instinctual. Sylas moved away and chopped his hand through the air, trying to summon the power again.

It didn't work this time.

"So it has to be in relation to brewing," he said as he turned back to the pots.

Keeping his focus, Sylas cracked the malted grains with a wave of his hand—another feat—and prepared them for the mashing process. Using the kiln, which Sylas was able to ignite with MLus, he brought the water to a boil. This was used to soak the grains for a moment as part of the mashing process.

Soon, he magically strained the mixture into what was known as wort, Sylas in such a deep concentration that he'd hardly paid any attention to the time that had passed.

"This is called lautering," he told Patches. "Normally, I'd need a lautering tun to do this, but that isn't necessary here. Honestly." Sylas looked down at the cat. "It makes me wonder what is possible once I really get the hang of this."

Patches blinked a few times, as if he understood him. Sylas wasn't certain if he could or not.

Sylas lugged the pot over to the kiln, placed it on the flat surface, and brought the water to a boil this way. He removed it from the heat. To cool it down he took hold of the Mana Lumens in the air around the pot and gestured as if he were stripping them away.

Much to his surprise, this worked, the wort instantly cooled. Now it was time for the yeast, the fermentation process.

Sylas figured this would take some time.

After trying numerous ways to kick-start the process and failing, he refocused and was finally able to ferment what would soon be the ale by simply thinking the word "ferment." Again, this was instinctual. It all happened in a way he'd later have trouble explaining.

The world around him sharpened as Sylas began the final process, the maturation of the ale. He felt that a great bit of time had passed even if it felt like just a few moments. His temples pulsing, Sylas placed his hand on the counter and bent his head forward, suddenly tired from all the MLus he had expended.

"Just got to check one more thing. Well, two more things," he told Patches as he found one of the cleaner casks. He looked at the small cask. "I still don't know why they're this size, but we'll try it anyway." He poured the ale in and cooled it the same way he had earlier, stripping the substance of its heat.

While it was his first batch, he sensed it was a process he'd be able to repeat and quickly perfect. "That does it," he told the pub cat, who mewed curiously in response.

Sylas accessed his stats, which had recently been filled by the second bread roll.

Name: Sylas Runewulf
Mana Lumens: 20/100
Class: Brewer

He ran the numbers in his head. "I had a hundred before thanks to Mira's second bread roll. That means it takes eighty MLus to make a cask of barley ale." Sylas found one of the cleaner pint glasses. He got a rag from a basket near the casks, made sure the rag was clean, and wiped the pint glass with it.

Once he was ready, Sylas placed the cask on the table, the head facing outward. Sylas took one of the taps, blew the dust off it, and used a wooden mallet to hammer the tap into place.

Patches watched, the pub cat wide-eyed as Sylas poured his first pint, examined the amber liquid, and finally took his first sip.

Sylas smacked his lips. "Not bad, not bad at all." He looked back around the storeroom. "Let's get rid of some of the old grains and call it a night."

CHAPTER SEVEN

PUBWARMING GIFT

Before heading to bed that night, Sylas ate more of the food that Mira had given him. He made a simple sandwich of cheese and bread, one that turned out to be filling. The sandwich didn't increase his Mana Lumens, but at least it hit the spot.

Especially when paired with the ale.

The brew was rich and robust, the distinctive sweetness of barley up front. The ale was strong too, much stronger than he had expected it to be. Sylas could tell he had a winner, and he was surprised it had turned out so well in his first attempt.

The rye ale he planned to brew would be weaker, yet it would have a certain spice and flavor profile that set it apart from the barley ale. Once he opened The Old Lamplighter, Sylas would have two ales, a strong one and a lighter one.

Now, he needed to figure out what he would charge for them.

Sylas thought about this as he lay in the bed, his hand petting Patches as he stared up at the beamed ceiling of his bedroom. There was a ton of work that needed to be done on the place, he could clearly see this. But at least he'd started the ale. He thought of the dozen small casks in the cellar below. Once he had most of them filled, he could properly open up.

"Not a bad day at all," Sylas told Patches as he got comfortable. "Not a bad day at all."

———

Patches waited until the big man was asleep. As carefully as ever, Patches slipped out from beneath his subject's hand. He sat on the edge of the bed for a moment cleaning himself, his ears twitching as he listened to the floors below.

Nothing of concern tonight, he surmised.

Patches turned back to the big man and watched him snore lightly. He was a bit of a brute, but he'd already succeeded in brewing his first batch of ale, which meant that the Tavernly Realm was one step closer to being filled with people yet again, which meant more power for Patches.

Now, it was time to do his part.

Patches approached the big man and got down on his belly, his paws tucked beneath his chin. He began purring, but this was a different purr than the one he'd used to thwart the rat. It was much deeper, the low resonance to the point that it vibrated his entire body. Soon, the piebald pub cat produced a golden energy, one that washed over the big man.

Patches kept this up until he was exhausted. He lay back onto his side and fell into a deep slumber.

Sylas came awake feeling entirely recharged, like he was ten years younger. But then the same glowing prompt he had received the previous morning flashed in front of him, souring his mood.

[You have 88 days until the invasion.]

"I'd better talk to Mira about this," he said as he rolled out of bed. Sylas spotted Patches resting in the corner and laughed. "Look at you. No rats last night? Heh. I guess I shouldn't say that until I check around the place."

The black-and-white cat looked up at Sylas, yawned, and went back to sleep.

"I'll see if I can't find you some milk today. Haven't seen any cows yet, but I haven't really looked around. I guess that's on the agenda for today, that and fixing some things around here."

Figuring he'd see how many Mana Lumens he recharged overnight, Sylas checked his status and was instantly surprised.

Name: Sylas Runewulf
Mana Lumens: 100/100
Class: Brewer
[Active Quest Contracts:]
Retrieve Halden Brassmere's hammer

"How . . . ?" He blinked a few times, figuring something was wrong with his vision. "Nope, topped off," he said as he skimmed through the information again. Was it the ale? Sylas considered this scenario for a moment. If he could brew ale that actually recharged someone's Mana Lumens, sort of like Mira's magical bread roll, it would be worth a lot.

"Imagine being able to get a nice buzz and your MLus completely refilled," he told Patches, who was still sleeping.

Sylas tried to recall if he'd actually checked his levels after tasting his first pint last night and couldn't.

"I guess I'll have to do some tests." As he sat there at the edge of the bed, Sylas's thoughts drifted to some of the people he would like to look for in the Underworld. The Celestial Plains were above, almost mocking those who hadn't made it there. Some of the people, people like his dear father, likely went there. But some of the other soldiers who had died, the swordsmen he had trained with, were here somewhere.

Unless they had moved on to the Chasm...

"Kael, Quinlan, and Raelis," Sylas said quietly.

But that search could wait.

Fixing up The Old Lamplighter and figuring out about the warning he had received twice now was what mattered at the moment. Sylas would also need to see to the quest contract he had taken, but he figured he had a few days before he did that to get more familiar with the Underworld.

After breakfast, Sylas deep cleaned the pub, sweeping and then mopping the wooden floor by hand. Once it was sparkling, he took care of some small repairs, things that wouldn't take too much time and wouldn't require more wood or tools.

He hammered in a few of the nails that had come loose in the floorboards, and chiseled out some of the crumbled bits of mortar of the fireplace so he could finish pointing it later. After cleaning the bar, it became clear that it would need sanding. "Later," Sylas said to himself as he moved on to fixing several of the chairs and some of the wobbly tables.

More supplies were in order. He needed wood, mortar, and a tool for sanding, which hadn't been in Mr. Brassmere's starter kit. In playing around behind the bar, Sylas saw that there was room for the small casks, yet there was also a way to run the ale taps all the way down to the basement and replace the casks there. This led him to cleaning and polishing the ale taps themselves.

He was just finishing up when he heard a knock at the door. As if Patches had been waiting for the visit, the cat appeared at the foot of the stairs and quickly took the steps down to the bottom to join Sylas.

"Look who decides to get up," Sylas told Patches as he mewed a few times.

Another knock.

"It's open," Sylas called out.

An older man entered. He walked with a slight limp, which made Sylas wonder if people appeared in the Underworld at the same age in which they died. If that was the case, it would almost be better to die young.

"Getting the old pub running again, eh?" the man asked as he sat at the bar.

Sylas took a position across from him. "I am. The Old Lamplighter is the name."

He wore a faded leather tunic adorned with some insignia Sylas hadn't seen before. While wiry and thin, the man's most distinct feature was his bushy eyebrows, which were thick and dark, unlike his gray hair. One of these dark eyebrows rose to the point that it looked comical. "The Old Lamplighter, eh? I like it. That'll brighten up Ember Hollow. We sure do need it." The man extended his hand to him. "Call me Henry."

"Sylas Runewulf."

"Sylas, Sylas. Now that's an Aurum name if I've ever heard one. You sure got lucky getting this place. This is the kind of assignment dead people dream of." Henry laughed at his own joke. "Unlike me. I was just assigned a home, no class. I've fixed up the home, mind you, joined the militia too. But no real assignment. No way to get enough MLus to really make a difference unless I want to save up."

"Ember Hollow has a militia?"

The man tapped his hand against the insignia on his chest. "We sure do. The Esteemed Coalition of Ember Hollow Defenders."

Sylas had heard plenty of long names when it came to guards and other military factions. Many of them belonged to the Shadowthorne Empire, which was a point of humor for Sylas and his men as they replaced certain words with vulgarities. "That's quite a name."

"Our leader is Tiberius Ravenbane. Met him yet?"

Sylas shook his head. "I can't say that I have."

"You've met his niece. I saw you with her yesterday."

"You mean Mira? That's her uncle?"

"Sure is. And I'm sure he's heard of you by now. You're practically the talk of the town."

"I am, am I? A town of three or four people?"

Henry's grin thinned. "Maybe it's more of a village. Tiberius likes to call it a hamlet, but you get the picture. We're small, but we get visitors, and this pub is going to bring them in by the droves. It'll be the only one between here and the Hexveil. The one in Cinderpeak is barely open, so I expect that this place will be busy."

"Yeah?"

"Everything from wayward warriors to the occasional escapee—"

"Escapee?"

Henry leaned forward as if this next part was a secret. "Sometimes, people and other things make it out of the Chasm." He whistled. "Right through the

Hexveil. Still don't know how they do it. I feel for them, I do, but if they come here, we have to take them back by force, if you get what I mean. That's one of the jobs the militia is tasked with."

"The Esteemed Coalition of Ember Hollow Defenders?"

"That's right." Henry touched the badge stitched into the front of his tunic.

"You occasionally fight off demons?"

"Not all are demons, but I do. I know I may not look it, but I'm pretty good with an axe. Even better with my mace. Good times, usually. But sometimes, bad times."

"Good times and bad times, huh?"

"Good name for a pub."

Sylas shrugged. "I like The Old Lamplighter."

Henry showed Sylas his palms. "That's your call, not mine. But do let me know when you're up and running. It's been ages since I had something fresh. Sure, I could go to Cinderpeak, but like I said, that place is barely open and sometimes, a man wants to get bladdered in his own backyard." Henry knocked one of his palms on the bar top. "Anyway, I'll let you get back to it."

"Wait. Would you like to have a pint now? It's early, but—"

"Never too early in the Underworld." Henry laughed. "If that's not a motto to live by, I don't know what is."

"In that case, wait here."

Patches hopped onto the bar, startling both of them.

"Holy—Look at this spectral surprise," Henry said. "This your cat?"

"It's the pub cat. His name is Patches."

"Fat as he is, I'm surprised he can jump this high."

"He's pretty agile for his size."

The heavy black-and-white cat strutted toward Henry, where he subsequently got a few ear scratches before moving on. "He'll do just fine," the sinewy man said as Patches went to his favorite window nook. "Might be too big to chase off a rat, but—"

"He's already left me a rat as a housewarming present."

"Heh, more like pubwarming."

Sylas looked past the man and grinned at Patches, who was already asleep again. "Wait here." He went to the cellar, grabbed a pint glass, and quickly used some of the water to clean it. "Linens," Sylas said to himself, another thing he needed to get. He filled the pint and carefully brought it upstairs.

"Well, would you look at that?" Henry's eyes lit up at the sight of the pint. "That looks absolutely marvelous."

Sylas placed the pint on the counter in front of the man. "Let me know how it is. And don't go easy on me. One more thing," he told Henry as the man

brought the pint to his lips. "I'm not asking how many MLus you have, but I want to see if this does anything to them."

"Does anything to my MLus?" Henry cocked a bushy eyebrow at him.

"Let me know if it fills your reserves is what I'm saying."

"That would be some ale indeed." Henry took his first sip and wiped away the foam on his lip. Sylas was about to ask how it was. Henry stopped him by taking another sip, this one much longer. He drank half the pint, admired the amber liquid for a moment, nodded, and finished it.

"Well?" Sylas asked.

Henry burped. "Apologies. And I'm going to be as honest with you here, mate."

"By all means." Sylas tried not to let the disappointment show on his face.

Henry started laughing. "I was just seeing how you'd react. The ale is great. It's the best thing I've had in years, better than the stuff they brew in Cinderpeak, I'll tell you that much. You have yourself a winner here, but it didn't do anything to my reserves, if you're wondering." He toasted Sylas and emptied the rest of the glass in one gulp. "Cheers."

"Thank you."

"I should probably get going. Once you're open, or if you need a taste tester, don't hesitate to ask me. I'm just a few doors down. The house with the blue door."

"Good to know," Sylas said. "Before you leave, can you point me in the direction of Mira's place? I'd like to meet with her."

"Wouldn't we all," Henry said with a sly grin and an almost creepy wink. "I'll tell you what. I was going that way anyway to meet with Tiberius. I'll tell her you were asking about her, and to stop by."

"Thanks. Anyone else I should know around here?"

Henry reached the door and turned back to him. "Certainly, but it's best in Ember Hollow to let people meet you, rather than you meet them. Folks are extra careful out here this close to the Hexveil. Anyway, I'll let Mira know."

Henry let himself out. He took a few steps away from The Old Lamplighter as the smile on his face disappeared. The ale was excellent, there was no doubt, but he still needed to have a serious conversation with Tiberius and the others about Sylas.

With the kind of people the pub could attract, not to mention how powerful it could make Sylas in a short amount of time, it was important they get a handle on it now.

The last thing Ember Hollow needed was a pub.

CHAPTER EIGHT

THE MYSTERY ROOM

The silver-eyed apothecary, who wore a beige dress and an apron, crouched to pet Patches. Mira looked upstairs just as Sylas came down, the rough newcomer in the sleeveless top he wore beneath his tunic.

"I thought I'd let myself in."

"By all means," he told her.

Seeing him now gave Mira a new look at how strong he actually was. His body, sculpted by combat and battlefield hardships and etched with veins, hinted at the warrior beneath. Mira knew those muscles hadn't come easy. Yet even with the sinewy terrain, there was a softness here too. His abdomen, while also muscular, bore a slight roundness that Mira found endearing. It softened Sylas's hardened exterior, smoothed out some of the edges.

"Just dealing with loose nails." Sylas set his hammer down and grabbed his tunic. He placed it over his head, the bagginess of his garb once again disguising his muscles. "Glad you made it. Henry tell you to come by?"

"Yes, Henry." Mira took a seat at the bar. She ran her finger across it and noticed it was clean enough. "Henry, my uncle's lackey."

"I got that vibe from him. Sort of a strange character too; there was something else there underneath his friendliness." Sylas stepped behind the bar and leaned back. He crossed his arms over his chest. "I can't imagine Henry fighting."

"You aren't the only one. He is certainly strong, though."

"Yeah? Doesn't look it."

"My uncle wouldn't keep him around if he wasn't."

"What was the militia's name again? Something unwieldy."

"The Esteemed Coalition of Ember Hollow Defenders."

"Like I said, unwieldy."

"Maybe." Mira removed a round sandwich from her bag, one that had already been sliced. "I wasn't able to enhance this one, but I thought you'd be hungry."

"I'm definitely hungry." Sylas said as he eyed the sandwich. He wanted to say something cheesy like *Any sandwich from you is already enhanced because it was made by you,* but realized that this wasn't very clever and even if she laughed, he'd feel stupid saying it. He went with a question instead. "You thirsty?"

"Henry said you brewed your first batch."

"I did, and it cost eighty MLus."

"Not bad at all, really."

"Ready for a pint?"

"Maybe later. You'll need to save some so you can officially open up. That's when things will get interesting."

"Actually," Sylas said as he took a slice of the round sandwich, "I've got a strange update for you and I figured you'd have some insight. I went to bed with twenty MLus. I woke up with my reserves topped off. Back to a hundred."

Mira looked at him curiously. "You recharged to your full capacity overnight? I thought only advanced lumengineers could do something like that."

"Advanced lumengineers? Whoever they are, I guess we have something in common." Sylas took a bite of the sandwich. It was good and grainy, flavored with just a bit of mustard.

"I doubt that considering theirs is a unique class. No, it must be something else. No one recharges like that, especially not newcomers."

"There's another thing." He licked some of the mustard off his thumb. Sylas caught the way that Mira was looking at him and cleared his throat. "Apologies. Not really used to eating around ladies so often."

"So I'm a lady now? I'm flattered. And what's this *other thing,* as you call it?"

"Do you ever get warnings?"

"Warnings?" Mira glanced over to Patches, who had just let out a loud yawn before falling onto his side.

"He's not as lazy as he looks," Sylas told her. He took another bite of the sandwich. "So, warnings. I'm getting warnings. They've come to me the last two mornings warning me about some impending invasion."

"Invasion?"

"You have eighty-eight days until the invasion," Sylas said, recalling the prompt. "That's what the warning told me this morning. Yesterday was eighty-nine, so it is clearly ticking down."

"An invasion warning? I've never heard of something like that, but my uncle may know more."

"I keep hearing about your uncle today, but we've yet to meet."

Mira offered Sylas a tight smile. There was a reason for this. Sylas and her uncle had been on the opposite sides of a war that had ultimately taken both of their lives. While Sylas seemed amenable, Tiberius was not. He had already had Henry come and check on Sylas.

She imagined there would be more altercations in the future, especially once Sylas opened.

Still, if anyone knew of such a warning in the area, it would be Tiberius. Mira's demon hunter uncle was well versed in system prompts because he received them himself. But never invasion warnings. At least none that he had mentioned.

"I'll see what I can find out," she told Sylas carefully.

"Because we're near the Hexveil, right? Maybe it has something to do with that."

"I'd prefer not to speculate."

"Maybe we could see the Hexveil today," Sylas suggested. "Also, I need to go to a market. Definitely in need of a few things. For one, some food. Anything simple will do. And I need something to sand the bar with as well. Wood, mortar, and milk for Patches. Linens. The list goes on." The cat looked up at Sylas, blinked his big eyes, and laid back down. "We really need a market here in Ember Hollow."

"We do. There's a space for one, but it closed before I arrived."

"Let me guess—years ago."

"Yes, years ago. How about this? I'll show you to the Hexveil, we can portal to Cinderpeak from there, grab supplies, and then return."

"You don't mind?"

"I do have a client to see later, but I'm free for the next few hours."

"Is the Hexveil really close enough for us to walk there?" Sylas asked as he joined Mira at the door.

"It is. That's why Ember Hollow is incredibly important in the grand scheme of things. Or maybe not so important, but we like to think of ourselves as important. That's why my uncle lives here. He's a demon hunter."

"Demon hunter, huh? That's really his class?"

"It is, and like his militia, he's rather proud of it."

Once they were outside, Sylas locked the pub with a wave of his hand. He joined Mira as she headed west, the apothecary now wearing a hood on her head. The strange luminosity from the Celestial Plains added a touch of melancholy to the empty cobblestone street of Ember Hollow. It removed the luster from everything it touched, a reminder that they were eternally between realms.

As Sylas looked up at golden clouds above, a question came to him. "Why aren't there children here?"

Mira paused, allowing him to catch up. "There are some children here in the Underworld, mostly teens, but few and far between. Children generally go to the Celestial Plains."

"Makes sense. And the ones here would be pretty bad."

"Not necessarily. Not everyone that is here did something bad. Did you?"

"Did I?" Sylas touched his chest. In that moment he saw a flash of all the things he'd done, the battles he'd fought, the split-second decisions he'd made and all the suffering, his included. It was a grim image that he had to blink twice to forget.

"Sorry—"

"No," he told her, "it is what it is. I was a swordsman in the Royal Guard. After the things I've done, I'm surprised I didn't get sent to the Chasm."

"Only the truly wicked are sent there initially. Others go because they run out of MLus. This is one thing you'll need to be careful of at your pub, especially if your ale is good."

"It is good. I'm almost offended you didn't try it."

"The ale will still be there when we return. People can easily drink themselves to death, in our former world and here. Remember, if you run out of MLus, you pass to the Chasm. And by 'you' I mean one of your 'patrons.' You won't run out, likely, especially if The Old Lamplighter is a popular place. But you do need to be careful of how much you serve."

"What did you do?" Sylas asked.

"What did I do? What do you mean?"

"To end up here. What did you do?"

Mira hesitated. The people of the Underworld kept their secrets. This was a given, but the reason she was here, the reason she'd found herself in the Underworld was a closely guarded secret, something that shamed her.

"We all have our reasons," she finally said.

They were quiet for a moment, both remembering their former lives. At least Sylas was. He decided to shift their discussion back to the pub. "There was a door upstairs that was sealed. Remember it?"

"I do."

"I think I'll pry it open today. I don't like having a mystery door."

"Something to add to your to-do list."

"No more mystery door." Sylas looked up at the golden clouds one last time. "Another question: Do people actually make it from here to there?"

"Some have tried. I don't know anyone that has succeeded, though."

The divide between the Underworld and the Chasm was a masterpiece of mystical forces. It provided a breathtaking panorama of shimmering light, one that held back hell itself, a swirling miasma of liquid silvers and vibrant blues. It pulsed every time Sylas looked at it, the Hexveil with a constant ripple to it like a great body of water beneath a full harvest moon.

Sylas felt drawn to the structure, like he could simply approach it and walk right though. Yet this was clearly an impossibility. Guarding the Underworld side of the Hexveil were towering sentinels clad in blackened armor that had been fashioned into sharp, geometric plates at odds with any gear Sylas had ever seen before. They were tall too, dwarfing Sylas and Mira.

"That's a big lot," he told Mira as he rubbed the back of his neck. Sylas was glad that he wasn't facing them on a battlefield.

"Those are the Hexveilian Guard. They are quite intimidating. As long as you don't bother them, they won't bother you."

"Are they human?"

"Hardly."

"And they just stand there, waiting for what, exactly?"

Mira nodded to the space beyond the veil. "For something from the other side to break through the barrier. I've only seen this once. The guards are much faster than they look."

"Yet things still get through."

"Always," she said. "That's why my uncle's class is important. He gets prompts when one has escaped. There's a whole system to it, but basically, he is informed, as are other demon hunters and they get MLus as rewards for handling the escapees, which he distributes to the militia."

Sylas took another look at the Hexveil. "The only thing keeping us from them."

"Yes, the only thing. It has served its purpose over the years."

"Shall we?" Mira motioned to a portal. The structure echoed what Sylas had observed just the day before: a ring of stone pillars circumscribing a circular rune.

"Certainly."

"I'll see you in Cinderpeak." Mira stepped onto the platform and vanished.

Before he did the same, Sylas took a final look at the Hexveil. Was this what the invasion warning was about it? It had to be. Or perhaps it was something else entirely. Hopefully, Mira's uncle would know more.

Sylas stepped onto the portal and was presented with two options:

- **Ember Hollow**
- **Cinderpeak**

He selected Cinderpeak and felt the same twisting sensation in his core. Before he could orient himself, he stood at the portal in Cinderpeak, the one not far from the farmer's market.

He joined Mira. "The budget is fifteen MLus. Whatever I can get with that. I need enough to brew another cask tonight."

"Eighty to brew a cask, right?"

"That's right."

"Leaving you with what, five MLus left if you spend fifteen now? That's pretty low."

"I'll be fine," Sylas assured her.

"I don't know."

"Don't worry about it."

They started with the wood, Sylas purchasing several random planks, throwaway pieces, according to the owner. It would do until Sylas had more to spend. He was also able to get some linens from the man, which would give him something to clean with later on. They weren't going to be able to find a sanding block at the market—he'd have to return later to the town itself—but they were able to get a small amount of food and some mortar.

In total, Sylas spent fifteen Mana Lumens, mostly due to Mira's bargaining, which meant he was right on budget.

"Back to the pub," he told Mira.

"Let me buy a pint when we get there," she said.

He turned to the apothecary and grinned. "Buy a pint? I'm not open yet."

"I'm aware, but your MLus will be lower than I'd like if you brew another cask tonight."

"Look at you, concerned about my well-being."

Mira turned away. She knew exactly how this sounded and didn't like the fact that it was partially true. "Maybe. Or maybe I'm just looking forward to Ember Hollow having some life breathed into it, which is exactly what The Old Lamplighter will do."

Sylas waited, his arms crossed over his chest as Mira looked down at her pint. They were back at The Old Lamplighter now, Mira seated at the bar, and Sylas standing in front of her. Patches was there as well, his head buried in a bowl of milk.

"It's been ages," she finally said. "How much?"

"I don't know. I honestly have no idea what to charge."

"And how many pints can you get from a cask?"

"Traditionally, seventy-two. But these casks are much smaller."

"Should we test it out?"

"What do you mean?"

"Let's pour out all the pints and transfer them into another cask. How much have you had?"

"Henry had a pint. I had about a half-pint."

"Well?" Mira looked at the ale. "What do you think? And then I'll have one pint, pay you, and be on my way."

"Sure. Actually, that's not a bad idea. And you don't have to—"

"I'm paying you for the pint," she insisted.

"In that case, let's head down." Sylas and Mira took the steps to the cellar, the apothecary careful not to spill her ale.

"You can put it there," Sylas said as he pointed at the old wooden table in the cellar. Patches appeared at the top step, the cat watching the two of them suspiciously.

"He's a strange one," Mira said as Sylas placed a different cask on the table. He popped the top open, saw that it was clean inside, conditioned perfectly. He was coming to expect this now from the Underworld, but always checked anyway.

"Let me do it." Mira came forward and carefully poured her pint into the new cask. "One." She used her empty pint glass to pour up another, which she deposited in the fresh cask. "Two."

"I'm going to guess there's a magical way to do this, right?"

She smiled as she carefully poured a third pint. "Yes, likely. But sometimes it's fun to do things manually. It feels human, you know."

"It feels human," Sylas agreed as Patches finally joined them. The piebald pub cat weaved a path through Sylas's legs as Mira emptied the cask pint by pint.

". . . And that's the half-pint. So if you've already had one and a half pints, that means a full cask has twenty pints."

"Twenty pints?" Sylas considered this for a moment as he looked at the small casks lining the wall. "So each holds twenty pints then. I'll need larger casks."

"I don't think you'll be able to get more in Cinderpeak. Maybe custom-built. You could talk to the pub owner there."

"The pub owner in Cinderpeak, huh? Good idea. If I can't get casks there, where would I do it?"

"Probably Battersea. It would take over a week to reach there by horse, longer on foot. There are other options, but I don't think you're at that stage yet."

"Small casks it is, for now. So, twelve casks, each with twenty pints. Two hundred and forty pints total." Sylas furrowed his brow. "Not great. My father's pub could do that in one night easy. Do you know what they used to charge here? Did Henry or your uncle ever say that?"

"Actually, they were talking about that today. Henry has been here longer, and he said the stronger ale went for ten MLus. The regular ale for five MLus. I think the pub in Cinderpeak charges something similar."

"Five and ten, huh?" Sylas did the math quickly in his head. "If I sell twenty pints at ten MLus each, I'll make two hundred MLus. If we deduct the cost of brewing up a batch, that would be one hundred and twenty MLus. Strong ale will have a decent margin."

"A hundred MLus if you sell all twenty regular pints, subtracting the brewing cost, would leave you with twenty MLus leftover."

"Right. So why would anyone brew regular ale?" Sylas surmised.

"Well, for one, you don't want people to get too drunk."

"That sort of comes with the territory of owning a pub," he joked.

"Remember that people will be paying MLus for your ale, meaning if you kill your customers because they get too drunk, thus spending all their MLus, you lose customers."

"I guess a real pub has to worry about that as well. But not really." Sylas scratched the back of his head. "You know, the word 'pub' is short for 'public house,' which is a place where the public can gather. So regular ale on tap is a good idea, it allows people to gather and enjoy themselves. I won't know people's MLus, right? My customers?"

"No, you will not. But there will be signs when they are low. Were you a bartender back at your father's place?"

"No, I was more of a bar runner and occasionally helped out at the bar. He did most of the bartending. Him and a buddy of his." Sylas grew silent. There was regret here, one he hadn't given voice to in a long time.

Sylas had missed his father's funeral because he'd been on the front line. It had always been something that had bothered him.

"Is everything all right?"

He cleared his throat. "Sorry. Is there a way to know who is actually here in the Underworld? A registry of sorts? Another question I've been saving for you."

"You're referring to the Book of Shadows, which a lumengineer would have access to in Battersea."

"The Book of Shadows? I remember you mentioning that."

She nodded. "Technically, we're all called shadows. Anyone you want to find will be registered in the Book of Shadows, and that's in Battersea, which is far. Remember, you could later portal there, but you have to physically visit the place first."

"Couldn't I portal there with you?"

"It doesn't work that way." Mira turned to the stairs. "I'm heading back up, where I'll have a proper pint. Care to join me?" Once she reached the stairs she stopped. "And don't forget, I'm paying you."

———

Mira raised her mug to Sylas, who did the same with his half-pint. "It's already been transferred."

"It has?" Sylas brought up his MLus to see that they had increased by ten. He should have had eighty-five MLus after what he'd spent in Cinderpeak.

Now, he had more.

Name: Sylas Runewulf
Mana Lumens: 95/100
Class: Brewer
[Active Quest Contracts:]
Retrieve Halden Brassmere's hammer

Sylas knew from a previous conversation with her that his total would increase if his reserve passed one hundred. He was almost there now, but by nightfall, his reserves would be low after he'd brewed another batch.

Mira brought the pint to her lips. She took a sip from it and her eyes widened. "Wow, that's strong."

"You think?" Sylas finished his half-pint in one gulp. "Not strong enough, apparently."

"Apparently. But that is why you need a lighter ale as well."

"Even if it makes me less MLus in the long run."

"It keeps people around and enjoying themselves, which is what you want, right?"

Sylas nodded. He remembered a youth spent basking in the warmth of the pub's hearth, the sounds of lively chatter from his bedroom upstairs, and the faint smell of the food cooking below. It was definitely what he wanted.

"Back to the Book of Shadows. I need to see that at some point. I have several people I need to look up. My mother too."

"Your mother?"

"I didn't know her," was all Sylas said as he used one of the linens he'd purchased to wipe the counter. "I don't even know how I'd find her, but if I can find my father, maybe there's something there. She died giving birth to me."

"I'm sorry to hear that."

"Not your fault," he said. "I never knew her."

"In that case, a trip to Battersea is in order. But first, you should get this place up and running. And you should know that it won't be cheap. The lumengineers who have access to the Book of Shadows are known to charge quite a bit to look things up. If you go to Battersea, it's best to go with as many MLus as you can earn."

"And then there's the invasion prompt."

"Yes, there's that. I will ask my uncle tonight."

"Tell him to stop by," Sylas told her. "Have a pint."

"I don't know if that is something he'll be interested in doing. But I'll let him know." Mira pressed away from the bar. "I hope you don't mind if I can't finish this? It's too strong."

"I'll give it to Patches." Sylas laughed as the piebald cat looked up at him, his ears twitching. "Kidding, I'll finish it myself. Then I'll deal with a few more things before I call it a night."

"I don't know if I'll be able to stop by tomorrow," Mira said as she reached the door, "but I'll try."

"I'll be here."

Sylas finished her pint after she left. He certainly felt a buzz as he completed more of the tasks he wanted to handle that day, including repairing the mortar on the fireplace. As the night dragged on, he used some of the spare wood he'd gotten to repair a table, and came to the conclusion he would need more. Sylas also needed a larger saw as well; but the smaller saw that came with Mr. Brassmere's kit worked well enough for now.

Just in case Mira visited tomorrow, Sylas went ahead and brewed up a batch of the regular ale using the rye he'd purchased. The process was the same, and in the end he was happy with how the regular ale tasted.

There was a hint of honeyed bread to it, yet it still carried that distinct flavor he knew to associate with rye, a hint of spiciness. The regular ale was smooth too, and he could see after having one of the stronger pints why this would be nice.

Another thing he noticed was the grain he'd used the previous day, the stuff he had put in the storeroom and planned to discard, had replenished itself. He would still arrange a grain delivery from the guy at the market, just to get a fresh supply, but this was a new development.

It would make brewing even easier.

Sylas looked at the small casks he had. There were ten still available. Until he was able to get more Mana Lumens, he'd only be able to brew one batch per day.

"Perhaps I can take some to the market in Cinderpeak two days from now and sell some of the stronger ale. There are some growlers over there," he told Patches, who now sat at the top of the cellar stairs. Sylas motioned to the growlers over on the wall. "It probably isn't as easy as me just showing up and selling pints, but who knows?"

Patches mewed.

"You're right, who knows? Worth a shot, anyway." Sylas whipped his linen over his shoulder and headed up the stairs. He was tired, but there was one thing he wanted to do before he officially called it a night.

Sylas took the stairs to the second floor and stopped in front of the door that was locked from the other side. The mystery door. He thought about shouldering through, but then he'd have to repair it later.

"No, there has to be a different way." He was just about to head downstairs to grab a couple of tools when an idea came to him. "Perhaps a magical way?" he asked Patches, who had joined him.

Sylas checked his Mana Lumens. He currently had fifteen, which wasn't so bad for the time being.

"How about this?" He squeezed the door handle and imagined pouring his power into it. The handle warmed, as if accepting his ownership over the room. That was the only way Sylas could describe it as he heard the lock click from the other side.

He brought his hand away and the mystery door opened on its own.

"Steady does it," Sylas told Patches as he hesitated in front of the new space. Rather than heed his warning, Patches rushed into the room, the door swinging wide open.

What Sylas found on the other side baffled him.

"How is this here?" Sylas wondered aloud as he took a wide step around what he recognized as a portal. But this didn't glow like the others he had seen, leading him to believe that it wasn't active. Aside from several crates, the rest of the room was bare.

Sylas approached the crates and found dozens of pint bottles. "Not bad," he said as he picked one up and wiped some of the dust off it. "Maybe tomorrow is a better day to visit the market and sell some of the stronger ale, just to get our feet wet."

He watched as Patches stepped out onto the dormant portal, stretched, and looked back up at Sylas. The cat took off, nearly colliding with the door on his way out.

Sylas laughed. "You're more comical when it's just you and me. As for this portal, I'll add figuring out where it leads to the to-do list." He yawned. "Are you already in bed?" he called to the pub cat. "In that case, I'm coming to join you."

Patches perked up once he felt a disturbance in the mana. He hopped down from the big man's bed and approached the door, determined to find out what was happening outside the Tavernly Realm.

His ears twitched as he homed in on a rustling sound.

I knew it.

The big man had made a mistake in burying the demonic rat. Creatures like this provided perfect vessels for the lesser-known, but more nefarious, beings of the Chasm.

He's new at this. And he did bring me some milk. Patches licked his lips. It was a forgivable offense.

He pawed at the bedroom door for a moment until it opened, Patches glad that the big man hadn't shut it fully.

Once he was out, he zipped through the hallway and down the stairs to the main room of the pub. Patches hopped onto a spot in front of the bay window, the one where he'd be able to see the well behind the pub.

He focused on the stepping stone that the rat had been buried beneath. The slightly humorous sight of his plump body was now a portrait of taut anticipation as Patches's ears flitted back, his whiskers straightening.

This is bad, Patches hissed as the stepping stone shifted to the side, the dirt bubbling up.

He bared his teeth as a wispy, smokelike entity took shape over the ground, Patches watching in horror as the dirt continued to spill out.

Pacing back and forth now, his fur standing on end, Patches wished desperately that he could go out there and do something about it, but he also knew better than to confront a demon of this nature.

Dread filled his heart as he pawed at the window. Patches began to yowl, but stopped himself when he realized he might wake his loyal subject.

Can't do that, Patches thought. *He needs his rest.*

Patches tensed up again as the tailless rat he'd killed pressed out of the soil. The wispy being hovering over it moved its claw through the air, which caused the rat body to split in two. This formed two smaller rats, their red skin stretched over sinewy muscle and punctuated with exposed bone.

A pair of bone-white razor-sharp incisors curved menacingly out of their snouts. The pair of demonic rats turned toward the pub.

The wispy, malevolent spirit that had conjured them brought a hand to its mouth as if it were laughing. It spiraled up into the air and disappeared into the well.

The rats took off toward the pub.

Patches hopped down from the windowsill and slid across the floor. He reached the steps at the top of the cellar and sailed down, his control over his own mana allowing him to effortlessly land on the ground below.

There were numerous places where the rats could get into the Tavernly Realm.

He had tried to point this out to the big man, but every time Patches came around, the big man ended up petting Patches. Even if he was able to repair the holes, the rats would find another way in. They always did. This was their nature.

Patches used his Mana Lumens to grow his claws and teeth. He took a low position in the center of the cellar and turned himself invisible just as the first rat appeared.

Patches hit it with a supersonic yowl, one that tore the rat off its feet. The second one charged past and reached Patches. He swatted at the rodent. The rat jumped back and bit into Patches's paw the next time he tried for another strike.

Patches bit back. But even with his enhanced teeth, the rat's new outer layer of skin was incredibly thick. It actually hurt Patches's teeth, which caused him to hop up into the air and shift backward.

He landed on the first rat, the one he'd already knocked away with an amplified soundwave.

The two tumbled into the shelf filled with casks and other supplies. Patches scurried to his feet and bit into the rodent's neck.

It stopped moving. Patches let up and turned to the other rodent, who was seething with animosity now.

You're next. Patches dipped his head forward, his eyes narrowing on the demonic creature. The rat presented its teeth with a throaty hiss. Patches did the same, his form growing larger.

The rat huffed. It took a step back.

Patches took a step closer to it.

The rat skittered to the side and took off toward the exit. Patches nearly caught up, but the rat was gone before he could fully reach it. The pub cat slid into the stone wall of the cellar and fell backward, dazed for a moment.

That was unpleasant.

Slowly as ever, Patches got back to his feet and took a few lumbering steps forward. He stopped in front of the dead rat's body. He wanted to bring it to the big man upstairs, but he knew that he would just bury it, which would lead to more troubles.

Patches glared at the rat and forced some of his Mana Lumens forward. It took a moment, but soon, the rodent's body faded away until nothing was left of it. Other than eat it, this was what the big man should have done to the rat Patches had left him a few days ago.

He looked down at his paw and saw that there was a bit of blood on it. Patches began licking the blood away. This turned into an entire session of grooming himself.

Once he was ready, he gingerly took the stairs to the second story of the pub. Patches found the big man sleeping on his stomach, one leg hanging off the bed. He approached the big man and began the power transfer process, even though he was exhausted from the fight. The big man needed the power to brew more ale.

The Tavernly Realm would be open any day now, and Patches couldn't wait.

CHAPTER NINE

PINTS FOR SALE

"Good morning to you too," Sylas said on the tail end of a yawn. This was in reference to the warning that flashed in front of him and was slowly starting to fade away.

[You have 87 days until the invasion.]

Sylas summoned his status. His Mana Lumens had been topped off yet again.

Name: Sylas Runewulf
Mana Lumens: 100/100
Class: Brewer
[**Active Quest Contracts:**]
Retrieve Halden Brassmere's hammer

Sylas was a man of his word, and he planned to deal with Halden Brassmere's hammer tomorrow. But he wanted to get his first taste today, to see what others thought of his stronger ale and hopefully raise a few funds for more production.

As he sat at the corner of his bed, he naturally dropped his hand on Patches's head, who rested by his side. "You're such a good cat," Sylas told the cat, who immediately started purring. "Even if you mostly just sleep all day."

Sylas had an easy breakfast of cheese and bread, which he magically toasted in the cellar over one of the burners that worked whenever he wanted it to.

After, Sylas shifted his focus to repairing more of the tables and chair legs, as well as covering a few of the holes that he'd found in various corners of the cellar. Patches joined him while he did this, the cat pointing out places Sylas missed by standing in front of them and staring down at the openings.

"You're so smart," Sylas told the black-and-white cat as he went in for another scratch. Patches let Sylas pet him for a moment before ultimately stepping away. The cat limped back up the stairs to the pub. "What happened to you?" Sylas asked, but by this point, Patches was already gone. "Probably got into something."

Sylas produced another cask of strong ale using the grains that had rejuvenated themselves, leaving him at twenty Mana Lumens. He retrieved the pint bottles he'd found upstairs and took the crate out back to wash them out. Patches joined him, the cat keen to sniff out one of the flagstones in the small backyard that had been overturned.

"That's not great," Sylas said as he looked at the hole that had been uncovered. "Something must have got it. Did you see a wolf? A fox?"

Patches mewed.

He set the crate down, found the shovel, and covered the hole in front of the well.

Sylas used a fresh bucket of water to clean the pint bottles. He took them back downstairs and followed this with several buckets of water to keep in the cellar. He filled fifteen bottles using his very first cask of strong ale. Sylas poured the two pints left into a growler with the idea that he'd hand out samples using shot glasses that he had also found in the cellar.

"But we're going to be stealthy about it," he told Patches as he brought the crate up to the main floor. "We'll set up outside of the Cinderpeak Market, make a few sales, and leave. Just a test." Sylas smirked at how much he was talking to the cat. It had been ages since he'd had a pet.

This thought brought a memory that caused him to tremble.

Sylas recalled the Battle of Willcrest, how the Aurum Kingdom's Royal Guard and the Shadowthorne Empire had been going at it for weeks on end. The memory was as sudden as it was strong.

Sylas had been on watch that morning when he'd seen two mangy dogs fighting over a hunk of flesh, the two just going at it, fighting over meat in an active war zone.

This image stuck with him, especially with what happened later that morning. It had been the day that the Royal Guard finally broke through the Shadowthorne forces. Thousands had died including Sylas's friend Raelis Sund, one of the men he hoped to find in the Underworld. But to do that, he needed access to the Book of Shadows, which according to Mira, was pretty far away.

"One day at a time," Sylas reminded himself as he took a seat at the bar. The motivation he'd just felt had left him. He looked down at the crate of ale that he'd just packaged up. "Come on. We've got to try something new."

Patches hopped into Sylas's lap, taking him off guard.

"So that's how you sneak up on rats, huh?" Sylas scratched behind the purring cat's ear. It made him feel better.

Soon, he was on his way toward Cinderpeak, crate in his arms and a leather satchel he'd found in the bedroom over his shoulder, the growlers and shot glasses inside. Ember Hollow was quiet as always, not a soul out. And aside from the way the Celestial Plains loomed overhead, the constant reminder of one's place in death, it was an otherwise peaceful morning.

Sylas reached the portal on the outskirts of the village and was presented with two options:

- **Cinderpeak**
- **Hexveil - Ember Hollow**

He mentally selected Cinderpeak and portaled away.

———

Sylas figured the shade of a tree would be the perfect place to set up. It was right outside the back entrance to the Cinderpeak Market, and there were signs that people had set up small operations here before, from the hollow sockets of tent pegs to oil stains on some of the larger rocks.

He found a stump, one large enough to keep the growler next to him, and took a seat. Sylas began greeting people as they came in and out of the market, making jokes when appropriate. Soon, he had his first customer, a woman who bought two pints for her husband.

"He'll like it even if it's bad. Hard to get a strong ale around here, and the pub in town is a load of rubbish."

[You have received 20 Mana Lumens.]

"Is it?" Sylas asked the woman, who had a cloth tied under her chin that kept her hair in order. "I haven't visited yet. I'm about to open my place in Ember Hollow."

"The Ugly Duckling is the name. Ale is good, but the place barely opens these days. Last it was open was probably two months ago. The owner acts like it's hard to brew a bit of ale when she's gifted with the power, like you are."

"Gifted with the power?" he asked.

"To brew. You have a pub, right? You're a brewer."

"The Old Lamplighter. I'm still renovating it."

"And it was assigned to you?"

"That's right."

"Then you get the power to make ale, which is rare in these parts. To my knowledge, it's rare for most of the Underworld. People are assigned jobs or they're not. Like me. I didn't get a job. But my husband did."

"And who is your husband?"

"Halden Brassmere. He runs the supply shop in town."

"I know him," Sylas said, now recognizing the woman's voice. She was the hardware store owner's wife. "I'm supposed to retrieve his hammer. Plan to do it tomorrow, actually. Wait, I think I'm supposed to keep that from you. Well, I suppose the hammer is out of the bag now."

She laughed at his terrible joke.

"You know what? Since I still haven't done the chore yet, the pints are on me. How's that?"

"No, it's fine. I'll let you sort your quest contract out with him. Besides." The woman gave Sylas a devilish look. "Who's to say this ale is for him?"

Sylas was pretty sure she was the one that had said that, but he didn't remind her. She soon moved on, ready to get home to enjoy one of the pints.

A new fellow approached, a man in overalls of about forty years of age. He carried a sack of grain over his shoulder. A deep network of creases lined his red face and his eyes, once bright, were now murky and bloodshot. He walked right in front of Sylas, paused, and slowly turned to him.

The man cleared his throat and swallowed in an attempt to stifle a thirst he hadn't felt in a while. How long had it been since he'd been tanked up? Nearly a month. It must have been a month or more. "Selling ale?"

"Strong ale," Sylas told the man, not yet sure of the vibes he was putting off. "Ten MLus a pint."

"And you have how many to sell? Been ages since I was properly rat-arsed."

Sylas grinned at this comment. "I have thirteen pints left. They're going fast this morning." He squinted up at the sky. "I think it's still morning."

"Past noon now. Let me see. Thirteen, so . . . would you take a hundred for the whole lot?"

"I'd prefer not to sell them all to one person," Sylas told the man. "I'm opening a pub in Ember Hollow in the coming days. It's called The Old Lamplighter. Selling my first batch here to raise funds, test the batch, and tell people about the pub I'm opening in Ember Hollow."

"Driving a hard bargain, eh?" the red-faced man huffed. "I'll give you one-twenty. You're out for the day, and don't have to sit here on the stump waiting for the next opportunity to pass you by, or for Constable Leowin to catch wind of you being here."

"Most I'll sell is . . ." Sylas hadn't actually considered this. A small part of him wished that Mira was there. She'd know what to do. "Three per person. I should have said that at the start."

The man licked his lips. It wasn't a tactic he wanted to resort to, but he'd been kicked out of The Ugly Duckling long ago, and the moonshine he kept trying to make with his friends was terrible. "You know you have to have a permit to sell at the market, right?"

"I did not know that. I guess I'm more of an ask-questions-later kind of guy."

"You need a permit," the man said, growing flustered. "And you don't have one, do you?"

Sylas got to his feet and felt like he was slipping back into a former version of himself. He pressed his shoulders back and took on the same demeanor he did when staring down enemy lines. It happened so fast that the red-faced man actually stepped back.

"How about this? I sell you three pints for thirty MLus, and you and I pretend this little meeting never happened."

The man ran his tongue over his teeth. "You're a newcomer."

"I am."

"You don't know the rules and procedures."

"I don't. But I'll learn them as I go. Now, do we have a deal or not?"

The red-faced man considered this for a moment. He could always buy the ale, see if it was any good, and report it to the people that ran the market later. Maybe he'd even get a reward for doing it.

The expression on his face changed into that of a forced grin, one that caused the sides of his eyes to twitch. "Sure. Three will do."

[**You have received 30 Mana Lumens.**]

Sylas grabbed the three pint bottles and gave them to the man, who put one in his pocket and kept the other two in his free hand, the one not holding the bag of grain.

"The Old Lamplighter, huh?"

Sylas slowly nodded. "But if you do stop by, leave any threats at the door. You only get one warning with me."

The red-faced man grunted, but ultimately didn't respond. He moved on and Sylas sat back down on his stump.

Sylas tried to withhold immediate judgment. It was impossible to know what a person had been through, or what they were going through that day, or what was in store for them once they finally decided to drag their feet out of their home or away from their work.

Not everyone was always having a good day, and everyone deserved a place where they could come and relax, have a few pints, talk, be merry, and leave their worries behind.

Yet it was equally important that Sylas run a tight ship. The Old Lamplighter wasn't going to be a family establishment, but it would be cozy, a place to ride out eternity in the abyss.

His next few customers were much easier to deal with.

Sylas ended up cracking open the growler and providing samples with the shot glasses, which certainly helped with sales over the course of an hour. A few people just took samples, promising to visit The Old Lamplighter when it was up and running.

[You have received 10 Mana Lumens.]
[You have received 20 Mana Lumens.]
[You have received 10 Mana Lumens.]
[You have received 10 Mana Lumens.]

It wasn't much longer before Sylas was down to his last three pints, two of which he sold to a nice man who ran a bookshop. The final one went to Mrs. Brassmere, who had come back after sampling the bottles she'd already purchased. Sylas went ahead and gave her what was left in the growler as well, which she gladly took.

"Be sure to share that with your husband," he called after her.

"He'll get what's left in the growler!"

"Tell him I'll see to his hammer tomorrow."

"That old hammer." Mrs. Brassmere waved Sylas's concern away. "He has plenty."

She left, and once she was gone, Sylas sat back down onto the stump. "Not bad." In total, he'd moved fifteen pints at ten Mana Lumens each. He had fully sold out, which was a great sign of things to come. Yet in checking his status, he saw the error he'd made.

Name: Sylas Runewulf
Mana Lumens: 170/170
Class: Brewer
[Active Quest Contracts:]
Retrieve Halden Brassmere's hammer

His total number of Mana Lumens had increased, just as Mira had explained they would. Yet Sylas had made a mistake in brewing a cask that morning.

If Sylas had started his little operation with 100 MLus, he'd now have 250, rather than 170. At least he understood it now. Sylas needed to be strategic about the time of day that he brewed so he could maximize how sales added to his power.

This also made him wonder how many Mana Lumens a person could possibly have. It was easy to think of it like money, but it wasn't money, although what he would be able to do if he got his operation running smoothly and smartly would be like printing money.

While the prospect of a near-constant stream of Mana Lumens would elicit a grin for most, Sylas bit his lip instead.

His years in the Royal Guard had unmasked the destructive potential of wealth and power. And his time on the battlefront had shown him how destructive it could be when the playing field was leveled.

Sylas took the empty crate and turned away. Earlier, he'd considered heading into Cinderpeak to do some shopping. Now, he felt like heading back to the pub instead. But then there was the little gift he needed to make for Patches.

"Just a quick trip to town," Sylas said as he turned in the direction of the volcano.

It wouldn't cost much.

Sylas finished installing the flap and ran his hand through, ensuring that Patches would be able to move back and forth freely through the back door. "See?" he told the cat as he finally came over to investigate what it was that Sylas was doing. "Kitty goes in, and kitty comes out. It's a cat door."

Patches mewed in either confusion or disinterest. It was hard to tell.

"Give it a try. I don't know how you were doing your business before, but I'm pretty sure it was by squeezing through the holes I am still covering up. So here's your new exit."

Patches approached the cat door and sniffed it. He looked up at Sylas, no visible emotion in his eyes, only that borderline acceptance of a cat.

"Just press your head through. You'll be able to get in and out. And you've been doing a great job protecting this place. This will give you something else to guard."

Patches returned to his perch near the window.

"Hey. Wait. Don't you see how this works. I'll go outside." Sylas stepped into the small backyard. "Patches," he called out. "Come on."

This didn't work. Sylas returned to the bar and got the rest of the milk he'd purchased the previous day. This got Patches's attention, the cat instantly perking his ears up. He mewed loudly and jumped down from the windowsill.

"Good, I've got your attention. But the only way you're getting this milk is if you follow me out." Sylas stepped outside before Patches could and shut the door. "The milk is out here," he called.

Patches darted out of the cat door, headed straight down the steps, and nearly faceplanted in the bowl of milk.

Sylas laughed. "Well, at least you know how the cat door works now."

Sylas was just about to head inside when he heard some voices in front of the pub. Rather than walk back through, he came around the front to find Henry standing there with another man dressed in the leather armor and badge worn by the local militia, the Esteemed Coalition of Ember Hollow Defenders.

The second fellow was much larger, with an oddly shaped head that looked like a wedge of cheese. He had an underbite and he carried a big club, larger than the one Sylas had propped up inside.

While Henry had a half grin on his face, the other man was all business. It grew increasingly clear that they were there to do more than check on how the renovations were going. Perhaps Sylas picked this up by the way Henry held his mace.

"Gentlemen," Sylas said. "The Old Lamplighter isn't open yet. But I believe it will be in a few more days."

"We're not here to have a pint." Henry adjusted his stance as if this would somehow give him confidence. Why, *why*, had Tiberius asked him to do this? Why not show up himself if he wanted to intimidate the newcomer? And to send Duncan with him, the dumbest member of the militia. Or maybe that was Cody... Either way, Henry didn't want to be there.

"We're here to deal with you," Duncan said, his underbite giving his words a slight lisp.

"Duncan—"

"You've come here to *deal* with me?" Sylas asked Henry.

"No, we didn't come here to *deal* with you. We're not bandits. We don't want you opening up the pub and we're here to, ahem, persuade you to move your pub somewhere else."

Patches came around and saw the two militiamen. He puffed his chest up.

"This your cat?" Duncan asked.

"It's the pub's cat," Sylas told them, just a hint of menace in his voice now. He would turn it up if he needed to. "You're here because of Tiberius, right?"

"What? No," Henry said. "No, this is our, ahem, this is our idea. Ember Hollow has enough issues being so close to the Hexveil. The last thing we need is a pub attracting the kind of rubbish an establishment like yours is fond of bringing in."

"That's strange. You seemed happy about the ale yesterday."

"You had some of the ale?" Duncan asked. "Didn't tell me that, mate."

"I didn't need to tell you that. I told Tiberius!" Henry blinked twice and bit his lip. "Enough of this. Grab your things; we'll be moving you along."

Henry took a step closer and Patches started to yowl. Sylas was surprised at how loud it became. It was instantly amplified to the point that he was afraid the windows behind him would shatter. "It's fine," he told Patches as he scooped him up in his arms.

"It's the cat making that noise?" Duncan asked, the large man dumbfounded. "Sounded like a giant banshee." Rather than take a step closer to Sylas as Henry just had, Duncan took a big step back. "I don't know about this one here."

Henry brought his mace around. "Sylas, we've been nice up to this point but—"

"Let me stop you right there. You're going to put that mace away, and if you ever—and I mean this, Henry—if you *ever* threaten me with anything again, you will wish you had been reborn in the Chasm." Still clutching Patches tightly, Sylas pointed his finger in the direction he was pretty sure they came from. "Now get out of here. If Tiberius has something to say, he can come around and say it properly. But he'd better bring more than the two of you."

Henry slowly lowered his mace and was glad to do so. His hands were shaking. He'd seen some things as part of the militia. Alongside Tiberius and a few of the others, including Duncan, he'd driven out some pretty nasty demons from the Underword. But what he just saw in Sylas's defiant blue eyes left him spooked.

And he didn't know why.

"I think we'll see what Tiberius has to say," he finally said.

"One more thing," Sylas called to them, changing his tone. Henry turned back to find him still holding Patches, the pub owner seemingly calm. "I'm opening in a few days. You all are welcome, but only if you're on best behavior. There will be none of this 'driving me out of town' nonsense. That's not happening. The Old Lamplighter isn't going anywhere, and if I wasn't already clear, it will be opening soon. Make sure Tiberius knows that."

CHAPTER TEN

TIME FOR A CHANGE

Mira sat on a stool near a shelf full of colorful powders, fragrant herbs, roots, elixirs in colorful glass bottles, and other concoctions she had crafted over the last couple of months. She had just finished augmenting a small pill for Miss Barrowsly, which helped the woman with her troubled knees. She placed this in a canvas bag, and set it with the others that were scheduled to be picked up in the coming days.

Mira checked her Mana Lumens just to get a read of where she was at.

Name: Mira Ravenbane
Mana Lumens: 767/2592
Class: Apothecary
[Active Quest Contracts:]
Deliver vision supplement to Andrew Foxsmart
Create Elixir of Easing for Evelyn Barrowsly
[Lumen Abilities:]
Flight
Lumen Beam
Mana Trace

Mira finished packaging up more of Miss Barrowsly's medicine.

She often overextended herself for her clients, and was proud to see that she hadn't pushed herself as far as she normally did with Miss Barrowsly's pills. Creating an Elixir of Easing would make it so the older woman didn't need the pills at all, but from what Mira had read in the books she'd picked up in

Duskhaven, it would take two thousand *fixed* Mana Lumens to create it, which was something that would create quite the tax on her system.

Miss Barrowsly had offered to pay for it, and had even offered to try to give her the Mana Lumens on a weekly basis, but Mira didn't want her to go through the hassle, and she certainly didn't want her to have to get loan from a Mana Lumen repository, like the one in Duskhaven. She could take it a day at a time for now until Mira had an additional two thousand to spare.

It was too bad the food Mira was able to imbue with Mana Lumens didn't work if she ate it herself. But it made sense that her job had limitations, or at least this was how she justified it. The system in place certainly was unfair at times.

Commotion outside drew Mira's attention. She approached the door of her shop, which was located at the front of the place she shared with her uncle, and peeked out.

Mira saw Henry and Duncan milling about, the two militiamen speaking in low voices to one another. Duncan kicked a stone, the big man tensing up as he heard Mira's door open. Henry looked up at her as she approached and quickly placed his mace behind his back. "Mira," he said with a wolfish grin.

"What happened?"

"Nothing," Duncan said.

"Why are you two out here with weapons, then? Was there a demon?"

"No demon," Duncan said, "just an ornery pub owner."

Mira glared at the two of them. "Wait right here. I'll get my uncle."

She stormed through the front door and headed out back, where she found Tiberius chopping wood.

Her uncle tossed a piece of wood to the side and sized her up with his one good eye. His other eye was milk pale and stemmed from an injury Tiberius had received in a battle years ago. This eye was a testament to his stubbornness. It was the kind of thing Mira could fix with her medicines, yet he refused to take anything, and had let it go to the point he could no longer see out of it.

A short man, Tiberius had a narrow frame and a squat build, which Mira knew was nothing like the tall, chiseled generals of the Shadowthorne Empire. Yet he had made it to this rank anyway, and in his lifetime, more people feared him than liked him. This feat extended to Tiberius in the Underworld, especially with his demon hunter class.

"Mira," he said with a huff that blew a long strand of his thick black hair free.

"After what I told you yesterday, you send your two lugheads to intimidate Sylas? He's getting some warning of an invasion, and rather than reach out, this is your solution? Really, Uncle?"

Tiberius brought his axe up and leaned it against his shoulder. He was an intimidating man, but Mira was long past the point that she would let him bully her. She'd seen him run good people out of town before based on nonsense, and she wasn't going to stand for it this time, no matter their past.

She was putting her foot down.

"Well? Do you have something to say for yourself?"

"Did he leave yet?" her uncle grunted.

Mira was almost beside herself. Before responding, she paced for a moment, her arms now crossed over her chest.

"Well? Did he?"

"Of course he didn't. Sylas was a soldier too, just like you—"

"He was a Royal Guard, a sworn enemy of mine."

Mira tried not to glare at him. She knew from past experience this didn't work. The angrier she got at Tiberius, the more he closed up. There were diplomatic ways to influence her uncle. "You know that doesn't matter here."

"It matters to some of us. And you don't understand what a pub will do to Ember Hollow."

"Why are you afraid of people moving here?"

"Ember Hollow has enough people living in it to be manageable. But that's not the part I'm afraid of."

"Then what?"

Tiberius settled the agitation he was feeling with a deep breath out. He liked having Mira around, but she was hardheaded, and she rarely understood the point of secrecy and especially the concept of a need-to-know basis. "It's important to limit certain kinds of influences in Ember Hollow," he said through gritted teeth.

"Is this about alcohol? You love having an ale in Cinderpeak when the pub is open."

"It rarely is," Tiberius said under his breath. "And that's not what I mean when I say limiting certain kinds of influences. I'm talking about MLus."

"MLus? What does Sylas being here have to do with MLus?" Mira's eyes went wide. Suddenly, she understood what her uncle was hinting at. This only bolstered her anger.

"Do you get it now, Mira? If this pub opens and it becomes popular, your little friend—"

"He's not little. He's taller than you."

"Those kinds of statements don't bother me and you know that by now," Tiberius hissed. "If the pub becomes popular, this newcomer of yours—"

"Mine?"

"He will quickly have more MLus than the rest of us. People will flood to Ember Hollow, and that will make the place harder to manage."

"It isn't your job to manage it."

"As head of the Esteemed Coalition of Ember Hollow Defenders, it *is* my job to keep it manageable."

"I'm not accepting that as an explanation. Come on then." She motioned for him to follow her.

"Come on?" Tiberius raised an eyebrow at his troublesome niece.

"We're going to the pub so you can meet Sylas. And we're sending Duncan and Henry home. You're not going to start trying to intimidate people around here. Not again, Uncle. It's time for a change."

Sylas had just started deep cleaning the bar when Mira entered with a short, agitated man. Part of Sylas wanted to continue cleaning for a moment, just to remind the pair of who was in charge here, but he decided against this in the end. He tossed his rag down and offered the two of them a firm grin.

Mira gestured to the man. "Sylas, this is my uncle, Tiberius."

Tiberius instantly sized Sylas up.

As a lord commander, he had seen dozens of soldiers that fit the same bill as the big man standing before him with his piercing blue eyes. It didn't impress him. To Tiberius, Sylas had pushed past the prime of his youth, and he probably should have ranked up. Yet something about his demeanor, the way the bearded man returned his gaze told Tiberius all he needed to know.

Sylas was unruly. It was best to deal with this now.

"I'll skip the pleasantries. Sylas Runewulf, yes?" A cracked grin formed on Tiberius's face. "Ember Hollow isn't in need of a pub. You can take your casks with you and find another place. Perhaps beyond Battersea. I've heard Wraithwick is in need of a pub."

"Uncle—"

"Mira, you don't understand."

"She's not the only one that doesn't understand," Sylas told Tiberius. "And as I told your henchmen—"

"They are *militiamen*."

"Same difference. As I told your lackeys, I'm not going anywhere. So if I were you, I'd get used to this fact." Sylas stepped around the bar. Patches joined him, the cat with his gaze fixed on Tiberius, his hair standing in agitation.

"I'm not one to be trifled with."

Sylas took a step closer to Tiberius and looked down into his dark eyes. "Mira says you were a lord commander, but she never said which army, and I'm going to go out on a limb here that we were on opposite sides. An Aurumite would never show up and start making demands of another soldier. Unlike the Shadowthorne Empire, we had respect for one another, from grunts to those at the very top. Mutual respect."

"You dare threaten me?"

"You're in my pub, are you not?" Sylas glanced at Mira. "Is there another authority who can settle this? Some village council, a mayor? Or are we really just a smattering of homes on the edge of the Underworld without any civil order?"

Mira smoothed her hands over the front of her dress. "I wouldn't describe it like that, but, no, there is no one—"

"I'm someone," Tiberius said with a stomp. "The Esteemed Coalition of Ember Hollow Defenders runs this village, and has for several years now! You, sir—"

"You really need to do something about that name," Sylas said with a chuckle that he knew would get under Tiberius's skin. It was clear that the small, black-haired man disliked him, which put Sylas at an advantage. He wasn't quick-tempered, but once his fuse was officially lit, things changed rapidly. If anyone wasn't to be trifled with, it was Sylas.

And showing up in his bar, demanding he leave was something Sylas wasn't going to allow to happen.

A spat of silence followed as Tiberius thought about the best way to go about this. Challenging the man would be foolhardy, even if he was reeling inside from being talked down to in such a way. And by an Aurumite! Due to his size, Tiberius had never been an intimidating figure. Yet he'd learned early on to make up for his ability to intimidate through sheer cunning.

"I see," Tiberius finally said. "So you won't leave peacefully in the night, then."

"I will not. I won't leave peacefully in the day either. Now, if you'd like a pint, I'd be more than happy to share what I'm brewing around here. Whatever war was happening when we were alive is over now. I don't care about the Aurum Kingdom any more than you should care about the Shadowthorne Empire. It's done. That war doesn't extend here. They had us fighting like dogs to please royals and to further divide two kingdoms that have a lot in common. It's over."

"This isn't about that war."

"Then what is it about?"

Tiberius started to back away. "You'll find out what it is about soon enough. Mira, let's go."

Mira's eyes flared with golden mana. "You will *not* order me around, Uncle. I will stay if I want."

Tiberius started to say something and stopped himself. "Fine. Enjoy your time with the newcomer." He pointed a finger at Sylas. "This isn't over." Tiberius stormed out the pub and slammed the door behind him.

Mira and Sylas stood there for a moment as Patches alternated between the two of them.

Finally, Sylas motioned for her to follow him down to the cellar. She took the steps without saying anything. Sylas patted his big hand on a stool and she sat just about the time that Patches started down the cellar steps.

"You made him a cat door up there?"

"I did." Sylas poured up a pint of the lighter ale. "And I made this for you. I mean, ahem, I took your suggestion and brewed a lighter ale. But I'll call it a regular ale, and the barley stuff is the strong ale. That's what I'm thinking, anyway. This stuff is made of rye. Figured you'd want to be the first to taste it."

"Pour yourself one and let's do this properly," she said as she took the pint glass from him. "We need it after that."

"Don't mind if I do."

"Sorry, about my uncle. He grows on you."

"Like a mold. I know the types. Did he say anything about this invasion warning I've been getting?"

She shook her head. "He found it curious, that's all."

"It's more than curious."

"I would agree with you there. Perhaps you can make amends with my uncle and his men as the pub opens and they see that you aren't a direct threat to Ember Hollow. You'll need them if there's an actual invasion."

"Why don't they have actual weapons?" Sylas asked, which was something he'd noticed. It didn't seem like anyone had the kinds of steel weapons he was accustomed to seeing. "All I've seen are maces."

"Swords and other kinds of weapons don't exist here. You'll mostly see people with maces and axes, but those axes are the same they use to chop wood. Some people have daggers, but that is about it."

"Weapons don't exist here?" Sylas gave her a funny look.

"They exist, but they deteriorate rapidly. Some people have managed to keep them from deteriorating using MLus. But I think it is how the Underworld is designed. It prevents widespread war."

"But people have maces and they can use magic."

"Yes, that is true. But the kinds of weapons we had in our world, you don't see them here," she said, not wanting to remind Sylas of the damage their people were capable of causing. "Are you going to drink with me, or what?" she asked, hoping to switch subjects.

Mira knew herself well enough to know that she wasn't ready to delve too deeply into their shared past, even if they hadn't known each other.

"Yes, not a bad idea." Sylas returned with his own pint. They clinked their glasses together and each took a sip.

"Very good," Mira said, just a bit of foam on her lip.

She caught Sylas looking at this and quickly wiped it away. She took another sip of the ale, and found it to have a unique robustness, its initial maltiness followed with caramellike undertones. It was unexpectedly smooth, light on her palate, which made it all too easy to take another sip.

"Well?" Sylas asked. "Looks like someone likes it."

"You have a customer in me," she said. "Will there be food?"

Sylas looked over to the oven in the cellar, which was vented to the outside by an iron pipe. "I haven't really thought of it. But I have what I need to cook. Maybe once we get up and running."

"You know that you can use MLus to cook, right?"

"I know. I use my power to heat the pots."

"What food do you have?"

"Right now? Just some bread, cheese, and eggs. I was going to make myself a sandwich. I've been eating lots of sandwiches lately. I never really was a cook."

Mira turned to the stove and quickly whipped up a meal of toasted bread and fried the eggs with melted cheese on top.

Mira gave Sylas the sandwich and he bit off a big hunk of it. "That's good."

Mira went for a small bite of her sandwich. She considered the taste for a moment. It wasn't bad, but she could have done better with the ingredients she had at home. Sylas seemed to like it, which was all that mattered. "You really haven't played around with MLus and their possibilities, have you?"

"Not really. I've been more interested in getting the pub ready for its opening and brewing ale. I did make some MLus today, though."

"You did? How?"

"I took a crate of the strong pints to the Cinderpeak Market and sold them. Netted a load of MLus. I realize now that I made the mistake of brewing in the morning. I'll need to remember the compound aspect of the way the MLus stack."

"You're not supposed to do that, Sylas."

"Do what?"

"You just showed up and sold the pints?"

"I did. What's wrong with that?"

"Sylas."

"What?"

"You didn't think there'd be a permit or something?"

"If there was, no one asked me about it."

Mira slowly shook her head. She took another sip from her pint and let it go. "Well, someone will find out at some point, and it will cost you."

"Are there jails here?"

"The Underworld is not the same as where we're from. But there are consequences. They'll fine you, and there are dungeons that the constables use."

"So jails."

"Yes, jails."

"Well, I'm not worried about it. I just need to sell pints for a few more days. It'll help me get all the casks filled, and then I can open."

"Be careful."

"You're worried about me?" Sylas grinned at her. Little did he know that he had a small piece of egg stuck in his tooth.

Mira turned away. "I suppose I should be getting back home. I have a few things I still need to work on."

"Wait, before you do. I wanted to show you something I found. Follow me." Sylas led Mira upstairs, to the bedroom where he had discovered the dormant portal. "What do you think?"

"This was what was in here?" Mira cautiously approached the outer rim of the rune that had been seemingly branded onto the floor. "I've never seen anything like it."

Patches exploded into the space. His girth took over from there, pulling him forward and directly onto the runic writing burned into the wooden floor. He rolled once, got up, tensed with embarrassment, and plopped back down on the rune.

Mira started to laugh. "I guess it is safe."

"He was resting on the portal last night. He didn't teleport anywhere or anything. Anyway, I thought you'd know what it meant."

"You might need a sigilist, and they aren't very common. I think there's one in Duskhaven."

"How far is that from here?"

"Two days or so. We could—"

"We could go together?" Sylas asked, finishing her sentence. "Sorry. If there are appropriate accommodations along the way, I could fund them. That is, if you're available."

"I could be," she told him. "Want to make it a quest contract?"

"A quest contract? Is there any reason to do that?"

"There is, actually. Oftentimes, completion of the quest contracts provide bonuses. There's one catch, however."

"Yes?"

"If you make a quest contract, it will remain on your status until you complete it or cancel it. So don't make too many or it will become unwieldy. Ready?" Yet again, Mira's eyes shone with golden light.

[New Quest Contract - Travel to Duskhaven with Mira Ravenbane to visit the sigilist. Accept? Y/N?]

"I accept."

"Good. We'll get this solved. To open a quest, simply focus on it. You'll notice changes in your environment when you do."

"Changes?"

"If you need to go somewhere, it will lead you. That's what I mean by changes. Now, let me get a sketch of the rune." Mira sat across from it and removed a small journal from the bag she carried. She looked up at Sylas. "Well? Don't you have something to do?"

"I could brew two more casks. That's what I was planning to do, anyway."

"Do you have enough MLus?"

Sylas checked his status just to be sure.

Name: Sylas Runewulf
Mana Lumens: 168/170
Class: Brewer
[Active Quest Contracts:]
Retrieve Halden Brassmere's hammer
Travel to Duskhaven with Mira Ravenbane to visit the sigilist

It would take 160 MLus to brew two casks. He had just enough. "I sure do."

"Good. Get started. I'll join you when I'm done here. And how many casks will you have after today?"

"Four," Sylas told her. "I'll open the pub when I have closer to ten. After that, I promise to quit selling at the market."

She gave him a dismissive hunch with her shoulders. "Don't say I didn't warn you."

Patches started in the cellar later that night. He checked the casks to see that four were now full, which was good. The big man was progressing, and he'd be able to open the Tavernly Realm soon.

Very good, Patches thought as he made his rounds. He came to his cat door, which admittedly didn't like at first. But it was growing on him. He even peeked his head out, intent on doing a bit of exploring when he sensed something in the small yard.

Spooked, Patches whisked back inside and quickly found his favorite lookout point by the window. What followed began with a curl of golden mana, one that turned a sinister hue as the trickster demon, the same that had resurrected the rats, formed into existence.

Patches flitted his ears back. He bared his teeth, and sent the power to them that made them grow. Doing the same to his claws, Patches prepared for the evil spirit to enter the pub. He watched the small door the big man had installed, aware that any moment the trickster demon would enter.

Then, it would be on. Patches would do whatever he had to do to defend his home.

Yet the demon never came to the back door. It merely floated over the backyard as if it were looking for the rats that it had brought back from the dead.

You won't find one of them, Patches thought, his whiskers now on edge. His senses were so heightened that he could almost hear the demon's thoughts as it debated if it should move on for the night or not.

Luckily for Patches, it vanished, and the trickster demon took with it any malice that had been lingering in the air.

But Patches had to be sure.

He waited thirty more minutes by the window. Once he was certain it wasn't coming back, he moved over to the cat door and stuck his head out.

Gone.

Patches slipped back upstairs, where he found the big man sleeping on his stomach. He lowered his chin and began transferring power to him. Soon, Patches started to feel a bit light-headed.

Thinking of his power brought the number up that he couldn't quite interpret. It seemed fine, so he pushed it even further until he was certain the big man had all the power he needed.

With a final yawn, Patches collapsed onto his side and fell asleep.

CHAPTER ELEVEN

AZOR

Sylas was up early the next morning feeling fully recharged and ready to see about Mr. Brassmere's hammer.

[**You have 86 days until the invasion.**]

The prompt was certainly alarming, but Sylas knew there wasn't much he could do about it at the moment. Besides, he had time.

He lay back down for a moment and began petting Patches. The piebald pub cat was sleeping in as he always did. Yet as Sylas scratched him behind the ear, Patches started to purr softly.

"You'll take care of the place today while I'm out, right?"

Patches continued to purr.

"Good. I guess I'd better get started for the day." Sylas headed downstairs. He made himself a simple egg sandwich, vowing to get more food later once he had finished with his first quest contract.

In the two hours that followed, Sylas continued his work at the pub. This included tightening the wobbly legs of two of the tables, dealing with the intrusive plants that lined the outer walls of The Old Lamplighter, checking and then counting the number of lumen lamps he needed to replace, fixing one of the squeaky doors upstairs, thoroughly checking the other casks for leaks, hammering down a loose floorboard, and cleaning and inventorying all the glassware.

He had several cases of bottles that he'd be able to sell at the market. After getting the business going, Sylas would figure out if more bottling was in order. If he had a surplus, it would be a great way to sell to other towns and people not wanting to visit the pub.

There was also the roof. Sylas knew he was going to have to head up there to deal with some of the shingles, but that could wait until the interior was ready to go. He still needed to sand the bar as well.

"Endless tasks," Sylas said, which wasn't a lament. Sylas liked the tasks associated with running a pub. It would become a bit more difficult when there were patrons, but that was something he could handle by hiring someone to help him out.

Sylas headed down to the cellar, where he filled twenty bottles of strong ale. If he sold them all, he would net himself two hundred MLus, which would go a long way in making more ale for tomorrow.

This time, he didn't fill up a growler to make samples, an act which paid off once Sylas reached the Cinderpeak Market and quickly sold all twenty bottles in little under an hour.

"Not bad at all," he said as he accessed his status.

Name: Sylas Runewulf
Mana Lumens: 370/370
Class: Brewer
[Active Quest Contracts:]
Retrieve Halden Brassmere's hammer
Travel to Duskhaven with Mira Ravenbane to visit the sigilist

Sylas had done this smart thing this morning in not brewing when he woke up, and he now had enough Mana Lumens to brew four of the small casks.

He wound through the market until he came to the guy who dealt grains.

"I'm Sylas," he told the man, who now wore a cap low on his brow. "Bought some grains the other day."

"I remember you, the guy with the new pub, right?" the man asked. "My name is Malcolm, by the way. Don't know if I introduced myself or not. Anyway, what can I do for you?"

"Because of my class, the grains have been rejuvenating themselves. At least that appears to be the case. I'm no expert."

"Not yet, you aren't, but that makes sense if you're classed as a brewer."

"Right, I'd still like to set up delivery of grains, however. Maybe once every two weeks or so."

"Refresh the batch?"

"That's right."

"That works for me," Malcolm said. "I need to stop by for a pint as well, been meaning to."

"By all means. We should be open any day now."

"Good to know."

"And we can set up a delivery then." Sylas and the grain supplier shook hands.

"Looking forward to it, mate."

Sylas left the market and focused on the active quest contract in question, just as Mira had explained to him.

He was suddenly familiar with the direction he needed to travel.

It was as if he had visited the place before, enough times that the location itself had been etched onto his very soul. West of Cinderpeak, the hammer was located on rolling farmland that was close to the Hexveil, a place known as the Seedlands. To reach it, Sylas would have to head through a forest.

"Easy enough." Sylas turned toward his destination.

Soon, the farms that grew up the slopes of the volcano beyond Cinderpeak disappeared, replaced by enchanting forest unlike any Sylas had seen in his world. The trees were astounding in size, their canopies bioluminescent through ethereal blues that blotted out the golden clouds above. Everything seemed to change color here including Sylas's hand, which now had a bluish tone to it.

This brought a memory from his past: a battle during the winter in which many on both sides froze to death. Sylas shook his head and quickly moved on from this thought. Although he did note that he needed to look for some people in the Underworld—Kael and Quinlan Ashdown, and Raelis Sund—who he hoped were somewhere accessible. There was also his father, but to find any of them, he'd need to travel to Battersea to view the Book of Shadows.

"Maybe I need to make a contract with myself for that one," he said.

Sylas walked in relative silence for the next hour. He grew cautious once he reached what he felt was the deepest part of the forest. Before heading in, he searched around for a stick and found one that would work as a club.

"Need to get a knife too," he mumbled as he reached a campsite. He was just about to pass by when he noticed a few embers flickering in the ash, the cinders barely strong enough to push back the spectral glow of the forest.

Sylas hovered his hand over the embers, causing them to spark.

"Thank you," came a female voice, one that Sylas initially took as sinister.

He stumbled backward and grabbed his club as a figure began to materialize over the fire.

Translucent and elegant, the fiery form was a symphony of curves and warmth, crafted from the whims of a fire that grew with intensity until it died down. The flames that composed her body danced lightly now, casting shadows that ebbed and flowed as she took a step closer to Sylas.

Naturally, Sylas brought his club to the ready, which caused the fire spirit to laugh. "You know that won't work against me, right?" she asked, her voice just a bit husky now yet without the malice Sylas felt he'd heard earlier. Perhaps it hadn't been malice at all. It could have been her dying breath for all he knew.

"Are you from the Chasm?" he asked.

"I am," she said, now curious as to why the man hadn't tried to extinguish her flames. She all but assumed this was what he would have done. The last adventurer she'd come across had tried, but he'd gotten spooked at the glowing embers. When was that? Days ago?

"You're an evil spirit?" Sylas asked, not certain of why he was questioning her.

"Hardly. Humans always think spirits are evil until they get to know them."

What Sylas should have done was run at this point. He was sure Mira would know what to do with something like this, but he certainly didn't. Yet something told Sylas that the fire spirit wasn't evil, not like the Demon Shifter that had first attacked him outside of Ember Hollow. "But you're from the Chasm."

"I am."

"Are all elemental spirits from the Chasm?"

"Some are, and some aren't. It depends where they were invoked or the contracts they have made."

"Contracts?"

"With humans like yourself."

"You want to make a contract with me?"

The fire spirit shifted to the right, her form like a flowing river of flames as it undulated back and forth. "I never said that. What is your name?"

"Sylas Runewulf. Yours?"

"Azor."

Sylas cleared his throat. "In that case, nice to meet you, Azor. I'm actually on my way to do something, so if you don't mind, I think I'll be moving along."

"You're just going to leave me here?"

"I don't know what to do with you."

"What do you do in the Underworld?" she asked.

If Sylas wasn't mistaken, it seemed like the fire spirit was sulking to some degree. "Here? I run a pub. Actually, it's not running yet but it will be in a few days. It's called The Old Lamplighter."

"And there is a fireplace in this pub?"

"There is."

"And you're running the place by yourself?"

"There's a cat there too. His name is Patches."

"Is he cute?"

"Incredibly so. Why?"

"Can I see the pub and this cat?"

"Can you see it?" Sylas asked.

"Yes. If there's a fireplace and it's a nice pub, and there's a cute cat, it might be perfect for me."

"I don't know what use a fire spirit would be in a pub, sorry," Sylas said, even if he could imagine how nice it would be if a fire was always going. Maybe she could help with food too? There were a couple of ways Azor could be helpful, but he didn't know her yet, and he wasn't keen on inviting fire into his pub, especially with most of the structure made of wood.

"How do I know you won't burn the place down?" he finally asked.

"Why would I do that?"

"Because you're fire?"

Azor looked down at her arms. "I suppose you have me there. There's always the contract."

"A contract between us?"

"Exactly. If we had one, you'd be certain I wouldn't burn the place down because we could put it in that contract. I just think I should see the pub first. What's the name again?"

"The Old Lamplighter."

"I am a lamplighter myself."

Sylas took a long, hard look at Azor. It was clear that she wasn't the kind of fire he was used to seeing. There was a golden glow to her silhouette, her form a serpentine allure. She was clearly magical.

"Well?" she asked. "What do you think? I'll join you for the rest of the day and we can see if we get along."

"Are you hard to get along with?"

"I've been known to be a bit fiery," she said, a joke that made her laugh long and hard. "I'm sorry."

Sylas smirked at the fire spirit. "You should be. I'll tell you what, you can join me, but only if you meet someone I know later. An apothecary."

"Are they going to try to cure me of something?"

"Not to my knowledge. I just want a second opinion."

Azor scrutinized Sylas for a moment. "You aren't the only one."

"So we have a deal?"

"I guess we do."

"We don't have to shake on it," she said, even though she produced her hand, flames licking off her knuckles.

"No, we do not. A verbal agreement then."

"Verbal agreement works for me."

"And how will you travel with me? I don't have a lantern or anything like that. I suppose I could scoop up some ash."

"Scoop up some ash?" While Azor didn't quite have pupils, the way her face shifted in the flames made Sylas feel as if she'd rolled her eyes at him. "I have a solution. I promise it won't hurt."

———

The flame tattoo felt warm yet it didn't hurt in any way. Azor had been right about that.

"And we can still talk like this?" Sylas asked as he looked down at the glowing tattoo on his forearm. Or was it a branding? He ran his finger over it. It was definitely smooth to the touch.

"You can hear me, can't you?" the fire spirit asked.

"I can. But others can't, right?"

"No, they cannot."

"And the tattoo isn't permanent?"

"No. Once I leave your body, the only sign that we ever bonded will be some redness that will fade."

"So you've done this before?"

"All elemental spirits have done this before. It's an easier way to get around, especially if you've bonded with someone. Not saying we're bonded. I guess the better word is contracted."

"And if we contracted, what would you get out of it?"

"Eventually I'd need to take some of your Mana Lumens, but I think there's a way around that."

"Oh?" Sylas looked down at his forearm again. The flame tattoo was of simple design, just three plumes lifting from a rounded point. He tried to think if he'd seen anyone else with this kind of marking, but was pretty sure he hadn't.

"So what are we doing anyway?" she asked.

"I have a quest contract that I plan to handle before heading back to Cinderpeak to pick up supplies."

"And you live in Ember Hollow?"

"Yes."

"I can't say I've heard of Ember Hollow, but I'm only familiar with the larger cities here in the Underworld like Battersea. That's where I was hoping to end up, but it's far away."

"You probably haven't heard of it. Ember Hollow is barely a village. More of an abandoned hamlet on the edge of the known world, right up next the Hexveil. Are you from this area? Wait, you're from the Chasm."

"I am, this is my first time in the Underworld. May I ask you something?"

"Sure."

"Why are we walking when you could fly? I thought most people here can fly."

"I don't know how to fly," Sylas told her honestly. "I am still getting used to the various ways I can use my MLus to enhance my abilities."

"So you're in a hoarding mode."

"Sure, you could call it that," he said as he swept a stray branch out of his way. "I'm hoarding because I would like to make four casks of ale tonight, two strong and two regular."

"This apothecary you know. Is she pretty familiar with the Underworld?"

"She is."

"Then I'm sure she would know more about flying."

"I'll have to ask her. Either way, we aren't much farther now," Sylas said. Even though he'd never been to the place they were going, he could sense they were close due to the quest contract. "What about you?"

"Me?"

"Your MLus? Do you have any?"

"Just a small amount. My power is tied to people I contract with. So I should be asking you if you have a lot."

"Getting closer to four hundred."

"That's it?"

"I've only been dead a few days," Sylas told her, which might have been one of the strangest sentences he had said in a while.

"I suppose that makes sense. With the pub, you'll gain loads quickly. Do you have food options yet?" she asked, circling back to an idea she had about gaining Mana Lumens. Azor didn't know if she'd ultimately form a contract with Sylas, but he seemed nice, and in doing so, she would be able to stay in the Underworld.

"Food options? Nah. I don't even have all the casks filled yet. I haven't thought of food. But a good pub should have something."

"I was a chef, you know. In the Chasm."

"The Chasm has cities?"

"It has similar things to the Underworld, only the place is filled with demons. Humans don't exist there. They become demons once they go there. But some are more civilized demons than others. Not all of them are plotting ways to break through the Hexveil and come to the Underworld. So yes, there are cities. And I was once contracted with a pair who ran a restaurant."

"I understand you can add heat to something, but how would you cook without being able to touch the pots and pans, not to mention the food itself?" Sylas asked.

"I can touch things."

"Without burning them?"

"There are types of gloves and aprons I can use. Fireweave cloth. That's what I need to cook and function more like one of you. They have tailors near volcanos who are able to make it. Are there any volcanoes around here?"

"Cinderpeak."

"Then maybe there is someone there. The material is woven by these fireweave tailors from the lava itself. If I had some, I could interact with objects just like you."

Sylas thought about this for a moment. He imagined the fire spirit with a pair of gloves and an apron on. "Fireweave cloth. Is it just for elemental spirits like you?"

"It is for a number of things, but yes, it's for us as well. You really haven't encountered one of us yet?" she asked.

"Not to my knowledge."

"And no one with tattoos?"

"Not that I remember."

"Well, you said it yourself, you're still new. But yes, I can cook, can cook very well thank-you-very-much, and I could do even better if I had some fireweave gear. But I'd have to agree to a contract with you."

"I feel like there's a bit more to it than you're letting on."

"In contracting? Perhaps," she said. "Some of it isn't so bad. Like the tattoo. Who doesn't want a glowing tattoo?"

"I thought you said it was temporary."

"It is right now. But if we contract, it'll remain permanently. We can travel together this way. You'll also have some immunities to fire and heat while we are contracted. Now, there is one limitation," she told Sylas as they finally came to a farm at the edge of the woods.

It was the farm he was looking for, Sylas could feel it. "Limitation?"

"If I'm somewhere else, I can't teleport to you, even if we're contracted."

"You mean if I was in Cinderpeak, and you were in Ember Hollow, and I needed your help?"

"Yes."

"Interesting. Give me a moment." Sylas looked at the ramshackle farm and considered his options. Perhaps this would be an easy exchange. Maybe the guy just forgot to give Mr. Brassmere his hammer back. Sylas really didn't know what he was about to get himself into, but he was fine with that. He had made it this far.

"How do you want to do this?" she asked.

"Let's just knock and see what happens. Unless he's in the fields." Sylas looked around the house but didn't see anyone working in the paltry fields beyond. He returned his focus to the front door.

Sylas knocked on the door and immediately heard a male voice on the other side.

"What is it?" the voice called out.

"Tell him you're here to buy his farm."

"Why would I do that?" Sylas whispered to Azor.

"To get him to come out."

Sylas cleared his throat. "Urgent message from The Old Lamplighter Pub in Ember Hollow."

Azor laughed at the back of his head. "What kind of urgent message could a pub possibly have?"

"I don't know. It's better than telling him I'm here to buy a farm."

After a few locks clicked, the doorframe opened to reveal a man with graying hair, wild tufts of which stuck out from beneath a threadbare hat. The man's clothing was shabby and covered in patches. His boots, which he wore in the home, were caked with mud. There was a dog barking in one of the spare rooms, the door shut to prevent him from attacking. "An urgent message, eh?"

Sylas placed his foot in the doorframe so the man couldn't close the door. "Actually, I'm here to collect Halden Brassmere's hammer. As for the pub, it'll be open in a few days and you're certainly invited to have an ale."

The man's face flashed pale. "You're a collector?"

"No, I'm just doing Mr. Brassmere a favor."

The man started to curse under his breath. He tried to shut the door on him but was prevented due to Sylas's foot. "You can't just barge in here—"

"I haven't barged in anywhere," Sylas said in a calm voice that had a menacing undertone. It came naturally to him, the same kind of voice he had used before in verbal encounters with soldiers of the Shadowthorne Empire. "The hammer, please, and I'll be on my way. What's your name?"

"Brom." The man shook his head in anger. "My name shouldn't mean anything to you."

"I'm Sylas Runewulf, and you're right, your name shouldn't. But now we know each other, which is something. The hammer, and I'll be on my way."

Brom's eyes began to glow with a golden intensity. This glow vanished once he saw the flames that had lifted off Sylas's shoulder, flames which morphed into an enormous fiery guardian that loomed over both of them.

He took a step back. "You'll . . . you'll never catch me!"

Brom took off into his home, Sylas quickly on his heels. He tackled Brom and the two smashed into a shoddily made dresser, which instantly splintered. It was only once they hit the ground that Sylas noticed the heat radiating off his own arms, the way the man screamed as if his face were being pushed close to a fire.

Sylas immediately let go. By the time he got to his feet, Brom was cowering in a corner, his dog barking madly behind a closed door near the two.

"Hammer," Sylas said as he swallowed a sense of savageness that had risen in his chest.

"It's in the shed out back." Brom pointed toward the back door, his eyes tracing over his arm. "What did you do to me?"

"I tackled you because you ran."

"The fire. How . . . ? Are you classed as an elementalist?"

"Nope. I'm just here to collect the hammer. Anyway. I'll be doing that now." Sylas turned away from Brom. He headed out the back door and immediately turned his focus to Azor. "I could have handled that myself, you know."

"He was going to attack you."

"How?"

"Didn't you see his eyes?"

Sylas thought back to what had just happened. The sudden action had both sped everything up and slowed down at the same time, just as he had experienced on the battlefield. He faintly remembered Brom's eyes glowing. "I did," he finally told Azor.

"And he would have used whatever MLus he had to flee. You got him before he could do that, and I helped. That's all."

"He called me an elementalist. Must be another class."

"An elementalist is your version of me," Azor told Sylas. "I've met the demon variety."

Sylas opened the shed and found the tool in question.

"This was a lot of work for a hammer," he said as he examined the piece. The hammer's head was made from a steel that he hadn't seen before, one with a slight turquoise glow to it in certain lights. "Anyway. We'll go to Cinderpeak now, then the pub. I wonder if there's a portal around here."

"You could always ask Brom. It's getting late."

Sylas looked back to the farmhouse. He entered through the back door to find Brom still agitated, the man clutching his arm around his knee while his dog continued barking in the other room. "I got the hammer. Listen, if you need a hammer, I'll get you one."

"I don't need your charity. I just liked that hammer."

"So you kept it because you liked it?"

"I was going to eventually return it."

Sylas shook his head. He didn't know the man's true reasoning, nor did he want to get further involved than he already was. "Is there a portal around here?"

"There is." Brom pointed with his chin to the back door. "Just head past my field, reach the next farmhouse, and you'll see it."

"One more thing."

"Yeah?"

"Stop by The Old Lamplighter in Ember Hollow in a few days. First pint is on me." Sylas approached the man and offered him his hand. "It's my pub, I'm a brewer."

Brom took it. "A free pint?"

"A free pint. And tell any of your farmer friends they'll have a free pint waiting for them as well." Sylas helped Brom to his feet. "Sorry about earlier."

Meanwhile, back at the pub, Patches's ears perked up when heard some disturbances outside. He bolted downstairs and took his place near the window that looked over the small backyard, where he found a masked man lurking about. The man looked through the bay window, pointed at Patches dismissively, and returned to sizing up the back entrance.

After taking a big step back, the soon-to-be intruder charged toward the back door, his shoulder flaring gold with Mana Lumens. The door blew off its hinges and ripped in two as the masked man reached the interior of the pub.

Not in my home, you don't!

Patches moved into action immediately. His form vanished, but not before he grew to twice his size, his claws and teeth ready to go.

Patches jumped all the way up to his masked face and wrapped his entire invisible body around the man's head.

His sheer girth and the surprise of his movement had the man on his back in a matter of seconds. The two scrambled for a moment, Patches still invisible as he locked his claws into the side of the man's face and bit down on his nose.

Patches jumped backward and triggered his supersonic yowl, the sound loud enough that it began shattering the pint glasses that Sylas had already stocked behind the bar.

Patches hurtled himself at the man's feet, which knocked him over. He clawed the man's legs and bit down into his thigh. The man tried to stab at him, yet Patches was constantly on the move, which caused the masked intruder to actually run his dagger against his own thigh.

Cursing, the man dragged himself toward the back door and left a trail of blood on the wooden floor. He stumbled out and was gone. Patches waited for him to return for a few minutes before finally reducing his size and becoming visible again.

This is bad, he thought as he surveyed the damage, from the shattered pints to the door that had been blown off its hinges and ripped into two large pieces. Patches approached the blood on the ground and sniffed it. *This is very bad.*

What was important now was that Patches guard the Tavernly Realm. With this in mind, the pub cat took a seat just beyond the open doorway. He kept his eyes trained on the exposed back entrance, barely blinking.

Patches would remain like this until his royal subject returned.

The big man will know what to do.

Sylas appeared at the portal just outside of Cinderpeak. He immediately moved to the town center, his first stop being the tool shop. Mrs. Brassmere was running the front when he entered, the woman a bit tipsy by the looks of it.

"I have the hammer," Sylas said in lieu of a greeting.

"You do?" Mrs. Bressmere looked from his face to the branding on his arm, the one that indicated Azor was with him. "That's new."

"It's temporary."

"Let me get my husband. We were just about to close shop too. Everyone is closing around now." She waved her hand toward the window in a dismissive way. "I keep telling Halden this place is too sleepy for me."

"Yeah? Try visiting Ember Hollow sometime," Sylas said.

"The only way I'm going to Ember Hollow is if and when your pub opens. Anyway, the other shops here in Cinderpeak. If you need something, best get it now. But we might have what you need?" She gestured around the shop, which was cluttered with tools.

"I need a larger saw, a sanding tool, more wood—I suppose I can get that later—lumen lamps, and some fireweave cloth."

Mrs. Brassmere motioned to the tools that were hung on the wall. "The tools we can do, and the larger ones my husband rents cheap. I don't know if he told you that already. The fireweave cloth we cannot. You're a newcomer, right?"

"I am."

"Well, no offense, but I don't think you'd be able to afford fireweave cloth at the moment. It's not cheap."

"How many MLus are we talking?"

"That, I don't know. Never bought it myself. Never needed to." Mrs. Brassmere approached the back door of the shop. "But I know it's pricey. Wait here."

"And where would I go to get it?" he called after the woman.

She didn't hear him. Soon, she appeared with her husband, who looked like he had just woken up from a late afternoon nap.

The older man coughed into his hand and greeted Sylas with a grunt.

"Your hammer." Sylas placed Mr. Brassmere's tool on the counter.

His eyes instantly brightened. "You got it back from Brom? How? He's been hoarding this thing for ages—"

Sylas missed a part of this statement as a prompt flashed in front of him.

[Quest Contract Complete – Halden Brassmere now owes you a favor.]

"I owe you a favor now, do I?" the older man asked, as if he too had received a prompt.

"That won't be necessary."

"No, it's not a bad reward, actually. At least I didn't have to give you any MLus. It's random, you know, these reward prompts," Mr. Brassmere told him. "Now, my wife said you needed some things."

"I do."

"But let's handle this favor first. Got anything you need other than tools?"

"I need fireweave cloth. Specifically—"

"An apron and gloves," Azor told Sylas so only he could hear.

"An apron and gloves."

Like his wife, Mr. Brassmere glanced down at the marking on Sylas's arm. Sylas would need a shirt with long sleeves in the future. It was clear that the glowing tattoo was something people would gawk at. "So you've contracted with an elemental spirit, yes?"

"I have not. Just formed a temporary alliance, that's all."

"Yet you want fireweave cloth."

"Just inquiring."

"In that case, I do have a fireweave tailor who owes me a favor, and that can cancel out the favor I now owe you." Mr. Brassmere nodded at his own cleverness. "Anyhow, come back tomorrow and I'll introduce you to him. Deal?"

"That works for me."

"Good, now what else did you need?"

Sylas rented a saw and sanding supplies, which cost him ten Mana Lumens, meaning he still had plenty to brew some casks once he returned to the pub. He left the shop and headed to the portal. Along his way, he noticed that Cinderpeak was indeed shutting down for the day. Still, he wanted to see something before he left.

"Where's the pub?" he asked a lanky man who had just walked past him on the street.

"The Ugly Duckling? Not open at the moment."

"But where is it?"

The man pointed to a street on his left. "That way. You'll find it at the end. But like I said, the place is closed. The lady that runs the place keeps strange hours."

"Thank you." Sylas turned in the direction of The Ugly Duckling.

"The Ugly Duckling? What kind of name for a pub is that?" Azor asked him as they continued on.

"I do not know."

"You just want to size up your competition, huh?"

"Something like that."

"Also."

"Yes?"

"About what you said back there in the tool shop. You really plan to get me some fireweave cloth?"

"Would it make your life easier?"

"It would," Azor told him. "I had some in the Chasm, but it melted once I crossed the Hexveil."

"Then I'll get you some."

"Regardless of if we contract or not?"

Sylas shrugged. "Why not?"

Sylas came to a large timber frame structure with a warm honey glow from the varnished wood. Overhead, a hand-carved wooden sign read *The Ugly Duckling*, the words over the body of a black swan that had been outlined in gold leaf paint. The stained-glass windows of the pub featured a trailing vine motif and the deep black door had a basket of purple flowers hanging from it. There was a small fence leading up to the door featuring swans wrought from iron, their wings spread in various states of flight.

"I need a sign," was all Sylas said as he turned away from the pub. The place definitely looked closed for the day. He would have to stop by later to try to meet the owner.

"I'm sure that's something I can help you with," Azor said. "I'm pretty creative, you know."

"Good to know." Sylas reached the portal outside of the town gates and was presented with several options, including the area he'd just visited to retrieve the hammer.

- **Ember Hollow**
- **Hexveil - Ember Hollow**
- **Seedlands**

He selected Ember Hollow and appeared there in a matter of seconds. "I should have gotten some food back in Cinderpeak," he said.

"You don't have anything?"

"Just some sandwich stuff. But it's getting old. Tomorrow. I'll get it then."

Sylas passed a few of the homes around the village center, a couple with their lights on. As always, Ember Hollow seemed entirely deserted and unwelcoming, which was something he had the urge to change. Did it have to be like this? Did people need to keep to themselves, holed up in their homes as they waited out eternity?

He would soon find out. The Old Lamplighter was going to attract attention, Sylas was certain of it.

"Here we are." Sylas stopped in front of the door to the pub. "Pub sweet pub." He touched the handle and it magically opened.

Sylas gasped once he saw that the back door had not only been blown off its hinges, it had also been ripped in two. Patches collided with his legs, the cat mewing as if he were trying to tell Sylas something.

The pub cat leaped back once Azor took shape, the tattoo on Sylas's arm completely disappearing. "Your place got broken into?" she asked as Patches hissed at her. "Who is the fat cat?"

"He doesn't like being called fat, and his name is Patches." Sylas placed his tools down and immediately turned to the cellar. He took the stairs down to find that his casks remained undisturbed. "So the thieves didn't make it all the way down for some reason," he said to himself. Sylas continued to check around the cellar to be sure.

Azor floated a bit closer to the hissing cat upstairs. "I know I can't pet you," she told him. "Patches, right? Sorry I called you fat."

Patches's nostrils twitched as if he were trying to smell her.

"If I can get a fireweave glove I can pet you and you'll see I'm pretty friendly."

Patches stopped hissing. He trotted over to Sylas just as he returned from the cellar. "The casks were untouched." Sylas stepped over to the back door and saw a trail of blood that led out. "Maybe they hurt themselves trying to break in."

"It looks like it."

Sylas sat at the bar. He looked with bitterness at the broken back door. "I really don't know. But if they didn't steal something, then they were likely trying to scare me, to prove a point."

"Is there someone around here like that?" the fire spirit asked. "Is there someone that wants to scare you?"

"There is. And I guess we'll have to deal with him tomorrow. His niece is named Mira; she's the one I wanted you to meet. Although now, now I don't even know if that matters."

"What do you mean?"

"You aren't going to burn the place down."

Azor laughed. "Not all fire spirits are mischievous, you know. We really get a bad rap. If anything, I'd use my powers to make sure all the vines growing along the outside of the pub are dealt with, but I won't touch the wood. You really thought that I'd torch the place?"

"You're the first elemental spirit I've met. I don't know what to think."

Azor hovered just a bit closer to him. Although he couldn't fully make out the form on her face due to the intensity of her flames, he could tell she was smiling. "It's nice to be trusted."

"It is. Anyway." Sylas motioned to the cellar. "I need to brew four casks. Once I've done that, I think I'll head to bed. Looks like I'm sleeping down here tonight. Do you sleep?"

"I'll just hang out in the fireplace," she said. "And if anyone comes, or if anyone tries anything, they'll regret it."

Sylas nodded. "I hope you stick around for a while, Azor."

"You do?" she asked, shrinking in size a bit.

Sylas rubbed his hands together. "I do. Now, it's cask time. By tomorrow morning I should have eight. We'll open the day after tomorrow. We should have plenty by then."

"While you do that, I think I'll work on your sign."

"My sign?"

"You'll need chains, but I can use a piece of the broken door. Just carry it outside for me."

"Sure," Sylas told her as he picked up the larger piece of wood. He carried it out back and set it on the ground, not far from the well. "Do you want it anywhere in particular?"

"That should be fine," Azor said, flames licking off her form. "And tomorrow? What will we do?"

"We'll get wood, get a new door, maybe sell another case of strong ale, and pay a visit to Tiberius, Mira's uncle. He lives somewhere in town here. I've actually never been to his place, but we'll find it."

"He's the one that did this?"

"I don't know," Sylas said. "But if he didn't, one of his lackeys did."

Patches didn't like the fact that the back door was wide open, but at least the big man was sleeping in the main room of the pub, and the fire spirit that had joined him was on guard. She was just a pile of glowing embers at the moment, but Patches sensed that she could come alive with relative ease.

After stretching, the piebald pub cat began his rounds. He started upstairs just to be thorough. He checked the bedrooms that were open and then headed down to the cellar, where he found that eight casks had now been filled.

Good, he should be opening soon. Patches returned to the main room and approached the back door. He stood at the threshold and stared out at the place where the rat had been buried. He watched this stepping stone keenly for a good hour until the fire spirit spoke to him.

He turned his head to the fireplace, his ears twitching. Her voice was sweet, but he had no idea what she was saying to him and right now, she was a distraction.

Luckily, she soon died back down. Patches returned to his place beneath the door frame. He sat there for several more hours, his tail softly grazing against the wooden floor of the pub.

Even though the big man and the fire spirit were there, Patches felt like the Tavernly Realm was entirely exposed, and it was his job to see the realm through the night, to make sure that nothing entered.

And that was exactly what he did.

Patches valiantly maintained his post until morning came and the big man began to stir. Before he was fully awake, Patches approached him and released the power he'd saved up over the last day.

It took even more this time, Patches all but light-headed by the time he'd finished transferring energy to the big man. His power levels flashed before him.

Mana Lumens: 425/1200

Patches yawned. He really needed to rest.

CHAPTER TWELVE

LAVALACE

Sylas kicked the blanket off and rolled to his side. He looked over to see the fireplace swell orange as Azor came alive. It hadn't been comfortable sleeping on the wooden floor, but he had made it work.

"Morning," said the fire spirit as her form took shape. She sat on the edge of the stone, one fiery leg crossed over the other.

"Morning." Sylas found Patches and scratched the cat's head.

"He sure gets busy at night."

"Does he?" Sylas asked as he finally sat up. He was just about to check his status when the prompt came.

[You have 85 days until the invasion.]

"What is it?" Azor asked once she registered a look of concern on Sylas's face.

Sylas ran his hand through his hair. "Ever since I came here, I've been getting this message about a pending invasion."

"A what?"

"Just now it came to me. It was a message that said I have eighty-five days until the invasion."

"That's not good."

"No, it isn't. And no one seems to know what it means."

"You think it relates to the Chasm? Some invasion? Maybe through the Hexveil near Ember Hollow?"

"I don't know. That would make sense." Sylas accessed his status to see that his Mana Lumens had been topped off. He was closer to four hundred Mana Lumens now. "There's another strange thing that has been happening."

"What's that?" Azor asked as she continued to observe the large man. He had a good heart, she was certain of it now. He also seemed quite even-tempered. The last person she'd contracted with would have been livid if he'd come to find his restaurant was trashed. But Sylas seemed to handle things differently.

"You won't believe this, I've been waking up with my MLus completely recharged. From what I've been told, they aren't supposed to fully charge overnight. Yet the last several mornings, I've woken completely charged."

"That's strange," Azor said. She'd drifted off herself late last night and hadn't seen anything out of the ordinary aside from Patches, who seemed entirely focused on standing guard. That had been a bit comical. The pub cat acted like he was some sort of guard dog. "I have a question for you."

"Yeah?"

"What were you before you came here to the Underworld? You never told me."

"Before I died—still weird to say that—I was a soldier in the Aurum Kingdom's Royal Guard. And before that, my father ran a pub and I helped him. So I grew up in a place like this."

"How did you die?"

Sylas blinked a few times as he remembered what he hoped would be the final battlefield of his life. He had gotten a second wind and had died shortly after. The details were blurry.

"Sorry—"

He shook his head. "It's fine. I died in a fight against an opposing army, the Shadowthorne Empire."

"And you came here and were given the deed to a pub."

"I was."

Azor pressed herself off the fireplace. She could sense that Sylas wasn't interested in sharing any more details with her. "What should we do first?"

"First? Right." Sylas took a look around. "We need wood and other supplies. So Cinderpeak is a must. But I don't want to leave the back door wide open like that."

"I could stay here."

"What about the fireweave gear? I figured we could look into that."

"You might not have enough MLus."

"Maybe, but I plan to sell another cask today at the market, which will also allow me to tell people about our grand opening tomorrow. We can at least see the cost of some fireweave. And I also need to confront Tiberius."

"The guy who knocked down your back door."

"Yes, him or his henchmen. They're responsible. Isn't that right, Patches?"

The cat let out a sigh.

"He's a cutie," Azor said. "I can't wait to pet him."

"I'm sure he'll love that," Sylas told her. "One thing I can do now is fix the lumen lamps. Let me do that first. Then, I'll deal with the bottles, eat something, and try to find out where Tiberius lives. I know a good place to start."

Sylas fixed the stray lumen lamps, which all came on with the wave of his hand. He filled the bottles, had a bit of stale bread for breakfast—he really needed to get some more food—grabbed his club, and headed to the door.

"If you're going to confront this Tiberius man, I'm coming with you," Azor said. "I don't mind staying here later, but you should have backup."

"Someone needs to guard the pub until we get that back door fixed."

She pouted. "Patches can guard the place."

"No, he can't. He's just a cat." Sylas looked over at Patches, who now rested by the window. "And I don't think he could stop an intruder."

"Who do you think stopped the intruder last time, hmmm? There was blood on the ground."

Sylas shrugged. "I think they just destroyed the door to make a point and hurt themselves in the process. I'll be back, and I might be with Mira."

"Mira?"

"The apothecary, the one I told you about. She may stop by. I don't know. This wasn't what I was expecting to have to deal with today, but this sort of thing can happen."

Sylas stepped outside. He recalled that Henry had said he lived in a house with a blue door. He found the house in question and knocked.

"It's early," Henry said upon opening the door, the thin man still rubbing the sleep out of his eyes. He noticed Sylas's club and took a step back. "What's the meaning of this?"

"You know what the meaning of this is. I need to speak to Tiberius."

Henry tried to shut the door. Sylas stopped him from doing so with his club.

"You can't just—"

"Tiberius. Take me there now," Sylas said, his voice with a hint of menace to it.

Henry noticed the golden glow radiating off Sylas, the way it made his eyes intensify. It was clear that the pub owner meant business.

"Sure," he said. "Wait here, mate."

"No. Take me there now."

"But I don't have shoes on."

Sylas shrugged. "Not my problem, Henry, *now*."

Mira had the door open to her shop as she often did in the morning. There wasn't often a breeze, not like there was in the southern town of Douro, but she liked to pretend there was anyway. The open door helped with that. Some commotion outside caught her attention just as she finished up a tincture she was working on.

She went pale once she saw Sylas stop in front of her home with Henry. "What now?" she whispered as she stepped outside.

"Morning, Mira," Sylas said, a hint of malice in his blue eyes. "I need to talk to your uncle."

"About what?"

"He won't tell me," Henry said.

Sylas stepped in front of him. "I'm going to guess that your uncle will know exactly why I'm here. Get him."

Mira placed her hands on her hips.

"Please," Sylas said, instantly interpreting the look on the apothecary's face. "Someone broke into the pub yesterday. They smashed through the back door."

Her demeanor changed instantly. "They did?" She glared at Henry.

"We didn't do that!"

"Why would I believe you?" Sylas asked Henry. He returned his focus to Mira. "I need to speak to Tiberius. He's in charge around here, right?"

"He thinks he is. I'll grab him."

She entered her home and found her uncle in the back room using an old rag to clean an axe. "You have a visitor."

He looked up at her with his good eye and raised an eyebrow. "A visitor?"

"Out front. Come on."

Tiberius almost set the axe down. He thought otherwise and took the piece with him instead. Upon reaching the front door, he also grabbed a dagger he kept in a drawer near the entrance and put it in the sheath at his belt.

"Tiberius. This is your one and only warning," Sylas said as soon as he stepped out. "You will leave my pub alone."

Tiberius squinted at Sylas, his milky white eye gleaming in the golden rays from above. "What now? And what do you mean by 'leave your pub alone'?"

The newcomer motioned in the direction of his pub. "The broken back door. I know it was either you or your two lackeys."

"I'm not his lackey," Henry said. "Maybe Duncan is, but I'm not. I'm a member of the—"

"I don't care," Sylas said, cutting him off. "I do not want to have to visit here again. Leave my pub alone. I *should* be making you fix the door, but I'm mad at the moment, and it's best that you don't come around for a while." Sylas let a deep breath out. "Even if we're opening tomorrow. I don't want people like you—"

"People like us?" Tiberius asked. "We have been in Ember Hollow much longer than you have, Aurumite. This is our little town, and we intend to protect it by any means necessary."

"This is hardly a town," Sylas started to say. "If anything—"

Mira stepped between the two of them. "Did you do it?" she asked her uncle. "Did you break into the pub?"

"This is our home and we will protect it, Mira. That is not up for debate."

"That's not an answer."

"That's the only answer you're going to get out of me!"

"Why do you hate having a pub here anyway?"

"Are you still this naive, Mira?" Tiberius hadn't ordered any intrusions into Sylas's place. That wasn't the way he operated. Perhaps Henry or Duncan had rounded up some of the militiamen and did this of their own accord. But if they did, Tiberius wasn't aware of it. And Tiberius wasn't about to let the newcomer storm over to his place and accuse him of anything. He drummed his fingers on the handle of his axe, which now rested over his shoulder.

"Your first and only warning," Sylas said. "And get used to people like me being around here. Ember Hollow is about to become a lot less sleepy once the pub opens."

Tiberius puffed his chest out as he looked up at Sylas. "We'll see about that."

"You have been warned." Sylas pointed a finger at the shorter man, and turned this finger to Henry. "Both of you have been warned. Now, I need to get back to the pub. Mira."

"Yes?" she asked.

"I have something I want to show you."

"You do?" Mira glanced at her uncle as if she was looking for permission. She remembered she was mad at him and stuck her nose in the air. "Fine. Let's go to the pub, Sylas."

"So you live there with your uncle," Sylas said as they neared the pub. As quickly as he had been agitated, he was now calm. There was no sense in holding the anger he'd felt earlier.

Mira nodded. "I do. I thought I told you that."

"And your shop?"

"It's in the front. There is a separate space."

"I'm sorry if I caused any trouble back there," Sylas said after it was clear in her tone that she was flustered.

"You don't need to apologize to me. I'd be mad too."

Sylas stepped in front of her.

"What?" she asked.

"Look. There's something else I need to tell you. Well, maybe 'show you' is the right phrase. Something happened yesterday."

"You finally got caught selling illegal pints?"

"What? No," he told her, a grin forming. "I'm too sly for that. Actually, I'm not that sly. I just think they don't really care. And besides. Today is the last day. One more case of strong ale and then the only pints I'll be selling will be out of the pub itself. At least for a while."

"Then what is it?" Mira asked. "What did you want to show me?"

"I encountered someone on my way to complete a quest contract for Mr. Brassmere. I got his hammer, and I had to pass through a forest to do so. Anyway, I guess—" Rather than say anything else, Sylas popped open the door of the pub and gestured toward Azor, who sat by the fireplace, one leg crossed over the other. His sudden appearance caused the fire spirit to flare up, which caused Mira to summon her powers.

"You contracted with an elemental spirit?" she asked.

"Not yet and it's fine. She's harmless." Sylas cleared his throat. "Well, she's not harmless, but she's not a bad spirit or anything, even if she came from the Chasm."

Patches, who hadn't been startled by Sylas's appearance because he could hear their voices outside, was startled by the tension that Mira brought into the pub, her shoulders pressed back, her eyes rimmed in golden energy. The cat took off toward the open back door, hit the steps, and tumbled out.

Sylas laughed. "Did you all see that? He's fast!"

Mira tried to maintain the serious look on her face, but finally gave in to the Patches's comical exit. She tried to stifle a laugh but couldn't. "This is . . ." She blew a strand of hair out of her face. "This is no laughing matter, Sylas!"

But it was too late. Sylas was already barreled over, laughing at the way Patches stared back at them, embarrassment evident in the way his whiskers were pressed back. "That cat. I swear. I really don't know how he got so fat. Poor guy."

Azor started to laugh as well, which caused small flames to flicker off her shoulders. "We really need a back door."

"Sylas," Mira said, her voice thinning. "You have to be careful about contracting with elemental spirits."

"We're not contracted yet, lady," Azor told her.

"You will refer to me as Mira!"

"You're the apothecary, right? Aren't you supposed to be kind and understanding, sort of like a nursemaid?" Azor leaned in closer, her fiery face moving into a squint.

"Nursemaid?" Mira composed herself with a quick breath. She fixed a strand of dark hair and smiled briskly at Sylas. "She's from the Chasm."

"Yes? She's not like that demon that attacked me several days ago."

"I'm definitely not a demon," Azor said. Yet she couldn't help herself, not when presented with such an agitated human. Demonic horns filled with purple fire pressed out of her fiery head. "Or am I?"

Mira rolled her eyes. "This is no laughing matter. My uncle is classed as a demon hunter. The militia hunt creatures and spirits like this," she told Sylas. "If they find out—"

"What if we contracted?" Sylas asked her. "Would that fix things?"

"That's a big commitment on your part. Eventually, you'll be sharing your MLus with her if you contract. She can theoretically take them all if she wanted."

"She could?"

"I wouldn't do that. I don't need that much to survive," Azor said as Patches reentered the pub. "I have my own ways to get MLus."

With a superior disdainfulness that only a cat can possess, Patches strutted between Mira and Azor and hopped up to his favorite spot by the window. He faced outward, his tail swishing in their direction.

Mira continued, "I'm being serious here, Sylas, be careful of who you contract with. She could kill you in an instant and take all of your MLus. You're harboring a fugitive here. If my uncle finds out, he'll be livid."

Sylas considered this. A livid Tiberius wouldn't bother him all that much. However, her first statement resonated with him. "Azor could kill me?" His brow furrowed until he couldn't hold it anymore. He started to laugh again. "I'm already dead."

"You know what I mean. The Chasm is a terrible place."

"It's not all that bad," Azor told Mira. "There are pubs there too. Not everyone in the Chasm is a demon, well, they are, but not everyone is demonic. I guess that's a better way to put it. I'd say the bad demons account for, I don't know, maybe twenty percent of what is there? And mostly, the demons are trying to get here."

"Why?" Sylas asked.

"Because demons are formerly people, they always want what they can't have. I guess in that regard I'm like them. I already can tell you that I like it here in the Underworld better. Besides, there was nothing for me there, especially after the restaurant I worked at closed up. Did I say twenty percent? That would account for bad demons, but there are also various types of mages there that like to exploit elementals to create more creatures to do their bidding. Creatures like Eldritch Horrors."

Mira shuddered at the mention of this.

"The Hexveil. You wouldn't believe how many want to tear it down. But the mages aren't strong enough. Anyway." Azor pressed off the fireplace and floated closer to Mira. "I won't take his power."

"And you believe her?" Mira asked.

"I do. In fact, sure, why not? Why not do it right now? We should form a contract," Sylas told Azor. "I could use the help around here, and if we're contracted, Tiberius can't do anything but stomp around and make demands."

A smile broke across Mira's face. "He would certainly be upset. But you're right. If you're contracted, he can't do anything to her lest she does something to you. Do you really trust her?"

Sylas looked over at Azor. She slinked away to some degree, as if she were being put on trial. He offered the fire spirit a firm nod. "I trust her. How do we do this? That is, if you're willing," he told Azor.

"I am," she said, her voice just above a whisper. Azor was trying to hide her joy, and the only way to do so was by lowering her voice.

"Then let's do it. After, we'll head to Cinderpeak, sell some pints, and get you some fireweave clothing. There's not a fire ritual or something, is there?"

"Not that I know of," Azor said.

"Fireweave is really pricey, you know."

Sylas waved Mira's concern away. "Brassmere says he has a fireweave tailor who owes him a favor, and Brassmere owes me a favor now for getting his hammer back. So we'll see the final cost. Maybe I can take a quest for the fireweave tailor too. I'll need the MLus to brew more casks for the opening tomorrow. The tailor might even want a cask himself."

The smile that had broken across Mira's face moments ago remained. It was a different smile now though, one of fondness for Sylas's drive and enterprising attitude. There weren't many people she'd met like that in the Underworld, and she found herself naturally wanting to be part of it.

"And who will watch the pub while you're gone?" she asked. "I'm assuming you'll be getting a new door."

"I will be. And, I was actually hoping you'd be able to watch it," he told her as he scratched the back of his head. "I could owe you a favor."

"You already owe me favors."

"That's true. I guess another couldn't hurt? Patches will be here with you. Who doesn't love Patches?"

"What about the contracting?" Azor blurted out. She brought her fiery hands up to her mouth. "Sorry. We were just talking about that, and it's sort of important."

"Yes, contract. Because I need you to come to Cinderpeak with me so you can pick out the clothing you'd like. Or the style. I don't know," Sylas said. "If I had my choice you'd end up in a suit of armor, heh, but I'm thinking you may like something else."

"Don't buy her a suit of armor," Mira said with a crossed look on her face. "And fine. Fine. I'll watch the pub so the two of you can go together. As for contracting, simply ask Azor if she'd like to contract with you. The system will take care of everything else."

Sylas turned to the fire spirit. "Um, right. Azor, would you like to contract with me?"

"I would," she said with a quick breath out.

[Azor, a fire elemental, has accepted your contract. Are you sure you would like to make this contract? Y/N?]

"Yes," Sylas said aloud.

He felt a sudden warm sensation on his arm. He looked down to the image of a fire with three plumes burned into his skin. It was much deeper than it had been before, the edges glowing orange red. Even after the warm sensation ceased, they remained red.

"You'll want to get a long-sleeve shirt in town as well," Mira said. "People get curious, you know. It's best to be able to roll the sleeves down if you don't want people staring."

"And it'll always glow like this?" Sylas asked as he examined the new marking. "I sort of like it."

"When we are together it will, yes," Azor said. "Like now."

"Fine by me." He turned to the cellar. "I'm going to get the bottles. We've got one more batch to sell and some word to spread."

Mira took a seat at the bar. "I suppose I'll stay here and guard the pub then. Speaking of which, who made the sign?" She gestured to the sign on the table. The hunk of wood from the back door now had *The Old Lamplighter* branded into its surface.

"I did," Azor told her.

"Really? It looks quite nice."

"Thanks!"

"And we'll hang it when we get back," said Sylas. "Just need to pick up a bit of chain." He rubbed his hands together. "Today is going to be a good day, tomorrow will be better, and after that, we'll figure out about this invasion."

Mira's brow settled. "I meant to ask about that. Still getting the warnings?"

"I am. Eighty-five days left," Sylas said, trying not to sound ominous. Unfortunately, with a message like that, it was impossible.

They reached the Cinderpeak Market, Azor tucked away in the blazing tattoo on Sylas's arm. He'd used a rag to hide it, which would work until he was able to get some proper clothing.

"Here we are." Sylas set up shop in the same place he'd been the last few days.

Soon, people started to approach, Sylas able to tell them about the pub opening. "Tomorrow," he told a man who bought two bottles, "evening until late. Stop by The Old Lamplighter in Ember Hollow."

"You're going to stay open late?" Azor asked.

"Just this first night, yes. I want to see how it goes. Are there days of the week here?" Sylas shrugged at his own question. "I probably should have asked Mira."

"There are days here and they match the days in the Chasm. Moonsday, Tombsday, Wraithsday, Thornsday, Fireday, Specterday, and Soulsday. Today is Wraithsday."

Sylas considered this with a huff. "So the middle of the week then, good to know. I wonder if it will be livelier on the weekend."

"I wouldn't know. I've never opened a pub before," Azor said as a woman approached.

"Two bottles," she said, a smile on her face as she looked Sylas over. The woman had fair features, orange hair, and her ears were just slightly pointed.

"Certainly. And my pub opens up tomorrow. Called The Old Lamplighter in downtown Ember Hollow."

The woman laughed. "Ember Hollow has a downtown?"

Sylas winked at her. "It does now. That'll be twenty MLus."

The woman transferred the Mana Lumens to Sylas and moved on. Business was brisk, and Sylas sold out of all his bottles about thirty minutes later.

Everything seemed fine until a man with short silver hair approached. He wore a dark cape and a deep blue tunic with a polished brass badge on it. At his waist was a sturdy truncheon, a whistle, and a set of heavy cuffs that were partially obscured by his cape. He smelled of some sort of strong musk that Sylas remembered older men wearing back in the Aurum Kingdom.

"Stop," the man told Sylas as he tried to slip away. His voice was authoritative and stern. As Sylas turned to him, he placed a hand on his truncheon. "What have you been selling?"

"Nothing," Sylas said, even though he held an empty crate in one hand.

"Nothing in the crate?"

"He's the Cinderpeak constable," Azor hissed. "Careful what you say."

Sylas looked at the crate. "Seems empty to me."

The man leaned in closer. "I've heard through a few fellows here at the market someone has been selling ale."

"Is that so?" Sylas asked. "Well, point me in their direction, because I could certainly use some. After all, I have a crate."

"Come again?"

"I just died a few days ago. I could do with a pint or two."

The constable scrutinized Sylas for a moment. "What is your name?"

"Tiberius," Sylas said. "Of Ember Hollow."

"I've known Tiberius for years, and you're not him. Impersonation is a crime, you know. One that can result in a fine. You might need to come before the magistrate if it goes too deep."

"Careful," Azor reminded Sylas.

"It was a joke. I'm new to Ember Hollow and, um, am thinking about joining his militia. The Exaggerated Battalion of Ember Hollow . . . No, that's not the name. But it's close. Sorry, I'm still new here."

"Are you now?"

The constable took a step closer to Sylas, giving him a view of the man's name, which was etched into his badge. "Leowin, is it? I'm Sylas. Sylas Runewulf, nice to meet you. I'd shake your hand, but I'll just wave instead."

Sylas waved.

Leowin was no fool. He knew that Sylas had been the one selling ale. He was also already aware of the newcomer in Ember Hollow who'd been given a deed to the pub. Leowin was good friends with Tiberius, and he knew Tiberius would be happy to learn that he had busted Sylas. But he also knew he didn't quite have a case. Not yet, anyway. Especially with Sylas standing there with an empty crate.

Leowin stepped just a bit closer to Sylas before ultimately moving aside. "I'll be sure to keep an eye on you, Sylas Runewulf. We have rules here in Cinderpeak, you know. You would be advised to follow them or face the consequences."

Sylas waved his crate at him. "Certainly. If I see anyone selling ale, I'll be sure to either buy some or run them off. Whichever you prefer, Your Lordship."

"Stop," Leowin said once Sylas was a few feet away. "There's a fine for disorderly verbal conduct, especially in the presence of a constable or other high authorities. That'll be fifty MLus."

Sylas tensed up. "Fifty?"

"You could have just gone on your way, but you chose to mock me instead." Leowin turned his palm around. "A fine has been issued for Sylas Runewulf of Ember Hollow." As those words left his lips, a prompt appeared.

[You have been fined 50 Mana Lumens.]

Sylas felt a strange pull at his chest, one that he had absolutely no control over. He immediately checked his status to see the additional Mana Lumens he'd received from selling the pints minus the fine.

Name: Sylas Runewulf
Mana Lumens: 520/570
Class: Brewer
[Active Quest Contracts:]
Travel to Duskhaven with Mira Ravenbane to visit the sigilist

"We keep things orderly around here," Leowin said as he moved on. "And you're lucky I didn't bring you before the magistrate or fine you more MLus. If found guilty, the magistrate can permanently remove some of your hard-earned Mana Lumens. Think about that next time you decide to be clever."

Sylas clenched his fists together as Leowin moved on, the thin man sweeping his cape back in a judicious way.

"I told you to be careful," Azor said. "Some of these constables let the power get to their heads."

"Noted," Sylas finally said. He relaxed his clenched jaw. "I learn something new here every day. Luckily it didn't cost me as much as I just took in."

"That's good."

"I don't like the fact he's friends with Tiberius, though. I'll have to ask Mira about him when we get back. Anyway. Let's go see about some fireweave clothing."

Sylas came to the tool shop to find Mrs. Brassmere running the front counter. She fetched her husband, who joined Sylas a few minutes later.

"Yes," the older man said, "the favor. I don't know what Godric will require, but we will soon find out." He glanced at the rag Sylas had tied around his forearm. "You're in need of new clothing as well, hmmm?"

"Take him by the shop I keep telling you about," Mrs. Brassmere told her husband. "They have good tops there. Get yourself one too. I'm tired of fixing all of your shirts."

"Yeah, yeah," he told his wife as he returned his focus to Sylas. "I know where to take you, but let's go to Godric first."

"I also need a door."

"A door?" Mr. Brassmere stroked his chin. "That I can handle. I've got a fellow who can install it as well. Inside door, outside door?"

"Outside. The back door. It was broken in half yesterday by an intruder."

Mr. Brassmere exchanged glances with his wife. "I'm sorry to hear that.

In that case, we'll get you a nice sturdy one. Perhaps a sturdier front door as well?"

"And it'll register with me?" Sylas asked. "My deed to the pub?"

Mr. Brassmere smoothed his hands together. "It certainly will."

"Both doors then. Mira is at the pub now, so if someone visits, she'll be there to greet them. Also I need a chain to hang the pub sign. What are we looking at here?"

Mr. Brassmere ran the numbers on a slip of parchment. "Let's call it forty MLus and a case of strong ale. Cheapest door you'll find this side of the Hexveil. But I happen to have some extra from an order for a farm that didn't pan out. Been sitting in the back of my shop for nearly a year now."

"You're not supposed to tell the customer that part," Mrs. Brassmere said.

"Well, I did. What do you say?"

Sylas extended a hand to the older man and they shook. "Works for me. Can you add in a cat door on the back? Just something for a cat to go through."

"I don't see why not."

"Good, Patches will like that."

"Patches?" Mr. Brassmere asked.

"The pub cat."

[Transfer 40 Mana Lumens to Halden Brassmere? Y/N?]

Sylas silently agreed.

"Great," Mr. Brassmere said as his eyes filled with light. "Dear? Will you handle this while I'm gone? Send John around to get the sizes and return with the doors and some chain. I need this done today."

Mrs. Brassmere smiled. "If it means you're taking me to the pub tomorrow night for an ale or three, sure."

"Sure, dear. If that's what it takes."

"Anyone there now?" he asked Sylas.

"Mira, the Ember Hollow apothecary."

"Yes, you mentioned that. The woman you were with the other day." Mr. Brassmere smiled at Sylas knowingly as his wife chuckled behind him.

They left the store, Mr. Brassmere guiding Sylas through Cinderpeak, the two headed in the direction of the volcano that loomed over the homes. Once they reached the outer edges of the town, Sylas turned to the older man. "The constable. Is he really as terrible as he seems?"

"Leowin? You had a run-in, eh?"

"I did."

"He is, but he also keeps the place safe, so I suppose we can thank him for that. The constable we had before, Catherina, she was great. Fair. And not too quick to fine either. She lives in Duskhaven now, I believe. Bigger city. You know how it goes. People get bored of these smaller places."

"Cinderpeak is huge compared to Ember Hollow."

"That's because Ember Hollow doesn't really have anything going for it. No industry, really. And it's close to the Hexveil. But I'm guessing you're going to change that with the pub."

"Opens tomorrow. And you and your wife should stop by. She's a fan of my stronger ale. I believe she'd like the lighter stuff too."

Mr. Brassmere grinned. "Yeah? Maybe we will. The Ugly Duckling hasn't been open in weeks."

"Is the owner still there?"

"She is. I don't know what her problem is."

"I'll have to meet her at some point," Sylas said.

The pair started up a small hill, one that soon morphed into the slope of the volcano. There were a few homes here, their walls and roofs coated in something that resembled obsidian, which glowed lightly beneath the shimmer clouds of the Celestial Plains above.

They reached a home with an open workshop out back. Sylas could already hear the sounds of someone pounding away, the noise reminding him of a smithy.

"Godric," Mr. Brassmere shouted as they came around to the back of the workshop.

Sylas took a cautious step back once he saw a burst of bubbling lava, one emitting from a hole in the ground surrounded by tools he'd never seen before.

He spotted Godric, who stood near a bench made of solid stone hammering a piece of glowing red fabric. Godric's skin, which had been permanently tanned from the proximity to the lava, had an ashen quality to it. He wore goggles made of thickened glass, which made his eyes beady.

"Godric!" Mr. Brassmere called out again. He waved his hands at the man. "He's practically deaf from all the hammering he does."

The tailor finally noticed them. He set his hammer down and pressed his goggles back, revealing white circles around his eyes. "Halden? Halden!" he said with a big grin. He came around the table and removed the thick gloves he wore, which had a woven texture to them.

"I've got a favor to exchange." Mr. Brassmere gestured to Sylas. "Godric, meet Sylas, the owner of The Old Lamplighter pub in Ember Hollow. Opens tomorrow."

"A new pub, huh?" Godric nodded. "Always could use one of those, especially with The Ugly Duckling being closed half the time."

"Most of the time," Mr. Brassmere chimed in.

"A real pity."

"A pity no longer," Sylas told the tailor. "Like he said, I'll be opening The Old Lamplighter tomorrow."

"The Old Lamplighter, huh?"

"That's right," Mr. Brassmere said to Godric. "And he has someone for you to meet, someone that could use your unique expertise."

"Yeah?" Godric raised an eyebrow at Sylas as he removed the rag around his arm.

Azor came alive, the fire spirit forming beside Sylas. The flames settled as they moved down her form, solidifying her body.

Godric didn't seem fazed in the least bit by the fire spirit. "You need some fireweave clothing then, is it?"

"I do," Azor told the tailor excitedly. "Gloves like yours so I can handle food and drinks. Also, an apron."

"Gloves like mine and an apron. How far up do you want the gloves to go?"

"Maybe to here." Azor pointed at the space where her elbow would be if she had elbows.

Godric scribbled something into his palm, as if he were taking an invisible note. "That much material won't be cheap," he told Sylas.

"I didn't expect it be. Perhaps there's something we can work out, a payment plan, or maybe you'd like a few casks of ale."

"A payment plan, huh?" Godric pursed his lips.

"Don't forget the favor I'm turning in," Mr. Brassmere said.

"I haven't forgotten the favor, Halden. The problem is finding the thread."

"The thread?" Sylas asked.

"I have some, but it's not easy to come by. Fireweave is made from a specific kind of lava, which I have access to here," he said as he gestured toward the pit of lava. "And a type of glass thread that occurs much deeper inside the volcano itself. These are woven together, which creates the material."

"So you need more of this volcanic thread to make fireweave?" Sylas asked.

"Yes. The material is called lavalace, and you'll find it in the volcano itself. Or better, in the caves around it."

"How will I survive?"

"You have contracted with a fire spirit," Godric told him. "It should be relatively easy for you to deal with the heat. And it shouldn't be too hard to gather several bundles of lavalace. The problem is the cinderspiders."

"Cinderspiders?"

"They are quite large. And they protect the lavalace because they feed off it."

"And I'm guessing you have something that I can smash them with if they get in the way?"

"I've got a mace." Godric gestured to a weapon resting against the outer wall of his workshop. It looked to be made of some charcoal-blackened bone of some underworld beast and infused with fireweave, the intricate latticework on display.

"Could I borrow that?"

"You could."

"So I'd bring you some lavalace?" Sylas asked Godric.

"Yes, and you'd pay me two hundred MLus for my supplies."

"That's a bargain," Mr. Brassmere said. "I assumed he'd charge upwards of two thousand MLus."

"Not quite that much, but not far off," Godric said. "Do we have a deal?"

Sylas nodded. "And you'll point me in the right direction?"

"I most certainly will. However, as you may know by now, accepting the quest will give you a natural inclination to where you should be going."

Sylas exchanged glances with Azor. "Definitely. Let's do this."

[New Quest Contract - Collect lavalace from the Cinderpeak Volcano. Accept? Y/N?]

Sylas grunted a positive response. "We'll be back in a few hours."

"Good, and take that satchel over there with you. You'll need it for the lavalace."

Sylas grabbed the mace and the satchel, which was much heavier than a normal bag.

"Good, good." Mr. Brassmere took a seat on a chair that seemed to be molded out of stone. "I think I'll wait here with Godric. I don't get to these parts as often as I should."

"No, you do not. I just got a bottle of flamefruit juice too from Bart. He was in Douro, you know."

"He was, was he?"

Sylas left the two men talking as he headed in the direction of the cave. "I can't believe we're about to do this," he told Azor.

Sylas approached the entrance to a cave with steam billowing out of the front.

It was hot now, Sylas at the point where he'd already removed his shirt and hung it from the back of his trousers. Aside from his mace, he had the heavy satchel made of fireweave over his shoulder, ready for lavalace.

"How are we going to do this?" he asked Azor, who floated beside him. "Godric seems to think you'll be able to help me."

"We are contracted. I can protect you from fire by extending my power around you."

"And it won't burn me?"

"It will be warm, but no, it won't burn you."

"Do you mean to say you'll be like a suit of fire armor?" Sylas pictured what this could look like and grinned.

"Something like that, yes."

"And my clothing?" he asked, an afterthought.

"Your clothing will be fine." She laughed. "Did you think that you'd have to get naked?"

Rather than answer, Sylas tapped his mace against a rock. It crumbled as if it were made out of ash. "Huh. I didn't expect that."

He saw a bit more of the rock that resembled charcoal and did the same, the rock crumbling.

"You're supposed to run a pub, not become a miner," she said. "Anyway, are you ready? You'll need me if we're going to go any farther."

"Ready as ever." Sylas stuck his arms out as if he were getting measured by a seamstress. He felt a sudden flash of heat that cooled before he could react. Blue flames now flickered off of his arms.

Sylas examined his body to see the same blue flames covering him. In doing so, he noticed that his vision had a slight glaze to it now, as if he were swimming in a crystal clear body of freshwater. "How am I not burning?"

"Nice, right?"

He turned the mace over in his hand. "Even the weapon?"

"Even the weapon. Well, if it were made of wood it might be a bit of an issue, but this mace is made from fireweave as well, meaning—"

"Meaning I need to get me one of these." Sylas broke away a bit more of the black stone. He pressed into the steam, all but expecting it to burn his eyes. It didn't, Sylas able to navigate the first chamber of the cave with relative ease.

He was lucky everything had a slight orange glow to it. This glow revealed patches of black on the ground that he suspected were the same crumbly stone he'd broken apart earlier. He tested this, and turned out to be right.

"We'll have to be extra careful coming back," he told Azor as they reached the next chamber, which had a bridge-like stone formation that ran over a stream of hissing lava.

"I wasn't expecting that."

"Incredible," Sylas said, who had never seen anything like it before. "If you had asked me a week ago what the Underworld looked like, I would have guessed it was something like this." He swept his hand out toward the lava. "But this is a small part of it."

"It's a very big part of it at the moment," Azor said, her voice all around him but somehow private, like it was when she had channeled herself into his tattoo.

"True." Sylas carefully stepped out onto the bridge made of stone. He had to be careful here, especially with the blackened patches that could potentially crumble under his weight. The lava spit out a ball of fire, one that passed directly beside Sylas. He stopped and only moved on once he got their pattern down.

"If I didn't have to protect you, I'd be able to do some pretty cool tricks with the lava," Azor said as they neared the end of the bridge made of stone.

"Like what?"

"Like dive into it."

"Can you control the lava?"

"I can. I'm sure some of the buildings in Cinderpeak were made by humans that contracted with fire spirits like me. Certainly the one Godric was living in, the walls of his outside workshop too."

"I didn't even consider how useful you would be for construction." Sylas stepped out into a chamber with crumbled stones on one side. At first, he assumed these were ordinary rocks, but then he saw the veins of lava running through them.

"Is that them?" Azor asked.

Sylas saw hundreds upon hundreds of glass-like threads sticking out from between the grooves in the lava rocks. "It has to be."

He started collecting them, Sylas stuffing as much lavalace as he could in the satchel Godric had let him borrow. "I wish he'd given me two bags to fill."

"Let's not get greedy."

"I want the mace too," he told her, "so I'd like to bring him as much as I possibly can." Sylas stopped collecting the lavalace and took a quick look around. "Keep an eye out for cinderspiders. Although I think we may be in the clear."

He got the satchel to the point that it was brimming with lavalace. Sylas rearranged the glass-like threads so they were stacked at the bottom, allowing him to add even more. Once he was finished, he hoisted the satchel onto his shoulder, and grunted at its weight. The lavalace was much heavier than he had anticipated.

"Here goes," Sylas said as he took a lumbering step forward. He was just turning around when he heard a tapping noise that sounded like tiny mallets hammering away.

There had to be twenty cinderspiders now standing opposite Sylas blocking his exit.

Each of the cinderspiders were easily as large as a goat, their bodies made of a stonelike exoskeleton that glistened ominously. Their eight legs were sharp and thick, tipped in what looked like blackened claws. Yet their hardened exteriors and their sharp claws weren't what suddenly had Sylas on edge.

Their thoraxes pulsed, Sylas understanding why once a few of them opened their mouths and began firing streams of liquid lava at him.

"Get to the exit!" Azor said as she came alive, the fire spirit flaring up all around Sylas.

Sylas did as instructed, swinging his satchel of lavalace into the spiders blocking his exit.

Thwack!

He hit the next cinderspider with the mace, which sent it directly into the spider beside it. His leg covered in flames, Sylas used his heel to kick another one to the side, a brazen move considering their sharp fangs.

Each stream of fiery venom that hit him was entirely absorbed by Azor, who then redistributed it into even more fire as Sylas charged through the cluster. He smashed the fireweave mace down onto another of the cinderspider's heads, killing it.

"I've got you. Jump!" Azor shouted.

Sylas leaped over its body, his movement augmented by the fire spirit, allowing Sylas to go up and over a few more of the spiders.

He landed.

The spiders turned to him, the sounds of their claws louder and louder as they began chasing Sylas.

"We're almost there!" Azor said as they reached the room of lava, the one with the stone bridge that ran across the molten river below.

A smaller cinderspider lunged for him. Sylas smashed the spider into the wall, causing it to spill backward onto one of its companions.

His eyes narrowed as a spider lowered directly in front of him. He cracked it with his mace and stepped out onto the bridge just as more spiders lowered from the ceiling, blocking his path. Sylas hesitated for a moment, and in that split second the stone beneath him began to crumble.

He fell backward and landed on top of one of the spiders.

Azor came to his rescue, the fire spirit rocketing him into the air. The two catapulted over the spiders and touched down on the other side of the room.

"Thanks!"

"Keep going!" she said as Sylas burst into the next chamber, the one filled with steam. He hesitated. Something enormous lurked in the shadows, a spider that was three or four times the size of the others.

Sylas stumbled backward as flames twisted around him. A huge bolt of fire exploded out of his shoulder and blew up in the large spider's face. Sylas took off, and just as he was nearing the final exit, just as he was almost free, a final spider came from the ceiling to stop him.

He whacked it with his mace and shouldered past, Sylas finally out of the cave, safe. He kept running for a few minutes before finally slowing down. After he was certain he hadn't been followed, Sylas slowed to catch his breath.

He turned to see that none of the spiders had followed him out.

"I guess they don't come outside." Sylas wiped his head, only then realizing that Azor had shifted away from him. He flicked some of the sweat from his brow to the ground. "You good?"

"I'm fine." She started to laugh. "That was insane."

He laughed alongside her, a nervous release of adrenaline. "It was. It really was." He showed her the satchel. "But we got what we came for."

"We did. Do it again sometime?"

"Maybe I'll take a rain check."

"A lava check?"

He grinned at the fire spirit and turned back toward Godric's place. "Wait until Mira hears about this."

CHAPTER THIRTEEN

OPENING

Sylas approached with the heaping bag full of lavalace slung over his shoulder. He hoisted it onto Godric's workbench as the tailor and Mr. Brassmere stared at him in disbelief. Azor, who floated next to Sylas, offered the two older men a big smile once she saw how surprised they were at his haul.

"Is this enough?" she asked.

"I've never seen so much in my life," Godric said, who was seated before a spread of meat and odd-looking vegetables that he had grilled up over the open pit of lava. "Usually, I'm only able to get a few handfuls."

"Well, this is much more than that," Sylas said, ignoring the prompt that told him the quest contract was complete. "Wasn't easy, either. I have a proposition for you."

"Yes?" Godric approached the workbench and began going through the satchel, admiring some of the individual strands. "It really is a lot, Hal," he called over to Mr. Brassmere, who was seated on a stone, just finishing a rib.

"I can see that," the shopkeep said. "It didn't take him very long either. We still have plenty of time to grab some clothing in town and head back to your pub, where your door should be installed. Anyway, this proposition?"

"Yes," said Godric, "I'm all ears. Also. Food. Help yourself."

"I want the mace." Sylas showed Godric the weapon to illustrate how serious he was. "We keep the same deal, two hundred MLus and all this lavalace for some clothing for Azor *and* this mace."

"You want to add the mace in?" Godric exchanged glances with Mr. Brassmere. It was a deal that was too good to be true. It would have taken Godric weeks to collect as much lavalace as Sylas had just brought him. He would have had to visit different caves to do so, where there were less spiders and unfortunately, less lavalace.

Godric exhaled audibly, as if this were a tough decision.

"Oh, come on," Mr. Brassmere said.

"Sure. That makes sense. A big fellow like you could use a mace like that, especially if people get rowdy at the pub. Heh. Sure." Godric extended his hand to Sylas. "We have a deal. You can keep the mace too. I'll make another one with the stuff you brought."

[Transfer 200 Mana Lumens to Godric? Y/N?]

Sylas grunted a positive response. He felt a sudden drain in his power, as if his heart had skipped a beat. The sensation was gone in a matter of moments. He sat down in front of Godric and grabbed one of the spareribs. Sylas ate it, the meat good and well seasoned, even if it was a bit cold now.

"Good, good, you'll enjoy that mace," Godric said with a grin. "And the cinderspiders?"

Sylas motioned the bone back toward the area he'd just come from. "There were a lot of them. I killed a few. I saw a rather large one and I ran. They didn't chase me out of the cave."

"They don't like to leave the cave. From what I've seen, they have a network of passages underground that run all the way to the Hexveil. Some people say that they're actually from the Chasm, but I don't believe them. They're just nasty creatures. You said there was a big one?"

"Really big," Sylas said as he tried to gauge the height of the creature with his hand. "I think. I didn't get a good look at it."

"That big, huh?" Godric shook his head. "Well, let's hope it stays in the cave. Anyway, your clothing." Godric turned to fire spirit. "The clothing will take me two days."

"That's fine. I have all the time in the Underworld." Azor grinned and proceeded to remind Godric of what she wanted. Once she was done, he approached her with a tape measure made from fireweave and popped his goggles down over his eyes. Godric measured her arms, her waist, and then the distance from her shoulder to her waist.

"That should be it," he said. "I'll see you both in two days."

"Wood," Sylas told Mr. Brassmere once they'd left Godric's workshop. The two were stuffed now, Sylas even managing to take a little of the meat for Patches.

"Firewood or wood for construction?"

"Both. There are just a few more things I'd like to take care of. And some shingles, if you have them. I don't think I need to replace the entire roof, not yet, anyway, but a few shingles need replacing."

Mr. Brassmere smacked his lips. "Wood and shingles. You should have told me. I could have had John deliver that today. Tomorrow morning, then. I'll get you what you need, and it won't cost you much either." He grinned at Sylas. "Thanks for what you did back there."

"What did I do exactly?"

"You just turned the favor Godric owed me into a new favor he'll owe me in the future."

"How so?"

"That lavalace. It's a lot. And I'll have him make me something as well with it." Mr. Brassmere's eyes lifted in delight at his own suggestion. "*A favor well done is a debt yet begun*. Or something like that. Come on, let's get you some new tops. And cover up your fire tattoo," he said as he pointed at Sylas's arm. "Remember, people are suspicious of elementals. At least this close to the Hexveil."

Mira gasped once she heard Sylas's story.

The apothecary had been in the pub all afternoon, and had been there when a bald man brought a pair of doors around and installed them. She certainly didn't expect to hear that Sylas had ventured into a cave and fought cinderspiders. Cinderspiders! Those were the things of nightmares, like most bugs to Mira.

Although she did laugh when he showed her the mace he'd acquired and performed a few practice swings as an example. "Cracking spider skulls."

"You're going to rip your new shirt," she told him.

"That's why I got two." He motioned to the other shirt, a dark gray tunic with long sleeves. It was currently thrown over the side of a barstool. Azor was with him—Mira still didn't know what to make of the fire elemental but she didn't seem so bad—and had already commented about Sylas not having any food.

"I keep forgetting it," came his reply. "But I'll be fine. I ate something at Godric's. A bunch of ribs and some other meat. Also brought some for Patches."

Mira watched as Sylas placed the meat on a plate. He took it over to Patches, who ate it at the windowsill. She could go home and make him a sandwich, but that would require going home and dealing with her uncle.

"So what now?" she asked as she sized Sylas up, Mira standing with her arms crossed over her chest. She only realized once she caught a glimpse of herself in the window's reflection how standoffish she looked. She smoothed them over the front of her blouse. "More plans for today?"

"Now? I'm getting lower on MLus. Three casks will give me just enough to make it through the night. That means I'll have ten casks for opening tomorrow. I'll probably go with five strong and five regular. If I get a magical delivery of MLus tonight, I could make some more as well. But I may hold off."

"How many MLus would you have left after brewing three casks?"

"Eight."

"Eight total?"

"Uh-huh."

Mira gave him a hard look.

"What?"

"That's not a lot," Azor chimed in. "Make two casks tonight and one in the morning, if you must. Just to be safe."

"Really?"

"Really," Mira said. Azor's comment had revealed something to her, namely that Sylas would possibly benefit from her being around. Mira still didn't know how she felt about a fire elemental from the Chasm, but at least she would be able to keep Sylas in line.

"Fine, fine. I'll do two tonight. But you all are worrying too much."

"You have to be careful," Mira reminded. "You don't want to overextend yourself. You'll end up in the Chasm before you sell your first pint."

"I've already sold my first pint."

"You know what I mean! And no offense about the Chasm," Mira told Azor as she approached the door.

"None taken," she said, her red-hot form softening to some degree. "The Chasm is doable, but the Underworld is much better. Plus there aren't as many demons here. Well, there are a few closer to the Hexveil, but that is to be expected. Don't worry about Sylas, I'll make sure he doesn't brew too much."

"I'm not worried," Mira said.

"Sounds like you are." Sylas laughed and Azor joined him.

Mira approached the brand-new front door of the pub, stepped out, and tried to slam it behind her but failed. It was really heavy.

"Bye!" Sylas called after her. He turned to the fire spirit. "Do you think we teased her too much?"

"Maybe," Azor said as Patches finally came around. The cat jumped onto the bar and approached Sylas.

"Do you like your second cat door?" Sylas asked the cat. He motioned to the back. "I'm going to have to teach you how to use it again, aren't I?"

Patches mewed.

"Fine, I guess I'll do that, and then brew a couple of casks."

"Two," Azor reminded him.

"Yes, a couple is two."

She smirked. "Just in case you were tempted."

Patches stretched for a while after waking up that night. He made his rounds, starting in the upstairs hallway of the Tavernly Realm. He headed down to the cellar, the piebald pub cat tiptoeing so he wouldn't wake the big man or the fire spirit.

He licked his lips, remembering the meat that Sylas had brought him earlier. *That was good. Very good.*

After checking all the corners one last time, Patches headed up the stairs to the main floor of the Tavernly Realm. He neared the back and slipped out through the cat door. His eyes immediately jumped to the space where the big man had buried the rat, just beneath the flagstone.

Patches approached cautiously and sniffed the ground.

Several rats have been here, he thought as he did a complete walk around the flagstone. *But when? I haven't heard or seen them.*

This troubled Patches to no end. He'd kept a good eye on the back of the pub for most of the day. The only time he hadn't been watching it was when the medicine woman had carried him around for a while, rocking him like a baby.

Patches sat there for a moment, disappointed in himself. He started licking his paws and stopped once he noticed a subtle change in the air.

Patches turned himself invisible. He stepped into the shadows cast by the pub and waited.

A swirl of mana came out of the well and formed into the subtle outline of a smoky, demonic being. Patches trembled. It was the same one he'd seen before, and this was as close as he'd ever been to one of these spirits.

Even though he was outside, the air seemed to constrict all around him.

Patches fought back the instinct to hiss, but he couldn't stop the hairs on his back from standing on end. His tail twitched, the only other outward sign of inner turmoil.

He remained frozen in a defensive position as the demon investigated the flagstone. It floated right up to the back door of the pub and examined the place, wisps of mana falling off the back of its head as the demon tilted its chin up toward the roof.

The monster turned toward Patches.

Still invisible, Patches grew his claws and teeth to twice their size. He narrowed his eyes on the demon as he prepared to defend the Tavernly Realm. In the end, the demonic being turned back to the well. It rose into the air and dropped back in, vanishing, but not before an evil smile took shape on its face.

It was another hour before Patches left the shadows and reentered the pub through the cat door.

He took the stairs to the big man's bedroom and found his favorite spot at the end of the bed. Before transferring Mana Lumens to the big man, Patches sat there in the early morning silence, his full focus on any sounds that came to him. He could sense that the malicious influence was gone, yet he had to be sure.

Patches traveled back down the stairs and through the cat door. He watched the well for another thirty minutes. The Tavernly Realm appeared safe, for now.

This should help, he thought once he was back in the bedroom upstairs. He began transferring his Mana Lumens to the big man.

Patches reached a point of delirium and stopped. He dropped to his side and let out a deep breath.

He didn't want to do it, and he probably shouldn't do it until he was stronger, but the well behind the pub would need to be explored.

The only problem was that Patches hated water.

A number that Sylas had been thinking of the previous night came to him upon waking that morning. That number was one thousand.

If Sylas reached a thousand Mana Lumens, which at his current rate wouldn't be very long, he could completely restock his casks every night or in the morning, and still have enough Mana Lumens to get by on.

[**You have 84 days until the invasion.**]

The system warning came to Sylas as he lay there scratching the back of Patches's head.

"Can't worry about that today," he said to himself as he sat up and checked his status.

Name: Sylas Runewulf
Mana Lumens: 570/570
Class: Brewer
[**Active Quest Contracts:**]
Travel to Duskhaven with Mira Ravenbane to visit the sigilist

He eyed his active quest for a moment. Sylas needed to visit the sigilist to decipher the portal writing in the room down the hall.

There was another quest not currently active, mostly because it was something that he had just made preliminary plans to handle at some point. Sylas needed to visit Battersea to speak to someone who had access to the Book of Shadows. According to Mira, the thriving city of Battersea was a journey that could take quite a while. A task like this would also require more Mana Lumens because he'd likely have to fork over quite a bit for information.

Sylas considered this as he lay in bed just a bit longer. There was also bartering, just like he'd done with Godric. Maybe he could do something like that in Battersea.

"Are you ever going to get up and get started?" Azor asked, who was suddenly hovering at the end of the bed.

"What day is it?" Sylas asked her in a playfully groggy voice.

"Thornsday. The day the pub opens! And guess what?"

"What?"

Patches turned to Azor, yawned, and then went back to sleep.

"Mira dropped off breakfast already."

"She did?"

"I think she likes you."

"She's just being friendly," Sylas told the fire spirit as he finally rolled over to the side of the bed. "I've got to get to work."

Sylas headed downstairs to find that Mira had made him quite the spread. There were breads, boiled eggs, meats, cheeses, fruit, and even some pastries.

"It's a gift basket," Azor said.

"It certainly is. Did she say anything?"

"No."

"Really?" Sylas asked as he took a seat at the bar. "Nothing?"

"Just that it was for you, and she'd stop in later once the pub was open."

He took a bite of cheese. "That was nice of her."

After eating some of the food, Sylas sanded down the bar.

He fell into a spell of intense work as he fixed any of the wooden planks in the floor that needed more attention. He still wanted to install a system to pump ale from the cellar up to the bar, but that could wait. And it wasn't like the small casks were heavy. Maybe it was something he'd never have to do.

A knock at the door signaled that John had arrived with more supplies.

"Courtesy of Mr. Brassmere," the bald man said. He motioned to a stack of wood and shingles. "Need help bringing them in?"

"I can manage, but I appreciate it. Stop by the pub if you can tonight."

"Tonight, yeah? I might not be able to come by tonight, but I'll certainly be by at some point." John placed his hands on his waist and looked up at the place. "It's looking good, especially that new door of yours. Anyway, I've got another delivery off in Douro. I'll be around. Cheers!"

John left. Sylas brought more of the wood down to the cellar and placed the firewood in a rack near the fireplace. He put some of the shingles in a satchel and carried the rest down to the cellar. Once he was ready, Sylas got the chain he'd purchased and installed *The Old Lamplighter* sign to the front of the pub.

Azor watched as he got the sign in place.

They were the only ones up at the moment, at least if the streets of Ember Hollow were any indication of who was awake. She didn't quite get why people wanted to live this far out, especially so close to the Hexveil, but she also knew that when people were given deeds to homes in the Underworld, they often didn't move.

It was different in the Chasm.

People weren't given deeds there, which meant that buildings often had to be defended. Azor had been partially lying when she told Mira that the Chasm wasn't as bad as it seemed. There was a reason that most preferred the Underworld and the Celestial Plains above.

"What do you think?" Sylas asked once the sign was properly hung. He stood back and admired his handiwork. "You did really well with the engraving."

"Thanks. And I think it looks great."

"But there's one more thing to add." Sylas went back into the pub to get the single lumen lamp he'd saved. He installed it in a fixture near the sign, so it would illuminate the text. "When the light is on, the pub is open. When it is off, the pub is closed. Easy, yeah? We should probably get a sign for that as well."

"Another sign?"

"A smaller one, yes." Sylas wiped his hands. "Time to get to the roof." He peered up at it for a moment. "I'm realizing now that I don't have a ladder."

"I can get you up there."

He turned to the fire spirit. "You can?"

"I did back in the cave."

"That's right. I really need to add 'learning to fly' to my to-do list."

Azor couldn't help herself. She had to tease him a little. "Maybe Mira can show you . . ."

"Stop it with that." Sylas stretched his arms out wide, a bag of supplies hanging from one shoulder. "Take me up to the roof, please."

Azor's fiery form engulfed Sylas. To someone passing by it would have looked as if he had spontaneously combusted. But there was no pain associated with her power, especially now that they had contracted. Flames flared beneath Sylas's boots mostly for dramatic purposes.

"Nice," Sylas said once they reached the roof, where she quickly released him. Azor moved away so she wouldn't catch the shingles on fire. Sylas, who already had a nail sticking out of his mouth, got started while Azor watched.

The hammering was loud, and soon, there were windows opening nearby.

Azor turned to see faces she didn't recognize, the strange people who lived in Ember Hollow.

There was a moment of hesitation on her part.

She was from the Chasm, yet she had also contracted with Sylas, which gave her a stake in the Underworld that would prevent people from taking her back to the Chasm.

She continued to watch Sylas pull up shingles and hammer in nails. If he had told her that he'd worked in construction back in his world, she would have believed it. He was efficient, and he moved fast and with determination. This was similar to how she'd seen him fight off the cinderspiders the previous day. It was a good trait to have.

"I think that about does it," he said as the morning started to shift into the afternoon. Sylas was getting more used to seeing the subtle changes in the sky, even if it always had the golden glow to it. He smiled at Azor, who seemed to be hovering close enough to him to catch Sylas if he happened to fall. "Almost time to open up."

"You certainly have drawn some attention." She gestured a flaming hand to some of the surrounding buildings just as a window slammed shut. "I wonder how many people live here."

Sylas leaned back against the roof. "I don't know. Everyone is so secretive, or maybe 'guarded' is a better word. Yes, guarded. Hmmm. Let's try something." Sylas cupped his hands around his mouth and began shouting. "Ember Hollow, good morning! The Old Lamplighter pub is open tonight! Stop by for a pint!"

Azor laughed. "If you're going to do a grand opening you should probably give something away."

"Good idea. Oi, everyone! Tonight, your first pint is on me at The Old Lamplighter!" Sylas shouted this again. He waited for a response, but never got one. "Well?" he said with a shrug.

"You did your part."

"I did do that." Sylas felt Azor's power envelop him, and soon, he stood on the ground looking up at the pub. There was exterior work he would have liked to do, and maybe he could get to that in the coming days, but it looked right. Everything was in its right place.

He entered The Old Lamplighter to find Patches eating the meat from Mira's gift basket.

"That's not yours—"

Embarrassed, Patches immediately hopped down from the bar and ran toward the cellar. The cat slid, his body weight pulling him forward. He hit the cellar stairs and seemed to tumble down from there.

Azor raced into the cellar. She came up moments later, relieved. "He's fine."

"The little monster," Sylas said with a chuckle. "He ate all the meat."

"You really need some food around here."

"I do, but there's still enough left for something tonight and tomorrow morning. Tomorrow. I'll get food. Just let me get the pub properly opened first."

"And I'll get my fireweave gloves tomorrow as well. Then I can cook something."

"You don't have to," Sylas started to say.

"I like cooking. There's something about putting ingredients together and seeing what they can become that brings me joy." A grin took shape on her face. "Especially when you add fire."

"Heh. Well, I'd better get down to the cellar too. Someone has to bring a cask or two up, especially now that I'm giving away free pints. That's a good idea, though. Give people a sample."

"And I'll keep track of who has already had their free pint," Azor said. "Regular or strong ale?"

Sylas considered this for a moment as he stroked his beard. "Strong. No, they'll have a choice. We'll give them a choice. No, regular. I'll think about it."

"Works for me. I won't be able to serve any pints tonight, but once I have my gloves, that will be easy."

"Then I'll be behind the bar, and you can take orders and run security."

Flames rose from Azor's shoulders as she grew in size, fiery muscles appearing and horns taking shape on her head. She deflated. "Sorry, I'm not *that* intimidating."

"I think you'd be surprised," Sylas said, who felt as if he'd just witnessed hell itself come alive.

Azor was much more intimidating than she thought she was. Even if they were in the Underworld, and things operated differently here, it was clear that the general human fear of fire was something people kept.

"Anyway, I'm heading down to grab some casks and then I'll do some more tidying up."

Azor laughed. "Try not to tumble down the steps like Patches."

"I'll do my best."

Sylas was ready. The lumen lamps were lit, and he'd even propped open the front door of the pub. He could see it in his mind's eye, all of Cinderpeak turning up, which would excite Ember Hollow and get some of the strange residents out of their homes.

He wasn't the only one that was ready for the action.

Patches strutted back and forth preparing to woo the people that stopped by the pub, the cat proud as ever.

Azor's excitement had shifted into nervousness. She floated near the fireplace, occasionally wringing her radiant orange hands out as she waited for people to begin arriving.

"Where is everyone?" Sylas asked through gritted teeth after The Old Lamplighter's doors had been open for an hour and it was still empty. He drummed his fingers on the bar.

"Should I go outside and start shouting for everyone that we have free ale?" Azor asked. "I could do some fire tricks too."

"No, or maybe? No, no, let's not do that. Yet. That little performance earlier was for the people of Ember Hollow who were watching me fix up the roof. We're overthinking this." Patches hopped up onto the bar. He mewed, his voice with a hint of confusion to it. "Don't worry," Sylas told him. "It's our opening day and we don't know many people, so we shouldn't expect too much."

"Should we have had food as well?" Azor asked. "Or cake? Humans love cake and pastries and anything sweet. Fruit? Fruit or cake? What about people that don't like sweets? Something salty. That will make them drink more ale—"

Mira stepped into the pub. "Ah, I guess I'm the first customer," she said before reading the room. "Ahem. Am I the first customer?"

"We're a bit slow tonight," Sylas told Mira.

"You're the first," Azor blurted out. "Where is everyone? We even offered the village a free pint! Who doesn't want free ale? Is there another party going on tonight? We could have hosted it here!"

Mira took a seat at the bar. "I don't know."

"All your drinks are on the house, in case you were wondering," Sylas told her as he poured up a pint of regular ale. "Or should I say, they're on Patches. He really liked the meat."

"It was your opening night. A gift basket was the least I could do. And thank you, Patches," she said as she greeted the cat.

"Sylas needs to get some food tomorrow." Azor was eager to join them, but she had promised Sylas that she would stay closer to the fireplace and only take orders later, once the place was packed. It was best not to scare off customers initially, even if they were contracted.

"What about your uncle?" Sylas asked. "Or any of his lackeys. Surely they are free tonight."

"Aren't they barred from the pub?"

"Barred? No, but I don't want people kicking down my doors. That reminds me, I still owe Mr. and Mrs. Brassmere a case of the good stuff. They are supposed to come tonight."

"Who else are you expecting?" Mira asked him.

"Um, a couple of people."

"Who, Sylas?"

"The people I've been selling pints to at the market, for one. Although Leowin fined me for doing that, no thanks to your uncle."

"The constable?"

"Is there another older man named Leowin who walks around with a salty attitude and an ugly cape?"

Mira eyes lit up at this description. "You could just get a permit and sell there, you know."

"When I have a pub here? Why would I do that? This place is ready to go, Mira. It's looking great, and it'll bring people to Ember Hollow. I just know it."

Mira didn't want to use her uncle's line of reasoning, but Sylas's tone pushed her to it. "What if the people of Ember Hollow don't want a pub?"

"Well, I was given a deed to one, was I not? And . . . and . . . I don't know," Sylas said, losing the thread of the argument. Luckily, he didn't have to pick it back up.

Brom, the farmer who Sylas had visited a couple days ago for the hammer, stepped inside with several other farmer types. "You're open, right?" he asked, suddenly nervous.

"We sure are. Welcome to The Old Lamplighter. Take a seat, mates," Sylas motioned to a table near the fire. "And don't mind Azor. We're contracted."

"Right, figured we would come for a pint. And, um, sorry about the other day."

"No problem at all," Sylas told him as Brom and the other farmers found a table. Azor spoke to them while Sylas poured a round of regular pints.

"First round is on me tonight," Sylas told the group as he approached, the pints all on a tray that he'd found in the cellar. "We have two types of ale at the moment. The strong stuff is made of barley, and it will be a bit more robust. The regular stuff, which we have here, will be lighter, a bit spicy as well. Less alcohol."

"Why didn't you bring the strong stuff?" one of the farmers asked.

"I've got to woo you in somehow, don't I?" Sylas grinned at the man as he placed a slightly frothy pint in front of him. "And besides, you'll love this. It's a rye ale, a bit different from what I've been selling at the market."

The man took a sip and the suspicion quickly left his face. "That's top-notch!"

"Let me taste," said another farmer, who quickly downed a third of his pint. "Not bad, not bad at all, mate."

It wasn't long before all four farmers had finished their pints and put in another order. At about this point, a couple more people stepped into the pub,

Sylas recognizing a few of them from the market. They got free pints as well once they took a seat at the bar.

"I guess this is as busy as it gets," Sylas told Mira once the two groups had settled into their pints.

"For now. But you do have some customers, and you'll likely have more later on. How late do you plan on staying open?"

"Until I turn the lamp off outside. I'll get another sign for that one at some point, but it'll be clear. I'll tell everyone too. Oi," Sylas said, drawing some eyes. "The Old Lamplighter is open if the light outside is on. It's closed if it's off. And don't be banging on the door if it's closed."

A few of the farmers laughed. "What if we're still inside drinking?" Brom asked.

"Then you've got to go," Azor told him to another bout of laughter.

"Like she said," Sylas told the farmer. "Anyway, continue, and let me know when you want another round."

The patrons drank several more pints over the next hour while Mira sat at the bar, aware that Sylas was disappointed in the turnout. She tried to cheer him up a few times, and he was certainly agreeable, but she could tell that he'd expected a bigger crowd.

A man with a pair of goggles on his head arrived and took a seat at the bar.

"Godric," Sylas said, his spirits instantly brightening as he recognized the tailor. "Glad you could make it."

"I know, I know, I should have finished the fireweave today and brought it with me. Talk about a surprise. But it's almost ready, and I figured I needed a drink. The lads will join me tomorrow, a couple of guys I know that live around the volcano. I promise we'll behave."

Sylas poured him up a pint, which just so happened to be the last one from the cask of regular ale. He handed it over. "A pint of the regular ale, on me. Be right back." Sylas took the cask down the cellar and returned with a fresh one.

"This is really good!" Godric told him, a bit of foam on his lip now. "And this is the regular stuff, yeah?"

"It is. The stronger ale is made of barley. Ten MLus for the strong, five for the regular."

"Not bad, not bad at all."

By the end of the night, Sylas had given away eight pints, he'd gone through his first cask of regular ale, had cracked open a second, and was at about the halfway mark with a cask of the strong ale. As he swept up, he took a look at his status.

Name: Sylas Runewulf
Mana Lumens: 755/755

Class: Brewer
[Active Quest Contracts:]
Travel to Duskhaven with Mira Ravenbane to visit the sigilist

"How'd we do, boss?" Azor asked.

"You don't need to call me that. And we did surprisingly well. We could have done worse is what I'm saying here. I'll head down and brew up a cask of the strong and two casks of the regular. Figure I'll head into Cinderpeak tomorrow, spread the word, and deliver the cask I owe to the Brassmeres."

"And pick up the fireweave clothing?"

"That too. But I think, yeah," Sylas said, a smile taking shape on his face. "I think this'll be fine. We'll give out ale daily, you know, to regulars and newcomers we like. We'll do a loose tally at night and brew from there. Nothing too serious when it comes to numbers. I'm dead, after all, and the last thing I want to do is stress over numbers. Anyway. It's a start. A good start."

"It is certainly that."

Patches, who had taken to the farmers earlier and gotten plenty of love, approached. He looked up at Sylas and nodded his head, as if he were congratulating him for a job well done. Sylas yawned.

He was tired, but there were casks to fill.

Patches was ecstatic now that the pub had opened its doors. While he didn't have a full understanding of the Mana Lumens system, he knew that his power grew exponentially when there were people in the pub, especially when they were enjoying themselves.

His status flashed before his slitted eyes.

Mana Lumens: 1072/1200

The numbers made little sense to him, but he could tell the first one had changed. Patches intuited that his power had grown, all thanks to the big man.

Sure, Patches secretly recharged the big man's powers overnight, but his loyal subject had wasted little time in fixing up the Tavernly Realm and opening its doors. He'd even installed a door for Patches to go outside.

You really aren't that bad, Patches thought as he looked the man over with adoration. The room was dark. As he often did, the big man slept on his stomach, his arm out at the side, the quilt covering half of his body. He snored lightly.

Rather than disturb him, Patches hopped off the bed and stretched for a moment. He headed down to the pub to find the fire spirit floating about.

She turned to Patches and spoke, but he couldn't understand her. Since she didn't seem angry, and since he certainly didn't want her petting him, Patches continued down to the cellar.

He sniffed the air. His ears twitched as he heard a noise in the walls.

Not today, you don't!

Patches rushed toward an opening the big man had yet to find.

He flashed invisible just as one of the demonic rats rushed into the cellar. Patches grew to two times his size as he took to the air with an incredible leap, one that shouldn't have been capable from a cat of his stature. He landed on the rat and drove his claws in.

The rodent bit him and Patches bit back.

Like the most recent rat he had encountered, this one was charged with mana, which enabled it to overpower Patches and slip out of his grip. The rat raced toward the center of the room and Patches took off after it.

The rat veered right. Patches slid into some of the supplies propped up against the wall, toppling the broom and dustpan. He turned visible again.

The rat raced to the table, which infuriated Patches. That was a sacred place. That was where the big man made his ale.

Patches was just preparing to jump to the table when a bolt of fire whisked down into the cellar. The fire spirit grabbed the rat and burned it to a crisp in a matter of seconds. All that was left by the time she was done was a pile of gray ash.

The fire spirit turned to him and grinned. She said something in a complimentary tone and then motioned for Patches to follow her upstairs.

Patches lifted his nose up at the smell. He considered his options. He could follow her up and listen to her say more nice things, or he could stay right where he was. Patches sat, his size returning to normal.

The fire spirit floated closer to him as if she were examining Patches.

To prove that he was in charge in the Tavernly Realm, Patches lowered to his front paws and yawned.

I go where I want to go, he thought as he stared up at her mockingly.

Rather than annoy her, this seemed to delight the fire spirit. She laughed, said a few more things, and left Patches in the cellar.

Once he was good and ready, Patches headed back to the big man's bedroom. He lightly hopped onto the bed and began the process of transferring his mana to his loyal subject. Much to his surprise, he didn't feel delirious this time.

I guess he doesn't need as much as he normally does, Patches thought as he got comfortable.

It was time to sleep.

[**You have 83 days until the invasion.**]

Sylas squinted at the glowing text for a moment. He yawned, checked to see that his Mana Lumens had been topped off, and got comfortable again. Over the course of what felt like a short night, he'd done a lot of thinking. Or dreaming.

Maybe both.

His thoughts centered around the ways that his father had brought people to the pub. There'd been pub quizzes and drink specials. Maybe Sylas could do something like that. But what kinds of questions would be asked? And who would host the quiz? Someone would have to pour the ale, and he couldn't do that and ask questions. Azor could host, she'd probably be good at something like that, but would this actually help bring people in?

A plan formulated in a matter of moments as Sylas lay there. He was heading to Cinderpeak anyway.

"I'm getting us some food today," he told Patches as he reached down to pet him.

The piebald pub cat let out a pouty little mew and started to purr.

"You're awake?" Azor asked as the fire spirit materialized in front of Sylas. "In that case, happy Fireday!"

"Is it Fireday already?" Sylas joked.

Azor whipped around the room, quick enough that she was able to burn the word Fireday into the air for just a few seconds. "Whew!"

Patches, who didn't appear to like the heat, hopped off the bed, scowled, and headed to the door. Once he reached it, he looked back at Azor, narrowed his eyes on her, and left.

"He's not really a morning cat, is he?" Sylas asked.

"That's because he's up all night defending the place."

"He is?" Sylas looked to the doorway, which he'd purposefully left open so Patches could come and go as he pleased.

"That cat has superpowers."

"Come again?"

"Patches. I saw him last night chasing after a rat. He was two times his normal size."

"The rat or Patches?"

"The rat was large, but I'm talking about Patches."

Sylas imagined Patches twice his normal size. "That would be a huge cat."

"He was huge. But fast. Fast like a fox. Faster. He can use Mana Lumens."

"Patches?"

"Patches," she said.

Sylas considered this for a moment and ultimately decided to think about it later. "Well, that is news to me, but Mira did say that sort of thing was possible. Anyway," he cleared his throat, "the agenda for today. I have something else that we need to do."

"Aside from getting the fireweave?"

"Aside from that. And also aside from delivering some pints to Mr. and Mrs. Brassmere. We need to put another sign out in front of the pub. We can use some of the spare wood in the cellar." Sylas showed her the dimensions of the sign with his hands. "About this big. The top part needs to say *Public House* and it needs to be burned deep enough into the wood that it's a dark black."

"And the bottom part?"

"The lamp outside. I was thinking some sort of pithy poem that I could carve into the sign and you could scorch it a little. *When the lamp is lit, come in and sit. If it's dark, best to depart.* Something like that. Or maybe we can just get the top part done here, and have the bottom part done in Cinderpeak, in cursive or something fancy."

"I like fancy."

"Who doesn't like fancy?"

"And we'll open as normal tonight?"

Sylas nodded. "Of course, we will. We'll be able to tell some people in Cinderpeak as well. That brings me to another thing I want to do there. The pub in Cinderpeak, The Ugly Duckling, as it's known. I'd like to find and speak to the owner, you know, get some tips."

"A day full of errands, it seems."

Sylas grinned at the fire spirit. "You'd prefer to be exploring lava caves?"

She laughed. "Of course I would. But this will be fun too. And once I have the fireweave clothing, I can help you."

"That reminds me, we'll need to get food."

"For you or for patrons?"

"Both," Sylas said. "And that's the final thing I'd like to discuss now in my . . ." He glanced around at the bedroom he was only now getting used to. "My office."

Azor laughed. "I suppose you could call it that."

"The food you come up with for the pub, that is how you'll gain MLus, so you don't have to pool from mine. I'll get the MLus from the ale, you'll get it from the food. Charge whatever you'd like, but I'd say keep it cheap so people come for the cheap yet delicious food and stay for the ale. Or come for the ale and get enticed by the cheap food."

"You mean it?" Azor asked, her mouth dropping. "You'd let me have that much power?"

"I cleared almost two hundred MLus last night alone. If there were fifteen patrons, or so, I'd probably pull in at least four hundred. It will take just under a thousand MLus to fill all the casks. That's plenty, *plenty,* of power on my end. So I mean it. Food sales are yours."

Azor bowed her head. "I don't know what to say."

"You don't have to say anything. Now, let's head down to the cellar so I can fill pint bottles, you can work on the sign, and then we'll head out. Wait, another thing."

"Should I start writing this stuff down?"

"No, I'm just thinking out loud here. I'll need more supplies at some point, I'm talking about pint bottles and glasses. I'm wondering if I can get some of the stuff in Duskhaven. I'll have to ask Mira. We have an active quest to go there anyway."

"And I can run the pub while you're gone."

Sylas slowly nodded. "Yes, yes, you can."

CHAPTER FOURTEEN

THWARTED BY A PUB CAT

It was a bit much to carry, yet Sylas managed to hold both the crate of pint bottles and the sign that Azor had started, the one that read *Public House*. Once the fire spirit had officially returned to the tattoo on his arm, he bid farewell to Patches, used his foot to shut the door behind him, locked the pub, and set off toward Cinderpeak.

Sylas reached the portal and was presented with several options:

- **Cinderpeak**
- **Hexveil - Ember Hollow**
- **Seedlands**

He selected Cinderpeak and instantly appeared outside the market, which was a bit more bustling than it normally was. "Not much farther now," he told Azor.

Sylas turned toward town, and had just started up the path that connected the market to the town center when Leowin approached.

"Back to sell more ale, are you?" The constable swept his cape over his shoulder, revealing his baton. He placed his hand on the grip. "I caught you."

"I owe Mr. Brassmere some ale," Sylas said calmly, even if he could feel his blood starting to boil. Sylas had nothing against authority, but he didn't like it when authority figures overstepped their boundaries. "We bartered for some supplies."

"What kind of supplies?"

"Supplies for my pub."

"I heard you had a pretty bad opening night."

"How—"

"Don't let him get under your skin," Azor said so only Sylas could hear her. "It's not worth it. He'll fine you again."

Sylas figured that Tiberius must have had one of his men check the pub last night, perhaps Henry. He shrugged Leowin's statement off. "It happens. Sometimes pubs are busy, sometimes they're not. But they're always a public house, a third place where people can gather. Just like my new sign here says. *Public House.*" He showed the constable the sign. "Anyway, unless there is something else you need, I have some errands to attend to."

"Errands? And you're not planning on selling that ale?"

"No, I'm not. Do you want to come with me to the shop so you can personally see me give Mr. Brassmere the crate?"

"Maybe."

Sylas motioned for Leowin to follow with his chin. "In that case, come on, then."

"Come on, then?" By the time that Leowin was able to say something about Sylas's tone, Sylas had already started off toward the tool shop. The Cinderpeak constable quickly caught up with him. "I can fine you for disobedience, you know. I've already done so once."

Yet again, Sylas had to bite his tongue for a moment to stop himself from saying what was really on his mind. "I have a lot to do today. How about we play a game?"

"A game? Do you know who you're talking to?"

"If I'm being honest with you, if I'm really delivering these pints to Mr. Brassmere, you come to the pub tonight with Tiberius or anyone, really. The first round will be on me. If I'm lying to you, then you can fine me, or take me to whatever magistrate you hinted at the last time we met, or toss me in whatever dungeon they have here in Cinderpeak."

"Dungeon?"

"There's some sort of dungeon, right?"

"The Ashen Hold?"

"Works for me. Anyway, I'm going to the tool shop." Sylas pressed on without waiting for a reply. Leowin came up with a number of excuses as to why he wasn't one to be bribed, Sylas ignoring them all.

They reached the tool shop and Sylas entered to find Mr. Brassmere just getting comfortable behind the counter. The older man wore a gray leather vest, almost the same color as his hair. "Sylas?" His eyebrows twitched. "Leowin?"

Sylas placed the crate on the counter. "He doesn't believe these pints are for you."

"They are for me," the shopkeep said as his face curved into a scowl. "I can't believe you followed him all the way here."

Leowin, who was clearly flustered, stomped his feet as he tried to make himself look bigger than the other two men. "I am merely doing my duty as Cinderpeak constable, Halden, and you know that. I do not have to explain my reasoning to you."

"Yeah? Well, he was being honest." Mr. Brassmere crossed his arms over his chest. "I believe you owe him an apology."

"An apology?" Leowin huffed. "Good day, good day to both of you!"

The constable had just reached the door when Sylas called out to him, "Be sure to stop by the pub tonight, we're open until I turn the lamp off out front."

Leowin slammed the door, leaving Sylas and Mr. Brassmere to laugh.

"Sorry I couldn't make it last night," the shopkeep said once he got control over his laughter. "My wife and I were planning on coming, but then she started an inventory count, and you know how that goes."

"Actually, I don't," Sylas said. "Or if I do, it's been a while."

"Well, you're lucky then. She gets on one of her benders and it's a count-all-night affair. The woman had both of us up until the crack of dawn." He yawned as if to illustrate his point. "But I'll be there tonight. We'll stop by. I won't let her touch these pints here until we've had a few at the pub."

"Good to know. In that case, I'm off to see Godric. I also need another thing."

"What's that?"

"Maybe two things. I need someone to make a sign for me. I've had Azor do the top part." He placed the wooden sign on the counter. "But I want the bottom part to look different, be stained in a way, maybe cursive or painted. Got anyone that can do that?"

"I sure do. What do you want it to say?"

"Do you mind if I write it down? It's a bit of a phrase."

Mr. Brassmere got out some parchment. Sylas wrote down the poem he'd come up with last night. *When the lamp is lit, come in and sit. But if it's dark, best to depart.*

"Not bad," the shopkeep said. "I always liked a good poem. I'll get my guy to do it now; should take about an hour."

"How much?"

"Just buy a couple of rounds tonight and we'll call it even. I'll try to bring John as well, the guy that put your doors in. He's a good lad who could use an ale."

"The more the merrier. Heh. Somehow, I end up owing you pints again."

"Somehow. But what can I say? Your ale is good, Sylas."

"Thanks."

"Speaking of which. How was the turnout last night?"

"It wasn't great, but that's an opening night for you," he said, recalling Leowin's comment. Sylas didn't want to go into detail.

"Was there something else?" Mr. Brassmere asked after Sylas was silent for a moment. He was still annoyed about the constable.

"Right. The pub here in Cinderpeak."

"The Ugly Duckling?"

"That's the one. I wanted to meet the owner, to get her take."

"Iron Rose?"

"Is that owner's name?" Sylas asked.

"I don't know if that's her real name, but that's what everyone calls her. I don't see her very often, just out to get groceries, really."

"I need to do that as well," Sylas said. "But after I meet Iron Rose and head over to Godric's place to pick up the fireweave."

"I'll bet Azor is excited."

"I sure am," she said, the fire spirit coming alive with a burst of flames that nearly caused Mr. Brassmere to fall off his stool. "Who doesn't like some new clothes?"

"But first, Iron Rose. She lives at the pub, right?"

"She does. But she mostly keeps to herself, so don't be surprised if she sends you away."

"I'll take my chances," Sylas said as he turned to the door. "See you tonight, and thanks again."

Sylas approached The Ugly Duckling. "What do you think?" he asked Azor after examining the building for a moment.

"It doesn't look open, but it also doesn't look abandoned. You could try knocking?"

"I could. But that would annoy me if it was my pub. Wait, what about you?"

"What about me?"

"You can get in, can't you? Look up there, the window is open." Sylas pointed to a window on the second floor of the pub. He glanced around to make sure no one was watching them and spoke again. "If Iron Rose is in there, just tell her the new pub owner from Ember Hollow is here, that I'd like to talk."

"What if she tries to attack me?"

"Fly back to me."

Sylas felt his tattoo start to warm as if Azor was considering his suggestion. "Fine, fine. I'll go."

She appeared in a small wisp of flame, no bigger than a dragonfly, and flew up toward the window.

Azor passed through the opening and stopped in a room without any furniture. "Strange," she said to herself as she came to the door, which was shut. Luckily, there was enough space for her to slip beneath the door.

Azor reached the hallway beyond.

She floated there for a moment, looking for signs that someone was actually home. None of the lights were on. There wasn't the sound of cooking food or anything coming from downstairs, nor was there any chatter. The place itself was nicely maintained, the floor polished, no art on the walls but no cobwebs either.

She heard a cough. Azor turned to the stairs that led down to the pub itself. She floated down cautiously and came to a room that was much larger than the interior of The Old Lamplighter.

There was plush seating against the wall just like Sylas had mentioned wanting to add to his pub, and the owner had gone with a swan motif, from oil paintings to details in the wood.

No one was on the main floor, which meant the sound she heard must have come from the cellar.

"Here we go," Azor said as she started down the cellar steps.

She reached the bottom to find a woman with dark hair that had been shot through with streaks of gray, her back to the stairs at the moment. She held an easel and she wore a black gown with an apron over it, one dappled with paint. Light coming in from several cellar windows provided the perfect ambiance for her art, which was mostly of swans.

Azor waited for the woman to lower her paintbrush, just so she didn't mess up her art. It was clear Azor was about to startle her.

"Excuse me," she said in a tiny voice.

The woman jumped so high she nearly touched the ceiling. She flipped around, her fists now rimmed in golden mana as she dropped her easel and her brush, paint splattering across the floor.

"Who are you?"

"I'm sorry! I'm just here looking for Iron Rose."

"That's me—"

"And to tell you that a newcomer named Sylas Runewulf has opened a pub in Ember Hollow called The Old Lamplighter and he wanted to meet you. He's outside. We're contracted," Azor said, the words flying out of her mouth and accented by blips of fire. "I'm sorry to disturb you!"

"A new pub?"

"The Old Lamplighter. We opened yesterday."

Iron Rose looked to her easel. "You could have knocked."

"We didn't want to disturb you."

"So you sneak up on me?"

Azor grew even smaller. "I'm sorry, Sylas thought it'd be better than knocking."

"Sylas, huh? Let's meet this Sylas of yours."

"You'll meet him?" Azor didn't dare shift back to her normal size even though she wanted to. She knew this could startle Iron Rose.

"I'll clean this up later. Come on." Iron Rose took the stairs to the top, Azor following after her.

Sylas, who had been standing outside wringing his hands in anticipation, smiled once the door opened to reveal a woman at least a decade and a half older than him. Her black gown would have been almost elegant had it not been partially blocked by an apron covered in splotches of colorful paint. The woman was tall and formidable, her eyes a shade of green that made Sylas uneasy.

"Come in," she said with a grunt.

Sylas entered and Iron Rose slammed the door shut behind him.

"Sit," she said as she motioned to the bar.

"Sure."

Sylas sat, and Azor morphed into her normal form once he was good and comfortable on the barstool. The fire spirit turned to Sylas, a nervous look on her face as Iron Rose rummaged under the bar.

Sylas heard the sound of her hand-pumping a cask. She returned moments later with a pint of dark ale. "Let it settle for a moment—"

"The foam takes a second," Sylas said, aware of the process.

"So you recently died?"

"I did," he said. "A week ago now." Hearing himself say this caused Sylas to pause. Had it already been a week?

Iron Rose noticed this. "I get it. It's strange to think of it like that. Anyway, you died and you were gifted the deed to a pub."

"That's right."

"Well, congratulations. You've just been given a chance to become more powerful than you could ever imagine. Or so they say."

"You mean the MLus?" he asked the other pub owner.

"Yes, you can net close to a thousand a night if you're doing it right. You could even bank enough to make yourself the richest, most powerful person this side of Battersea. Or you can be like me. Only open when you're feeling like it and spend most of your time painting."

"You paint?"

"She makes beautiful pictures of swans," Azor said. She slinked back. Sylas gestured for her to come forward and join the conversation fully.

"Swans, huh? Did you do that one?" He pointed to a painting of a swan at dusk. The swan had its head tucked into its feathers, the sky beyond a canvas of dark blue speckled with emerging stars.

"I did. The sky never looks like that here, but I remember."

"Where did you live back in our world?"

"Victoria."

"You were from the Aurum Kingdom?" Sylas asked, familiar with the city. There were loads of artists who lived there.

"I was."

"Same. Died fighting the Shadowthorne Empire."

"I've heard that story before," she said as she nodded to the pint. "It's ready."

Sylas took a sip from it. There was a touch of sweetness, followed by undertones of caramel and subtle hints of honey. The sweetness lingered as Sylas put the pint glass down. The ale was amazing.

"Well?"

"I love it," he said.

"Every brewer has their own twist as long as the basics remain the same. What are you brewing up at The Old Lamplighter?"

"I'm keeping it simple at the moment. A strong barley ale and a lighter rye ale."

"That's a good option. You'll get more creative in the future. Or you won't. I've been to places in Battersea where they've served the same ale for years."

"How many pubs are there in Battersea?" Sylas asked. "It's the biggest city in the Underworld, right?"

"It is by far. And there are plenty of places. They have tougher regulations in Battersea, though. They don't want people like us getting too strong. That's another thing about having a pub. Sure, it's a great gathering place, but those in power know what we're able to do. Even if we charge three MLus for a pint, it'll still add up. Especially because the most it will ever cost us is nine hundred sixty MLus to brew twelve casks."

"Can I get bigger casks?"

"You can try, but the ale will disappear. The cask size is due to the Ale Alliance and agreements they made with lumengineers a very long time ago. I do not know how long ago, nor do I know the details. But let me save you the trouble. You're stuck with the small casks."

"That's fine. I'm sort of getting used to them."

"They do grow on you, and they're easy to transport."

"So it's rare to get a deed to a pub?"

Iron Rose nodded. "It is. People get deeds to all sorts of places, and they are gifted all sorts of classes when they arrive here. They can sell things and do well, but a pub, once you get it up and running, can really make an impact here in the Underworld. Wait. You died a week ago, yet you're already open? How?"

"What do you mean?" Sylas asked Iron Rose as he took another sip from his ale.

"Everyone starts out with a hundred MLus. People get stronger over time, of course, but I've met people that have been dead for hundreds of years that don't have as much power as someone who owns a pub can have. You started with a hundred. Did you just go quest contract crazy or something?"

"Quest contract crazy?"

"You know, trying to do as much as you can so you can gain as many MLus as possible in a short amount of time."

Sylas nodded. His mind had just circled back to something that she'd said moments ago. Hundreds of years. Of course people could be in the Underworld hundreds of years, if not longer. He hadn't yet thought about that. "My MLus completely refill overnight," he finally said. "That's how I've managed to do it."

"Overnight?"

"Strange, right?"

"I've never heard of that," she admitted. "That is one thing that keeps people from powering quickly. They expend MLus, only a small amount refills, and then they use that amount to do other things. But that would explain how you were able to open so quickly. How are the Ember Hollow villagers taking it?"

"What villagers?"

Iron Rose laughed. Azor did as well, her laugh just a bit too loud. "It really is empty there," the fire spirit told Iron Rose. "Maybe that's why they gave Sylas the deed to the pub."

"So close to the Hexveil too."

"Doesn't bother me," Sylas said. "There is a militia, however, that's giving me a hard time."

Iron Rose shook her head. "There's always a militia, especially this far out. Some are worse than others."

"I've met the constable."

"Leowin? He's not officially associated with the militia but he technically is. I mostly ignore him. He stopped bothering me years ago. Wait. How does he even know about you?"

Sylas took another drink from his pint. "My power recharges overnight, but I needed to get MLus quickly, so I started selling bottles at the market. He busted me, or tried to, and ended up fining me for disorderly conduct or something."

"You need a permit to sell there."

"I'm aware, now. But I got away with it for a few days, so that helped."

"That makes more sense. I was doing the math moments ago thinking, well, his power refills, but how did he get so much? Makes sense. And your pub already had supplies?"

"It has some things. I'm almost out of pint bottles, though. I'd like to get new glasses as well because some have seen better days. But they work."

"You'd have to go to Battersea for that. That's where the suppliers are."

"I need to go to Battersea for a number of things," Sylas said, thinking of the Book of Shadows. Something else came to his mind as he enjoyed the ale. "Your pub doesn't happen to have a portal, does it? I found a dormant one in a locked bedroom upstairs."

"Yes, that's a direct line to Battersea. But you'd have to first get their approval to activate it, which will require a sigilist. And to do that, you'd have to join the Ale Alliance. They're the ones I mentioned earlier."

"The Ale Alliance, huh?"

"Yes, a guild of brewers."

"But it would take me some time to reach there, right?"

"Yes and no. It's sort of a rite of passage. With as much MLus as you'll be able to accumulate, you should be able to fly there."

"Fly that far?"

"I've told you about flying already," Azor reminded Sylas.

"Where would I learn how to do something like that?"

Iron Rose glanced from the stained-glass window back to Sylas. "There are people here in Cinderpeak, but your best bet would be Duskhaven. At least that is closer to civilization. You'll want to speak to what is known as an archlumen. There are many there in Duskhaven, but the best one is named Tilbud. He's eccentric, but he's the best."

"Archlumen Tilbud."

"That's him. He can show you certain techniques, but it will cost you. He's easy to find too. The man lives in a house shaped like a sphere. Can't miss it."

"Good to know, I was planning on heading to Duskhaven soon anyway." Sylas finished his pint. "What do I owe you?"

"On the house."

"You're too kind," he told Iron Rose. "Whenever you're feeling like stepping out, I'll have a seat at the bar and a pint with your name on it at The Old Lamplighter."

She shrugged. "I've got a lot of art I'd like to do before then. But maybe. I have something coming up and we need a place to drink."

"Why not here?"

"It's more fun elsewhere. This is my home."

Sylas stood. He could tell it was time to go. "Been a pleasure," he said as he headed to the door. Azor joined him once he reached it, the fire spirit returning to her tattoo.

"Next time, knock," Iron Rose called after him.

Sylas reached Godric's place in the shadow of the Cinderpeak Volcano. The fireweave tailor was seated out front, a big smile on his face, his goggles on his forehead.

"Didn't know when you'd come," he said, "but I figured it would be soon. Ready to see it?"

"We are," Sylas told him as Azor appeared.

He rubbed his hands together. "This way, then."

They followed Godric to his outdoor workshop. "Has anyone said anything about the cinderspiders?" Sylas asked the tailor.

"What do you mean?"

"They definitely weren't happy with all the lavalace I took."

"As long as we don't go into their caves, they'll be fine. They're smarter than they look, you know," he said as he approached his workbench. Godric motioned to a pair of long gloves and an apron. "Before she puts it on I want you to touch it," he told Sylas. "It's some of my best work. Actually, all of my work is my best work. But this is certainly up there."

Godric brought Sylas one of the gloves.

Azor moved in closer, examining his fine craftsmanship as Sylas held the fireweave glove. The fabric itself almost resembled chainmail. It was surprisingly soft and flexible, the weave loose enough to allow full freedom of movement.

"This is brilliant," Sylas finally told the tailor.

"With as much lavalace as you brought, stringing this together was surprisingly easy. Go ahead, try it out," Godric told Azor as he placed the long glove on the bench.

She picked up the first glove and slipped her fiery hand in. The glove ran all the way up to her elbow, which gave it an elegant touch, especially after she'd slipped her other hand in the second glove. Azor placed the apron around her neck and let it drop over the front of her body. She tied it at the back and did a complete turn.

"What do you think?" she asked Sylas.

"It looks great!"

"It does?" Azor glanced down at herself, gauging the look. She flexed her fingers and turned her head to Sylas. "Shake my hand."

"Sure."

Sylas reached his hand out to the fire spirit. Her hand was now cool to the touch even though there was a raging fire within the glove. She squeezed his hand and grinned, blue flames flickering off her face as a familiar warmth reached Sylas.

"Since we were contracted, I wouldn't have been able to hurt you anyway. But you see what I mean. This will be perfect," she said as she let his hand go. "I can help you now, I can serve things."

"You can. But we can't travel like this, right?" he asked, a question for Godric or Azor. "I mean in public, when you've reduced yourself to the tattoo."

"No, you'll have to carry the stuff for her in that case," Godric said. "It's a little heavy. But I've got a bag that will handle it. Not made of fireweave, but extra strong. Hold on." He turned to his home. "I'll be right back. I hung it by the door figuring you'd need it."

The tailor left Sylas alone with Azor, who was still brimming with joy. "I've always wanted fireweave clothing."

"You didn't have any in the Chasm?"

"I did, but it wasn't as good as this. People there would talk about it, and at first, I didn't believe them that it could be this good. Now, I see they were right." She flexed her fingers again. "I can't believe it's mine."

"It is," Sylas said, "and it looks great. I can see you now, serving up pints and cooking up delicious food."

"I've got to think of a menu."

"You do, but keep it simple. Also, I'll show you how to correctly pour a pint of ale. It's not too difficult, like you saw Iron Rose do back there, but there is a bit of a trick to it. And don't forget: you have to let ale settle for a moment."

Godric returned with the satchel, which was made out of just about the thickest hide Sylas had come across yet. It was rugged, the entire piece an aged brown leather that looked like it had existed since the dawn of the Underworld.

"What kind of leather is this?" Sylas asked.

"Underox. You probably saw some out toward the Seedlands."

"I don't think I saw anything like that," Sylas said.

"Yeah? Well, you'd know if you did. But think a huge ox. The hugest of oxen, with thick skin perfect for leather goods. Anyway, that should work to store the clothing while you travel." He grinned at Sylas. "Are you open tonight?"

"I sure am. We'll probably open up in a few hours, once I get back and get settled. We'll have food soon too."

"You will, will you?" Godric grinned. "That sounds even better. I'll have to stop by then."

"Is there a place to get any fish around here?" Azor asked.

"Fish?" Godric considered this. "You won't want to get any from Cinderpeak. The good fish is in Duskhaven or beyond, but that's a bit of a journey unless you can teleport. Actually, Douro, south of here, has fish too. But Duskhaven has the Finmarket, and that's where the best deals are."

"Are you suggesting what I think you're suggesting?" Sylas asked Azor.

The fire spirit beamed a big smile over at him. "I believe I am. What kind of pub doesn't offer fish-and-chips?"

"Fish-and-chips, eh?" Godric asked. "Been ages since I even thought about something like that. And we've got plenty of potatoes in the Seedlands. Once you get to Duskhaven and you can portal back and forth, that will solve your fish problem. You'll be able to set up a delivery as well."

"It's certainly on the to-do list," Sylas said. "Maybe in a couple days. I want to make sure the pub is running smoothly first."

Sylas finished installing the new sign, which he'd been able to pick up on his way out of Cinderpeak.

He lowered his hammer and took a step back to admire the finished project. It hung beneath the lumen lamp outside the pub and read *Public House* on top, with cursive beneath it featuring the phrase Sylas had come up with: *When the lamp is lit, come in and sit. If it's dark, best to depart.*

"Are you open yet?" came a voice.

Sylas turned to find the face of a man he hadn't seen in a few days.

His was still a troubling visage, the man's face defined by splotchy redness, wrinkles, and bloodshot eyes. He was the same fellow that Sylas had been forced to get a little stern with back when he was selling bottles at the Cinderpeak Market, the man who had demanded he sell him more ale.

"We are," Sylas said as he waved his hand over the lamp, which instantly illuminated. "Head on in and your first pint is on me."

"Sure, thanks," the man said as he started to shuffle past.

"What's your name?" Sylas called to him.

"Anders."

"Enjoy, Anders. And hopefully, people will be joining you soon."

Sylas didn't know what kind of turnout to expect. He hoped there'd be more than a handful of people, but he had yet to figure out a good way to advertise the pub aside from the people he'd met. "People," he said as he looked at the sign. "That's a great idea."

Sylas popped into the pub to find Anders sitting at a chair near the back door. He now had a pint, a bit of shame in his eyes. "Azor," Sylas said to the fire spirit, who was behind the bar. "I'm going to make some rounds."

"Rounds?" she asked.

"Head to the houses in the vicinity and tell them we're open. Hold the pub down while I'm gone." He took one more look around. "Where's Patches?"

"Upstairs, last I saw him," she said as she wiped a pint glass clean with a bar rag. "I'm sure he'll be down soon enough."

"Be right back." Sylas started with the door closest to the pub, the building nondescript aside from some old paint claiming that it was a general store. He knocked and no one answered. He took a look at the boarded up windows, decided it was abandoned, and moved on. Sylas finally got a bite at a door a block or two away.

Duncan opened the door and immediately stumbled back, as if he were about to go for a weapon.

"I'm not here for that," Sylas said as he showed the militiaman the palms of his hands. "Not here for conflict. I'm actually here to tell you and Henry, if he's around, and anyone you may know, that the pub is open. Feel free to stop by. First pint is on me."

Duncan, who looked like he had just woken up even though it was late afternoon, grunted a positive response. "Yeah? I'll tell him. Tell my mate Cody too. He lives here. Sleeping at the moment."

"Cody? I don't believe I met him."

"A relative newcomer like yourself," Duncan said with his unique lisp.

"Great, thanks."

Sylas moved on and ended up telling several people about the pub opening. None were particularly friendly. Even if he told them his name, they didn't reciprocate. Sylas was fine with that. He could learn more about them at The Old Lamplighter if they actually showed up.

By the time he returned to the pub, Sylas found Azor serving drinks to Mr. and Mrs. Brassmere, who sat at a different table with Godric and John, the man who installed the doors. Brom and some of his farmer buddies were gathered at one of the tables, enjoying drinks with Anders.

Sylas noted that Mira wasn't there as he stepped behind the bar and began pouring pints.

More people came, including a couple of locals. A quick head count told Sylas that there were fifteen people in the pub now, The Old Lamplighter growing increasingly lively. He was excited, and didn't mind giving out the occasional pint, especially to key people.

Eventually, Patches strutted down and a few of the farmers clapped. The pub cat sashayed over to them and got his pets. His ears twitched at some point when Anders coughed. Patches immediately jumped down from one of the patron's laps and began hissing at the red-faced man.

"I don't know what's gotten into him," Azor said.

Patches started to yowl.

Azor rushed around the bar and shooed Patches away, who ultimately headed upstairs, tail tucked between his legs.

Sylas looked to Anders to see the man recoil a bit, but Sylas soon became too distracted with another couple of patrons to really check in on him.

Later that night, after the Brassmeres had left, Anders stumbled to the bar. He plopped down on one of the seats, his eyes filled with shame. "I'm drunk," he told Sylas.

"I can get you some water," Sylas offered. They had water available in pitchers with cork tops. Sylas reached down to grab one of the pitchers.

"No, I'm fine. I need..." Anders hiccuped. "Apologies, mate. I'm so bloody sorry."

"Let's get you some water," Sylas said.

"Water won't wash away my sins."

Sylas turned to him. "What are you going on about?" By this point, one of the farmers had noticed Anders's strange behavior, the others still listening to one of Godric's stories about the volcano.

"I need to confess something," Anders blurted out. "Only thing to do. And if you want to take it out on me, I understand. I bloody well deserve it."

"Confess?"

"I was the one that did it," Anders said in a low voice. He nodded his head to the back door. "I was the one that broke it down, the back door. That cat of yours beat me back. Never seen nothing like it. I—"

"You're the one?" Sylas asked. He glanced over to Azor, who quickly appeared at his side. It dawned on him why Patches had made such a commotion earlier.

"What's going on?" she asked Sylas as flames flickered around the crown of her head.

"He's the one who broke into the pub. It wasn't Tiberius or his men."

"Who?" Anders asked.

"Don't worry about that part," Sylas told him.

"What do you want me to do to him?" Azor asked, her tone shifting caustic.

Sylas was a nice man. He was the kind of man that had taken Azor in and trusted her. He didn't deserve to have his property damaged, not with all the work he had put into it. Azor tensed her shoulders, the flames burning brighter. This brought the attention of all the patrons.

"Hold on a moment," Sylas told her.

Azor looked at him in shock. If they had been in the Chasm, she would have already handled someone like this by now. She was his security. Yet Sylas seemed calm. Agitated by the man's confession, yes, but ultimately calm.

"You were trying to steal my ale?" Sylas asked Anders.

"I was. And it was wrong of me. Bloody wrong of me. It was just so good and, I know I can't go around doing things like that."

The door swung open and Leowin stepped in. The constable dramatically swept a part of his cape over his shoulder and instantly turned to the bar, his already sour expression souring even more so. "Anders? What in the blazes?"

"Constable." The red-faced man tensed, his eyes bulging.

"What's going on here?"

"Do you want to tell him, or do you want me to tell him?" Sylas asked Anders as Godric, Brom, and a few of the farmers approached, all curious to see what was about to happen.

Anders had nowhere to run, but it didn't seem like he wanted to run at all. He held his head high instead, his eyes partially closed. "I'll confess."

"Here I am coming in for a free pint, and I get a confession instead," Leowin said, annoyed. "Let's hear it then, Anders. Go on."

"I broke into the pub a couple of days ago. Destroyed the back door." Anders pointed to Sylas. "Ask him. He'll tell you. Door is fixed now, though."

A hawkish grin formed on Leowin's face. "And?"

"That's it, Constable. I was planning on stealing me a cask, just until they opened. I was going to bring it back, honest. But I didn't make it that far."

"Why not?" Leowin asked.

"The pub cat."

Godric and the farmers burst out laughing. "Patches took you down?" Brom asked, the farmer nearly dropping his pint. "Thwarted by a pub cat!"

"That's no ordinary cat," Anders started to say, but by this point Leowin had stepped up to him and placed a hand on his shoulder.

"You know I've got to take you to the magistrate now, right?"

"I know," Anders said. "I'm sorry," he told Sylas. "You've got a nice place here, and I almost ruined it."

"You will have your MLus permanently docked," Leowin said.

"I know, I know." Anders looked down at his big hands. "Don't have that much to begin with. But I deserve the punishment."

"Do you want him to pay you back for your repair costs?" Leowin asked Sylas.

Sylas wasn't a vengeful man. He had also met enough people to know when someone was beaten down to the point of desperation. Desperation was a consistent killer of men. In a way, it had been how Sylas had died himself. Rather than tend to his mortal wound on the battlefield, he had moved on in desperation to rally his men.

Anders deserved whatever punishment he got. Yet Sylas didn't want to add onto it.

Everyone got one chance with him, which was a phrase that Sylas liked to say from time to time. But some people got two chances or more. Call it soft, call it coming from a place where'd seen the best and worst of people. But Sylas was a forgiving man, and it seemed like Anders was the type that needed one more chance.

"No need to pay me back. The doors are already repaired."

"Let me do something else then, anything," Anders pleaded. "I'm a carpenter by trade."

"A carpenter?"

"I was back before I died and classed as one here."

"Make him pay you back," one of the farmers said.

"Make him pay you double," said another.

"Let me handle this," Azor said, her flames intensifying to the point that a few of the farmers stepped away from her.

"No, no," Sylas said. "I'll let Constable Leowin take it from here. You're free to return once you've cleaned your act up," he told Anders. "I could always use a carpenter."

"So be it." Leowin grabbed Anders by the arm and shuffled him out.

"Well?" Sylas said with a grin to the farmers and the other people who had gathered. "The show's over. Back to your seats. We'll be closing in about thirty minutes—"

"Give us another hour," Brom said. "Just one."

"No, thirty minutes. I have things to do tomorrow."

"Like what?" one of the farmers asked.

"For one, I need to apologize to someone myself," Sylas said, thinking of Tiberius. He clapped his hands together. "And I have a few other errands. Anyway, that doesn't matter now. Back to your seats, gents. These pints aren't going to finish themselves!"

Sylas was up bright and early the next morning, his hand naturally coming to Patches's head to scratch the pub cat behind the ear.

[You have 82 days until the invasion.]

He stared at the ominous prompt for a moment as the words started to fade away. Maybe it was something he could figure out in his visit to Duskhaven.

From there, he checked his status to see that his levels had been topped off. He had breached one thousand Mana Lumens, which was cause for celebration. While he had given away a good number of regular pints last night, he'd also sold a fair amount as well.

Before bed, as was becoming his tradition, Sylas had brewed up several casks to maximize the number of MLus he could gain without spending any during the day. He currently had eleven and a half casks in the cellar below, almost a split between regular and strong ale.

"Maybe I'm just blessed," he told Patches, referring to how quickly he was gaining power.

Azor entered the room. How did she always know when he was awake? Sylas suspected she checked on him more often than he thought.

"Happy Specterday," she said with a spin.

"Same to you. Anything to report after I went to bed last night?" he asked. "Did Patches kill any more rats?"

"No, but he was pretty curious about something outside. He seems to be very interested in the well out back. I don't know why. He circled it several times and hopped to the top. I thought he was going to jump in but he didn't. I might have played a part in that. I actively tried to make sure he didn't jump into the well."

"I don't even know if he'd fit in the well," Sylas said. "Anyway, we did good last night. Earned just over three hundred MLus. Now I have enough that I could refill all twelve casks in one night."

"Is that something you'd like to actually do?"

"If I sold out, sure." He yawned. "Anyway, all good news."

"I made breakfast with the food you got yesterday."

"Did you?" Sylas got out of bed. "You don't have to do that. I know how to cook."

"I'm sure you do, but I can cook better than you," she said in a teasing tone. "Come on. I figured you'd want a full stomach before you head over to Mira's place."

"I'm pretty sure it's her uncle's place, but point taken. And you're right. Sure. That sounds doable. What about you, Patches? You heading down with us? Want some milk?"

Patches perked up. Soon, Sylas was seated at the bar eating scrambled eggs and a side of toast while Patches lapped at a bowl of milk at his feet.

"Last night was so fun," Azor said. "Even with that one guy."

"Anders?" Sylas asked. "I wasn't expecting that at all. But it's not the first drunken confession I've witnessed. Considering my profession, it's probably not the last. We'll see if he actually comes to help with some carpentry work."

"You'll really just forgive him like that? I suppose it comes with the territory, but aren't you afraid you'll get burned?" A fiery grin appeared on her face, Azor proud of her pun.

"We'll see what happens." Sylas brought his plate down to the cellar and washed it in the sink there. He returned to the main floor to find Patches on his back, Azor carefully scratching his large belly using her new glove.

"He's starting to *warm* up to me. There I go again," she said, laughing at her own comment. "I guess it's just that sort of morning. How long do you think you'll be?"

"That I don't know, but when I'm back from Mira's, we'll do a sweep of the pub and see if there's anything that could use a little work. Hold the place down while I'm gone."

Mira, who had just finished working on a balm for a woman who lived a few doors over, was surprised to look up and see Sylas approaching. "What does he want now?" she asked as she moved to the front of her shop.

That last time he'd shown up, it had been to confront Tiberius. She hoped this wasn't something like that. Her uncle had only recently dropped the subject.

"Mira," Sylas said. "You're one of two people I need to see."

"That's not a proper greeting."

"I meant to say good morning, happy Specterday. And what a fine morning it is." Sylas swept his hand toward the dark golden clouds above, the Celestial Plains mocking the Underworld as always. "I'll bet it's an even better morning up there."

"In the Plains? I'm sure it is." A wry smile took shape on Mira's face. "If you're here to confront my uncle about something—"

"No, not confront, apologize. But I'll get to that. First, I wanted to talk to you about Duskhaven. I need to go there for several reasons now."

"Several reasons?"

"Yes. And I wanted to know if you wanted to go on . . ." He paused for a moment, as if he were trying to remember the name of the day.

"Tomorrow? Soulsday?"

"No, the day after tomorrow. I'm still getting used to the names. I only know today because Azor told me."

"Moonsday."

"That's the one. Although I haven't seen the moon at night."

"That's because we don't get to see it. The Celestial Plains do, though," Mira said. "What do you need in Duskhaven aside from the sigilist?"

"I need to get fish for Azor at the Finmarket. I also need to speak to an archlumen. I got a recommendation from the pub owner out of Cinderpeak, Iron Rose. I'd like to improve some of my powers. Or learn powers. Maybe I should start there. I want to be able to fly, so I can go to Battersea more easily."

"And why Battersea?" Mira asked, her interest piqued.

"The Book of Shadows, for one. But also because I was recently told there is an Ale Alliance there. Again, Iron Rose. Know her?"

Mira shook her head.

"She told me about the Alliance, and that I'd need the sigilist to first get the portal activated after their approval. So I don't need the sigilist in Duskhaven yet. I'll need them after I go to Battersea."

"You need the Ale Alliance's approval for what exactly?"

"So I can become part of the network and get certain supplies, like pint glasses, that sort of thing."

"And Azor would run the pub while you're gone?"

"She would. She has her fireweave gear now. I thought you'd stop by last night to check it out."

"I'm not normally one to visit a pub nightly," Mira said.

"I have a new sign as well. You'll like that."

She couldn't help but grin at Sylas. "Will I?"

"I'm certain of it. It's quite pithy, if I do say so myself."

"We'll see. As for my uncle, what is this about an apology?"

The front door of their home burst open. Tiberius came out with his sleeves rolled up, clearly looking for a fight. "You aren't supposed to come around here," he told Sylas. The short man brought his fists to the ready and clenched them so tightly that his knuckles turned red. "I warned you."

"Uncle, please—"

"Mira—"

Her eyes flared with golden mana, enough that Tiberius lowered his fists. He had seen his niece get this way before and knew what she was capable of.

The former lord commander of the Shadowthorne Vanguard narrowed his gaze on Sylas. He didn't like him, and he especially didn't like the way Sylas held himself, always with the confidence of a bigger man.

Tiberius certainly thought that Mira could do better, if those were her intentions in the first place. More important, Tiberius knew what would happen if Sylas's pub was successful. It would change Ember Hollow, and Sylas, *not* Tiberius, could become the most powerful person in this region of the Underworld.

"What is this about?" he finally asked.

"It's about the pub."

"Of course, it is." Tiberius almost gestured for Sylas to wrap it up but stopped himself once he caught how Mira was looking at him. "What about it?"

"The break-in. That wasn't you or your people. We found the culprit last night."

"We?"

"He confessed to it, and Leowin took him in."

"That's *Constable* Leowin to you. And what was he doing at the pub anyway?" Tiberius asked.

"I invited him. I invited Duncan yesterday as well, but he didn't show up. What I'm trying to say here is that whatever this is," Sylas motioned between them, "I'd like it to stop. And I was wrong to accuse you of breaking into the pub. I'm, ahem, I'm sorry for that."

"Even if it seemed like it was something I would have ordered my men to do?"

Sylas showed him his hands. "You said it, not me."

Tiberius kept his arms crossed over his chest. "So you came here to apologize?"

"I did. My apologies," Sylas said. "Come by the pub, both of you. And Mira, Moonsday. Let's head to Duskhaven. See you later." He turned in the direction of The Old Lamplighter.

"He sure is confident," Tiberius said as he glared at Sylas's back with his one good eye.

"He came here to apologize, Uncle."

"You're really going to join him on a trip to Duskhaven? That will take at least a day on horseback."

"And we happen to have two horses."

"You're not taking my horse."

"Sylas has already ridden your horse. But fine, we can walk."

Tiberius tried not to grow flustered at this statement. "He rode my horse? When?"

"When I first took him to Cinderpeak. Relax, Uncle. He's actually not a bad guy. He didn't have to apologize to you. Speaking of which, you could have told him it wasn't you who ordered the break-in."

Tiberius ran his hand along his smooth chin. He had shaved that morning, and he could still smell the ointment Mira had made him as an aftershave. "I could have, but sometimes it's best for an enemy to think one thing so you can hit them with another. It's all strategy, Mira."

"Strategy? This isn't war. We aren't at war with him."

"Maybe you're not—"

"You aren't either," she said. "Let Sylas be. I think things will get better with him around. They already are."

"How?"

"I don't know," Mira said, not ready to tell him it was just something she was feeling about the pub's addition to Ember Hollow.

"He'll get too powerful."

"You're the only one that seems to worry about that, Uncle."

"You haven't seen what these high-powered lumenists can do. I have. You say there are no wars, but that simply isn't true. Never mind the battles fought in the Chasm. There have been skirmishes here, and not just chasing down creatures that have broken through the Hexveil, which I'm supposed to do today."

"What escaped this time?"

Tiberius grimaced. "A C-Rank demon. Nothing big, or nothing too big. It will be large, but I've seen worse. I just received a message from the Hexveilian Guard."

"Are we safe?" Mira asked, aware that like Sylas, Tiberius also got messages. But her uncle's prompts didn't warn of an ominous invasion, they only told of active demon hunts he could join.

"I think so. But I may need to ask Leowin if he'll assist on this one."

An idea came to Mira, evident in the way the look on her face shifted. "Why not ask Sylas?"

"Sylas?"

"I'm sure he would help."

"But then he'd get part of the reward."

"You could negotiate that with him. In fact, yes. Yes, Uncle. If you don't ask Sylas, I will walk over there right now and ask him myself. His fire spirit can—"

Tiberius gasped. "He has a fire spirit?"

"You didn't see his branding?" Mira thought back to what Sylas was just wearing and remembered he had long sleeves covering the marking.

"Sylas contracted with an elemental spirit?" he asked, in a tone that meant to relay to his niece that Sylas was already becoming powerful.

Mira didn't take the bait. "He did. And she is quite helpful. She'll run the pub while he goes out with you and the others. I think this is a great idea. It will give you two a chance to bond."

"I'm not trying to bond with the man."

"Sylas was able to get lavalace from a cave near the Cinderpeak Volcano and apparently, he fought of a good number of cinderspiders to do it."

"He did, did he? Hmmm." Tiberius considered this for a moment. "That's not an easy battle."

"No, it is not."

"Perhaps you can make the introduction. You are, ahem, more familiar with him."

Mira placed her hands on her hips. She was about to say something about men and their senseless pride but came to the conclusion that going along with this would be best. The odds of her uncle botching the invite with his ego were high; this was a chance for him to see that Sylas wasn't a bad guy after all.

"Do you want me to go ask him now?"

"Sure," Tiberius said. "We'll see what kind of man he actually is."

CHAPTER FIFTEEN

THE ESTEEMED COALITION OF EMBER HOLLOW DEFENDERS

Sylas had just finished wiping down the floor when he heard a light knock at the door.

"I'll get it," Azor said, who had been behind the bar cleaning pint glasses. She zipped to the other side of the bar just as Mira entered. "Hi, Mira!"

Patches, who had been on the windowsill, hopped down and rushed over to the apothecary. He purred and rubbed his body against the side of her leg.

"Good to see you too, Patches." Mira scooped the cat into her arms. He purred even louder.

"Do you want something to eat?" Azor asked the apothecary. "I could make you something. We have food now."

"I'm fine. Actually, I'm here to talk to you about something," she told Sylas.

"Yeah?" Sylas approached the bar and motioned for her to sit. Mira remained standing so she could easily cradle Patches in her arms. "What did I do wrong this time? Wait, don't tell me, this is about your uncle."

"How did you know?"

"I figured he'd have something more to say about me accusing him. But honestly, it made sense in my head, and I apologized and—"

"It's not about that. You're the owner of a pub, a brewer. And I'm an apothecary."

"Yes . . . what are you getting at?" Sylas scrutinized her for a moment.

Azor, who felt a tension between the two, decided to act. "I'm going to make a little snack anyway. I'll be right back!" The fire spirit rocketed away, heading straight for the cellar. This caused Patches to begin struggling until Mira set him down.

"Anyway," Sylas said. "You were saying, Mira."

"Not everyone has a class assigned to them in the Underworld, but many do. My uncle was assigned the class of demon hunter. This is one of the reasons he created the militia, as you know."

"Ah, the Esteemed Coalition of Ember Hollow Defenders. I feel like that would benefit from an acronym. E-C-E-H-D? No, that doesn't have a ring to it."

Mira tried not to roll her eyes at Sylas and failed. "Yes, that militia. The people in the militia, people like Henry and Duncan, join him on demon hunts. They are all rewarded from a pool of MLus when they successfully kill the demon. These cuts are negotiated, of course, but my uncle gets the most because of the role assigned to him. They rank these demons in various ways as well, from F to S, the larger or more difficult ones being A, B, and S-ranked. That's why I'm here."

"At the pub?"

"At the pub, your pub."

"The Old Lamplighter."

"I see the name hasn't changed."

"I thought you were here to see me," Sylas told her with a grin. He couldn't help himself. It was fun to flirt with Mira, mostly because she became so flustered when he did so. Even now, she was already starting to blush.

"I'm here to tell you that my uncle has invited you to go on the hunt with him and a few of his militiamen tonight."

"Tonight? What about the pub?"

"Azor can run the pub, can she not?"

Sylas considered this. "I mean . . ."

"You told me that she'd run the place while you and I go to Duskhaven, so it sounds like it's in her wheelhouse."

"I wanted to give her a few more days to learn the ropes."

"What ropes? Serve pints and make sure no one does anything crazy."

"Well, when you put it like that." Sylas shrugged. "Did Tiberius ask for me to join him, or is this you trying to make us play nice?"

"He asked," Mira said, leaving out the fact that she had prodded her uncle to some degree. "And I think it would be a good chance for you to show him that you're not a bad guy after all."

"How do you know that?"

"Please. You know what I'm saying, Sylas. You have a weapon, do you not?"

He glanced behind the bar to the fireweave mace he'd received from Godric. It was currently under the counter, but Sylas knew it was there. Like most weapons, he felt it had a presence. This wasn't something that was rational, but he'd been around the items long enough to feel as if he could sense them. "I do."

"You can bring that. You'll also get to learn what some of the other classes do here in the Underworld."

"You said they share a cut of MLus, would I get any of this?"

"I'm certain you could work something out," Mira said, which meant that she would work something out for him once she spoke to her uncle again.

"And we hunt the demon and come back?"

"That's usually how it goes, yes."

"What if I say no? What if I say I'd rather just stay here at The Old Lamplighter, where it's comfortable and safe, and where I can happily make my own MLus."

"Then..." Mira bit her lip. "Then I won't be able to go with you to Duskhaven on Moonsday."

"It's like that, huh?"

She nodded. "You're going to be living here in Ember Hollow, and it's important for everyone to get along. I read your sign out front. I saw that you added the *Public House* above the poem. If The Old Lamplighter truly is a public house, a place for the people of Ember Hollow to gather, then making these connections will help the community embrace you."

"Yeah," Sylas said, a bit dejected now even though he knew she was right.

"And who wrote the poem?"

"I did."

"You wrote that? I could have sworn it was Patches. Kidding. It's clever, I'll give you that."

He grinned at the apothecary. "That's all I get?"

"It's enough, isn't it?"

"It's something. How do these hunts normally go?"

"You know this warning that you've been getting?" she asked.

"I most certainly do. We'll need to do something about that soon because I'm guessing this invasion relates to Ember Hollow."

"Likely, but we have time. At least right now we do. Anyway. The warning you get is similar to what my uncle gets. He gets notified if there is a demon that escaped the Chasm, and these notifications tell him of their ranking. At that point it becomes a race to get the demon before other hunters and adventurers try for it. We're so close to the Hexveil, though, that we have somewhat of an advantage."

"And then he has this sixth sense or something as to where the demon is, right?" Sylas asked. "Like when I take a quest and know which way I need to go. I noticed that with Mr. Brassmere's hammer."

"Exactly like that, yes. It's like a sixth sense. This is his advantage being classed as a demon hunter, something that someone like an adventurer wouldn't have. Duncan and Henry? They aren't classed, and it helps them to partner with someone like Tiberius. Same with anyone else who decides to join the hunt tonight. They partner with a demon hunter to share in the MLus."

"That's all starting to make sense now. And you think we'll be home sometime tonight? Because I'll have to brew before I go to bed."

"He said it was a C-Rank demon. That's normally one that they handle in a single night, so yes, I believe you'll be back. I'll even sweeten the pot."

"How?"

A light smile lifted Mira's cheeks. "I'll stay at the pub and keep an eye on the place. I can help Azor if she needs me."

This statement came as a surprise. "You'd stay and help?"

"If she needs me, yes. So, what do you say? Will you do it? Will you join my uncle on his hunt?"

Sylas returned her smile. "I get this feeling I don't really have a choice in the matter."

"You don't."

Azor raced up from the cellar holding a plate of toast with jam and butter on the side. "I hope this is fine," she said as she frantically placed the two plates on the counter. "I figured you would like a small meal."

"Sure," Mira said, "I'll have some toast. Then I suppose I'll head back."

"When should I come over to join your uncle?" Sylas asked.

"A couple hours from now."

"What's going on?" Azor asked Sylas, the fire spirit barely able to hide her concern.

"I'm going on a demon hunt tonight, and you're in charge of the pub."

Hours later, Mira met Sylas in front of her home just as they had planned. "My uncle is out back. I negotiated for you as well."

"You did?" Sylas asked her.

"It's your first hunt, so he wanted to give you a standard adventurer cut. I got a little more. Forty MLus."

Sylas gave her a skeptical look. "Forty? That's all? That's like four strong pints at the pub."

"I know it's not a lot."

"No, it isn't." Sylas shifted his mace to his other side. "But if it eases the issues we have, maybe it is worth it."

Mira relaxed a little. It was only through the way her shoulders shifted down that Sylas saw just how tense she had been when he approached. "Thank you.

I'll head to the pub now to help Azor. My uncle is out back. You can just walk around the place." Mira passed beside Sylas and stopped. She turned her head to him. "Really, thank you."

She stepped away before Sylas could reply. After a deep breath out, he circled around their shared home to find Tiberius doing a few practice swings with a mace that resembled the one Sylas had, albeit larger and made of a blackened steel. The former lord commander also had a baton tucked in a sheath at his waist.

"You're here," Tiberius said as he lowered his weapon. His eyes traced over the mace that Sylas carried. It was a rather impressive piece, especially in the way the metal had been welded to the bone. "How did you get that?"

"A friend. Who is joining us?"

"Just Henry, Duncan, and our youngest member, Cody. They should be here soon. A few others were supposed to come, but they all got caught up with things."

"How many people are in your . . ." Sylas cleared his throat, he nearly said *little* militia. "How many people are in your militia?"

"There are ten of us," Tiberius told him, pride in his voice. Even if it was a paltry number, he wanted Sylas to know that his men were highly qualified. At least by Underworld standards. They paled in comparison to the quality of soldier Tiberius had commanded when he was alive. The Vanguard were a truly elite force. But they were fine for the Underworld.

"Were any of these men soldiers before?"

Tiberius glared at Sylas with his good eye. Of course the Aurumite would ask him this question. He had been part of the Royal Guard. He would want to know how qualified his fellow soldiers were. "I trained them."

"So they weren't."

"Henry was, but the others, no. I've since trained them, and I've trained them well. They train every other day. Are there any more questions?"

Sylas started to formulate another question as he thought of Henry and Duncan. He stopped himself and nodded instead. "I'm guessing demon hunting is different from the kind of battles I'm used to."

Tiberius sheathed his mace at his side. "It is. And unfortunately, whatever powers that be here don't let us use the kinds of weapons that would actually help us against these kinds of monsters. At least we have our abilities. Swords would be helpful, though. The bloody rulers that be." He cleared his throat. "We make do."

"You've been to an archlumen?"

"Of course I have. And I make sure all my men go. As soon as I saved up the MLus, I went. It wasn't easy either, saving up. I had to hunt with blunt objects at first. Nearly lost my Underworld life to a C-Rank one. But I got better."

Sylas shrugged. "Adapt or die."

"Heh. Something like that."

"So what do you want me to do tonight? This isn't my realm of expertise, it's yours. Where do you want me? How do you want me to help?"

Tiberius gave Sylas a wolfish grin. "Right up front. Yes. Best to take these things head on."

"Head on?"

"Adapt or die. You said it best yourself, Aurumite. You'll do best up front, especially with your size."

"And you'll command from the back?"

"Not a lot of commanding to do. We find the demon, we kill it, MLus are then distributed. If we're lucky, we're back in Ember Hollow by dinner. Or, at the very least, a late dinner."

Another man came around the corner in the same militia clothing that Sylas had seen on Henry. Judging by his handsome, youthful appearance, this had to be Cody. Around twenty years old, Cody had light blond hair that was at odds with his dark beard stubble. He was thin, his neck defined by an Adam's apple that looked almost heavy. He immediately straightened up upon seeing the two men.

"Tiberius, sir!" He saluted the shorter man.

"At ease," Tiberius told him.

Sylas looked the young man over once again. Cody reminded him of the new recruits, the ones that were fresh from training and ready to sacrifice their life for the kingdom, only to find out later just how grueling a hundred-year war could be.

"Nice to meet you," Sylas said. "I run the pub in town."

"There's a pub in town?" Cody asked, although his tone told Sylas that he already knew the answer to this question.

"There is now. It's called The Old Lamplighter. Maybe if we get back early tonight, all of us can have a little nightcap."

Tiberius opened his mouth like he was going to say something but ultimately didn't. Soon, Henry and Duncan appeared, the pair also in the kind of leather clothing that Sylas had once worn beneath armor.

"What's he doing here?" Henry asked, his skeptical gaze pinned on Sylas. Duncan crossed his big arms over his chest and grunted a hello to Sylas.

"He'll be joining us today." Tiberius motioned for the four men to follow him into what Sylas originally thought was a shed. It turned out to be an armory, one with numerous pieces of crude armor made of a type of metal Sylas had never seen before.

"It's called gloomsteel," Tiberius said before Sylas could ask. "Put it on. It's better than it looks and it's less heavy than what we're used to in our world. Trust me there."

Sylas found a gambeson that would fit him. Cody helped him put the breastplate with tassets hanging from it next. This was followed by rerebraces, which would provide protection for Sylas's shoulders and upper arms. Finally, he was given a peculiar helmet, one that resembled a bucket with two eye holes carved into it.

"You're joking," Sylas said.

"It's the only spare helmet I have," Tiberius told him.

"I thought you said there were ten members of your militia. Where are their helmets?"

"We don't share helmets," Duncan told him. "All our heads are shaped differently. Newcomers get that helmet until they get something proper made."

Sylas begrudgingly put the helmet on. It didn't give him as much of a field of view as he would like, but it would work.

Duncan and Henry started to laugh. Cody glanced at them. "What's so funny?"

"Nothing is funny, Cody. Get your armor on," Tiberius said, who now wore most of his armor aside from a helmet. All of it was black and well fitted, the individual pieces clearly custom. They made him appear bulky, especially with his short stature. "I'd like to have this hunt finished in the next three to four hours. It's a C-Rank, and we've dealt with plenty of C-Ranks before. We'll be fine, lads."

Sylas wasn't great with directions, but he was pretty certain they were heading in the same direction of the forest where he'd first encountered Azor. Since he didn't have a sheath, Sylas carried his mace in his hand. It was heavy, but not heavy enough that it made him feel any strain.

He had a strong sense that he was getting the short end of the stick when it came to the gear he'd been given. But the armor seemed solid enough, and was surprisingly flexible. Perhaps his hesitation had to do with the fact that they'd kept him front and center, where he'd take the brunt of whatever was to come.

Sylas knew this was some sort of test, and he had to keep this fact in mind. Men did things like this, especially soldiers. He'd done these sorts of tests with people numerous times. Of course, they'd never been going up against some C-Rank demon, and he certainly wouldn't have put someone front and center. Yet this sort of hazing was common.

Sylas just needed to pass the test. It would earn him some respect, and hopefully that would cool tensions across Ember Hollow.

"Had my first kill somewhere around here," Henry said as they came to a stream. He pointed his mace at a particular stone. Sylas remembered the first time he'd seen him, when Henry had been sent to check on him and report back to Tiberius. Even with his armor, he still wasn't anywhere near an intimidating figure, especially with his comically dark eyebrows. "That stone right there."

"How?" Cody, the youngest of the group asked.

"You'll laugh if I tell you, but it was a while ago and I'm fine with it. I tripped over the stone. Wasn't any water at that time, and as I fell back the demon jumped forward. It smacked its forehead on the rock. Knocked it out. I took care of things from there."

"Did you beat it?" Cody asked.

"No, I made friends with the demon, took it to The Ugly Duckling in Cinderpeak, and bought it a round. Ha! Of course I did. Like I said, my first kill. Keep up, Cody."

"Quiet," Tiberius said as they started down a hill with exposed roots. "We're getting closer."

"Are we going to try to trap it like we did last time?" Duncan asked. "Easier to kill that way."

"No, not a great place to spring a trap," Tiberius told him. "Had we had more forethought, maybe we would have done something like that."

"Do these demons often escape into these woods?" Sylas asked Tiberius.

"They do."

"Then why not prep some traps so you can more easily set them?"

Tiberius snorted at Sylas's audacity. "A member of the Royal Guard would say something like that. Charging ahead with no compass."

Sylas didn't take the bait. He wanted to; he would have liked nothing more than to come back at Tiberius with a pithy quote or a challenge. But he had to do this for Mira and The Old Lamplighter. Framing it that way made the medicine go down, Sylas ultimately pushing ahead through Henry and Duncan's snickers.

"Here," Tiberius said after they had walked another twenty minutes. "It headed in this direction. The two of you are there," he said to Henry and Cody, gesturing toward a spot about fifteen feet away. "Duncan, you're there. Sylas, right here."

"So you don't want me to hide with the others?"

"No, I want you here next to me," Tiberius said as his eyes started to glow. "Right here."

Sylas tensed. He assumed the militiamen were going to ambush him until he felt a tingling sensation. Every subsequent beat of his heart sent this strange, vibrational energy through his body. In looking down at his hands, Sylas saw them flicker and fade.

"What have you done to me?"

"Quiet," Tiberius hissed. "You're invisible. The demon cannot detect you, nor can it smell you. It will smell the others. That is what will bring it in this direction. And then you and I will handle it."

The directions made sense. What made them hard to process was that Sylas could no longer see Tiberius. He also couldn't see himself.

"Did an archlumen teach you this?"

"Of course they did," Tiberius said, his voice now off to Sylas's right.

"You can seriously turn invisible?"

"What does it look like?"

"How do I swing my mace if I can't see the tip?"

Tiberius groaned, albeit quietly. "First-timers always have this trouble. Close your eyes for a moment. Open them again, and you'll be able to see yourself. Just remember that you'll be invisible until you make contact. At that point, it will be able to see you. Now, no more talking. We only have a few more minutes."

Sylas did as instructed. Upon opening his eyes again, he could now see his arms and legs, as well as his mace. He turned to Tiberius, who was crouched, awaiting the demon's arrival. Sylas did the same on the other side of the pass.

Just as Tiberius had said, a demon no larger than Azor floated forward, its darkened body filled with sinewy muscle and pulsing veins. It paused, as if it sensed this was some sort of trap.

Sylas went for it, his first strike strong enough to send the demon straight to the dirt path. The creature ballooned in size as Tiberius came forward and cracked it across the shoulder with his mace.

The other militiamen ran out from their positions and all surrounded the demon, which huffed with anger, its claws uncurling.

It moved like a whirlwind straight toward Cody.

Sylas instinctively came forward to protect the younger man through a downward strike that hit the same shoulder Tiberius had already injured.

Duncan yelled and charged toward the beast, the biggest of their group delivering a huge strike to the demon's back. Frantic, the demon lunged for Henry, and was able to bite down onto his mace. Much to Sylas's surprise, the demon actually bit through the weapon, the mace breaking in half.

Henry moved away with what was left of his broken mace and Tiberius cut forward, his next strike amplified by Mana Lumens. It was as if he had summoned a shooting star, the tip of his mace blazing with so much power that Sylas had to look away. This did a number on the demon, but it didn't fully take it down.

It tried for Sylas one last time, and brought a claw across the front of Sylas's helmet. His face was fully protected, Sylas glad that he wore the bucket-like helmet even as he was tossed to the side.

The demon tried to flee.

As Sylas got back to his feet, his head spinning, Henry went on the attack.

He brought his arm back, his wrist amplified with golden energy. Henry released the bolt, which seared toward the fleeing demon. His attack struck the monster in the back and thrust it into a tree, the force of its movement causing the tree to fall. This led to more falling trees, the forest coming alive as they crashed into one another.

Using this distraction to its advantage, the demon rushed toward the falling trees. By this point, Sylas was chasing after it alongside Cody, the youth fast and nimble. He was the first to catch the demon, and delivered another solid hit that caused it to flip forward. Cody went in for the kill, only for the demon to quickly whirl around and latch onto him with its claws.

Screaming, Cody tried to beat it back but was unable to.

"I've got it!" Tiberius said as he shouldered past Sylas. He released a ball of pure golden mana, one that flew right over Cody and struck the demon in the head. Most of it exploded. Viscera spritzed the air, and what was left of the demon's body collapsed to the ground.

Cody stumbled away, and was quickly met by Henry and Duncan.

"Are you okay, son?" Henry asked as he began examining Cody's wounds. The demon had managed to dig its claws into small spaces between his armor, deeply cutting the young man's side.

"Mira can do something about it," Tiberius said in a tone that told Sylas he'd seen this sort of injury before. The leader of the militiamen sheathed his mace. "She'll have a balm. It will take a few days to heal, but we did it. We did it, lads." Tiberius brought his hands in front of him and dispersed glittery energy toward the four of them.

[You have received 40 Mana Lumens.]

Sylas sat down on the ground for a moment. Not only had he just seen what Tiberius and his men were capable of, he'd come face-to-face to a demon from the Chasm. It had put up a pretty good fight. And as much as hated to admit it, the militiamen had impressed him.

Sylas could only imagine what a B-Rank demon or above would be like.

Sylas headed back to the pub after dropping the armor off. He had invited the members of the Esteemed Coalition of Ember Hollow Defenders to join him, but they'd ultimately decided to stay with Tiberius as he unpacked the hunt and what they could have done better.

Once he reached The Old Lamplighter, Sylas peeked his head in to see Mira sweeping and Azor wiping down the bar.

"You're back," the fire spirit said, excitement in her voice.

"Slow night?" he asked.

"Pretty slow," Mira said as she leaned on the broom.

"But we handled it." Azor stashed her rag behind the bar and bolted to the space directly in front of Sylas. "We finished the half cask of strong ale and went through an entire cask of regular ale, with just a few free pints thrown in."

"Two of those were for me," Mira said. "Azor's idea to loosen me up a bit." The apothecary hiccuped and placed her hand over her mouth. "Sorry."

Sylas started to laugh. "I was not expecting that, not at all."

"And the hunt? How did it go?" Azor asked as she flitted around Sylas, making sure he hadn't been injured. "You seem to be in one piece."

"I am indeed. It went well enough. The C-Rank demon we encountered was pretty tough." He grimaced. "And your uncle is much stronger than I thought he'd be. Same with the others."

"Henry and Duncan?" Mira asked.

"And some kid named Cody. He had some injuries, but Tiberius seems to think you can handle it."

"They brought Cody? He's still technically a trainee. I'd better get home."

Sylas nodded. "The kid did his part. Anyway, it sounds like I have two casks to brew down there. I'll do that, and call it a night."

"Are you sure you don't want a pint yourself?" Azor asked in a playful tone. "You look like you've been through it."

"You know what? I have. And sure, let me bring up a cask of the strong stuff. I still need to get the piping fixed so we don't have to carry casks up. Another day. Another week. Maybe another month."

"We have plenty of those ahead of us," Mira said as she placed the broom against the wall and joined the two of them. "I'm glad you survived the hunt."

"You had your doubts?"

"I wouldn't say that. But I didn't know exactly how it would work with you and my uncle. If he would play nice or not."

"He played nice enough. Although he did give me some pretty bad armor."

"The bucket helmet?" Mira laughed. "He would do that."

"It worked." Sylas said, recalling how it had protected him from the demon's swiping claws. He stepped around the bar and placed the fireweave mace in its spot. "And maybe I'll go out with them again."

Mira left. Sylas ended up drinking two pints of the strong stuff before he took care of what he needed to brew for the night and headed up to bed. He hadn't netted as many Mana Lumens as he had the previous day, but he had done alright, and there was also the forty he'd received from Tiberius.

Sylas fell asleep thinking about the hunt. He had a feeling it would be the first of many, but he definitely wasn't going to join the Esteemed Coalition of Ember Hollow Defenders.

Especially with a name like that.

———

Patches waited until the big man was fully asleep to finally hop down from the bed. The man snored now, likely because of the ale that he had drunk.

He deserves it, Patches thought as he headed over to the door.

While the pub hadn't been too busy last night, Patches had been able to absorb plenty of Mana Lumens from the guests. He was certain that the number hovering before him had increased.

He was ready to check out the well again.

I've killed several of the spectral rats, but there may be more. And if there are, I believe that well has something to do with it.

Before he could do that, Patches needed to make his rounds.

He started in the cellar, where he saw that the big man had made a bit of a mess brewing earlier. Other than that, there was nothing in the cellar that was cause for concern. From there, he headed up to the main floor of the Tavernly Realm, where he saw the fire spirit resting in the fireplace.

I still can't believe she can pet me now.

After pausing for a moment to groom himself, Patches headed to the door that led to the outside world. He sat on the stoop for a moment, his eyes trained on the spot where the rat had been buried.

His whiskers twitched.

The dark elements in the air were unmistakable. Patches was certain they were still there and he was entirely sure where they were coming from.

Patches circled the well a few times, his tail hooked in the air. He could jump to the rim but he wasn't ready yet. While adventurous, Patches wasn't the type to head into the unknown. And how would he get out once he took care of whatever was causing the dark elements to pool behind the Tavernly Realm?

Someone has to defend this place, Patches thought in an effort to steel himself. *The big man is doing his part, and the fire spirit is helping. This is my part.*

He hopped up to the rim and peered down into the well. Patches was big enough that he could probably descend into the well with relative ease. The problem remained his return. Could he stretch his body long out in a way that would let him shimmy his way back up the top?

He sat there for a moment and considered this. His ears flinched. Patches jumped off the rim of the well just as the fire spirit appeared in front of him.

She placed her fiery hands on her waist and peered down at him. She spoke in a playful way, pointed at the well, wagged her finger at him, and spoke again.

Patches's whiskers pressed back, joining his ears as he bared his teeth.

Out of my way, he hissed.

The fire spirit seemed to find his behavior humorous.

I'm warning you! Patches started to grow larger, his fur bristling as if electrified. His already substantial frame bulked up, his silhouette stretching and elongating, claws doubling in size.

The fire spirit stopped laughing. She said something in a soft voice, wagged her finger at Patches again, and pointed it toward the back door.

He hissed again and the fire spirit swooped forward, her body suddenly that of a flaming banshee.

Patches felt the warmth against his face. He leaped backward, twisted in the air, and took off through the cat door.

He burst into the pub, skittered into the leg of a table, and ignored the pain that bloomed as he tore up the steps to the big man's bedroom. Patches reached the room, hopped onto the bed, and turned, all but expecting the fire spirit to come after him.

But the fire spirit never made it up to the big man's bedroom.

Even so, Patches waited with bated breath, prepared to engage her if forced. Once it became clear this wasn't going to happen, he turned to the big man and released some of his power.

This relaxed him to some degree, but the pub cat never slept that night.

Patches needed to be ready.

CHAPTER SIXTEEN

THE WELCOME INN

Sylas was a bit groggy the next morning when the prompt came to him.

[You have 81 days until the invasion.]

"I've got to get this figured out," he mumbled to himself. While scratching the side of Patches's head, Sylas accessed his status to confirm that everything was in place.

His eyes fell to the single quest contract he had active. Sylas would travel to Duskhaven with Mira tomorrow, a trip that would take a couple of days. He was looking forward to this trip. The Underworld fascinated him to no end. It was a place ripe for exploring.

"Happy Soulsday," Azor said as she came into the room with her typical flare. Her appearance caused Patches to bolt toward the door, the cat hissing along the way.

Sylas laughed. "What has gotten into him?"

"I had to scold him last night because he was trying to jump into the well."

"The well?"

"He was perched there like he was planning to hop right in." She rose higher into the air and dove forward to illustrate her point. "So I told him not to, and then he did that thing where he turned bigger and bigger to try to get me to leave him alone. Well, I'm not one to be bullied by a cat. Even a cute one."

"So you threw a fireball at him?"

Azor was horrified by the suggestion. "What? No! I'd never do something like that. I just scared him enough that he came rushing back inside."

Sylas glanced back at Patches. "He's a strange one."

"He is, and I hope he doesn't hate me. Anyway, what's on the agenda today?"

"What's on the agenda today?" Sylas looked out at the golden glow coming in through his murky window. "Let's work around here. We can open early. But before we do, I'll head over to Mira's just to talk about tomorrow. You'll be good running the place while I'm gone, right?"

Azor's flames grew brighter, radiating an unwavering confidence. "Of course I'll be fine to run the place. It was easy enough last night. I can't wait to start serving some food, though."

"That will be nice. I'll look to get a supplier in Duskhaven." Sylas ran his hand over his beard. "There's a lot to do in Duskhaven. Should be fun."

The idea to paint the interior wall came later that morning, after Sylas had eaten breakfast and briefly spoken with Mira. He planned to do some other things around The Old Lamplighter, but something about the way the light was coming into the pub told him it was time.

"I'm heading to Cinderpeak to get some paint," he told Azor. "Shouldn't be very long."

Sylas didn't want to get wrapped up in anything, especially with the big trip he had planned tomorrow. Who was he kidding? It probably wasn't as big of a trip as he felt it could be in his head, and Mira had already told him they'd go on horseback. So why did he feel a bit of apprehension?

Rather than dwell on any of this, he grabbed the tools he planned to return to Mr. Brassmere and headed to the portal, leaving Azor alone in the pub.

"Patches," she said as she cautiously approached the cat, who now rested in the windowsill. "Are you still mad at me?"

Patches seemed to pretend as if the fire spirit wasn't there.

"I don't think you should go into the well. For one, you're too large. You could get trapped in there. Also, that's where we get water from. It's not a place for a cat."

Patches's ears folded back. He stood, and turned to watch as Sylas moved away from the pub.

"Fine, be that way," Azor said as she went back to her work.

She wiped down some of the tables that Mira had missed the previous night. The apothecary didn't seem to have an eye for this sort of detail, but at least she'd stuck around for Azor's first night and kept her company. "That was nice of her," the fire spirit said to herself.

Not long after, Patches stood and approached the cat door.

"You better not be thinking about that well."

Patches stuck his tail in the air and headed out.

Azor followed after, keeping her distance. She didn't want the cat to hate her, but she really didn't want him going down the well and causing trouble. She could imagine Sylas doing everything he could to get Patches out, and how angry the overweight cat would be once he was finally rescued, likely drenched with water.

Luckily for Azor, Patches turned back to the cat door, went back into the pub and straight to his favorite windowsill, ignoring her all the while.

Sylas returned an hour or so later with the paint. Judging by the dab on top of the paint can, Azor saw that he had chosen a warm brown, much lighter than the pub's current walls.

"Miss anything?" he asked her as he set the can down on one of the tables that Azor had just cleaned. He noticed this and immediately moved them to the floor. "Sorry."

"Not a lot. No visitors. Patches is still mad at me," Azor said, the fire spirit a bit deflated. "I'm only trying to protect him."

"Are you being mean to Azor?" Sylas asked the pub cat. Patches looked up at him and started purring as Sylas scratched the back of his head. "Be nice to her. It'll be the two of you for the next few days, and I don't want this place turning to rubbish."

"I won't let that happen," Azor assured him.

"I know you won't. But a cat in a well is the last thing we need. Anyway. Paint. This a public house, as the sign outside says, and one thing I want to do is create a warm environment. A place where people can come and relax awhile. It's too dark in here. Let's warm it up, shall we?"

"It *is* dark in here," Azor said as she examined the walls. "I never really thought of it like that, but it's quite dingy."

"Exactly. Let's start here." Sylas motioned toward the back wall. "And we'll work our way around. If we open the front and back doors, we'll be able to air out the place. It should be dry by tonight if we're lucky. Brassmere said this stuff dries really fast, not like the paint from my world."

"And you brought two paintbrushes?"

"I sure did," Sylas told Azor. "I would have brought a brush for Patches if I thought he'd be a help."

She shook with excitement. "I've never painted anything before."

Sylas gave her some pointers and the two started up. They moved quickly, as did Patches, who huffed his way up the stairs, clearly not a fan of the light brown paint. By the time The Old Lamplighter opened later, the paint was dry, and Sylas was ready to serve up some pints.

Now behind the bar, Sylas threw a clean rag over his shoulder and waited. Azor floated near the window, Patches's normal perch, looking out at the street.

"Anyone?"

"No one is coming," she said dejectedly.

"And the light is on out front? Of course it's on. I'm the one that turned it on. They will come. I'm expecting someone," Sylas said, who had briefly talked the pub up in Cinderpeak.

They waited another twenty minutes, Azor checking the window occasionally, Sylas busying himself by cleaning pint glasses even though they were already clean. Patches came down, sniffed the air, and decided the paint was dry enough to take his usual place. He found Azor there and sat on the floor instead.

"Patches," she said, speaking softly to the pub cat. "Be nice to me."

He got up and turned the other direction.

Azor approached cautiously and was finally able to pet him. Patches had just started purring when his ears perked up. Azor noticed this and moved over to the window.

"People are coming," she told Sylas.

"People?"

"Yes, a group. And it's Iron Rose leading them, the pub lady from Cinderpeak!"

"Iron Rose?" Sylas glanced over to the door. "Really? How many people?"

"A lot," Azor said. "Like a whole group."

"Are they an angry mob?"

"They look happy."

"In that case, I'd better start pouring up pints."

Iron Rose pushed into the pub and threw her arms out wide. She spun a few times in her black gown, took a deep breath in, and turned to Sylas. "Nice place, mate!"

Her party moved in after her, a collection of men and women, all of whom seemed to be a little tipsy.

"Right this way," Azor said as she led the group to the back, where she'd already pressed two tables together.

Iron Rose approached the bar and dropped down in front of Sylas, who had already poured up four pints and was waiting for them to settle. "Nice to see you," he told her with a smile. "What are you celebrating?"

The woman grinned. "We're celebrating my deathday."

"Deathday?" Sylas asked as he poured up another pint.

"Should be self-explanatory. Deathday is the day you died. People celebrate it once a year."

"And you came here to celebrate?"

"I sure did," she told him with a smile. "You're going to Duskhaven soon, right?"

"Tomorrow."

"Even better. We'll spend some MLus, and you can go with a bit more than you figured you'd be able to go with. Lessons from an archlumen aren't cheap."

"For now, I just want to learn how to fly," Sylas said, even though he also wanted to learn how to do some of the techniques he'd seen during the hunt the previous night. Those seemed like they would be useful, especially that ball of mana Tiberius had produced.

"Flying is fun." Iron Rose hovered off her barstool. Still remaining in a seated position, she floated around the room to a song that her friends started singing up, one of them pounding a table.

"Down in the depths the shadows dance, the embers glow and the specters prance," the group sang.

"And the specters prance!" Iron Rose chimed in, now conducting her party.

"Stomp your feet and clap your hands, we're the long-lost souls of the underlands! The heavens above can laugh and mock, but they'll never be part of our worthy flock!"

A smile on his face, Sylas finished pouring the final pint and motioned for Azor to come get them. "First round is on me!" he shouted over their song. "Happy deathday, Rose!"

"Aye!" the group shouted. "The deathiest of days!"

It became a whirlwind of activity from that point forward, Sylas so busy that he had little time to process how happy the proceedings had made him. *This* was what he'd always enjoyed about his father's pub, the way people would show up in large groups celebrating something, how their happy voices would fill the space, how contagious it all would be.

And how unpredictable it could become. There was an excitement to this, an adrenaline rush as more people came to the pub and joined the merriment. Connections both good and bad could be made. It was manageable yet mercurial. And it made the time fly by.

"You've got to go to this guy I know, the one I told you about, Archlumen Tilbud," Iron Rose said at some point as she returned to the bar. "Also, I've got to say, from one brewer to another . . ."

Sylas tensed, prepared for her review of his ale.

"This swill is the dog's bollocks!" she said, her true accent making itself known. Sylas could tell she was from a particular area of the Aurum Kingdom, where they were known for losing their inhibitions. "Joking with you. It's absolutely amazing! You'll have all of us fuddled and gaddled before long. Better make it another round of regular ale, mate!" she said after squinting back over to her group and getting the confirmation.

"Sure, cheers," Sylas said. "And what were you saying about a man I need to know?"

"Tilbud. The archlumen. Lives in a home shaped like a spear. Ha! I mean sphere. Ale has my tongue twisted and my brain trousered. Might need to cut myself off after a few more or I'll be so skunked that someone will need to carry me back to Cinderpeak."

"Get over here, Rose!" a guy from her party shouted over to her.

"I'm coming, you loaf!"

"I do have an extra room upstairs if you need it," Sylas offered.

Iron Rose gave Sylas a flirty look. "You do, do you?"

He shrugged off her suggestive gaze with practiced ease. "A guest room."

"I'm a guest now, am I?" The woman snorted. "Don't bloody look at me like that. Just having a laugh. Another round, please!"

Later, after the group was good and sloshed, drunk to the point that any other patrons that came to The Old Lamplighter that night decided to leave early, Sylas flickered the lights. "Last call," he announced.

"Last call!" Azor said, her hands cupping her mouth.

Patches, who had been having an absolute blast with the group, scowled at the fire spirit. He was currently in Iron Rose's lap as she listened to one of her friends tell a story, the pub cat happy and content.

The group had a final round and sauntered out, two of them helping Iron Rose stand, all still singing a song that Sylas had never heard before.

Azor turned off the lamp outside and rushed back in, the door shutting behind her. "The Old Lamplighter is officially closed for the night," she said as she playfully fell onto the ground in a puddle of fire, her apron and gloves falling beside her. She whooshed back up before anything could catch fire. "Whew!"

Sylas laughed. "Deathday. We'll have to do something like have a special rate for people celebrating their deathdays. Or maybe allow them to rent the pub out? A free pint? Just ideas." He rubbed his hands together and yawned. "Anyway, time to tally up and fill the casks."

Sylas headed to the cellar and brewed two casks of strong ale, and one regular ale. They had drunk less than he thought, but he still had netted nearly five hundred Mana Lumens, the most yet.

Not a bad night. Not a bad night at all.

After a bit of stretching, Patches tiptoed to the top of the stairs. He peered down into the Tavernly Realm and saw a glow of red near the fireplace, his mood instantly souring.

Is she asleep? he wondered as he sat there for a moment. Patches started licking his paws, the pub cat always one to keep clean. *The fire spirit isn't going to stop me again.* Patches huffed as he thought about how she had thwarted him the previous night.

He waited another thirty minutes, his keen focus homed in on any activity downstairs. He could hear the subtle crackle of a fire, but Patches didn't know if that meant she was asleep or not.

Does she even sleep?

That was another unknown.

After considering his options yet again, Patches turned himself invisible. He crept down the stairs, avoiding the planks that made noise, and softly touched down in the pub.

It became a waiting game at that point, Patches moving a step at a time, as slowly as possible. From what he could tell, the fire spirit still hadn't noticed his presence. Yet one obstacle remained—the cat door.

Patches sat in front of it for a moment, considering his options. It didn't make much noise to go through to the other side. But if he wasn't careful, he would alert the fire spirit. He glanced from the fireplace back to the door.

I can do this quietly.

Patches shifted his weight to his back heels. He shook his rear and stood, wobbly at first, but then he placed his front paws against the door and was able to stabilize himself.

He shimmied over toward the cat door and slowly pushed it open. Patches squeezed through, and winced at the way the top of the cat door came down on his spine and the pressure the frame put on his belly. He reached the halfway point, where he was able to stretch his front legs forward and touch the step.

As carefully as ever, Patches pulled his hind legs through the cat door.

He tensed up as the hinge caused the door to come down onto his tail. Patches held it there for a moment, his tail throbbing, the pub cat waiting for the pain to subside. Gradually, he began to pull his tail out, Patches able to close the flap without making any additional noise.

He hopped off the steps and approached the well. Patches looked up to the rim of the well.

You have to do this, he told himself, *even if you hate water.*

As he was preparing to jump, the fire spirit appeared in front of him.

She made a strange sound that resembled a bark. Patches couldn't make any sense of it. He pressed back, prepared to strike her with an amplified meow when the fire spirit ballooned several times her size. The heat and the sudden plumes of purple fire had Patches charging back toward the pub.

As he had the previous night, he exploded through the cat door and rushed up to the big man's room, where it was safe.

Angry and upset that his plan had failed, Patches paced back and forth, tensing and untensing his paws. He finally relaxed onto the bed, only to realize he hadn't checked the cellar.

Patches got back to his feet, turned invisible again, and headed out the room. Once again, he took his time tiptoeing down the stairs and into the cellar. He checked the space, and after he was certain that nothing was afoul, he went back to the big man's room.

Before Patches drifted off to sleep, he recharged the big man with as much Mana Lumens as he could give him.

It was the least he could do.

[You have 80 days until the invasion.]

"And so I do," Sylas said as his status appeared before him, his Mana Lumens topped off.

Name: Sylas Runewulf
Mana Lumens: 1775/1775
Class: Brewer
[Active Quest Contracts:]
Travel to Duskhaven with Mira Ravenbane to visit the sigilist

Sylas was glad to see his overall count moving up. He knew he was going to need all the Mana Lumens he could get, especially with the trip he had planned. Azor didn't rush into his room as she normally did, and Sylas almost went back to sleep. It was Patches who finally woke him, the cat licking his face.

"What is it?" he asked as he finally set up.

Patches meowed. Sylas couldn't tell if it was a happy or annoyed meow, but it sounded different than it normally did.

"I'm up, I'm up. Let's see if we can't get you some milk." Sylas came downstairs to find Mira seated at the bar in front of scrambled eggs, breakfast potatoes, and strips of crisped bacon.

"Look who finally decides to wake up," Mira said, a smile forming on her face. Her black hair was pressed behind her ears now. She had clearly curled the ends before coming to the pub that morning. "Azor should have your plate ready soon."

The apothecary had a backpack with her, one made of leather and held together by black straps. It was packed to the brim.

"You're not bringing anything?" she asked once she interpreted the look on Sylas's face. At least she thought he was scrutinizing her travel gear.

"I don't have that much," he told her as he sat at the bar.

"Grab a pack anyway, and believe me, that will change once you visit Duskhaven. They have a really good shopping district there. That's why I packed an extra bag."

He raised an eyebrow at her. "An extra bag in your backpack?"

"Yes. I might as well get some things while we're there if we have time to shop."

Azor came up from the cellar with a plate for Sylas. "Morning. Happy Moonsday!" She set the plate before him.

"I wished you ate so I could cook you something," he told the fire spirit.

"Just get me the fish supplier I need in Duskhaven and we'll be even. Also, that cat of yours." Azor squinted up to the top of the stairs, where Patches sat, watching her with disdain. "He tried to sneak out again last night, but I caught him." She started laughing. "You should have seen him! He can turn invisible, as I told you, but I'm able to see his outline. He actually made it out of the cat door without making any noise, but I scared him back inside at that point. Before you leave, is there a latch or something you can put on the cat door so I can close it at night?"

"A latch?" Sylas looked over at the cat door. He could think of a number of ways to make sure it couldn't open at night. "Sure."

"What's wrong with him going out at night?" Mira asked Azor.

"He keeps trying to go into the well."

Now it was Mira's turn to laugh. "Go into the well? Why would he do something like that? Can he even fit?"

Azor shrugged. "I think he can fit, but I don't know how he'll get out."

"And I don't want to have to figure that part out," Sylas added. "Sure, I'll figure out a way to latch the cat door, and we'll head out. Hopefully, this will only take a couple of days. At least after we arrive, I'll be able to open the portal and teleport back to brew some casks."

"Don't worry about it," Azor said. "Patches and I can run the place, as long as he isn't running it from the bottom of that well."

Sylas and Mira set out on foot this time, the two heading in a southeasterly direction. "No horses?" Sylas asked once they reached the outskirts of Ember Hollow.

"Unfortunately, no. My uncle wouldn't let me borrow them for a longer journey like this, especially since we can just teleport back."

"That makes no sense to me. It seems he would let us borrow them for something like this over a quick trip to Cinderpeak."

"I never said he made sense," Mira told Sylas.

"It has something to do with me, doesn't it?"

"No comment. Let's just enjoy the walk." She knew they would reach what was known as the Gloomflower Meadow soon, and that the view there would impress him. She wanted to see how he would react, so she walked a bit faster, Sylas having to keep up.

"Are we in a race to get there?" he asked. "We're both carrying packs. And I've got this thing," he said, referring to the mace he had resting against his shoulder.

"I told you that you didn't need the weapon."

"We're venturing into the unknown. Usually, that is the very definition of a time that is appropriate for a weapon."

"It's only the unknown to one of us."

Sylas didn't press this point. After what he'd seen in his fight alongside the militia, he felt it was safer to be prepared. Then again, Mira had some magical powers that he wasn't fully certain about. Maybe he was a bit overprepared.

He didn't have time to address this as they came up a hill, where Sylas was presented with a view he wasn't expecting. Stretching before him were fields upon fields of ghostly luminescent flowers. The pale light and its eerie glow contrasted heavily with the gold-rimmed clouds above. An almost bittersweet smell met Sylas's nostrils as they started through the field, the two following a path that had been worn over the ages.

"The Gloomflower Meadow," Mira said as she turned to him, her hands behind her back and tucked under her the bottom of her backpack. "I thought you'd find it interesting."

"It's amazing. Do they do anything?"

"The flowers?"

"I mean, are they edible, do they have any properties?" He sniffed the air again. "I feel like I could maybe make a unique ale with them. Do they always bloom?"

"They are always in bloom. There aren't seasons in the Underworld like there were in our world. A day can be cold and it can be warm, and there are storms that come through occasionally, but we don't have a winter, and sadly, we don't have a fall. They do up there," she said, nodding toward the heavens. "At least that is what I've heard."

"And their properties?"

"I use the flowers for certain concoctions. I wouldn't know about using them to brew but they are a bit sour."

"Interesting. Maybe it is something I could use at some point. Anything else I should know coming up? Any interesting landmarks?"

"We'll reach the Shadowstone Mountains in a few hours. That's actually what we're aiming for today. There's a small settlement there where we will spend the night. We won't travel through the mountains themselves. I've never done that. We'll take a path I know and continue on from there."

"What's the name of the settlement?" he asked.

"It doesn't really have a name. There's a portal there, though, and once you activate it the portal will be listed as Shadowstone Mountains."

"And the inn? Does it have a name?"

"I don't believe so, at least last I checked. But you can't miss it. It's practically the only establishment in town. Most of the people that live in those parts portal to Duskhaven for supplies. So it will seem more outfitted than Ember Hollow, if that makes sense."

"They could portal to Cinderpeak too."

"They could, but why would they? Duskhaven is pretty large. Just about anything you can get in Battersea, you can get in Duskhaven, but you'll have less options. Cinderpeak, even less. And the farther out, as you know, the more expensive things become."

"Even if people can simply portal between the places once they've visited them?"

"Even with that," she said. "Someone still has to carry and transport the goods. There are porters and porter services, which you'll likely use for the fish that Azor wants, but that costs MLus."

"Everything costs MLus."

"Correct." A faint smile appeared on Mira's face. "Funny, that."

"What's funny?"

"We basically had to pay to keep alive in the real world, and we more or less do the same here. Anyhoo, onward and upward."

"Are we going upward?" Sylas asked her with a raised eyebrow.

"We will be. It's all uphill from here."

―――

Sylas understood exactly what Mira meant once they reached the settlement outside of the Shadowpeak Mountains. For the last two hours, it had seemed as if they were constantly heading uphill. His calves hurt now and Sylas was glad to finally be able to rest for the evening.

The inn she had mentioned was in the center of town. It had a restaurant and a general shop attached to it, which gave Sylas the spark of an idea even in his tired state. Perhaps once he really got The Old Lamplighter up and running smoothly, he could invest in other businesses in Ember Hollow. Was it possible to channel his MLus into purchasing other places? Maybe he could grow them out as part of The Old Lamplighter.

At least that appeared to be what the innkeeper had done.

"Nice, right?" Mira said, her hands now on her hips as she looked up at the three-story inn.

The inn stood tall and proud, the large building towering over anything in its vicinity and casting a long shadow at its feet. It appeared to be a masterwork of stone masonry, all held together by an oaken door heavily banded with iron speckled in silver. The windows on all three of the stories glowed, and the chimney at the top had smoke coming out of it, the rich aroma of food wafting down to Sylas and Mira.

"It is certainly something. And you've stayed here before?"

"Loads of people have stayed here before. It's sort of a rite of passage," Mira told him. "Newcomers that are reborn near the Hexveil, at least anywhere in the vicinity of Ember Hollow, all come this way toward Duskhaven. Anyway, let's get inside and see what they're cooking up."

"One more thing," Sylas said just as she was turning away. "Whatever the cost is tonight, room and board, food, it's on me."

She grinned at the earnest look on his face. "Of course it's on you. You're running the most successful pub Ember Hollow has seen in years. Come on, let's get in there."

Once they were inside, Mira and Sylas were greeted by an older man with bushy eyebrows. He wore a tight leather vest and a strange necktie. "Welcome in to the Welcome Inn," he said, cracking up at his own joke. "I keep telling the owners of the place they should name it that. The Welcome Inn. There currently is no name. Imagine that, a nameless inn."

"You aren't the owner?" Sylas asked as he took a seat at the bar.

"Nope, but I run the place. Anyway. A room, I'm guessing. We also have a honeymoon suite if that's what you're looking for."

"Two rooms," Mira said, her cheeks instantly flush. "No honeymoon suite necessary."

The innkeeper whistled. "As you wish. That'll be two hundred MLus for the night, and that includes dinner and breakfast. We've got a very good meal planned tonight, a roast, made by the man who lives a few doors down. He makes the roast twice a week, on Moonsday and Thornsday. People come from all over to eat it. You'll see. They should be showing up within the hour. In fact . . ." The innkeeper produced a small booklet and leafed through it. "Whew, you're in luck. There just so happens to be a canceled reservation for two."

"Great," Sylas said.

"I brought food," Mira started to tell him.

"We're enjoying ourselves," Sylas reminded her. "Payment now or in the morning?"

"If you pay now, there will be a five percent discount. If you pay in the morning, you'll pay the price in full," the innkeeper said. Sylas nodded. This made sense to him, a way for people to maximize their Mana Lumen expenditure and a way for businesses to cater to them. "In the morning then."

"Great. I'll have Chip here show you to your rooms. Chip!" The man called out. An even older fellow with a cane hobbled out of a back room. He wore a leather vest as well and a square little hat without a brim.

"Right this way, right this way," he said, his voice hoarse, like it had been raked over the coals.

"Don't forget their keys, Chip!"

"Apologies." Chip returned to the front desk and grabbed a pair of keys. He led Mira and Sylas upstairs, the man putting much of his weight on his cane as they came to the second floor. From there, it was to the end of the hallway where Sylas and Mira's rooms were across from one another.

"This will be fine," Mira told him as she approached the door on the right. "Thank you."

"Which room do you want?" Chip asked, the man scrutinizing the two of them.

"Which is better?" Sylas asked. "Give her the better room."

"The one on the right has a view. The one on the left doesn't. Otherwise, they're the same."

"I'll take the one on the left," Sylas told him. Soon, he had disappeared into his room, leaving Mira with the older inn clerk.

"I guess that means you're on the right." Chip dangled the key in the air for a moment in front of her. "He your boyfriend?"

"No, just a friend," she said as she took the key from him. Before Chip could respond, or possibly flirt with her, she entered the room and shut the door behind her.

Mira dropped the key on a table and approached the drapes, anticipating the view to follow. She swept them aside and frowned.

"Seriously?" she asked as she stared out at another building being constructed directly behind the inn, one that was completely blocking the view.

Apparently, the Welcome Inn was expanding, and not in a logical direction.

There were no drinks to be shared that night. The Welcome Inn, as the innkeeper kept calling it, didn't have a supplier. Sylas planned to remedy this, but he never got a chance to speak to the man alone, especially after the topic of discussion turned to death.

"I told you mine, you tell me yours," Sylas told Mira in jest. His comment had been triggered by a man entertaining the locals and guests with a song about the many dumb ways to die.

Mira, who had been picking at the food left on her plate, set her fork down. "My death? It's not a great story or anything, not like yours, dying valiantly on the battlefield."

"I don't know if I'd call it that. Looking back . . ." Sylas never finished this statement. His life had changed so radically since arriving in the Underworld that he hadn't had a chance to look back. Just about the only thing he'd thought about was seeing if his father and some of the men he'd served with were here, which would require a trip to Battersea.

"Yes?" she asked.

"Never mind. I died, and now I'm here. And I'm happy here, strangely enough. I don't know what all the fuss is about the Celestial Plains," Sylas said, even though he hadn't actually heard much about the heaven that constantly loomed over them. "But life here isn't too bad."

Mira used the napkin to wipe her mouth. "I was executed."

"Executed?" Sylas asked, nearly choking on the bite he'd just taken from his plate.

"For treason."

"Do what now?"

"It gets worse."

"How? I mean, sorry. What happened exactly?"

"You know the city of Riverpool, near the Morgan Plains."

"Right on the border between our two kingdoms," Sylas said. "I know it."

"Riverpool's citizens are a very mixed group. Some are loyal to the Aurum Kingdom, where you're from. Others, the Shadowthorne Empire."

"Where you're from."

"I had friends on both sides of the city. I knew after a family gathering that my uncle was leading his forces through Riverpool, intent on clearing out anyone loyal to the Aurum Kingdom."

Sylas nearly choked on his last bite. "You betrayed Tiberius?"

Pain flickered across her eyes. "It gets worse."

"Does he know?"

"Oh, he knows. We hashed that out a year ago. We don't speak of it now, but it's there. It's there beneath all of our interactions. He hasn't gone as far as to say that he would still be alive if it weren't for me, but I'm certain he feels that way."

Sylas finished chewing his food and swallowed. He set his fork down as well, an act of solidarity. It was clear that what Mira was telling him was hard for her to reveal.

She wiped her mouth again, even though there was nothing to wipe away. "My uncle invaded and he was killed in an ambush. The people I had warned, my friends that supported the Aurum Kingdom, had spread the word and brought backup. They betrayed me in the end."

"How?"

"Only a small group of Aurumite soldiers came. They were able to ambush and kill my uncle because he had arrived in the city with just a few men. He thought the city was mostly under Shadowthorne control, that he was just there to weed out any stragglers. But he had a huge force with him beyond the walls, thousands of men. And once word reached the group outside the city, they invaded. They killed the Aurumite soldiers and rounded up anyone loyal to your kingdom."

"And they tortured them until they revealed how they knew Tiberius was coming," Sylas said.

She nodded. "Which led them to me. I was publicly executed, beheaded."

"Beheaded?"

"And I ended up here as an apothecary."

"How? Why weren't you sent up there?" He motioned toward the ceiling. "I'm not trying to say you're an angel or anything, but that seems more logical."

She smirked at Sylas. With one statement, he'd been able to lighten the mood. This conversation could have turned heavy. "I believe it was because of the deaths I was responsible for, my uncle's included, the soldiers, the people—my friends—who were tortured and killed. Anyway. That's what happened."

"I really wish we had a couple of ales at the moment," Sylas said. "They make stories like this easier. But I'm glad you told me. And I think if anyone deserves to move on to the Celestial Plains, it's you. But who am I? I was a grunt in our world and I run a pub here. So take what I say with a grain of salt. Make that two grains."

[You have 79 days until the invasion.]

"Seventy-nine days until what invasion?" Sylas asked as he rolled to the side. "What invasion?" The bed wasn't as comfortable as the one back at The Old Lamplighter, and he hadn't slept so great. As he sat there on the edge of the bed, getting his bearings, he checked his status. "That's strange."

Name: Sylas Runewulf
Mana Lumens: 2013/2020
Class: Brewer
[**Active Quest Contracts:**]
Travel to Duskhaven with Mira Ravenbane to visit the sigilist

The Mana Lumens he'd spent just being alive and traveling, which hadn't been very much, hadn't been topped off like they normally were back at The

Old Lamplighter. "So maybe it has something to do with resting in the pub," he mumbled as he performed a quick calculation in his head as to what he had sold the previous night.

Yesterday, Sylas's Mana Lumens were just under eighteen hundred. Now he had pressed past two thousand, yet he'd also lost a little too. Perhaps from his poor sleep. "All in all, somewhere in the range of two-forty or two-fifty," he said. "Not bad for a night away from the pub."

It dawned on him once he went downstairs for breakfast and to settle the bill that the Mana Lumens he had netted last night would be gone as quickly as they came.

[Transfer 200 Mana Lumens to the innkeeper? Y/N?]

Sylas mentally confirmed this and saw his power tick down the next time he checked his status.

Name: Sylas Runewulf
Mana Lumens: 1813/2020
Class: Brewer

"Breakfast is right over there," the innkeeper said. "It seems like that lady friend of yours is getting her beauty rest. We'll keep a plate hot for her."

"Thanks," Sylas said. "Also, I was meaning to talk to you about this last night, but you were busy."

The innkeeper grinned. "It was a good night, wasn't it?" The smile on his face thinned. "Was something wrong?"

"No, nothing like that. I run a pub in Ember Hollow called The Old Lamplighter. I'm in the process of getting to Battersea to register with the Ale Alliance, among other things."

"Yet you are going in the direction of Duskhaven."

"I have to go there first for various reasons. Anyway, my pub. We have pint bottles and once I get more, I'd like to discuss selling the ale to the Welcome Inn. I thought there may be some interest."

The innkeeper grew serious. "There is interest! We were getting ale from Duskhaven but they charged us the same price they were charging their patrons, which started to add up. There's always wine from Douro, but my contact there moved to Lilihammer, of all places."

"We'll work out a wholesale price," Sylas said. "But give me a few weeks."

"That sounds like a great idea to me," the innkeeper said. "I can't tell you how many complaints we've gotten about the lack of alcohol."

"We'll work something out."

"Before you leave," the innkeeper said as Sylas was turning away. "Don't forget to activate the portal. Head behind the inn and keep walking. It's in a little grotto there. You can't miss it."

CHAPTER SEVENTEEN

ONWARD TO DUSKHAVEN

The next landmark they came to was the Ebonwood Pines, known for its black pines that stood higher than any tree Sylas had seen yet. It was a majestic forest, one that Sylas enjoyed walking through.

"This is the best part of traveling to Duskhaven on foot," Mira said once she had seen Sylas look up at the trees with appreciation for what must have been the fiftieth time. "And it is pretty much all we will see until we reach the city. So get used to it."

Sylas took a deep breath in through his nostrils. "It's so fresh," he said as a piney scent reached him.

"It's a great place to gather supplies."

"I'll bet. Are there demons this far out?"

Mira glanced at the forest. She knew from some of the things her uncle told her that there was no telling where the demons were at any given time. It wasn't something that was entirely predictable unless someone had classed as a demon hunter.

"I'm going to take your silence to mean that they could be anywhere."

"Then you're better at reading silence than I thought you would be."

Sylas laughed and strolled ahead, his mace resting against his shoulder as if it were an axe. It had been a good morning thus far, and the breakfast at the Welcome Inn had turned out to be better than he thought. He was full, and ready for a long day of walking and getting to know Mira.

The temperature in the Underworld was perfect, at least in the woods. Not too hot, with a slight breeze, but not cold enough for Sylas to feel like he could benefit from a jacket.

The walk continued after they rested for a bit, Mira sharing some food she had made the previous day. Later that evening, they came out of the forest to find the city of Duskhaven.

[Quest Contract Complete - You now owe Mira Ravenbane a favor.]

"I give you Duskhaven," Mira said, oblivious to the prompt he had just received.

"Quest contract completed, I now owe you a favor." Sylas smirked. "Sorry, just got the notification."

"Did you?" She playfully brought her hand to her chin. "I'll have to remember that."

Sylas checked his status and saw that it didn't mention anything about a favor. "Am I just supposed to remember that I owe you a favor."

"I won't let you forget," Mira said.

"In that case, is there a way to modify a contract?"

"Of course, there is. Why?"

"I already told you, we no longer need a sigilist because Iron Rose told me what the upstairs portal did. Now, I need to see a sigilist after visiting with the Ale Alliance, meaning our reasoning for coming here to Duskhaven is different than it was when we made the contract."

"Next time," Mira said, "simply change the contract. Now, you owe me a favor."

"You should have asked me to change the contract, then."

"It must have slipped my mind."

Sylas looked out at a city humming with life.

Nestled in the wide bowl of a shadowed valley, one hemmed in towering bluffs and weathered rocks shaped like pillars, Duskhaven was an amalgamation of practicality and artistry. The buildings, which varied in height, stood like uneven stalagmites shaped in ways that Sylas had never seen before, all of which were situated around an enormous citadel in the center of the city.

"Crazy compared to Cinderpeak, isn't it?" Mira asked, who yet again felt a spark of joy in seeing the pleasure on Sylas's face.

"What's with the citadel?" Sylas pointed out to the building in the center, its spires glistening with gemstones arranged in mosaic patterns. In doing so he also noticed something else. A dark river flowed through the city, which made it necessary for bridges and walkways over the canals that it formed. Sylas had been so mesmerized by the sheer size that he hadn't yet noticed this detail.

Mira stepped forward. "You're not going to believe it if I tell you."

Sylas finally shifted his gaze away from the city and to the apothecary. "I'll believe just about anything at this point."

"It's a Mana Lumen Repository, the MLR Bank."

"A bank?"

"Yes, exactly. People who have lived in the Underworld a long time generally use it so they can save MLus and earn interest and loan MLus to others. It also allows them to travel without carrying too many MLus. You can also get mortgages and other loans through it."

"And why would they not want to travel with too many MLus?" Sylas asked.

"In the bigger cities, especially closer to Battersea, there are thieving mages who are able to strip people of their power. We don't have to deal with that where we are, but we have to deal with demons." She shrugged. "There's always a trade-off. Come on. Let's get to the Archlumen District."

Mira wasn't one to linger. The apothecary took Sylas straight there and had the notion to grab his wrist at one point so he didn't wander off. "You'll have time to explore later," she said as they passed by a market. "And, hopefully, I will as well."

"I could really outfit the pub here."

"You just painted the place, right? Does it need outfitting."

"It needs new furniture, at least something nice and plush and built in to the wall near the back door. I've got a guy, Anders, who owes me a favor, but he hasn't been around. We'll see if he comes through, though."

"And he's a carpenter?"

"He claimed to be," Sylas told her as they passed under a wrought iron gate.

"We're looking for a spherical building, right?" she asked.

"We are, according to Iron Rose."

"I'll bet it's that one," Mira said as they circled around a fountain to a home constructed from darkened pine. Tucked away in a quiet district, practically in the shadows of the MLR Bank, the home in question had lustrous mother-of-pearl accents around its windows and its massive circular door, which was made of polished black iron.

"You are probably right." Sylas approached the door, looked back to Mira, and knocked.

As if it were on a spring, the door pushed open slightly. A whisper escaped, Sylas fairly certain that whisper was inviting them in.

"Shall we?" Mira said as she shouldered past Sylas. Having visited archlumens before, she was well aware of the things they did to enchant visitors. "Hello?" she called out once they came into an atrium of the home, one with a spiraling staircase that led to various levels within the sphere. "What was his name?"

"Tilbud."

"Tilbud!" Mira called out, not at all worried if she would disturb the numerous scientific testing instruments, which she knew were mostly for show. Archlumens had access to a more advanced system, allowing them to sell certain kinds of powers and use the proceeds from their sales to buy new abilities.

"Do you think he's even here?" Sylas asked.

A flash of golden energy had Sylas bringing his mace to the ready. He lowered it once the smoke settled, revealing a man with an imposing stature yet a twinkle of mischief in his hazel eyes as he spoke in a rich, baritone voice, "Ah, visitors. Next time, announce yourself through the bell outside."

"There was a bell?" Sylas asked.

Tilbud gave him a curious look. "There was supposed to be. Anyway, Octavian Tilbud at your service, but you may call me Tilbud. How may I help the two of you? And do make it fast. I have plans for the evening."

Archlumen Octavian Tilbud was draped in a flowing purple robe, which would have looked dignified had it not been for his trousers, which were tied off at the knee revealing a pair of skinny legs covered in patchy hair. To complicate the look, he wore polished leather shoes with buckles that were shaped into narrow dragon faces. To further complicate the look, a quirky hat, much smaller than it should have been, sat on his head, barely covering a glorious mane of silver hair that matched his oversized mustache.

"Well?" he asked after Mira and Sylas had stared at him for too long.

"Sorry," Mira said.

"I'm here to learn how to fly." Sylas only realized after these words left his lips how utterly ridiculous they sounded.

"Are you, now?" Tilbud asked, a grin forming on his face. "Then you've come to the right archlumen. The others may charge you less, but it will take you longer to learn the skill and there will be mishaps." He indicated what he meant by this by lifting his finger and spiraling it in a downward pattern.

"Iron Rose sent us. I don't know if that means anything to you," Sylas told the archlumen.

"Iron Rose? Doesn't ring a bell," he said. "But I meet a lot of people from all over the Underworld. What kind of power are you looking for? Would you care to see a menu?"

"You have a menu?" Sylas asked.

Tilbud turned to a table. "Somewhere around here."

Mira clasped her hands behind her back. "He is interested in flying. He already told you that."

"Right! I'm sorry, I can be a bit forgetful. Sure, flying. I'm the best flight instructor west of Battersea," he said. "It will cost you two thousand fixed MLus. And I have availability—"

"Two thousand?" Mira crossed her arms over her chest. "That's a bit steep. I'm fairly certain I paid eight hundred. Did you say fixed?"

"But that must have been years ago."

"It was last year."

"Ah, so it was." Tilbud cleared his throat. "Did I mention I am the best flight instructor between Duskhaven and Battersea? No, well, I meant to. Two thousand is my rate."

"What's a fixed MLu exactly?" Sylas asked.

Mira raised an eyebrow at him. "No one told you?"

"You are generally the one that tells me things," he reminded the apothecary.

"And Iron Rose didn't tell you?"

"She just said he's the best. She didn't mention anything about a fixed MLu."

"Fixed MLus are permanently spent. Meaning, if you spend two thousand, your MLus, whatever number they're at right now, will *decrease* by two thousand. And they won't regenerate. You'll have to do whatever you've done in the past to earn more."

"That's right," Tilbud said, "and I am the best. With the power of flight comes all sorts of tasks you are able to perform. What is your class exactly?"

"I was given the deed to a pub in Ember Hollow. I'm classed as a brewer."

Tilbud's eyes lit up. "Ah, like Iron Rose!"

"So you do know her?"

"I do now. I just needed to hear the right word, which in this case was *pub*, to remember who she was. Anyway. I'm late for a date. Yes, I may look wise beyond my years"—he ruffled his gray hair, careful of his quirky hat—"but I'm still an eligible bachelor. A *most* eligible bachelor. And who wouldn't want to spend time in a wondrous place like this?"

The skepticism on Mira's face didn't seem to bother Tilbud as he spun around and pointed out some of the high points of his home, from his library to his bed up top. "Which just so happens to be circular as well! But as I said, a date. I must go. The price is two thousand fixed MLus, nonnegotiable. Be here tomorrow morning if you agree, and I will add you to my calendar." He ushered them toward the door.

"We can find someone else," Mira told Sylas.

"I truly hope you don't," the archlumen said as he swung the door open and gestured for them to leave. "It will be the biggest mistake of your life. Ah, and one more thing."

"Yes?" asked Sylas.

"The portal is closed for tonight. They're doing some maintenance. Might I suggest the bed-and-breakfast a few blocks away? It is quaint, affordable, the food is passable, and I've had students stay there before to rave enough reviews. You'll know the place when you see it. That red roof has been the talk of Duskhaven ever since the owner had it repainted. Until then, bye!" Tilbud slammed the door, leaving Sylas and Mira on his porch.

"Well?" Sylas asked Mira, who couldn't wipe the critical look off her face. "What do you think?"

"What do I think? You'd be bloody mad to pay him two thousand fixed MLus."

"He comes highly recommended."

"He's eccentric, and clearly has a screw or two loose. We should price around. These are fixed MLus we're talking about here."

"Why didn't anyone mention fixed MLus to me earlier? This is the first time I'm hearing about it."

Mira turned in the direction of the bed-and-breakfast. "I can't tell you the answer to that question."

"You were sort of my tutor," he joked.

"Ha! I'll be sure to remember to teach my future pupils about fixed MLus early on, then. But yes, it is a thing, and you'll find these kinds of payment requests more frequently in the larger cities of the Underworld. Especially when it comes to grander things, like powers and property."

"Powers and property, huh? I guess that makes sense," Sylas told her. They came around a large gate and spotted a two-story building with a bright red roof at the end of the lane. "That's the place. We can rest and return tomorrow."

"You're really going to pay him, huh?" Mira asked.

"I trust Iron Rose. I don't know why, but if she says he's the guy, then he's the guy. So yes, I'm going to pay him."

"Do you even have enough MLus?"

Sylas nodded. "If the pub sales go well tonight, or well enough, I should be fine."

"And who is paying for the bed-and-breakfast?" Mira asked.

"Why don't you get yourself a nice room and I'll just sleep outside." Sylas glanced around. "There has to be a bench here somewhere."

"Outside? Absolutely not. You may be dead, Sylas, but you should still be civilized. I'll take care of lodging, but you owe me on top of the favor."

"Free drinks for life?"

"You kid, but I'm serious."

"I am too. One other thing we need to take care of in the morning. Fish. I need a fish supplier."

"In that case, we'll head over to the Finmarket. Plenty of fish mongers there."

———

It had been a slow night at The Old Lamplighter, yet Azor had been able to sell a cask of the strong ale to Godric and a group of people who lived along the slopes of the Cinderpeak Volcano. She'd also managed to sell a few regular ales to some folks from Ember Hollow who never introduced themselves.

Before she headed to her fireplace, where she planned to rest after her long night of running the pub by herself, Azor locked the cat door.

"Patches," she called out, the pub cat nowhere to be found. "Good night!"

With that, Azor settled and soon found herself in a deep sleep, what was left of her form glowing red.

Patches, who was upstairs when the fire spirit called for him, remained on the big man's bed. He was furious about the cat door. He'd tried it last night, and it wasn't open. He could go out during the day, but there didn't seem to be a dark influence during that time.

Why can't she get it through that fiery skull of hers that it is my job to protect this place? Patches thought, the cat stewing in his anger. *And where is the big man? Why has he been gone for so long?*

A twist of despair ran through Patches, enough that it caused him to stand up. His whiskers folded back. He really hoped the big man hadn't died. The fire spirit could run the pub, but she couldn't brew, and once they were out of ale, people would stop coming. Then Patches would be back to where he started, a cat in an abandoned pub chasing magic-powered rats.

Speaking of rats...

Patches turned invisible and headed downstairs. He did this just in case the fire spirit was still up. She kept trying to pet him and it annoyed Patches to no end, especially with the fact that her pets and scratches felt good, yet he was mad at her.

I'll never forgive her! Patches thought once he reached the cellar.

He had been so focused on his anger with the fire spirit that he hadn't paid attention to the signs of an intruder. Yet now, he could hear the sound of a rat below. Was it one of the demon ones? He didn't yet know, but he certainly had to do his part in slaying it.

Patches prepared himself at the top of the stairs. He remained invisible yet he doubled his form, his claws growing thicker, his teeth sharper.

He could see the rat now, and based on the energy radiating off its form, it was certainly of a demonic nature.

I really need to get into that well, Patches thought as he watched the rat approach the table where the big man brewed his casks. The rodent looked up to the tabletop and prepared to jump.

Patches wasn't going to let that happen.

As soon as the rat was in the air it was struck by the pub cat.

The two hit the ground, Patches able to twist his body in time to avoid a painful collision with the table leg. Yet doing so also twisted him in an awkward position, Patches not able to hold onto the rat with his claws as well as he would have liked.

The rat took off toward its exit, Patches soon in hot pursuit.

The rat was just reaching the hole it planned to escape through when the fire spirit appeared. She swooped down in front of the rodent and it caught fire. Patches skidded to a halt as the rat ran in circles for a moment before it ultimately expired.

The fire spirit bent down, her legs floating in the air as she examined the rat. She turned to Patches and said something in a soft voice.

Rather than listen to her—it wasn't like Patches could understand her anyway—he raced upstairs to the main floor of the pub, hoping that the cat door was open. It was locked, yet before the fire spirit could reach him and say something about it, Patches headed back up to the big man's bedroom.

Patches jumped onto the bed and turned in the direction of the door, his hair standing on edge. The piebald pub cat would remain agitated like this for some time before he finally drifted off to sleep.

He missed the big man.

CHAPTER EIGHTEEN

FLIGHTCHECK

Sylas all but ignored the message the next morning.

[**You have 78 days until the invasion.**]

"I know, I know," he said on the tail end of a yawn. He checked the most important details of his status and frowned.

Name: Sylas Runewulf
Mana Lumens: 2028/2035
Class: Brewer

The pub hadn't done as well as he would have liked the previous night, netting just about two hundred Mana Lumens. This put him above the two thousand he needed to learn to fly, but it also put Sylas in a tight spot. After he settled up the archlumen's bill, he'd have less than thirty Mana Lumens to his name. That was risky, and he knew Mira wouldn't like it.

"What's that face mean?" she asked over breakfast later that morning. They had already had coffee, which wasn't readily available out near the Hexveil, and were now waiting on the main course.

"Which face?"

"What's wrong, Sylas?"

"Just figuring out the numbers."

"The numbers? What does that mean?"

"I'll have just a few MLus left if I learn to fly, but I need to learn to fly so I can go to Battersea and meet the Pub Alliance and check a few names in the Book of Shadows."

"You could wait," Mira suggested. "Go back to the pub for a week, sell more, portal back here, and learn to fly at that point. You'd have to activate the portal, of course, which will also cost you."

"Why would it cost me here in Duskhaven? Portals are free in our parts."

"Because this is a larger city, and they charge for things because they can. It costs fifty MLus."

Sylas drummed his fingers on the table.

"You're thinking?"

"I am," he said as their breakfast came, which consisted of poached eggs over a bed of greens. "I don't like being impulsive."

"Then don't be."

"But I feel like now is the time to learn how to fly if I'm going to do it."

"You literally have the rest of your life to learn to fly, which is basically infinite years, as long as you take care of yourself. It can definitely wait."

"We should talk to Archlumen Tilbud," Sylas said as he cut into his eggs. "Maybe he'll take a partial payment. I'd like to get started now."

"He won't take a partial payment. Once he unlocks the power, you could simply fly off, never to return."

"I wouldn't do that. Besides, he knows I run a pub in Ember Hollow. I'm not exactly a difficult person to find."

"Fine, let's talk to the archlumen after breakfast. But I'm telling you now, Sylas, he'll want payment up front."

Once they finished their meal, they left the bed-and-breakfast and took the short walk to Tilbud's spherical home. This time, there was a doorbell. Sylas pulled the lever to hear melodious tones that seemed to echo inside the strange home. Tilbud came to the door a few moments later.

"May I help you?" he asked. The archlumen was in a nightcap that matched his evergreen gown. He yawned. "Well, get on with it."

"We were here yesterday," Sylas said.

"Yesterday? Has a day already passed? Yes, it has! Good morning." He squinted at Sylas. "Some sort of adventurer right?"

"Brewer."

"Ah, yes! You are the pub man, and you are . . ." Archlumen Tilbud drew a blank as he looked Mira over. "I don't remember that part. But I do remember that you wanted to fly. That will be two thousand fixed MLus."

[Transfer 2000 fixed Mana Lumens to the Archlumen Octavian Tilbud? Y/N?]

"Not so fast," Sylas said. "Two thousand is too steep. I know you've said you're the best, but we have checked with other archlumens in the area, and they're all at about the thousand range."

"The thousand range?"

Mira, who was unaware that Sylas was going to lie, quickly joined in. "Yes, the thousand range. It only cost me eight hundred."

"And who taught you?"

"An archlumen out of Douro named Julia."

"Julia from Douro. Can't say I've heard of that archlumen."

"I can fly."

"Can you?" Tilbud asked Mira.

"Do I have to prove it to you? Let's go, Sylas." Mira turned away, and by the force of her swivel Sylas knew he'd better turn with her. He caught up with the apothecary just as Tilbud called out to them.

"Wait!"

"Should I?" Sylas asked.

"Let's see what he has to say," Mira told him under her breath.

They approached Tilbud once again. "I will have you know that my normal rates are two thousand MLus for flying. That is standard. If I recall, you've yet to see my menu of things I can teach you." He pointed at Sylas's mace. "Want to turn your mace into a magical axe, er, at least something axe-like? I can show you how to do that. Want to shrink yourself to one-tenth your normal size? Easy! Want me to show you a place where you can get a sheath so you don't walk around looking like a brute? I can do that free of charge."

"I get it," Sylas said, yet Tilbud continued.

"What about a Mana Lumen shield? Want to learn how to craft one of those? Or how about create a ward? Or maybe you just want to be super strong and fast the next time those sorts of physical traits are needed? What I'm trying to say here, good man, good lady, good man and good lady, is that other archlumens can show you these things. But notice I said *other*. As in plural. As in you'll have to travel around piecemealing your way to Mana Lumen harmony. But with me, the best in Duskhaven, and dare I say the lands west of Battersea, you get the whole package."

"Are you sure about that?" Mira asked.

Tilbud threw his arms out to illustrate his point. His robes moved back, revealing the bright blue tattoo on his arm that was a sign of an elemental spirit. A golden glow traced down to his fingertips. His spherical home lifted from the ground and settled. Sylas heard the sound of glass breaking inside. "Well?"

"Well, what?" Mira asked him.

"How about fifteen hundred MLus? No, Seventeen," Tilbud said, madness in his eyes. "Seventeen."

"Fifteen works for me," Sylas told him.

"Seventeen."

"Fifteen-fifty."

"Seventeen."

"Sixteen-fifty?" Sylas asked.

Tilbud puffed his cheeks out, the ends of his silver mustache lifting. "Fine. Wait here."

[Transfer 1650 fixed Mana Lumens to the Archlumen Octavian Tilbud? Y/N?]

"We're doing this out here?" Sylas asked the archlumen. "This is where you teach people to fly?"

"No, of course not. Are you insane? We'll be fined. The Duskhaven constables are no joke. I have a space where we can do it."

"And you want us to wait here?"

"I need to prepare myself. How about this? Come back in an hour. Surely, you have something else to do in the city."

Sylas and Mira exchanged glances. "We can head down to the Finmarket," she suggested.

"Good, yes, do that," Tilbud told her. "A lovely day for fish and other dry goods."

"We'll be back in an hour." Sylas extended his hand to the archlumen who took it readily and shook. This wasn't necessary with the system, yet it felt right to Sylas.

"Yes, sixteen-fifty, and if anyone asks you, tell them you paid full price. The two of you are lucky I had a good date last night, and I'm in a relatively good mood." Tilbud bowed his head to some degree, which caused his nightcap to fall off and reveal a bald spot on the crown of his head.

"We'll be back in an hour," Mira said after Sylas transferred the Mana Lumens.

"I know that." Tilbud held his chin high, grinned at the two of them, stepped back, and shut the door. "One hour!" he called from inside.

The Finmarket was relatively easy to navigate, especially with Mira, who always seemed to know where she was going. It was set in an enormous structure that seemed to be a conglomerate of previous structures that they continually gutted and expanded.

"He really tried to wow us back there," she said, her first comment since reaching the market.

"You mean when he levitated his own home? Because that was pretty impressive. Heh. Wish I could do that with the pub."

"Archlumens can do things like that, you know, party tricks. I don't want to call them show-offs, but they do need to show new clients what they're capable of."

"Why do they want fixed MLus? Does it matter?"

Mira turned to Sylas, and was nearly struck by a man pushing a barrel of fish. The fishmonger said something under his breath and moved past. "It's the system they use. They can't teach you a power without sacrificing some of their own power. Your exchange of fixed MLus directly pays for the new skill. If you didn't exchange, it would come out of his overall total."

"But he wants a profit?"

"Of course, he does. And we certainly didn't get a bargain back there."

Sylas grinned at her.

"What?"

"He was impressive though, right?"

"That's not what we're talking about here." Mira looked around. "Let's find the fish. Did Azor say what kind of fish?"

"Now that we're here and I can teleport, maybe I should just bring her."

"Now you're thinking. You have to be strategic with these things. You're down nearly seventeen hundred MLus."

"I can earn more next week," Sylas said.

"It's already Wraithsday. Next week is sooner than you think."

"Well, I have seventy-eight days until the invasion, so as long as I'm strong or prepared by then, it doesn't matter to me."

"Seventy-eight days now?" Mira asked, a hint of alarm in her voice.

"It seems like a long time, but the days are dwindling. And I still don't know what the warning means." Sylas glanced around. "Do you think I could learn more about that here?"

"At the Finmarket?"

"No, I mean here in Duskhaven."

Mira's shoulders sank.

"What?"

"If someone knew, it would probably be Tilbud."

"So I'll ask him. But I think it's best if I hold off buying any fish until I know what the MLu situation is going to be." Sylas bit his lip. "Better to be safe and get exactly what she wants."

"Azor can fund them."

"Once she's selling food, yes, but right now I'd be funding the first few batches. Do fish come in batches?"

"I believe they come in schools." Mira laughed at her own joke. "Come on. Let's take a look around, and then we can head back to the archlumen's place."

About an hour later, Mira and Sylas approached Tilbud's spherical home to find the bell outside was gone. There was a letter tucked under the doormat, one that had been sealed with wax.

Mira tensed up immediately. "He did a runner, didn't he?"

"You think?" Sylas picked up the letter, his spirits deflating as soon as he broke the wax seal.

Dear Sylas and his unknown female acquaintance,

I'm terribly sorry to have to leave in this manner. It turned out the date I went on last night did NOT go as well as I thought it had. I can explain later, and I promise that I will. You said you owned the pub in Ember Hollow, yes? If so, I will visit this weekend once things have cooled down around here. At that point, I will teach you how to fly, and I will also let you select something from the menu, free of charge. Of course, there are limitations. Perhaps I will select for you. Either way, lucky you! In fact—well, I probably should leave now before I'm discovered.

Yours in luminous laughter and relentless whimsy,
Archlumen Octavian Tilbud

The walk to the Duskhaven portal only took them a few minutes. During that time, Mira lit into Archlumen Tilbud, loudly too, as if she wanted other people to hear about their experience.

"Let's just see if he comes this weekend," Sylas said.

"He took your MLus. If he knew that he was having some issue—whatever that issue may be—with some date, then he should have made arrangements with you. Who would even date him? And we were only gone for an hour. What could have happened?"

"I don't know," Sylas told her as they approached the portal. Like the others Sylas had encountered, the portal featured a large rune surrounded by monolithic stone formations. There was a small line leading up to it, one that moved quickly as people teleported away.

"What do you mean, you don't know?" she asked.

"I'm going to give him the benefit of the doubt for now. *For now.* If he doesn't follow through, then—"

"Then what?"

"We'll figure that out then."

"There are legal options, you know. But it won't be cheap."

"I'm already in the hole when it comes to MLus."

"You are. He more or less tricked you, and you should keep that in mind if he actually comes around again," Mira said as they neared the front of the line. She turned to Sylas. "I'll stop by the pub tonight."

"You don't want to come now?" Sylas asked. After two days with the apothecary, he was growing used to her company.

"No, I have important things to do, Sylas."

"Important things like shopping?"

"Maybe."

"When you do get back, let your uncle know that I am available for more hunts. I've got some MLus to recover."

"I'll let him know, but I won't let him know that second part. See you back there." Mira waved goodbye and turned in the direction of the city center.

Sylas was presented with a prompt.

[Transfer 50 Mana Lumens to use the portal? Y/N?]

"Yes," Sylas grumbled. He was presented with several options:

- **Ember Hollow**
- **Cinderpeak**
- **Hexveil - Ember Hollow**
- **Seedlands**
- **Shadowstone Mountains**

Sylas selected Ember Hollow and felt an immediate pull in his stomach. Energy swirled around the vortex, distorting around him, an array of kaleidoscopic colors momentarily blinding his senses. Suddenly, the hustle and bustle of Duskhaven was gone, replaced by the quaint quiet of Ember Hollow, a place that seemed both sleepy and on the verge of its last breath.

No one was out. Sylas was used to that.

"I was supposed to be able to fly by this point too." Sylas laughed cruelly at his own misfortune. He reached The Old Lamplighter, and was nearly tackled by Patches once he opened the door. "You missed me that badly, huh?" he asked as Azor came to greet him.

"Heya, Sylas! You're back!"

"Indeed I am," he said as the pub cat mewed incessantly.

"I tried my best. Gave plenty of free pints away too. Didn't sell as much as I would have liked. And Patches. He makes me so mad. Ever since we dealt with the cat door, he has hated me with a passion. You would think that I tortured him or something."

Azor floated closer to Sylas, her form flaring with delight. She felt a bit like Patches at that moment. She had truly missed Sylas and his calming presence.

"He's just a cat being a cat. Don't let him get to you."

"Hungry? I can make something? Wait, can you fly now? Want to go for a flight? I can fly too, you know. Of course, you know that." To illustrate what she meant, Azor did a complete loop, her fire coming a bit too close to Patches's tail, which caused the cat to scatter toward his favorite windowsill.

"That's a long story," Sylas told her as he dropped his backpack on the bar. He came around and placed his mace where he normally kept it, Sylas instantly noticing how good of a job Azor had done in keeping the bar nice and tidy. "Actually, it's a short story. First, learning to fly cost fixed MLus."

"Really?" Azor asked. "I wasn't aware. Then again, I've never paid an archlumen for anything."

"Well, that was a surprise. And the guy Iron Rose recommended wanted to charge me two thousand. Two thousand! But I was able to talk him down to just under seventeen hundred. We agreed to meet an hour later, and during that time, Mira and I checked out the Finmarket."

"Yes, any leads there?"

"Not really. I figured you'd want to come with me. We can do that this week. I'm also low on MLus because of the archlumen, who, if you haven't figured it out yet by the way the story is going, was gone when we got back to his home. He left this letter."

Sylas placed the letter on the bar. Azor approached it, and was just about to pick it up with her bare hand when she laughed. "That wouldn't have been a good idea. Let me grab my glove." She did just that, the fire spirit quickly reading through the message. "So he'll be here this weekend?"

"Apparently," Sylas said.

"And if he doesn't come?"

"I don't know."

The fire licking off Azor's form grew with intensity. "If he doesn't come, we'll pay him a visit. He has a home in Duskhaven, right?"

"Yes, and you should have seen the place," Sylas said, recalling its unique spherical shape.

"Don't forget I am a fire spirit." A pair of devil horns grew from Azor's forehead.

Sylas laughed. "I see what you're hinting at. Mira said there are legal options too. I can't believe there are lawyers in the Underworld, but if there are magistrates, I guess that makes sense."

"Burning his place down would be easier." Azor's mirth masked an underlying seriousness. She didn't like the idea of someone exploiting Sylas's goodwill. It was already becoming apparent to her that people took advantage of his kindness.

Sylas nodded. "Always an option. Anyway, we need tonight to be a success. Let's push strong ale because it will net me more MLus. I wish we could do something like a pub quiz, but..." Sylas's eyes lit up. "That would work!"

"What would?"

"Everyone is from my world. Meaning they'd likely know answers about the Aurum Kingdom and the Shadowthorne Empire." Sylas ran his hand over his beard. "Although that could create conflict if there are people from both realms here and they get drunk. Nope, that won't work. I can't run the pub quiz anyway. We need someone who had a better knowledge of this world to do something like that."

"Maybe you could have quizzes for each individual realm?"

"That's an idea. I'm just trying to think of ways to get people to come in tonight aside from free ale. Maybe I made a mistake not bringing back some fish. We could have had a dinner service tonight if I had." Sylas rubbed his hands together. "Definitely a mistake."

"We can *still* have dinner service. Head into Cinderpeak, grab me a bunch of potatoes and whatever meat is on sale. I know a recipe. We can charge for it tonight, the MLus can go to you, and that will add on to whatever pints we sell. Hopefully strong pints."

"Potatoes and meat? What are you planning on making?"

"Shepherd's pie. I can use a pot and crisp the potatoes on top. Or I can cook the pieces separately," the fire spirit speaking faster now, clearly excited. "Get vegetables too. Wild onions, carrots, peas, and garlic should do the trick. We can do a set menu. Something like a strong ale and some shepherd's pie for fifteen MLus. That will get people started on the strong ale, they'll get a meal, and they'll want one to wash it down with more pints after."

"Brilliant idea, Azor." Sylas stepped around the bar and turned to the front door. "I'll be back in an hour or so."

"Wait, before you go."

"Yes?"

"Make sure you tell everyone at the market and everyone you know in Cinderpeak that we're having a dinner menu tonight." She smiled at Sylas. "Tonight will be a success. I'm sure of it! And wait!"

"Yes?"

"One more thing. Let me get you a list."

———

Sylas hustled. He hustled for hours in Cinderpeak and the surrounding areas, visiting the few people he knew and spreading the word to anyone he ran into in between. He wished at one point he had a flyer, but that didn't seem possible at the moment. And where would he find a printer anyway? Likely Duskhaven, but to travel there would cost fifty Mana Lumens, and he was looking to conserve as much as he could.

Especially with food costs.

It wasn't too expensive considering his haul, Sylas able to get twenty pounds of meat, dozens of carrots and onions, cream, a large sack of potatoes, flour for thickening the meat gravy, and some seasonings that Azor had requested. It was too much for him to carry, so he paid a nominal fee of five Mana Lumens to have it delivered.

All in all, he spent over seventy Mana Lumens, which reduced his stored power even further. "Still enough to brew a few casks," Sylas said to himself as he checked his status.

Name: Sylas Runewulf
Mana Lumens: 247/385
Class: Brewer

He knew that he just needed to get through the night. If it was a success, if Sylas could bring in a pretty big haul, he would be up and running again in no time. Then things could go according to plan.

This thought made Sylas laugh.

"As if there is a plan," he said to himself as he headed back to the pub. He arrived in Ember Hollow and ran into Cody, Henry, and Duncan, the three men wearing leather tunics that told him they'd recently been training. "Tonight, we're having a special at the pub."

"A special?" Cody asked, the youngest of the group with his hair slicked back and some grime on his face.

Duncan, who looked like he'd been through a pretty tough fight, crossed his beefy arms over his chest. "What kind of special?"

"Shepherd's pie and a pint of my strongest ale for fifteen MLus. So save some room for dinner, it will be worth it."

"You're a cook now?" Henry asked, the scrawny, eyebrow-heavy man as suspicious as ever.

"Me? Not really. Azor. She is a chef."

"By trade?" asked Cody.

"Does it matter? Stop by tonight, and I'll be sure to take care of you all. And next time, let me know if you're going on a hunt." Sylas grinned at the three.

"That was surprisingly fun. One more thing," he called after he'd stepped away from them. "Invite Tiberius if you see him. And Constable Leowin. Everyone is invited. We're having a Wraithsday Feast!"

"A Wraithsday Feast?" Cody looked to his counterparts. "Is that what you're calling it?"

"I am now. And it'll be a great time."

"We'll see," Henry said. "We'll see."

Sylas moved on, not in the mood to deal with Henry's general skepticism. Of Tiberius's men, Henry seemed to treat Sylas the worst. Duncan was a bit dumb, and Sylas had been around enough men who had been recruited due to their size to know how to get along with someone like that. Cody, while young and perhaps naive, was the friendliest of the group.

It was too bad Henry held so much sway.

Sylas reached the pub and burst inside, his heart filled with excitement. All the hyping he had done in Cinderpeak was contagious.

"I think tonight will be the night," he told Azor as she hovered over to him. "Food should be here in an hour. I'll help you prep in any way I can. In the meantime, let me mop up the place and, I don't know." Sylas laughed at his own exuberance. "I'll figure it out."

The next couple of hours seemed to pass in the span of a few minutes. Soon, Sylas was turning on the light outside, ready to welcome guests, the smell of Azor's cooking filling The Old Lamplighter. It was strong but prying open one of the windows seemed to air the place enough to keep it tolerable.

"Ventilation system," Sylas said, which, like the pumps he wanted to install, was a long-term task. For now, it would be fine. "Get ready," he told Patches, who had just come from outside. The pub cat hopped onto the bar and approached Sylas. He placed his hand on the cat's head and eventually scratched the side of his chin. "Tonight is going to be fun."

The night started slow, but then something that had never really happened at The Old Lamplighter quickly took shape. From just a few patrons to a room full of people. It was that fast. The tables all ordered the special, and laughter and loud talking soon filled the space. More pints galore.

Sylas barely had time to speak to Mira, who sat at the bar in what looked like a new dress, picking at her plate like she was disappointed he couldn't pay more attention to her. He said just a few words to Godric, the fireweave tailor, and his group; Brom, the farmer, and his friends; Mr. and Mrs. Brassmere and Malcolm, the grains dealer; Iron Rose and her crew; and even Henry, Duncan, and Cody. There were simply too many people.

A head count at one point told Sylas there were forty patrons crowded into The Old Lamplighter, most of whom got the special.

"The special is the way to go," Sylas said to Mira at one point as he waited for the ale to settle in one of the pints.

"You seem to be enjoying yourself."

"I'm just glad this actually worked. We can make a thing of it, the Wraithsday Feast at The Old Lamplighter. Something like that."

"Azor will have food every day in the future, right?"

"Yes, but I don't know if we'll do something like this. Something special. That will be harder to replicate. So maybe we'll do it once a week," Sylas told her. "Some new meal. Anyway, I'm glad you came. I was hoping Tiberius would come, but at least his men did."

"My uncle is with Leowin right now."

"Doing what?"

"Private hunt."

"A what?" Sylas raised a finger to her. "Sorry. Hold that thought. Let me hand this off." He brought the pint over to Iron Rose. "And we need to talk about Archlumen Tilbud."

"He's great, isn't he?" Iron Rose asked, her mouth full of food. She swallowed. "Sorry. Tell Azor this is really good."

"Tilbud took my payment, and then left before I returned. He said he'd stop by the pub."

Iron Rose shrugged as if this was something totally normal. "Then he'll stop by. He's the best around, you'll see."

Sylas returned to the bar, to Mira. "Sorry, you were saying."

"A private hunt. My uncle sometimes takes bigger hunts worth high-level MLus and does them with just one or two people so he can maximize the reward."

"Isn't that dangerous?"

"It's incredibly dangerous." Mira took a sip from her regular ale. She still didn't like the stronger version. "But he does it from time to time, and I've stopped worrying about him."

"That's probably for the best. Worrying isn't good for anyone."

As always happened at any pub at any time in any history of any world, eventually, people began to clear out. It was a slow trickle at first, but more followed until all that was left was Sylas, Mira, Azor, and Patches, who looked as drunk as some of the patrons in his perch by the window.

"Well, how did we do?" Azor asked after Sylas turned off the light outside.

He checked his status, the moment of truth.

Name: Sylas Runewulf
Mana Lumens: 1152/1152
Class: Brewer

Sylas clapped his hands together. "About nine hundred MLus. We cleared nine hundred MLus tonight! Whoo! That's a record."

"Yes!" Azor said, the fire spirit doing a complete spin, one filled with tiny bursts of flame.

"Let me head down and check the casks really fast." He did just that and returned. "With a few free drinks, we sold through three casks of strong ale and one of the regular stuff. I'll have to brew five casks of strong ale tonight and four regular ones, but we should be just under twelve tomorrow morning. Back to where we started."

"That's great!" Azor said.

Sylas did the math in his head. "Nine casks should cost me seven-twenty to brew. I'm back at the pub, so my MLus should refill tonight. Things are looking up. They are really looking up. And it's all thanks to you," he told Azor.

A fire spirit shouldn't be able to blush, but it seemed like Azor did so anyway. Mira was joyful as well, the apothecary a bit tipsy but happy for Sylas, especially after how he'd been taken advantage of earlier that day. She pressed away from the bar and yawned. "I should probably get going. Any big plans tomorrow?"

"Tomorrow." Sylas shrugged. "I haven't thought that far ahead yet, but I'm sure I'll be getting into something. Thank you for coming, and for taking me to Duskhaven." He cracked his knuckles. "Alright. I'm going to brew the casks we'll need for tomorrow."

Patches purred until the big man drifted off to sleep. He kept purring for several minutes after, until the point that he knew it was time to make his rounds.

He also wanted to check on something he had seen earlier.

Hopefully, the fire spirit didn't notice it...

Patches reached the cellar, the pub cat delighted to find that the big man had indeed restocked the casks. This was what kept people coming to the Tavernly Realm.

While he didn't quite understand the Mana Lumens system, nor could Patches read numbers, he knew that the more he was able to siphon off people, the better. And he only ever took a little, his own system tripling the amount he had received.

Over the last few days, he'd pulled in quite a bit, especially because he hadn't needed to recharge the big man's power. The numbers flashed before him and Patches was certain he was getting stronger.

Mana Lumens: 1421/1421

Patches would never know about the Mana Lumens system, its intricacies, its hidden classes and their strengths and weaknesses. But he understood that more visitors was a good thing, and he felt better, more agile, ready for anything that tried to disturb the Tavernly Realm.

He checked his usual spots with a bit of pep in his step, feeling energized after such a successful night. He even thought about heading up to the main floor and openly challenging the fire spirit. It was not her job to decide if he went in or out. She was not the master of his free will.

His chest puffed out, Patches thought of doing just that as he took the steps out of the cellar. He turned invisible. It was instinct, and it made him feel more confident.

His spirits lowered once he saw the window they had opened earlier while the fire spirit cooked was now closed. That had been his plan, to hop out the window rather than use the cat door and get back into the pub after the big man opened the cat door in the morning.

The fire spirit said something to him, and it sounded sweet.

Patches ignored her.

He kept his tail erect as he turned back to the stairs. Once he was in the big man's room, he paced angrily by the door, considering his other options.

There were no other options.

Well, there is the option of running away during the day. But I wouldn't want to worry the big man like that.

Patches hopped onto the bed. He approached the sleeping human and gazed at him fondly for a moment. He then started the transfer. Patches kept this up until his legs trembled.

Blurry numbers flashed before Patches's eyes.

He had to make sure the big man had enough.

―――

Sylas awoke feeling well rested.

[**You have 77 days until the invasion.**]

An idea came to him as he lay there looking at the invasion warning. It was something he could do later that day. He reached his hand down and placed it on Patches's head. The piebald pub cat made a sound with his throat like he was in pain.

"You alright there?" Sylas looked down at him to find the cat sleeping peacefully on his side. He assumed Patches was dreaming and moved on, Sylas checking his status to see the Mana Lumens he had used last night had been topped off.

Name: Sylas Runewulf
Mana Lumens: 1152/1152
Class: Brewer

What was it about the pub that recharged his power? Yet another mystery.

He thought of something else. Had Mira mentioned something about assigning himself quest contracts? If she hadn't, he was pretty sure she had hinted at it.

As of right now, Sylas had several things he needed to get to the bottom of. There was the invasion and its ominous message. Then there was his nightly recharge. Sylas also needed to go to Battersea for a couple of other pieces to the puzzle.

In Battersea, he could learn the fate of his father and his three closest friends, Kael, Quinlan, and Raelis. He could also find out more about the Ale Alliance. If he joined them, he'd have access to a new set of supplies, which would allow him to sell to places like the Welcome Inn. That would mean more Mana Lumens, which would give him more options like purchasing property and learning new skills from archlumens.

This reminded Sylas of Archlumen Tilbud. Yet another active quest he would give himself if the man didn't show up that weekend.

A smirk traced across Sylas's face as he ultimately decided *not* to start using the quest system like a to-do list. Even if he was dead and running a pub in the Underworld, he was sort of retired. Why give himself more tasks? Aside from figuring out the invasion warning, everything would work out in due time.

Sensing he was awake, Azor burst in with her typical morning flare. "Happy Thornsday!"

Patches jumped into the air, high enough that it seemed like he would hit the ceiling. The cat landed, hissed, and curled away from the fire spirit.

"He seems especially grumpy this morning," Sylas told her. "Was he up causing trouble last night?"

"I saw him sneak down the stairs to the cellar. He came back up to the pub, took a look around, gave me a dirty look, and headed back to your room." She offered Sylas a fiery shrug. "I don't know what his deal is. Anyway. Breakfast. Hungry for anything in particular?"

As if on cue, the two heard a loud knock at the front door below. It was much louder than a morning knock should have been, the sound instantly putting Sylas on edge.

Azor turned to the door, intent on racing down there and seeing who was being so aggressive in the morning.

"Wait, wait," Sylas called after her. "I'll join you."

CHAPTER NINETEEN

PUB DEFENDER

Sylas opened the front door of the pub to find Anders, the red-faced carpenter who had once broken into The Old Lamplighter. He had a hand cart with him full of tools and other supplies.

"Morning," he said, his eyes dropping a bit upon seeing Sylas. "Finished my sentence in Ashen Hold yesterday, and wanted to take care of the second part of my punishment. You said you needed some work, right?"

"I do. I've been thinking about adding some booths at the back. Something cozy."

"Banquette seating, I believe it's called. I call them comfy seats. I figure they'd be affixed to the wall?"

"Works for me." Sylas grinned at the carpenter. "Please, come in. I'll help you get your stuff."

"Have you eaten anything?" Azor asked, the fire spirit picking up on Sylas's tone. She also felt something else at that moment, a flash of appreciation for Sylas and his forgiving nature. He could have run Anders off. He could have done much worse, considering Azor was in his company. Yet he had forgiven the man, trusted him, and now Anders was here to do exactly as he said he would do.

This flash of appreciation was double-sided once Azor realized that not everyone Sylas met would live up to their end of a bargain. She was certain someone would take advantage of him in the future, and she wanted to be there to protect him, even if he would likely laugh it off.

"I've not yet eaten, no," Anders told her. "But you don't need to trouble yourself. I brought a sandwich."

"I will trouble myself. Breakfast is my specialty. Actually, all meals are my specialty."

"She's not lying," Sylas said. "There was a little bit of the shepherd's pie leftover. How about warming that up with some eggs?"

"Sounds great," Azor said. While Sylas helped Anders unload his cart, Azor raced downstairs and got the oven going. She was surprised to see Patches join her, the pub cat seated at the top of the stairs and occasionally watching her as she cooked. "I'll make you some too," she said.

The cat swatted his black-and-white tail against the stairs in response.

"And once we get to Duskhaven and get some fish, I'll always have something good for you, Patches." Now wearing her fireweave gloves, Azor poured a bit of cream into a bowl and set it at the bottom of the stairs. "If you want milk, you have to play nice."

Patches played nice. Even though it took him a minute to get to his feet, he eventually crept down to the bowl of cream and lapped it up, purring as he did so.

"Such a strange kitty," Azor said as she returned to the shepherd's pie. She fried up some eggs, plated the food, and took it up to Anders and Sylas, who had just finished bringing all the supplies in.

"And you think you'll finish today?" Sylas asked Anders.

"Most of it. I'll be back in the morning, if not."

"Good, in that case, let's eat and then I plan to head out. Azor will be here," Sylas said, "and I'll be back later."

Sylas set off in the direction of the Hexveil. He carried his mace with him just in case. Having now encountered demons from the Chasm twice, he felt like it was safer to travel with a weapon, especially if he was going to the border of hell itself.

As he traveled through a wooded area, Sylas dipped into a mode that he had fallen into countless times before. It was that of a warrior, someone who could sense danger and knew to keep his guard up. Any sound, be it a branch breaking in the foliage or the leaves rustling above, caught his attention.

"Relax," he told himself at one point. Yet he couldn't. He had spent ten years on the front line, and had been ambushed a handful of times by Shadowthorne mercenaries. He couldn't lower his guard. Sylas physically couldn't do it.

So he didn't, not until he made it to the Hexveil, where he saw the Hexveilian Guard standing around the barrier, the sentinels in their unwieldy black armor. Maybe they would know something about the invasion message.

Mira had said they weren't exactly human, but what did she mean by this? Were they native to the Underworld or were they perhaps something a group of archlumens had conjured up?

Sylas had a feeling it was the latter.

He was the only person at the Hexveil aside from the guards, which made it easy to approach them.

Sort of.

He first placed his weapon down to let them know he wasn't there to pick a fight. Once he'd done that, Sylas came to the first guard as casually as possible. He offered the man or woman, he couldn't tell with the armor, a subtle wave.

"Hello, I was wondering—"

"Move along, mortal," said the Hexveilian guard in a deep male voice.

"Yes, I was planning to move along. But I've been receiving a message about an—"

"Move along, mortal," said another Hexveilian guard, this one with the exact same voice as the first who had spoken. He joined his counterpart, the two shoulder to shoulder and creating a wall of muscle and armor. They brought their swords to the ready, the blades gleaming in the Celestial Plains' golden glow.

This annoyed Sylas. He had been approached by civilians before when guarding something, and while distracting, it was important to not treat them like hostiles unless it was warranted.

"I was a soldier, you know," he told the two.

"Move along, mortal," the first said, the second repeating his command.

"Move along, mortal."

"And I'm here to report something." Sylas took a step closer to the two Hexveilian guards, which drew the attention of more. He had never seen movement like this before as the other guards swarming around in the way a peacock opened its plumage. Sylas was quickly surrounded by dozens of members of the Hexveilian Guard.

"Move along, mortal," the first said, the group around him all repeating the same phrase.

Sylas wasn't stupid enough to test them. He backed away, showed them his palms one last time, picked up his fireweave mace, and left.

Next stop, Mira's place, where he was certain she would laugh about his encounter. At least he had that to look forward to. Her laughter, even at his expense, brought Sylas joy.

Mira's shop was closed when he approached. Sylas thought about walking around the back, to the place Tiberius hung out with his militiamen, but thought otherwise. He'd already had one encounter that morning that could have turned violent and he didn't want another.

With this in mind, he knocked.

The door opened, revealing a short man, his black hair slicked back and one good eye instantly scrutinizing Sylas. "Oh, it's you," Tiberius said.

"Morning. Mira in?"

"If she was in, she'd be in her shop."

"So, she's out?"

Tiberius's left eye twitched. "What do you think?"

"Any idea of where she went?"

"Do you think I'd tell you if I knew? Look, we may have gone on a hunt together, but that doesn't mean we're friends. I have other duties."

"Aware," Sylas said, maintaining the firm, yet not quite confrontational look on his face. Tiberius spoke to Sylas like he was his commanding officer. He knew how to deal with people like this from experience.

Tiberius cleared his throat. "She told me yesterday that you are interested in going on more hunts."

"I am."

"But not in joining the militia, hmmm?"

"I never told her that."

"You didn't ask me about it."

"It hadn't crossed my mind."

"You live in Ember Hollow. You are good enough with a weapon. It would make sense for you to join the Esteemed Coalition of Ember Hollow Defenders."

"It would."

"Especially if you want to go on more hunts. That is what the militia does, you know."

"Aware."

Tiberius grunted as he looked Sylas over.

He had seen potential in the man during their hunt, even if he was from the Aurum Kingdom. Sylas's size alone made him a force in any battle, be it against a demon or another human. But he had a penchant for bucking authority. Sylas thought of himself as a maverick, and Tiberius knew better than to trust people like that. Maybe if he could get him to join the militia, then he'd be able to mold Sylas in some way.

Until then, Tiberius would treat him like he would the sellswords he occasionally employed as a lord commander for the Shadowthorne Vanguard.

"Is there anything else?" Tiberius asked once the silence between them had grown awkward.

"Ever heard of Archlumen Tilbud? Is he any good?"

Tiberius squinted at Sylas.

For a moment, Sylas thought that he was scrutinizing him again, yet it appeared to be the way that Tiberius searched his own thoughts.

"I have heard of him. He trained at the same academy in Battersea where my guy trained. They do better if they go to these academies, you know."

"So you've heard of him, then."

"I have, and I've heard he's a bit eccentric. Lives in Duskhaven. Why?"

"No reason. Enjoy the rest of your day, and let Mira know I stopped by." Sylas was just turning away from Tiberius when he stopped. "Also, you should drop by the pub sometime. Your men were there last night and they had a great time."

Tiberius watched Sylas walk away, a sudden flash of jealousy causing his eye to twitch again. He hadn't forbidden his men from going to The Old Lamplighter. He was disappointed they hadn't invited him, even if he was busy on a private hunt.

Yet this was the life of a commanding officer. Even though he knew that, part of him longed for the simpler times among the ranks, the camaraderie of the common soldier.

Tiberius shut the door and went back to what he had been doing before Sylas had appeared.

Absolutely nothing.

The Old Lamplighter opened its doors later that afternoon. Now behind the bar, apron on, Sylas prepared to pour up pints in the only way he knew how—polishing pint glasses. There was little to do at the moment aside from wait for patrons to come, which made him doubly glad when the door swung open and Godric entered with a group of people who lived around the volcano.

"We've got an issue," the fireweave tailor told Sylas instead of hello.

"An issue?" Sylas motioned to the back of the room, where one of the two booths that Anders had worked on was ready to go. The carpenter, who had left an hour ago, would finish the second one tomorrow afternoon. "Why don't you all take a seat and we can talk."

"Good, let's get a round going too. Strongest you got."

Soon, Godric and the others were seated, a few keeping the distraught looks on their faces even as they complimented Anders's handiwork. While Azor poured up five pints of strong ale, Sylas listened to Godric's story.

"It happened last night here to Bart." He motioned to a man next to him. Bart had broad shoulders that stretched the front of his tunic. His hair was white and his ears were pierced. Sylas sensed he was some sort of artisan. "Bart lives near me, just a bit down the lane and closer to that cave. Holes appeared behind his workshop."

"Holes?" Sylas asked, crossing his arms over his chest.

"Great giant ones," Godric said.

Bart nodded in agreement and showed Sylas exactly what he meant with his arms. "Cinderspiders came up like marmots, big ones. They attacked my place," he said, his voice with a musical undertone to it, a bit of flair.

"They did what?" Sylas asked as Patches came around. The pub cat hopped into Bart's lap and settled so the man could apparently pet him. A half grin formed on Sylas's face. Patches sure was a smart cat. He shook his head to wipe the smile away. "Is your place okay?"

"Barely," Bart said. "They burned down a part of my workshop, nasty buggers. I was able to beat them back but, as you can see, that didn't go so well." Bart, who had been wearing a cape over his shoulder, moved it aside to show Sylas his arm, which was mangled and now held in a sling. "Someone recommended Mira the apothecary out of Ember Hollow here. We sent word and she came and fixed me up."

"I know her," Sylas said, connecting the dots in his head as to where Mira was that morning.

"But I'm still in the healing process. And the spider holes are still there."

"We want to get a group together," Godric said after Bart trailed off. "But I suggested we talk to you first."

"Why me exactly?"

Azor appeared, the fire spirit with five pints on her tray. She placed them in front of each of the men, none of them bothered by her fiery presence in the least bit. Once she was done, she joined Sylas.

"Well, you were successful with them before," Godric said after he took his first sip of the strong ale. "So I thought that you would be interested in taking a quest contract. You don't have to. And it's not like I'm asking you to go back into the cave where you said there was a big one. You said that, right?"

"I did," Sylas said as he remembered the enormous cinderspider he'd seen lurking in the steam of the cave.

The door of the pub opened and Mira stepped in. She sat at the bar, and just about the moment she settled, the door opened again revealing Cody and Duncan, the two militiamen. Rather than sit at the bar, they took a table near Godric and the others.

"I just figured, ahem, *we* just figured that you were good at clearing the cinderspiders out then, and you'd be good at doing it now," Godric said. "We can help if you'd like, but we're not fighters. I had that mace, you know, but that was a last resort kind of thing."

"I'm definitely not a fighter," Bart said. "Back in our world, I was a bard. Bart the bard, ahem, former bard. I can still sing, you know, if you ever need entertainment."

"Actually, put a pin in that," Sylas said as he glanced over to Cody and Duncan, both of whom had taken an interest in the conversation even if they had only heard a small portion of it.

"Come on, Sylas," Godric said. "Are you going to make me beg here? We have pooled together a reward for you, you know, for your troubles. Eight hundred MLus. It will be worth your while. Not only that, we'll owe you a favor. All of us will," Godric said.

The men huffed in response.

"We could go with you," Cody volunteered. Sylas expected Duncan to shush him in some way, but the big man nodded in agreement instead.

"The three of us?" Sylas asked. He remembered seeing Cody and Duncan fight the demon a few nights back. Cody was brave and Duncan was a tank of a man, which was always good to have around.

"The three of us," Duncan said with a firm nod. "No plans tomorrow. Tiberius gave us the day off."

"Four of us," Azor said. "I'm going too."

"In that case, sure," Sylas told Godric. "Make it nine hundred MLus and we'll deal with the cinderspiders at Bart's place tomorrow morning."

[New Quest Contract - Handle the cinderspiders at Bart Walker's place. Accept? Y/N?]

Sylas nodded. "I'll let you gentlemen get back to it. As for you two," he told Cody and Duncan, "first round is on me. Thanks for joining the cause."

"Not a problem at all," Duncan said. "I'd much rather fight off a spider than a B-Rank demon."

A ripple of trepidation stirred Godric and his companions upon hearing this comment, their curiosity piqued. They ultimately refrained from delving deeper, allowing Duncan's unsettling remark to linger longer than it should.

"Anyway," Sylas said, his gaze drifting toward the bar, where Mira patiently awaited his companionship, "I should get back to the front. Let us know when you're ready for another pint."

Sylas awoke the next morning to find Patches purring next to him, the pub cat close enough that he could have tucked him under his arm.

[You have 76 days until the invasion.]

"More like, I have seventy-six days to figure this invasion out or else. Seventy-six days, Patches."

The cat mewed softly, almost sympathetically.

Sylas checked his status to see he now had 1362 Mana Lumens, his levels topped off. He also saw his new active quest.

[Active Quest Contracts:]
Handle the cinderspiders at Bart Walker's place

Last night had been slower than he would have liked, yet he had still netted over two hundred Mana Lumens. This was more than enough to brew the two regular casks. And now, as had become the norm when he slept at the pub, his power was topped off.

"Maybe the building itself is magical," he told Patches as he continued to pet the pub cat.

Azor appeared, her fireweave apron with flour splattered across the front. "Morning. Happy Fireday!"

"Is it Fireday already?"

"It is, and Cody and Duncan are already downstairs waiting for you."

"In that case, give me a minute and I'll be down there."

Soon, Sylas joined the two militiamen, who had just finished a big breakfast that Azor had whipped up. There was a plate for Sylas as well, one filled with pastries, eggs, and grilled meats.

"You two look ready to go," he told the pair, who wore thick leather armor stitched with metal plating.

Duncan seemed to take this comment as a compliment. "Just something we have lying around. Good stuff out of Battersea. Or good enough." He admired the leather vambraces, the metal plating of which was stitched with a thick red thread. The large man knocked his fist against the metal. "See?"

"Not bad," Sylas said, secretly noting that it wasn't the same armor they had worn during the demon hunt. This told him that they probably hadn't run their little side quest by Tiberius. "It won't do much against the fire they spit, but it will at least protect you from their fangs."

Duncan didn't seem bothered by this comment, but Cody reacted differently. The younger man's complexion noticeably paled.

"Don't worry," Sylas said. "We'll be fine."

Once he locked up the pub, Sylas, Azor, and the two militiamen headed to the Ember Hollow portal. They arrived in Cinderpeak moments later, Azor now tucked away in the glowing tattoo on Sylas's arm so she wouldn't bring attention to them. From there, it was a straight shot through the town to the upper slopes of the volcano, where they found Godric the fireweave tailor's home.

Godric paced outside, his thick goggles on his face as he patrolled his property with a blunt weapon about the size of a baton. He also had a buckler, the small shield affixed to his arm. "You're here."

"We certainly are." Sylas handed Cody his mace so he could pull his sleeve back. Azor formed into existence, wispy flames twisting around her body.

Godric pointed away from his home. "Just head down that way. I'm honestly surprised the spiders haven't moved over to my place. I was certain they would."

"But you were at the pub last night," Cody said.

"Of course I was! Have you seen a cinderspider? No?" he asked after Cody shook his head. "I needed a stiff drink just to keep my thoughts together."

Godric's front door opened, startling the tailor. Bart stepped out, the former bard with a large wrench. "They're here. Good."

"Good is right," said Godric. "Anyway, we can come if you'd like, but—"

"It's fine," Sylas told him as he read the look on the fireweave tailor's face. "We can handle the spiders. Cody, Duncan?"

The two militiamen grunted a positive response.

"One more thing." Godric removed the shield from his arm and handed it to Sylas. "I have two more inside. Bart?"

"I'll grab them," the other man said.

"They're made of fireweave," Godric told them, even though Sylas could already tell by the unique texture of the shield. "I crafted these up from the lavalace you brought. So that one is yours. You two can have the other shields as part of your reward."

Sylas affixed the shield to his nondominant arm. He brought it up, shifted it back, and nodded. "I could have really used something like this when I went into the cave."

"Yes, you could have. My apologies there," Godric said with a toothy grin. "But you have it now. Good luck."

"Cody, Duncan," Sylas said after the militiamen had fastened their shields onto their arms. He paused, surprised by the words about to leave his lips. "On my lead."

The two militiamen fanned out as Sylas approached Bart's house, Cody on his left, Duncan on his right. The home didn't appear to be infested by cinderspiders upon first glance. But then one of the spiders, about the size of a small dog, crawled up the side of the home and settled on the rooftop.

Cody froze. Sylas didn't blame him.

"Just remember that you are bigger than it," Duncan said. "And don't let the spiders burn the place down."

"I'm surprised they haven't done so already," Sylas said as they carefully moved to the right of the house. They came around the back, where they found several large holes in the ground and what was left of Bart's workshop.

The nest.

As soon as they arrived, dozens of eyes locked on them.

The largest of the group pushed out of their holes and were immediately met by Azor. She whirred forward in a flash of blistering flames. This was mostly for distraction. The cinderspiders lived in the caves around a volcano. The heat meant nothing to them.

Sylas advanced, shifting in front of Cody and Duncan. He struck the first cinderspider and killed it. He kicked its body to the side and smashed another. Sylas turned to block an incoming bolt of flames with his fireweave shield.

His actions, as they had done before, inspired the others to move in.

Duncan was first. The large man gripped his mace with both hands and brought it down onto one of the spiders. He stomped on another even as it tried to bite at him, his leg protected by the greaves he wore.

Cody lunged at a cinderspider just as it jumped for him and was able to bat it out of the air.

Azor rushed by the younger man, as if she could sense that he was the most vulnerable of the group. She struck a spider hard enough to knock it over, allowing Cody to crush the underside of its thorax.

One of the spiders aimed its spinneret at Cody and hit him in the face with a net of webbing.

"Arggh!" Cody shouted as he stumbled in the opposite direction. He tripped over a stone and cracked his chin on a bench that was pressed up to the side of the home, the young man out cold.

"We've got this," Sylas told Duncan. "Azor, keep up the distractions!" Sylas swung his mace at a cinderspider and blocked a ball of fire with his shield. "Try to knock over as many as you can!"

Azor blazed forward comet-like. She smashed into the rank of cinderspiders, Sylas able to see her use her hands to flip individual spiders onto their backs. This was no easy task. They were heavy, and she strained to flip them, yet her work was what soon gave them the upper hand.

Charging forward, now wielding both his mace and Cody's weapon, Duncan smashed the spiders left and right. One managed to hit him with its venom, and his arm caught fire. Yet he continued to clear a path into their nest.

"Beat the flames out!" Sylas told him as he came to his aid.

Sylas bashed one of the spiders across the face just as it was about to sink its fangs into Duncan. He followed this up with a boot that crushed its body. Sylas ignored the crunch, its sound and the feel—too gruesome to focus on. Instead, he fell into a version of himself he was intimately familiar with, that of a warrior, of a machine trained to advance no matter the cost.

Sylas crushed another spider and dove to the left to avoid a net of webbing. He came back up and struck a spider charging toward him, Sylas able to protect Duncan while he beat the flame out.

Azor continued flipping them over, Sylas only just noticing how much he was sweating, just how hot it was, after Duncan roared something about the heat.

The large man beat back several of the spiders, giving Sylas a split second to catch his breath.

He sucked in a deep inhale through his nostrils, found his next target, and moved in for the kill. One of the spiders came out of its hole just as Sylas rushed past. It snapped at his legs and sunk its fangs into Sylas's shin.

The pain was instant. The pain was fiery. The pain soon became unlike anything Sylas had ever experienced before. It spread quickly, down to his foot and up to his thigh, Sylas's entire leg burning from within.

Sylas limped toward his opponent with a bloodlust that had the spider second-guessing what it had just done. He smashed it and another one jumped for him, only to be knocked to the side by Cody, who struck it with the sharp side of his shield.

"Are you alright?" Sylas asked as he struggled to stand.

"Me? I'm fine. Are you alright, mate?" came Cody's reply.

Rather than answer, Sylas crushed another cinderspider, Duncan doing the same until there was just one left.

It backed away from the three men.

"Let me finish the job." Cody turned his palm around and Duncan gave him his mace. He took off toward the cinderspider, which tried to run, its escape blocked by Azor.

Cody killed it with two quick strikes. He turned back to Duncan and Sylas, a haggard look on his face.

"We did it," Duncan started to say. "Let's—"

Sylas fell to one knee, the pain too excruciating for him to stand. Duncan came to his aid and helped him stand.

"I'm fine, I'm fine," Sylas said, his voice growing weak.

"Sylas?" Azor was suddenly hovering in front of him, her fiery face a mask of genuine concern. Her fingers elongated into bladelike fire knives, which she quickly used to cut Sylas's pant leg away. "Oh, this is bad," she said as Duncan helped Sylas down.

The puncture wound was black and blue, as to be expected. Yet this wasn't what concerned the fire spirit. It was the glowing veins that had appeared, the ones that looked to be spreading.

"I'll be fine," Sylas told her, feeling delirious as he continued to sweat profusely.

"I'll be able to hold it off. For now." She immediately returned to her tattoo, her voice now at the back of Sylas's head. "But you need to get to someone who can help."

"Someone who can help?" Sylas asked.

"Mira," Cody said. "Let's get you to Mira!"

"But that means . . ." Duncan cleared his throat. "Tiberius will—"

"It doesn't matter," Cody told him.

"Mira? Right. Apothecary," Sylas said, a bit breathless as he got to his feet. He felt a bit stronger now, but each step felt like he was walking on a limp leg. Azor was clearly helping to keep him stable. "Get me back to the pub and get her. She'll know what to do," he gritted. "We'll grab our quest rewards along the way."

Patches was immediately concerned to see the big man limp into the pub. He approached, and with one sniff, the pub cat recognized that he'd been poisoned.

Patches started to mew once he saw the strange orange veins pulsing on the big man's exposed leg.

This is bad, this is really bad!

The big man and the fire spirit spoke to Patches, but he never could figure out what they were saying.

What bit him? Some sort of insect? Patches continued to try to better understand the smell. There was something sulfuric about it, but it had the distinct acidity that he'd come to know from insect bites.

Terrible. Simply terrible!

Patches hated insects. There had been a few when he had first settled into the pub, but he'd killed all of them early on.

He started to pace nervously as the big man rested on the floor of the pub. The fire spirit brought a blanket down for him and a pillow. He protested. She insisted.

The big man pointed to the stairs as if to say he wanted to go up to his bedroom. The fire spirit raised her voice.

Patches was familiar with this raised voice. It was the same stern tone she used with him about the well, which he'd still not been able to explore. The big man pointed to a window. The fire spirit opened it and was immediately distracted by a knock at the door.

A new man entered, one with a red face. He was the one who was building the comfy seats at the back of the Tavernly Realm, the one Patches was now starting to trust even though he'd once been an intruder.

Is he here to fix the big man?

Patches was just about to approach his loyal subject and transfer power to him when the door swung open again and the medicine woman appeared.

Patches could sense the terror she was experiencing, the way her heart beat rapidly upon seeing the big man lying on the ground, one knee bent, the other sticking straight out.

The medicine woman moved into action.

She gave the big man something to bite down on and applied a balm that had a wintergreen smell to it. There was something much deeper as well, an earthy aroma that almost reminded Patches of the forest outside of the village. He then noticed a honey scent, but more floral than honey that he'd smelled before, which caused Patches's nose to scrunch up.

But if it worked, and the big man would be fine, then he was happy.

He was so happy, in fact, that he approached the medicine woman to rub his body against her in appreciation. She nudged Patches to the side and focused again on what she was doing.

But I'm trying to thank you, Patches told her as the fire spirit came in with her big metal gloves and shooed him away. He hissed at her, which caused the big man to laugh. He reached his free hand out to Patches and the cat approached.

Patches collapsed headfirst into the big man's hand and began purring. He lay there next to him, watching as the orange veins in the big man's leg stopped pulsing. Soon, they were gone, and all that was left was the puncture wound.

The medicine woman applied something to that as well and then wrapped it.

Patches was happy. The big man was going to survive.

Sylas didn't like having to sit on a stool behind the bar that night, but Mira insisted, and to make sure he stayed put, the apothecary sat on a different stool across from him.

"I'm fine, I can walk," Sylas told her. He got off the stool to demonstrate what he meant.

"I know you can. I'm the one that healed you, remember? It's precautionary. And it's just for tonight. Azor can serve ale and if you need a new cask, she can get one."

"I'm stronger than I look," Azor said as she flexed her fiery muscles.

The door swung open and Mr. and Mrs. Brassmere entered, the two discussing their inventory yet again. She snipped at her husband to some degree, but Mr. Brassmere complicated things too in the way he grunted answers at the woman.

Sylas and Mira exchanged smirks.

"To run a business with your spouse," she said under her breath.

Rather than reply, Sylas poured up a pair of regular pints. The pair took one of the new booths at the back of the pub while he waited for the ale to rest. "On me," he told Azor once she placed the pints on her serving tray.

The fire spirit brought them over to Mr. and Mrs. Brassmere, who waved back at Sylas in appreciation and continued their discussion.

"And tomorrow?" Mira asked once Sylas relaxed onto his stool, his arms crossed over his chest. "You probably shouldn't make plans to kill more cinderspiders."

"I think I'll stay around the pub and hope that our favorite archlumen shows up."

The night grew busier, especially once Godric, Bart, and some of the other men and women who lived near the Cinderpeak volcano arrived. They joined Mr. and Mrs. Brassmere and soon became a lively group.

"You know I owe you a favor, right?" Godric told Sylas later that night, the fireweave tailor half drunk. "Really, Sy. Can I call you Sy? You really helped us out today, saved our—" He burped. "Apologies, mate. Where was I? A favor is in order!"

"You told me that earlier," Sylas reminded him. His eyes jumped to Mira, who was in the process of leaving.

"I'll be around tomorrow to check on you," she said. "Good night."

Godric waited until she was gone and gave Sylas a wolfish grin. "I think she likes you."

"What? Mira? No way. We're friends."

He laughed and beat his fist on the bar. "Friends, is it?" Godric grew serious. "Actually, I guess that is a possibility as well." He sneered at how serious he had just become. "Anyway, a favor. You let me know when you want to collect. Perhaps I'll make you a fireweave suit of armor for that favor I owe you. What would you say to that?"

"How long would that take?"

"A few days if me and the boys worked on it." He produced a tape measure. "Let me get your measurements."

"That was your plan all along, wasn't it?"

Godric snorted a reply. "It was, you got me."

Godric had just finished taking measurements when he was interrupted by Bart, who now stood on a chair. *"La-la-la-la-la-la-la-la,"* he sang, warming up his vocals. He placed his hands behind his back and began: *"A maiden so fair from the Garden of Dreams, danced in the meadow where the everlight beams. With hair of gold and cheeks of cherry, she moved with grace 'midst rows of berries."*

Sylas felt a quiver in his heart. It had been years, *years* since he'd heard the song. How old was he when he last heard it? A boy? He remembered now, a troupe of bards performing the love song in his father's pub. He hadn't thought of it in ages. He had forgotten it.

Yet in hearing the tune, the memories returned.

It was like they had been there all along. A warm smile crossed his face, Sylas realizing in that moment that he was happier than he had ever been. He had created the exact environment he had hoped to create with The Old Lamplighter, a public house, one where people could unwind and connect.

He might have technically been dead, he might have nearly been killed by a cinderspider earlier that day, but in that moment, Sylas felt like his life had only just begun. The Underworld was more than a rebirth for Sylas, it was a place where he had found his joy and his purpose.

His reverie was interrupted by Patches, who charged toward the window that Azor had opened earlier and hopped out.

Bart stopped singing. "Did the bloody cat just hop out the window?"

The others in the pub began to hoot and laugh.

"What is wrong with that cat?" Sylas asked.

"I'll find him!" Azor raced out the window in pursuit of Patches.

Patches watched the fire spirit from the dark. She had been hovering around for the last thirty minutes looking for him. He didn't know how she saw him when he was invisible, but now, as he hid in a nook in the pub's stone foundation, he was certain she wouldn't find him.

Patches waited.

Cats were good at that, as patient as they could be seemingly impulsive.

He waited until she ultimately gave up. Patches remained in the nook until the last patrons stumbled out and the light in front of the pub flickered off. He needed to take a look at the well, no matter how dangerous it was, even if he had to stay outside all night, even if he got wet.

I hate getting wet.

Regardless, it was his duty to protect his home.

The fire spirit came out again. This time, she used the cat door, which she moved in and out of in what looked like an attempt to tell Patches that the door was open. She called to him a few more times in desperation and slinked forward as she ultimately gave up.

Patches didn't let this perturb him. It could have been a trap.

He waited and waited, anticipating that the fire spirit would come out one last time.

She never did.

As he sat in the dark, Patches noticed a subtle change in the air. It grew heavier as a wisp of golden magic curled out of the well. To the naked eye, the energy was the same color Patches had noticed when he used his own powers.

Yet he knew it was different.

It was an illusion, meant to mask something far more sinister. The smoky being that Patches had seen once before took shape. About the size of a child, it was clearly demonic in nature, with sharp teeth and a face shaped like that of a bat.

Patches's ears flitted back, his whiskers following suit.

He crept out of the nook he had been hiding in and doubled in size, his hair on edge, Patches prepared to strike. His boldness quickly shifted to fear as the demonic being turned to him, its mouth dropping open as an evil smile formed on its face.

Patches's throat constricted as he choked back the sound of panic. He couldn't alert the big man or the fire spirit. This was his burden to bear.

He charged toward the demonic being. It zipped up into the air where Patches couldn't reach it and dove straight into the well. Patches hopped up to the lip of the well and returned to his normal size. He couldn't hesitate this time. If the fire spirit was watching, she would prevent him from going in.

Patches was going to have to risk it.

He gathered all the courage he could muster and jumped into the well.

Patches stretched his arms out wide, hoping to slow his descent. This helped to some degree and he was able to control his fall. He got close to the middle of the well when a terrible sound reached his ears. It was the sound of bones cracking against one another, one that came coupled with a smell that reminded Patches of the wounds the big man had earlier that day.

The demonic being appeared directly in front of Patches face, its eyes narrowing on the cat.

This was all it took. Summoning a strength he didn't even know he had, Patches thrust backward and managed to move several feet toward the opening at the top of the well.

The demon lunged at him, gnashing its teeth as Patches performed the same maneuver, the pub cat backtracking the way he had just come. He reached the rim of the well and pulled himself out.

With a speed he had rarely harnessed before, Patches bolted back toward the Tavernly Realm and exploded through the cat door.

He bounded up the stairs, taking two steps at a time until he reached the big man's room. Patches hopped onto the bed and buried himself beneath the covers, safe.

Luckily, he didn't wake the big man.

Hours later, when Patches was finally ready to peek his head out, he transferred some of his power to the big man before falling into a deep, yet troubled, sleep.

Sylas had already been awake for a few minutes when the prompt came to him.

[You have 75 days until the invasion.]

He sat up, careful not to disturb Patches. Sylas gingerly removed the blanket from his leg to find that it was fully healed. He also checked his status to confirm that The Old Lamplighter had done pretty well last night.

Name: Sylas Runewulf
Mana Lumens: 2008/2008
Class: Brewer

He had gone through a cask of the strong ale and over two of the regular ale. He'd also given away a good number of drinks. All in all, Sylas had brewed three casks before going to bed, one strong and two regular.

He also had noticed something else about his power, a detail that hadn't really been as prevalent until yesterday's injury.

Sylas did the math. He had started the previous day with nearly fourteen hundred Mana Lumens. He had netted three hundred from the quest contract, and had cleared over four hundred from the sale of alcohol. He should have been closer to 2100 Mana Lumens, yet he was about a hundred off.

"I should have checked after my injury," he said to himself, "But I likely lost some there. And that meant the MLus added didn't push me as high." He clenched his eyes shut for a moment.

The thought of numbers made him want to go back to sleep.

Azor wouldn't let him. Just as he was about to drift off, the fire spirit rushed into the room with her usual morning exuberance.

"Happy Specterday," she told Sylas as she darted her head to Patches. "You should have seen him last night!"

"Did he come ripping through the cat door like he'd seen a ghost?"

She gave Sylas a confused look. "How did you know?"

"He's a cat. And it was a lucky guess. Anyway, we'll keep an eye on him today, but he seems to be fine. Tired, but fine."

"And you? Are you feeling better?"

"Much better. I think I'll still take Mira's advice and stay around here today. There's some wood I can chop. I'll sweep upstairs and wash some clothes and linens."

"I can help dry them."

"I'm sure you can." Sylas clasped his hands together and stretched his arms over his head. "Hopefully, it will be an uneventful day."

This statement caused Patches to stir, even though he didn't understand their language.

"Heh," Sylas said as he scratched the side of the cat's neck. "I probably shouldn't say stuff like that."

CHAPTER TWENTY

QUILL AND WINGS

Sylas had just finished tightening up the bolts on a barstool when he heard a knock at the door.

"I'll get it," Azor called from the cellar below. She whooshed up to the main floor of The Old Lamplighter, opened the door, and flared back.

"Oh my," came a voice that took Sylas a moment to recognize. Archlumen Tilbud stepped into the pub, the ends of his purple robes sweeping the floor as he stepped in. The mustached archlumen wore a tiny lavender top hat that barely covered the crown of his head. "You didn't say you had contracted with a fire spirit."

"I'm Azor." She extended her gloved hand to the archlumen.

Tilbud didn't hesitate to take it. "It is a pleasure, no, an honor! I am contracted with a spirit as well." He pulled his robe back to reveal a glowing blue tattoo. "A water spirit named Horatio. But he doesn't come out very often. He prefers Battersea, the lake there. He can be a little difficult, isn't that right, Horatio? Anyhoo." The archlumen smiled at Sylas. "Fancy place you have here!"

"I was wondering when you'd show up." Sylas, who had been crouched by the chair he was working on, placed his tools on the table and got to his feet. "You really left in a hurry back there in Duskhaven."

"Ah yes, that. Trouble, I tell you, and trouble that had nothing to do with me. Well, it had something to do with me. If you must know—" Patches trotted down the stairs. "Ah, what a beautiful cat!" Tilbud cast his hand toward the cat.

He produced a node of light that Patches chased up and down the stairs for a moment until he got bored.

"Maybe I can do something like that." Azor conjured a marble-sized ball of fire. She sent it toward Patches and he ignored it. The fire spirit deflated. "He hates me so much."

"He doesn't hate you," Sylas said as he approached the archlumen. "He's just mad because he thinks you're preventing him from going out at night."

"There are archlumens in Battersea who can use MLus for what I would describe as love potions," Tilbud suggested. "But perhaps that isn't the relationship you'd like with the cat. I'm here for something. Ah, yes. To fly. Are you ready to fly? Wait." He flicked his finger and produced a scroll. Tilbud read through it. "I owe you something else, don't I?"

"According to your letter, yes."

"In that case, I'll teach you to fly now, and tomorrow I'll teach you something else. Yes, that will work. Let me have a think about that. Do you have a place for me to stay?" Tilbud looked to the stairs.

Sylas raised an eyebrow at the archlumen. "You want to stay here?"

"Is there a hotel in Ember Hollow? I think not. And the air in Cinderpeak is far too dusty for my taste. I can't go back to Duskhaven, not tonight. Still having issues there."

Sylas didn't press the archlumen on what these "issues" might be. Instead, he motioned toward the second story of the pub. "I have a guest room up there you're more than welcome to use." An idea came to him. "How long have you been in the Underworld?"

"Time is different here than it is where we're from. But if you're meaning how many deathdays have passed, it has been a good many." Tilbud started counting his fingers. He gave up. "Why?"

"So you know a lot about the Underworld?"

"I would say that is the case, yes."

"Would you be interested in hosting a pub quiz tonight? I know it's impromptu, but I figured it would be something you like. Of course, you don't have to if you don't want to."

"A pub quiz?" Something lit behind the archlumen's eyes. "Yes, I can see it now. A battle for the ages! Wit against wit! Only the brave, only the strong, only the intelligent will survive!" He threw his hands out and produced a spark of magic that caused Patches to race upstairs. Tilbud cleared his throat. "I'd be glad to host. I can prepare questions this afternoon after you've learned to fly. Also, about flying."

"Yes?" Sylas asked.

"It will take you several days to get the hang of it. I suppose, in that way, it is like walking. Actually, it is not like walking. I've never had a baby so I don't know how long it takes to learn to walk, but I'm assuming more than a few days. But it is like walking. Or maybe it's like walking and then learning to run."

He shrugged. Sylas shrugged. Tilbud continued:

"Anyway, it will take some time to get good at it, flying. And you'll want at least a week under your belt before you do something like fly to Battersea. But you should fly there. It's a beautiful city." Tilbud swept his robes to the side and turned to the door. "Come. It is time I give you wings." Confusion traced across his face. "What was your name again?"

"Sylas Runewulf."

"Ah, good. I didn't write that part down in my notes. Just 'pub in Ember Hollow.' Heh. Luckily for both of us, it was easy to find."

Tilbud led Sylas out of the village, or at least in the direction the archlumen assumed was out of Ember Hollow. They ended up in a forest, which they explored for a moment until the archlumen found a small meadow.

"This will do." He turned to Sylas and grinned. "Now, you may be wondering why I asked your fire spirit to stay behind."

"Someone has to watch the pub?"

"Well, that. I suppose. Actually, I don't know if that's a necessity. I asked her to stay back because I don't want you to have a safety net. She could theoretically catch you or simply take over your body and stop you from a crash-landing. If you didn't know, the threat of a crash-landing is one of the main motivating factors in learning to fly here in the Underworld. Will you die? That depends on how high you were flying. Will it hurt? Yes. It will hurt. If you do fall, aim for the trees."

"Aim for the trees," Sylas said as he glanced at the foliage around them. In doing so, he caught a glimpse of the Celestial Plains above and its golden glow.

"No, unfortunately, you won't be able to fly all the way up to the Celestial Plains," Tilbud said, misreading the look on Sylas's face. "Many have tried. None have succeeded. It is much higher up than it appears. Anyway, to fly. Spread your arms out like a bird."

Sylas did just that.

"Now flap them."

Sylas flapped his arms and Tilbud burst out laughing. "I'm sorry. So sorry. That's an old archlumen joke. Did I mention most of us have a sense of humor? If not, now you know. You are familiar with MLus. I'm assuming you have several thousand."

"Just above two thousand," Sylas said.

"Flying uses MLus as a fuel source. I would estimate in our lessons today that you will probably spend two to three hundred MLus. Give or take. Just so you are aware. Another thing to be aware of: Once I unlock this power, it will appear on your status screen under the heading Lumen Abilities. So don't be alarmed if you have more text the next time you check."

"Good to know."

The archlumen raised his hand toward Sylas. A gold glow took shape at the center of his palm. "Do you know how archlumens work?"

"Sort of, but not really."

"We are given a list of powers that we can purchase with fixed MLus. These aren't cheap. We then sell these powers to those who can pay us fixed MLus to use them. Once the exchange is made, we transfer the power to you, and immediately use the fixed MLus you've given us to repurchase the power. That is what I'm about to do. We then show you how to use the power. That is what I plan to do next. Prepare."

The archlumen gave Sylas little time to prepare. And how would he have prepared anyway?

Tilbud thrust both palms forward and struck Sylas with a flash of mana.

It was like Sylas had been hit by a bull. His heels dug into the ground as a great beam of power poured into him, one with spiraling golden tendrils along its outer edge.

After the initial impact, Sylas felt his core warm up. This soon turned to a luminescence that spread outward, completely covering his body.

"Look down," Tilbud said, the archlumen's tone increasingly serious. "And relax."

It wasn't until Tilbud pointed this out that Sylas realized how rigid he was, like he was bracing himself for an impending onslaught of enemy soldiers.

Sylas gasped. He was now floating just a few inches off the ground.

"Yes?" Tilbud asked.

"This is crazy," Sylas said.

"Are you ready to go higher?"

Sylas glanced up to the gold-hued sky above. "Only one way to go."

As Sylas soon discovered, the problem with flying was in understanding how to move through space without any barriers. Once he was above the tree line, he found that he shifted too hard if he wanted to move forward, which resulted in him actually moving downward. There was a subtlety of control here that Sylas didn't quite grasp. This coupled with the butterflies he felt every time he veered in the wrong direction made it harder to perform the feat.

Tilbud settled in front of Sylas, the archlumen having no difficulty in keeping himself steady. "People dream of flying until they can actually do it. You won't believe this, or maybe you will, but some give up before they reach the point of mastery. I've had that happen before."

"Is this why I don't normally see people flying?"

"Do you spend a lot of time outside stargazing?"

"I don't spend as much time outside as I'd like."

"If you did, you'd see people moving through the air at times. But they're pretty high up, at least the experienced ones. Some even look like comets. Actually, I'll show you what I mean. Stay here."

"Sure," Sylas said. In trying to maintain his position in the air he ended up bending forward until he was completely horizontal. He tried to right himself, but couldn't figure it out, so he simply turned around onto his back as if he were floating on top of a body of water.

Energy flared around Tilbud as he moved skyward. The archlumen reached a point far above any reasonable height Sylas would fly and took off toward the west. He reappeared a few moments later and lowered in front of Sylas.

"Let me help you," he said as he twisted his wrist in front of him. Sylas felt an invisible force move over his body and shift him into a vertical position. "There, that's better."

"How do I turn it off?" Sylas asked.

"Ah, that's not as hard as it sounds. Simply lower and *will* the power away. It will take a few days, but eventually, it will be like running. Or maybe skipping? You don't skip when you walk around, do you? Did I already use the walking and running analogy?"

"You did, and I haven't skipped in ages," Sylas said as he tried to force himself down.

"You should try it sometime. It is quite fun."

Lowering wasn't as easy as Tilbud made it sound. The only thing that seemed to work was imagining a great pressure on his shoulders. This had a way of pushing him down to the point that he could reach his toes out and touch the ground.

"Good," Tilbud said as he hovered before him. "Start to think of it like that. If you want to skip, you skip. If you want to fly, you fly. Now, I want you to fly. Follow me. I'll go slow and we won't go too high."

"Sure," Sylas said, thinking about feathers lifting him up seemed to help him levitate.

"Ready?"

"Actually, should I be visualizing this in some way? To lower myself, I thought of weights pushing my shoulders down. To float, I thought of feathers. Is this normal?"

The archlumen laughed. "Nothing about what we do here in the Underworld is normal. If it works, it works. And I would encourage it. Now, come. We'll fly for a bit, and then I need to prepare for the quiz tonight. I do wish I had brought a different hat, but that's fine. This outfit will do."

Sylas noticed how Tilbud's hat hadn't shifted at all, even though his long silvery locks of hair had moved in the wind. "How are you keeping it on your head?"

"An archlumen doesn't reveal all their secrets early on." He hovered forward. "Try to keep up."

Tilbud kept a relatively slow pace as he traveled over the woods. A few birds passed them, but none of them seemed bothered by the two floating humans.

"I've been wondering about the animals here," Sylas said.

"In the Underworld? You're wondering if they did something bad and were sentenced here, hmmm?"

"Yes." Sylas shifted forward and nearly found himself horizontal again. To correct this, he imagined standing upright which seemed to help.

"They weren't bad back in our world, I can assure you that. I believe many of them were already here. Or perhaps they were gifted to us by those in the Celestial Plains. They certainly aren't Chasmastic creatures, although there are beasts—not demons, mind you!—out there that you would think were from the Chasm."

"Good to know," Sylas said as he sent his arms out and did a complete spin. "I think I'm getting the hang of this."

"It does come more naturally to some. But I would advise against trying anything too daring for a week. And certainly don't attempt a trip to Battersea unless you go on foot. Give yourself time. Come, let's go a little higher."

The wind rushed past Sylas as he began his ascent. It was clear how useful flying would be in the future. He only hoped he could master it.

The Old Lamplighter was buzzing with activity that night. It wasn't as full as it had been several days back when Azor had made food, but it was certainly lively, and that was before Tilbud started the pub quiz.

"Now, quiet down," the archlumen said as he raised his glass of regular ale to those that had gathered. Mira, who sat at the bar, looked over at Sylas and shook her head playfully.

"What?" he asked her.

"I can't believe he's hosting a quiz. Did he say—"

"Ahem!" Tilbud looked around for something to ding his glass with. "No silverware. Never mind. We have three teams here. What is your team name?" he asked Godric and a few of his friends who lived around the Cinderpeak Volcano.

"Definitely not the spiders," Bart joked.

They brainstormed some names and eventually came up with the Lava Boys, even though there was also a woman at the table. Another table, this one with some people Sylas hadn't seen before, called themselves the Veilians, and the final table of three went with the name the Underdogs.

"Now, the prize. All of you have put in ten MLus, and since there are eleven of you, that means the winner will be rewarded one hundred and ten MLus. Your table will also have the next round of drinks covered by the house."

"Wait, I'll join the table of three," Mira announced. She sat at the table, the group known as the Underdogs, which included Brom the farmer and two of his friends. Patches soon joined her and found a place in the apothecary's lap.

"I guess they aren't the Underdogs anymore," Azor told Sylas, who hovered near the bar, ready to serve drinks.

"Good, then the prize is now one hundred and twenty MLus, plus a round of the best ale west of Battersea!" Tilbud took a sip from his pint and smacked his lips.

"You need to bring him around more," Azor said to Sylas, who nodded in response.

"There will be three rounds. The first is on Underworld geography. The second will be on flora and fauna. The third and final round will be on cities in the Underworld. Each of your tables has a piece of paper. I will ask the question, and you will have one minute to discuss the question and write down the answer before I move on to the next question. After the question is asked, it will not be repeated. So listen carefully. I will collect the paper at the end and I'll tally up your scores."

After the teams selected the person responsible for writing answers, the quiz began.

To Mira, it soon became apparent that there was a method to the archlumen's unique form of madness. He would start off with low-hanging fruit, asking simple questions like what mountain range was between Ember Hollow and Duskhaven. Then he'd move to insane questions, like travel comparisons between cities in the Underworld that Mira had never heard of before.

"Why do I have to be the one to write answers again?" she asked as Brom and the other farmers flung answers at her.

But she knew why they'd chosen her. Mira had a knack for dealing with a group of people, from gauging what her group was saying to getting it all down in time before Tilbud moved on to the next round. She handled it all in stride.

"Answers, please," he told her as approached the table to collect the piece of paper with her scribbles. Once he had the three papers, Tilbud calculated the scores out of a possible ten points. "The next round will have a bonus question worth three points," he announced to the group as Azor zipped around with fresh pints of ale.

"Wait, who won the last round?" Brom asked Tilbud.

"The last round? Ah, right. Of course you'd like to know the winner. Let's just say that two of the groups are neck and neck. The other has a ways to go," he said, his eyes glazing over Mira's table, "but this group can still turn it around."

"He means us," Brom said.

"We don't know that," Mira told him. "And you all are farmers. At least, I think you are, right?"

Brom and the other two men nodded.

"And I'm an apothecary. This next round is about flora and fauna." She beamed a smile at the three of them. "This is our round to win."

Sylas, who had quietly approached behind them to see how they were doing, saw how focused she was and thought otherwise. He returned to the bar and filled up more pints in preparation for the round to come.

"Ready?" Tilbud asked. He brought his answer card closer to his face and read the first question, "This animal thrives in hot environments and is known for its heat-resistant skin popular in leather goods stores in Battersea."

"Oh, I know that one. Charcoalmander," Brom whispered to Mira, who was already starting to write it down.

The questions that followed were easy.

In order, the answers were wispwillow, a tree with bioluminescent leaves known for their aphrodisiac properties; emberfern, which Mira used for upset stomachs; nightdrake, which was a small bird-sized dragon that lived in the hills surrounding Battersea; echolilies, which people gave to loved ones after whispering words of affection into the flower itself; and gravemoss, a moss that grew in the shade and was used to cure hangovers.

"This round is definitely ours," Mira said once Tilbud got to his final questions.

"Often found near quartzblossoms, this animal is known to collect the flowers to brighten up its nest."

Mira smiled at the group. "I know that one." She wrote down the answer, phantomoa.

"And finally, as promised, a bonus question worth three additional points. Kay's Rose, which only blooms near the Hexveil, can cause powerful hallucinations. Write the part of the plant that causes the hallucination for one point, the colors of the petals for an additional point, and for the final point, the remedy."

Godric the fireweave tailor cried out in frustration. "No one here knows the remedy," he said, his group nodding along.

Mira couldn't hide the smile on her face as she jotted down the answer.

"Write down what you know," Tilbud reminded them. "That's all that's asked. One round to go!"

Tilbud collected the cards and tallied up the scores. "In first place with a whopping eighteen points is the Underdogs. But second place is close. The Lava Boys have fifteen points. In last place are the Veilians with ten points. This is still anyone's game! Well, ahem, sort of. Let's make this final round one to remember, yeah?"

It was indeed a pub quiz round to remember, one that was neck and neck all the way to the end. Ultimately, the Underdogs took the win with twenty-five points, beating out the Lava Boys's twenty-four.

Brom and the farmers celebrated as the free round came. "Someone can have mine," Mira called over to Sylas.

As often the case when the pub got busy, the next hour at The Old Lamplighter blazed by in a boozy blur of bluster-faced revelry and increasingly crass songs from Bart alongside playful yet batty Mana Lumen demonstrations from Tilbud.

Mira left at some point after telling Sylas she would stop by tomorrow. He offered to walk her home or have Azor do it, but Mira declined. "I know how to handle myself," she told Sylas. "Remember who saved you on your first day in the Underworld, hmmm?"

"Whatever happened to that demon?" Sylas asked as he waved goodbye to Godric and some of the others.

"The one that tried to attack you? My uncle handled it later that day. It was a pretty low-level shape-shifter. I don't know the ranking, but low-level."

"Makes sense."

"Anyway. Good night." Mira left and Sylas turned his attention to Brom the farmer, who was now having what looked like a heated discussion with Tilbud. Upon tuning in, Sylas realized this wasn't the case.

"I'm ready to get rid of it," Brom said, wringing his hands out.

"Your entire farm?"

"Sell it and move to Battersea. The land is bad, or I can't seem to take care of it right. Barely produces anything. Pretty sure there's something in the soil there cursing the place. The other farmers do better than me. Should be easy. It should be bloody easy!" He pointed a finger at Sylas. "Look how well he's figured it out in such a short amount of time. Should be easy."

Tilbud listened for a bit longer before he finally looked up at Brom. "It will work out. Battersea has its own issues, especially when it comes to housing. There are those given deeds, the lucky ones, but the rest usually have to live outside the city center. If you are persistent, and if you perhaps seek the service of a manaseer, I'm certain you'll do just fine."

"I don't mind that at all. Back in the Aurum Kingdom, I never lived in the city center. What's the benefit of that anyway? I like the quiet." Brom threw his hands in the air and turned to the door.

"Don't mind him," Azor told Tilbud once the farmer was gone. "He always gets a little complain-y when he's had a few too many."

"Well, he certainly had that tonight." The archlumen approached the bar and sat. He smiled at Sylas. "How did I do?"

"The quiz went great. Thank you, again, for hosting it."

"You know, there's one thing I'd like to do before I head up to bed."

"What's that?" Sylas asked.

"See your brewing process. I've never seen that before. Over the years, I've found myself fascinated by the classes given to people here in the Underworld. Now, don't look at me like that."

"I'm not looking at you in any way," Sylas said as placed his rag on the bar top.

Tilbud laughed. "I can't steal the power or anything. Even if I could, I don't think I could do this every night. Do you ever close?"

"We haven't closed yet," Sylas said. "I suppose we'll pick a day to close in the future, but right now, I'm fine with the hours."

"I see. Where were we?" Tilbud's eyebrows lifted and lowered. "That's right, brewing and classes. We are all given a unique class. You are a brewer. I am an archlumen. I bet you're wondering if you can change classes."

"Actually, I'm happy as a brewer," Sylas said. "I had a similar job before."

"Really? I always fancied you as a soldier of sorts considering your size."

"I was that too."

"Well, if you did ever want to change or even add a class, you can do that in Battersea. There are lumengineers there who are able to grant additional classes. It isn't cheap, and it will cost you fixed MLus."

"Why are you telling me this?"

"Because you seem like an entrepreneurial fellow. And there may be a farm for sale soon."

"Brom's farm?" Sylas asked. "Why would I want that?"

"If you could get it running, it would increase the MLus you are able to take in daily. You may be able to grow something that would make your ale even more unique, not that it isn't excellent. To be clear, your ale is excellent."

"Thank you. I'm not really here in the Underworld on a power trip." Sylas laughed at this statement. "I guess I should have prefaced that sentence with saying it wasn't my idea to come to the Underworld to begin with."

"But certainly you'd like more power. You'll be able to do so much more with the system."

"If I could do anything with the system, I would ask it to stop warning me of an impending invasion every morning."

Tilbud leaned in closer. "Do what now? An invasion?"

"Every morning I get a message that an invasion is set to happen. This morning it said I had seventy-five days until this invasion. Tomorrow morning, it will likely say I have seventy-four."

"An invasion message? How peculiar."

"No one can figure it out," Azor said, who appeared beside the two of them. She set her tray down on the bar. "I've never heard of anything like it before."

"Nor have I," Tilbud said after a moment of consideration. "But I have heard of strange messages generated by the system."

"What kind of messages?" asked Sylas.

"Warnings, but less intense than the one you are getting daily. A manaseer might be able to interpret the message, but there are not many of them, and none that I know live in these regions. Many end up moving between here and the Chasm."

"People can do that?" Sylas asked. "Why?"

"A manaseer can. Some go to take part in wars that take place in the Chasm. These wars prevent the Chasm from spilling over to the Underworld. It was through the spiritual guidance of manaseers that lumengineers made the Hexveil. They are also the ones who have created the Hexveilan Guard," he said.

"I'm confused. Do I need to find a lumengineer or a manaseer?"

"Lumengineers are easy to find," Tilbud told Sylas. "That is who you would see to change or add a class and look someone up the Book of Shadows. Manaseers are not as easy to find. As for the message itself, I believe you should interpret it at face value until you visit a manaseer. It is likely a warning that the Chasm, or something nefarious from the Chasm, will invade. What else could it be? I would also take it as a sign that you have seventy-five, now almost seventy-four days until this invasion comes to pass." The archlumen grew serious. "I will be here on that day, even if it isn't my weekly pub quiz."

"You want to do one weekly?"

"For all the ale I can drink and room and board for the night out here in the sticks? I would love to. But maybe biweekly. I do get wrapped up into things and I am one to overcommit."

"As long as you give me a day's warning so I can actually tell some people."

"Certainly, a day's warning. I can send a message." Tilbud smoothed his hands together. "Now, brewing. Please, show me your process. It's one of the processes I've never seen before."

Sylas led Tilbud down to the cellar, Patches following after the two. Azor stayed above to sweep up.

"Four ingredients," Sylas said as he came to the table where he made his ale. "Traditionally, you need four ingredients to make ale. They are barley, yeast, hops, and water, which I get from the well out back. If this were the real world and not the, ahem, Underworld, it would be a process that takes weeks. Malting, milling, mashing, lautering, fermentation, maturation, filtration—I could go into detail, but I won't. Now, I just do this."

Sylas went through the process that had become second nature to him. Soon, he filled a cask and then motioned to the others. "I'll do that with them. Strong ale is made from barley, regular ale is made from rye."

"If you don't mind me asking, have you thought about new infusions? I can imagine you could brew some very interesting things with spirit ingredients."

"Ingredients imbued with MLus, right? Mira mentioned them two weeks back. I haven't heard anything about them since."

"Yes, something like that. But other ingredients, different infusions. I'm no brewer, but I'm sure there are things you can do, especially with such a good base."

"I'll have to think about that," Sylas told the archlumen. "It could certainly be something we use for certain nights, like the pub quiz or the meal Azor makes on Wraithsday."

"Fascinating, fascinating, truly. I appreciate the demonstration, and I will have to try to get here for one of the food nights as well." Tilbud rubbed his hands together. "Oftentimes, no, most times, I prefer my life here in the Underworld. It is quite the cozy abyss, if you ask me."

"Yeah?"

"What about you?"

Sylas slowly nodded as a flash of battlefield images came to him. "There's no comparison."

[You have 74 days until the invasion.]

"And so I do," Sylas said as he rolled to his side. He stared down at Patches, who seemed completely exhausted, the pub cat sleeping on his side.

Sylas checked his status.

Name: Sylas Runewulf
Mana Lumens: 2258/2258
Class: Brewer
[Lumen Abilities:]
Flight

As Tilbud had said, Sylas had expended power in learning to fly. This had reduced his overall Mana Lumens, even with the nearly six hundred he had gained through the sale of about thirty strong pints and a good fifty regular. Add to that the five casks he had to brew later, which cost him four hundred Mana Lumens at eighty a cask, Sylas's overall count since the previous day had only grown by a small amount.

But at least they had been topped off. Which was another thing he wanted to ask Tilbud about.

"Morning," Azor said as she floated into the room. "Happy Soulsday."

"How do you always know I'm awake?" he asked her.

"Because we're contracted. Once you wake up, my energy levels lift. Usually, I'm up before you, so I can do things like cook and chase Patches away from the exits."

Upon hearing his name, Patches blinked one eye open, scowled at the fire spirit, yawned, yawned again, stretched his front paws, and went back to sleep.

"Is Tilbud up?"

"He is," Azor said. "He's down at the bar eating scones and drinking a tea that he had me make. I made scones. Did I tell you that?"

"You did not, and thank you." Sylas smiled at the fire spirit. "Thanks for all you do. I couldn't do this without you." Sylas meant this, but he also found it funny when Azor blushed, her fiery face growing cherry red.

"Anyway, we're down here when you're ready." Azor rushed downstairs, leaving Sylas alone in his room with Patches.

"I guess I should go down there," he told Patches as he scratched the back of his ear. The cat immediately started purring. "Rest, buddy."

Soon, Sylas joined Tilbud at the bar. The archlumen wore the same set of purple robes, yet his hat was different, Tilbud now in a small green cap that had intricately detailed flower stitching. Sylas noticed he'd also twisted the ends of his mustache so they arced upward.

"I was just telling Azor here about the hat," he said as he caught Sylas looking at the strange accent piece. "I picked it up in a place far north of here known as Lilihammer."

"Lilihammer," Sylas said. "I've heard that name before."

"Do you know the basic geography of the Underworld?" Tilbud asked. "Because if you don't, I will show you what it looks like with the same power I plan to transfer to you before I depart. I really must get going, you know. But I'm a sucker for a geography lesson."

"The basic geography? I do not," Sylas said as he took a seat.

Azor slid a scone over to him, one baked with dried fruits. Before he could thank her, she also poured some hot tea into a pint glass. This made it difficult to hold, but Sylas was fine with that.

"Actually, before we start, I've been wondering something," Sylas told the archlumen.

"Oh?"

"My MLus are refilled every night."

"They are? That's something I haven't heard of before, at least not without a power that quickens your recharge time."

"Here's the strange thing. It only happens while I sleep here at the pub. When I was in Duskhaven, it didn't happen."

"Yet again something peculiar," Tilbud told him after a long pause. The archlumen clasped his hands together. "You had a deed to the pub when you received it, but we all, or at least those of us who received property, had a deed. So it can't be that."

"It can't?"

"At least to my knowledge, no."

Patches came down the stairs, louder than usual. He saw them seated at the bar and immediately started mewing.

"I'll get you some milk," Sylas said.

"Already did it," Azor told him as she brought a bowl around to Patches.

"Where did you get the cat?" Tilbud asked. "It isn't often that someone new to the Underworld instantly has a familiar."

"He came with the pub."

"Did he now?"

"Is that normal?"

"I don't know if there is a normal here in the Underworld," said the archlumen. "So, he came with a pub. A familiar that came as part of the deed."

"His name wasn't on the deed. He was just here." Sylas remembered that Mira had sensed the cat's presence before Sylas. It seemed like so long ago he was standing a few feet away from where he sat now, wondering how he was going to fix up the place yet still up to the challenge.

"Then that is your answer," Tilbud concluded.

"What is my answer exactly?"

"Patches is the one that is refilling your powers nightly. Your cat is the culprit."

"Patches?" Sylas could barely hide the skepticism on his face.

Azor burst out laughing. "Patches? Sure, he'll fight stuff and he can turn invisible—" she trailed off, her eyes going wide. "Wait. Maybe it is Patches."

"Does he sleep with you?" Tilbud asked Sylas.

"He does."

"Then that will be an easy test. Lock him outside the room and see if your power is topped off overnight. It should increase slightly, it always does when we rest, but see if it is completely refilled."

Sylas ran his hand along his beard as he considered this. "I guess it is worth a shot. But not tonight. We're visiting Duskhaven tomorrow to go to the Finmarket."

"Are you, now? Too bad I'll be gone. Otherwise, I'd invite you over for tea." He squinted at Sylas for a moment. "Now, where were we?"

"Patches? Geography?"

"Ah, Patches. Run a test. Do it on a night that you don't need to brew much. Now, onto geography. Today, as promised, I'm going to teach you a new power. Luckily for both of us, I can use it for our little geography lesson. This power is called Quill, and it works like this." Tilbud's finger illuminated. He traced it through the air with expert precision, soon forming into something that resembled a map. "We are here, Ember Hollow." He touched the map and a dot lit up.

"And this power is called Quill?" Sylas asked. "Magical mapmaking?"

"Not exactly. Quill is an ability that will let you leave a mark in the air, one that you have control over."

"Meaning?"

"Meaning it could be a reminder to you about something, a reminder that only you can see. Let's say you find yourself in a labyrinth for some unknown reason and you want to note the paths you have already traveled. You can use Quill to do this. Let's say you want to leave instructions for Azor here or someone else. Quill can do this as well. The advantage of Quill versus leaving a note is only the person or people you designate are able to see what you have written, or in my case, drawn."

Sylas nodded, impressed. He didn't know exactly how he would use this power, but he could see how it would come in handy in certain situations.

"But we'll get back to Quill. I want to show you the map here. Where do you think the Chasm is?"

"It has to be here," Sylas said as he pointed at a spot west of Ember Hollow. Everything seemed to be east of the village, so this made sense.

"It is, but it is also here." Tilbud tapped a place north of their current location, toward the center of the rough-looking circle he'd drawn. "And this is the northern city I mentioned earlier, Lilihammer." He tapped this location as well and the spot illuminated. "Do you see?"

"So the Chasm is west and north of here?"

"No, the Chasm *surrounds* the Underworld on all sides. This is Battersea." He tapped in a place northeast of Ember Hollow. "And even if it is next to a body of water that appears to be endless, if you were to swim as far east as you possibly could from Battersea, you'd eventually reach the Hexveil as well as a smattering of other small locales."

It dawned on Sylas what Tilbud was explaining to him. "So the Underworld is completely surrounded by the Chasm."

"Even worse, the Underworld exists *within* the Chasm. It is a zone that was carved out long before you or I or anyone we would likely ever meet journeyed to this place. It was carved out for souls that were neither good nor bad."

"Not all souls in the Chasm are bad," Azor told the archlumen. "I'm from there, you know."

"Most elemental spirits hail from either the Chasm or the Celestial Plains, I am aware of this fact. Take no offense by it, and take no offense yourself," he said to Sylas, "for being somewhere between bad and good. We all are, or should I say, *were*."

Sylas grunted a response. "So we're in the middle of the Chasm."

"Yes, precisely. Some don't believe this, but if you travel far enough, you will see that the Underworld is entirely surrounded by the Hexveil, which means that it must exist within the Chasm itself. There is even a pilgrimage that some powerful archlumens will take. They'll fly around the entirety of the Hexveil, thus circling the Underworld."

"Would you consider doing something like that?" asked Sylas.

"Me? No, I'm more of a people person. Not only is that an arduous journey, but it is also a lonely one." He cleared his throat. "Anyway, geography. Never forget we are an island in the depths of hell with heaven gloating above." Tilbud laughed at his own statement. "That sounded darker than it should have been."

"It's not a bad island."

"No, it is not," Tilbud said, "but the knowledge of this fact does make me wonder more about your invasion message. If it is a warning about an invasion from the Chasm, where will the demons break through? I suppose you have seventy-five—"

"Seventy-four."

"Right. Seventy-four days to figure it out. Anyway, Quill. I'll leave you with this ability and be on my way. It shouldn't be very hard to use, and certainly not like flying. Let me see your finger."

Sylas placed a hand on the bar.

"I meant for you to point your finger at me."

Sylas did just that with the finger on his right hand. A warmth came over him, one that accumulated into a swirling golden glow at the end of his fingertip.

"It is all here," Tilbud said as he tapped his temple. "Whatever you want to write, just start writing. If it is a message for you alone, then your scribblings will only be viewable by you. If it is for others, then only those who you designate will see it. This won't, however, have a prompt or anything. It's all instinctual. Try it."

Sylas lifted his hand into the air and wrote a message for both Azor and

Tilbud. *Thank you.* His words didn't glow as brightly as Tilbud's had, but it was bright enough to read even with the light coming through the pub's windows.

"Good, and you're very welcome." Tilbud stood. He grabbed his bag, which had been resting on the barstool next to him. He tipped his strange hat at Azor and Sylas. "I'll be back later this week. You'll get the message when the time comes."

"How?"

"An advanced form of Quill. I've already left the message, actually. Did I mention you can schedule messages with Quill? No? I must have forgotten. Anyway, you can, and you should."

"I'll try to do that as well," Sylas said.

"And you'll practice Flight?"

"I was planning to do so after you left."

"Good, but do so alone. As I said before, early on, it helps not having a safety net. Later, you and the fire spirit can flit around in the air to your heart's content." The archlumen grinned at the two of them. "Azor, Sylas. It has been a pleasure. I await my return to The Old Lamplighter."

CHAPTER TWENTY-ONE

B-RANK

Sylas lowered to the ground and let out a deep breath. It was strange how quickly he went from hovering to standing. Over the last several hours, he had practiced flying in the forest near Ember Hollow. Sylas had kept low at first, but soon found that he could go increasingly higher with good control.

"It definitely burns a lot of MLus," he said as he took a quick look at his status.

Name: Sylas Runewulf
Mana Lumens: 1851/2258
Class: Brewer
[Lumen Abilities:]
Flight
Quill

"A lot."

For a moment, Sylas felt like finding a nice patch of grass under a tree and simply staring up at the heavens for a while. Literally. The Celestial Plains above emitted golden beams over the Underworld that were consistently enchanting. But he also knew relaxing here was a bad idea, especially this close to the Chasm.

After all, he didn't have his mace with him.

Sylas remembered the map that Tilbud had conjured out of thin air and the explanation that followed. It was wild to think that the Underworld existed *within* the Chasm. This thought reiterated in the back of Sylas's mind that he himself had to do something about this impending invasion.

Sylas liked it here.

He *really* liked it in the Underworld, and he didn't want to see it go away. He also didn't want to see the Underworld torn apart by war, especially one where demons were on the other side.

Sylas had received the invasion message for a reason, and he planned to act on it.

Things were pretty slow that night at The Old Lamplighter.

Brom and the farmers never stopped by, nor did Godric and his friends. There were a few new faces, however, people that Sylas wasn't familiar with. He was cordial as always, but this new group didn't seem too keen on opening up.

"At least they're buying drinks," Azor said as the door opened and Mira stepped into the pub, which drew everyone's attention as it often did.

The first thing the silver-eyed apothecary did was crouch as Patches came running. She scooped the pub cat into her arms and held him like a baby as he purred.

"I was wondering when you'd stop by," Sylas told Mira once she took a seat at the bar. This was increasingly becoming her favorite stool, the one right at the end of the bar, closest to the door. Surprising Sylas, the door popped open again and Leowin, the Cinderpeak constable, stepped in.

"Sylas," the man said as he shifted his dark cape back over his shoulders. Leowin looked like he'd recently had a haircut, his silver hair even closer to his head. "One ale. Regular." Leowin joined the group that had come in earlier, most of whom didn't seem too keen on the constable's appearance.

Sylas poured a regular ale and let it sit for a moment. "You want one too?" he asked Mira.

"Not tonight. I can't drink every night, you know."

"I get it," Sylas said.

She continued, "But this is becoming my favorite place to hang out. Especially when there is entertainment."

"Like the pub quiz last night?"

"That was fun." Her eyes lit up. "Oh! I meant to ask: What Lumen Ability did Tilbud teach you?"

"I'm glad you asked." Sylas quickly ran his finger through the air as he wrote the word *This*. Only Mira could see the letters, which soon fizzled out. He still didn't quite understand how this sort of command worked, but like the brewing process, it all felt instinctual.

Mira leaned forward. "He taught you Quill?"

"You know this power?"

"It is one I've been meaning to get, but it isn't cheap."

"How much do you think it is worth?"

"I never really think of powers that way, but I believe my archlumen told me it would cost somewhere around five thousand MLus."

Sylas nodded, impressed. "I did not expect that. Although I don't quite know how I'm going to use it yet."

Azor approached. "Hey, Mira. Is the pint ready?" she asked Sylas.

"Ready."

"Oops, I mean they want a full round. The whole table and the constable."

"Right, I'll pour those up now." Sylas poured up five more pints. He caught Leowin giving him the side-eye and ignored it. Ale needed a moment to sit.

The word that he had written in the air in golden mana slowly dissipated as Mira told Sylas about her day, which mostly consisted of helping some people she knew in Cinderpeak and finally delivering a vision supplement to a man named Andrew Foxsmart. "Never a dull moment," she said as Azor brought the pints over to Leowin and his group.

Later, Anders entered The Older Lamplighter, the carpenter turning a shade redder once he saw that Leowin was in the pub. He quickly took a seat at the bar.

"Don't worry about him," Sylas told the carpenter. "You did your time, right?"

"I did," Anders said as Sylas began to pour him up a pint. "Ashen Hold. It was terrible."

The night unfolded at a leisurely pace, but Sylas was fine with that. Mira was there, they were busy enough, and it seemed like he would at least earn back the MLus he had spent flying earlier until the door swung open and Cody burst in, the youngest militiaman's eyes wide with terror.

"We need you," he told Sylas breathlessly. Cody spotted Leowin. "You too. I've been"—he sucked in a deep breath—"I've been sent to get whoever I can. You too," he said to Anders, whom he apparently recognized. "Tiberius sent me. They have cornered a B-Rank Eldritch Horror. But we can't do it ourselves."

"You can't?" asked Leowin, his words laced with urgency.

Cody brought a hand to the back of his neck. "Not this one. We need help."

Leowin quickly spoke to the guests surrounding him, letting them know he would be departing.

"I'm going too." Mira pressed away from the bar and a golden glow cycled around her hands. "That's my uncle out there."

―――――

Sylas grabbed the fireweave shield and the mace that Godric had given him and joined the others outside. "You're in charge," he told Patches, who stood in the center of the pub, alarmed. As soon as Sylas closed the door, Patches immediately turned to the cat door, which Sylas had left open.

"Ready," Sylas told the others.

"We need to run by my place as well," Mira said. "I can grab some supplies."

"We could get more weapons there," Cody said.

Mira shook her head and gestured for everyone to follow her. "I don't have access to my uncle's armory. He keeps it locked."

"I'm not going to suggest we smash our way in," Anders chimed in, "but that's always a possibility."

Even with the tension, Sylas almost laughed at Anders's suggestion, especially with how he had once done the same thing to The Old Lamplighter. "How bad is this demon?" Sylas asked Cody. "What should we expect?"

"This was supposed to be a D-Rank Shifter. Nothing too big. Instead..." He swallowed hard. "I've never seen something like this before."

"A B-Rank Eldritch Horror," Leowin said, repeating what Cody had announced earlier. "As to what we should expect, we should expect one hell of a fight," the constable told the group once they neared Mira's home.

"Wait here. This will only take me a moment." The apothecary produced a key and disappeared into her home, leaving Sylas, Anders, Leowin, and Cody waiting outside. Sylas felt his tattoo warm as Azor took shape.

"We need to hurry," she said. "I've seen these things before. They grow stronger the longer they are beyond the Hexveil. No time to grab more weapons. That won't help us here."

"It won't?" Cody asked the fire spirit. "Then how?"

"We just have to keep hitting it until the Horror tires, and then the demon hunter will be able to handle it, Mira's uncle."

"Tiberius," Leowin said.

"Yes, him, the short guy." Azor used her fiery hand to estimate his height.

This statement bothered Leowin, but he didn't say anything as Mira came out of her home with a satchel under her arm. She also had a mace for Anders, the only one who wasn't armed. "I keep this one in my room, just in case." The carpenter gladly took it, gauged its weight in his hands, and nodded to let them know he was ready.

"Let's go," Cody said. "Those that can fly should go ahead. Follow this." He produced a glowing orb. "The rest of us can go on foot."

Azor rose into the air, Mira and Leowin did so as well. This left Sylas, Cody, and Anders still standing.

"Come on, Sylas," Azor said.

"Right." He floated up to join them. "You coming?" he called down to Anders.

"I can't fly, but I'm plenty fast."

Cody hovered. "In that case, you can follow the orb."

The orb lowered in front of Anders. He gave the group the thumbs-up. "Will do. And don't any of you count me out. I'll get there."

It soon became apparent that Sylas had a long way to go before he could be considered a true flier. Leowin was an expert, and Cody and Mira seemed well versed in the skill. Mira's powers made sense, considering she'd been there for a while. Sylas assumed Cody had gained his through being part of the militia. Azor was a natural, the fire spirit whisking around them as the group made a beeline toward the fight.

But Sylas could barely keep up.

"Not bad," Mira told Sylas. He couldn't tell if she was joking or not. At the moment, he was flying with his head forward as if he were bending over, which was the only way for him to keep their pace.

"I'm terrible at this!" he called back to her.

"You've only had the skill for a day or so. On my second day, I could barely hover. But you'll get it." To demonstrate what she meant, Mira did a quick spin and rushed ahead to catch Leowin and Cody.

Sylas kept his slower pace even as he wished he could go faster. He didn't want to crash in front of the others and, if there was a big battle ahead, he had to be prepared. Leowin and Cody arced toward the ground, Mira following. Azor waited for Sylas, the fire spirit illuminating the sky as he caught up with her.

"We have to tire the Horror out," she said, fear in her voice. A trail of flames whisked down her shoulders and to her arms. "It's the only way."

"So hit it with all we have?"

"Hit it with all we have."

Sylas landed on the outskirts of the fight to get his bearings. He found Mira, who was charging up a blast of mana, the kind she'd used against the Shifter Demon that had first attacked Sylas over two weeks ago.

Leowin and Cody stormed ahead, joining Tiberius, Henry, Duncan, and several other militiamen that Sylas didn't recognize.

It was dark, but the scene was still visible.

Night in the Underworld wasn't the same kind of night Sylas had grown up with. It was more of a twilight, the glow of the Celestial Plains painting the world in a mystic blue hue. It was in this cerulean shroud of not quite bitter night that Sylas saw the B-Rank Eldritch Horror.

The creature's body, if Sylas could call it a body, was covered in dozens of ferocious mouths that pulsed in its pitch-black flesh, the monster's shape constantly shifting. Each of these mouths seemed to function independently, gnashing, laughing, shrieking, and salivating as they attacked Tiberius and his men. The Eldritch Horror had multiple appendages, its arms ending in menacing razor-sharp talons. The claws snapped open and shut, cutting through the fabric of reality and leaving a sickly golden hue in their wake as they swatted at Tiberius and his men.

Whoosh!

Mira's opening shot struck the Horror near what Sylas would guess was a shoulder. This forced it back and allowed Tiberius to hit it again. The myriad mouths all roared in pain as the Eldritch Horror staggered backward, the caterwaul maddening.

"Mira, my men!" Tiberius shouted to her. "Backup is here, lads!"

Mira rushed toward the militiamen on the ground, those who had already been wounded. Sylas moved forward with her and joined Cody. The pair attacked some of the Horror's claws, while Leowin beat at the creature with his mana-powered baton.

"We have to tire it!" Sylas shouted for anyone who could hear.

"You think I don't know how to kill an Eldritch Horror?" Tiberius cried.

Azor flew over the demon hunter, just inches away from the top of Tiberius's head, and collided with their enemy. The burst of flames that followed forced all of them backward as tendrils of fire flared around them to the smell of sulfur and smoldering resin.

"Tell your blasted fire spirit to be careful of the trees!" Tiberius hissed at Sylas.

Rather than listen to him, Sylas went on the attack. He dove to avoid the Horror's next strike. Back on his feet, Sylas put everything he had into delivering a hit to its midsection. The monster's numerous mouths went from seething and screeching to moaning and groaning as more strikes came in, the biggest being from Duncan.

"That's it!" Sylas called to the large man.

"Oi!" Henry shouted to Duncan as the Horror's claws came inches away from his face. "Watch your head, mate!"

Leowin sent power into his baton and threw it into the air, the constable's weapon spinning several times before it struck the Horror, causing the beast to slip to the side. The weapon returned to his hand, smoking.

"Keep it up, keep it up!" Tiberius swung his mace, his attack amplified by Mana Lumens that produced a flash of brilliance that momentarily blinded Sylas and the others.

"You'll be fine," Mira told the militiaman she had just partially healed with a balm. The flash her uncle had caused was so bright she looked away, shielding her face with an arm.

Once the lingering mana died down, Mira saw Sylas charging toward the Eldritch Horror seemingly without a care in the world. Or was it a fully-fledged care, Sylas showing his true nature, the battle-hardened man who was accustomed to sacrificing himself for the sake of others?

He brought his fireweave shield up to take the brunt of an attack, which protected Cody, allowing the younger man to get away.

A flash to Mira's right caught her attention.

She gasped as Anders reached the battle and struck the Horror with such alacrity that he forced the monster into a row of trees that soon fell, a long path ripped into the ground, roots and soil filling the air.

"He's that fast?" Mira asked herself as she moved to another of Tiberius's men.

Anders answered her question with his next attack as he bolted around the Eldritch Horror, the creature turning increasingly mad as it tried to track Anders and cut him down.

"More, more!" Tiberius shouted. "Everything you've got, lads!"

Sylas and the militiamen used Anders's distraction to pummel the Eldritch Horror with attacks. They surrounded the monster, the group taking turns, and using its confusion to their advantage as they continued to beat it down.

The sound of sickening strikes and terrified wails was soon replaced by a primordial rumble as the Eldritch Horror tried to portal away.

"Not today, you don't!" With a guttural shout, Tiberius thrust his hands forward and released a concentrated ball of mana that whisked forward like a meteor. The air filled with a thunderous roar as the ball of mana struck the Eldritch Horror.

For a moment, Sylas and all those that gathered, held their breaths.

It appeared as if the Horror had *fully absorbed* the ball of mana. But then its body began to glow. A shock wave erupted from the point of impact, the explosion sending discs of wind through the trees around them.

Tiberius stood, panting, a faint golden smoke coming off his hands. He loomed over the creature's body, which was slowly melting away.

Sylas didn't like the man, but in that moment he saw everything he needed to know about Tiberius to understand that he was a formidable opponent.

He saw Tiberius on the battlefield, the kind of lord commander that Sylas would have feared as a member of the Royal Guard. There were those who stayed back with their advisors, with the noblemen and the higher ranked officials.

Then there were those who got their hands dirty.

Tiberius was the type to get his hands dirty.

After a deep breath out, Tiberius turned to the others. "We'll divide the MLus for this one evenly. Good work, everyone."

"Not so fast," Sylas said.

Tiberius shot an angry glare over to him, a glare that softened once he heard what Sylas said next.

"Once we're ready, everyone is free to join me at the pub. Drinks on me. Let's close this night out with something a little less terrifying. What do you say?"

The militiamen murmured, the group ultimately looking to their leader.

Tiberius smiled. "I say, that's a grand idea. Good job, all of you." He cleared his throat and produced his version of a smile. "Cheers."

The Old Lamplighter thrived again that night, although the light wasn't on out front. This was a private affair, meant for those that had helped kill the B-Rank Eldritch Horror. The celebration began with a toast from Leowin.

"The Chasm wants what it can't have," the constable told those that had gathered. As Sylas looked around the room, he noticed someone was missing.

"Azor," he said quietly as Leowin continued his toast.

"Yeah?" the fire spirit asked.

"Have you seen Patches?"

She looked from the window to the cat door. "We must have forgotten to bolt it."

Sylas grimaced. "Well, leave it unlocked tonight. Maybe we aren't going to be able to prevent him from going out. He is a cat, after all, he likes to explore."

Leowin cleared his throat and continued, "Ahem. As I was saying, we all play a part in defending the Underworld, even if we aren't all members of the Esteemed Coalition of Ember Hollow Defenders." He raised his pint. "Here is to your militia, and here is to our most recent hunt. May the Hexveil protect us all."

Some of the militiamen loosened up after their first pint.

Others, like Tiberius and Henry, barely touched the pint they had been given and maintained their composure throughout the rest of the night. Mira, who sat at the bar, was a bit less talkative than usual, likely due to the presence of her uncle.

Anders, who had really helped with his speedy attacks, was the first to leave that night, the man stumbling out after bidding farewell to Sylas.

Tiberius followed, and Mira joined him.

"Good luck tomorrow," she told Sylas in reference to his planned trip to Duskhaven to procure a fish supplier.

"Thanks!" he called to her. Sylas almost wanted to lob an offhand remark at Tiberius to let him know the next time he'd like Sylas to swoop in and save the day. He almost did, too. Ultimately, Sylas thought otherwise. Their relationship was already a bit rocky.

Leowin and most of the militiamen cleared out, leaving Cody and Duncan behind to finish their pints. "We appreciate your help earlier," Cody told Sylas as he chugged what was left of his ale. "Glad you were able to rally the troops."

"I did what I could do. And thanks to both of you as well. I couldn't have taken those cinderspiders out with your help."

"Your leg is clearly better," Duncan said, referring to where Sylas had been bitten. The big man burped and excused himself.

"What can I say? Mira works wonders."

"That she does," Cody said.

Once everyone was gone, Sylas turned to Azor. "I'll head down and get brewing."

"Should I go out and look for Patches?"

"He'll be fine. The cat is going to do what the cat is going to do." Sylas brought the empty casks downstairs to the cellar. As he set everything up, he went over some of the numbers for the day.

He did the math in his head.

Sylas had received 250 Mana Lumens from the hunt, but he'd spent just under 300 flying around. He hadn't sold a lot that night, just a handful of strong pints. And he'd given away nearly a cask and a half of regular ale. In the end, he would have to brew one strong ale cask and three regular ale casks, which would cost him 320 Mana Lumens.

Sylas started up the process, and once he was done, he checked to confirm everything.

Name: Sylas Runewulf
Mana Lumens: 1897/2258
Class: Brewer
[Lumen Abilities:]
Flight
Quill

He would have almost broken even for the day had it not been for the Eldritch Horror hunt. Then again, without the hunt, he could have stayed open later and sold more. Plus, there was the free ale he'd given out.

"Not a bad day at all," he told Azor as he headed up to bed.

"Do you want to test Patches tonight?"

"What do you mean?" he asked.

"I mean how your power keeps refilling here at the pub. You can shut your door, and I can make sure he doesn't get in. We can even lock him out for the night."

"We could," Sylas said as he brought his hand to his beard. "But let's not. Not tonight, anyway. We need all the MLus we can get for our trip to Duskhaven tomorrow. Let's definitely perform that little experiment this week. I'd like to know how my powers are being replenished. It's fine if it is Patches doing it, but I don't want to exhaust him."

"What do you mean?" Azor asked.

"Sometimes, not every morning, but some mornings, he looks pretty bad. You know, like he's had a rough night."

Azor glanced to the back door of the pub and crossed her arms over her chest. "Why do I get the feeling he's going to have one of those nights tonight?"

Sylas waved her concern away and started back up the stairs.

Patches waited until he was certain the fire spirit wouldn't come out. For a moment, he wondered if she'd stopped caring about him. She hadn't even peeked her head out, nor had she floated around like she usually did, calling him by name.

But then he assumed the two had finally understood how important his task was, especially as the caretaker of the Tavernly Realm.

Patches puffed his chest out and approached the well.

He circled it, sniffing the air. Patches could sense the dark influence coming from below and had thought up a new way to investigate it.

After stepping away from the well, Patches began licking himself. He started with his tail and worked his way as far up his back as he could. He licked his legs, and once he had enough, Patches hacked up a hairball.

He animated this hairball and sent it in.

Rather than plop down to the water below, the hairball slicked down the side wall of the well collecting data. Patches's ears twitched. Controlling it without being able to see it wasn't easy, yet he managed. Just as he suspected, there was a new opening along the side of the well, just a few feet above the waterline.

The opening was large. Patches slicked the hairball around it, his eyes closed as he monitored the exploratory mission.

It's a tunnel.

This was the tunnel that held the source of the evil, and it was certainly where the demonic spirit he'd seen was hiding. Patches felt a rumble. This wasn't felt by his own body; rather, it was sensed through the hairball.

Something was coming. His hairball returned to the top of the well and scooted its way back toward Patches. It was soon trampled by a horde of demonic mice that came tearing out of the well.

But Patches was ready.

He took his largest form and activated his auditory power, which froze many of the mice in place, confusing them. Patches went on the attack, slaughtering the mice left and right. Those that were eventually able to move scattered. Something happened as they did so.

As Patches leaped for one of them, his body split and a *second* pub cat of equal girth and courage lunged for the other mouse.

His replicant killed the rodent and whisked back toward Patches, as if he had inhaled his sudden clone.

That was strange.

This was the only thought Patches gave his newfound power. He was familiar with the way these kinds of skills worked. They came to him in the heat of the moment, a moment like this, one in which he was doing everything he felinely could to protect the pub.

Patches's form never split again as he finished off what was left of the mice. The final rodent to come at him, one that was closer in size to the demonic rats that he'd faced before, was thwarted by Patches's hairball.

It dropped onto the mouse just as it was preparing to fight Patches and suffocated the rodent.

Patches was left with a backyard filled with dead mice.

He thought about trying to incinerate them, but he figured the big man would be proud to see what he'd done. Before heading back in, Patches sniffed his hairball to see if it had picked up anything else in its exploratory mission. Yet again, he noticed the same scent that he'd smelled on the big man after he was bit by an insect.

What could it mean?

After considering this for a moment, Patches grabbed one of the mice and snuck back inside using the cat door. He headed upstairs and deposited the dead mouse at the foot of the big man's door.

From there, he hopped onto the bed and sat for a moment looking at his loyal subject, the one who had brought so much life to the pub.

It worried Patches that the big man didn't know that something was happening beneath the ground.

The tunnel in the well.

It wasn't that big yet, but soon the tunnel would be large enough for a human to fit through.

What was making it? And how were they doing it? Was it the demonic spirit Patches had encountered? He shook his head. He'd sensed these kinds of spirits before, but they generally weren't able to do something like dig a big hole. So it probably wasn't that. Then what was it?

Patches would have to keep an eye on the well and investigate it further.

Maybe once he figured out how to fully control the replica he'd made of himself, Patches could send his replica down into the well and monitor it from above.

One last thing to do.

Patches turned to the big man and released Mana Lumens into the air until he felt light-headed. He staggered a bit and dropped right next to the big man's body, where he fell into a deep Dream Nap, as he called it.

The Tavernly Realm was secure for another night.

───────

[You have 73 days until the invasion.]

Sylas grumbled at the text in the blue box. As he scratched the back of Patches's ears, he checked his status to find that his Mana Lumens had been topped off.

"Was it you, buddy?" he asked Patches.

As she did every morning, Azor burst into Sylas's lofty bedroom after hearing his voice. She did a complete spin, the fire licking off her shoulders turning into blue wisps. "Happy Moonsday."

She stopped moving, and waited for the smile she got every morning from Sylas. There was always a twinkle in his blue eyes upon seeing her. Azor hadn't asked him much about his life before he was dead, but she knew he'd been a soldier. She also knew that he was happy here, content, which made her feel the same.

It was funny how a simple grin could reflect all of this.

"Duskhaven," Sylas said with a yawn. "The Finmarket. I'm guessing we'll have to pay to portal there because we'll certainly be paying to portal back. But that's fine. Do you have a list of what we need?"

"It's here." The fire spirit tapped the side of her face where her temple would be.

"Where all good lists should be."

"Exactly. I've also whipped up something for breakfast. We might as well get some new food and spices at the market. It will give me some variety. And before you say, 'you don't have to cook for me,' I like cooking, and I'm up anyway."

"I didn't say anything," Sylas told her, showing the fire spirit his hands. "Any Patches activity last night?"

"Actually, there is something. But I figured you'd want to see it. Also, he left you a dead mouse but I already took care of it."

Sylas sniffed the air. "I don't smell anything."

"It was early," she assured him. "Come with me."

Azor waited outside the door for Sylas to get ready. Once he was fully dressed, she led him to the back door. The fire spirit stopped and turned to him.

"What's going on?"

"You have to see this to believe it." She opened the back door to reveal numerous dead mice in various states of butchery.

"Patches did all this?" Sylas ran his hand over his mouth, gawking at the sight. "He's a monster." Sylas laughed. "That cat is a monster."

Azor floated over the mice, her gloved arms drooping as she counted them. "There are twenty. Plus the one I took care of upstairs."

Sylas grabbed a shovel that leaned against the side of the pub.

"You're going to bury them?"

"What else—wait, that's right. I'll put them in a pile and let you do the rest." Sylas returned the shovel to its spot. "He was protecting the pub. So I can't knock him for that. Maybe it's fine if we leave the back door open at night so he can go out and hunt."

"You'd call this hunting?"

"Good point," he told her. "This is a bit more than your typical hunt."

"This is slaughter."

"It is. And I'd rather him do that out here than let these mice into the pub. That's the last thing we need."

"Agreed," Azor told him once he'd gathered all the rodents. "Your food is at the bar. I'll handle this, and we'll go to Duskhaven." The fire on her arms flared. "I'm looking forward to a trip!"

CHAPTER TWENTY-TWO

FINMARKET

Sylas was presented with a list of places he could portal to. In seeing the list, he was reminded that he needed to make good with the Pub Alliance in Battersea so he could sell pints to the Welcome Inn, located at the foot of the Shadowstone Mountains.

- **Cinderpeak**
- **Hexveil - Ember Hollow**
- **Seedlands**
- **Shadowstone Mountains**
- **Duskhaven**

Sylas selected Duskhaven and was prompted again.

[**Transfer 50 Mana Lumens to use the portal? Y/N?**]

"Yes," he said begrudgingly, an appropriate response for anyone forced to pay a toll.

"Here goes," Azor said with excitement.

They appeared in Duskhaven, Sylas instantly wishing he'd set their trip up as an active quest. "Can I still do that?" he asked himself, unable to remember the exact path to the Finmarket.

"Do what?" asked Azor, who was tucked away in the tattoo on his arm.

"I'll just ask someone." Sylas saw a man pushing a wheelbarrow. "Excuse me. I'm looking for the Finmarket."

The man gave Sylas an *Are you really that dumb?* look as he gestured to a sign pointing toward the market.

Sylas didn't say anything and moved on.

"The locals are certainly friendly," Azor noted.

"I might have deserved that," Sylas told her.

"He could have at least been nice about it."

"You're right, he could have. But it's fine. People have bad days and they don't know how to handle them."

"It's still morning."

He shrugged. "People have bad mornings and they don't know how to handle them."

"How do you do it?"

"Do what?" Sylas asked her as he followed a flagstone path until he reached a large dirt road, one that was brimming with activity. From people moving supplies to small restaurants, there was a bit of everything here.

Sylas recalled seeing it last time with Mira, but he hadn't paid as much attention as he did now. That, or he was just seeing it for a second time and more details were popping out to him.

"You're so nice, forgiving of people. Even when you shouldn't be."

"I don't think I am."

"You are."

"Am I?" he asked, trying not to seem like he was talking to himself. His fire tattoo was covered; Sylas had yet to see anyone wandering around with an elemental spirit.

"Maybe it comes from your past?"

"My past? What do you mean?"

"As a soldier, and the fact that you grew up in a pub. You were probably forced to be social at a young age."

Sylas thought back to his youth. He had helped his father serve guests and do various pub tasks ever since he could remember. As a soldier, he'd been forced to get along with different people from different backgrounds. "Maybe you're right."

"I just find it admirable, that's all. There are people you've dealt with since I've known you that I would have likely torched by now."

"Yeah?" Sylas asked, imaging Azor growing her purple devil horns.

"Leowin, Tiberius, the guy that just gave you a dumb look. Even Anders for breaking into the pub."

Sylas grinned. "I might still need you to *torch* Tiberius and Leowin, as you say. Henry too. He still seems skeptical of me. At least the other militiamen I've met are coming around. We're here."

He stopped in front of the entrance to a grand building, one that was hard to size up due to the clutter of businesses around the river that passed through Duskhaven. The structure was constructed of different buildings seemingly pressed together, their outer facades the only way to distinguish differences. Viewing it from the front reminded Sylas of looking at a bookshelf filled with books, how the individual spines and shapes formed a unique pattern in a lineup.

He entered the market, and was immediately greeted by a buzz of activity, one coupled with the briny pungence of fresh fish and various spices. The Finmarket felt larger than it had been during his last visit.

"It's wild in here," Azor said. He could feel her influence a bit closer to the side of his head now. Azor was all around him like a fine mist, yet he couldn't feel her heat and he knew others couldn't see her.

"I have an idea." Sylas ran his hand through the air and made an X using his Quill power. "I'll mark places along the way so only you and I can see them. We'll use this to get back and also to navigate the booths." Sylas had a burlap sack that he'd picked up the last time he visited the Cinderpeak Market. He looked down at it. "I hope this is large enough."

"It will be fine," Azor told him. Sylas moved along and stopped first at a vegetable market, where he found several booths. He noted the prices of some of the peas and potatoes, but also checked other root vegetables like carrots. "Good. I'll come back and get everything all together," he said after making his marks.

"I didn't see any lemons. They had those in the Chasm but that's fine. Maybe we can find some in Battersea. You're still planning to go there this week, right?"

"I am. But I want to make sure I have enough MLus to actually get what I need there," Sylas said, referring to supplies and however much it would cost to view the Book of Shadows. He rubbed his hands together. "What now?"

"We'll need more flour, oil, baking powder, and spices. And we already have the ale for the batter. I have the perfect recipe. Trust me."

"I trust you," Sylas told the fire spirit. They headed toward the cooking supply section of the market, where he also used Quill to note prices and take notes in the air. While this would have looked strange where Sylas was from, no one seemed to notice him at all. He reached the fishmonger section of the market and was immediately overwhelmed.

"There is a lot here," Azor said, "but luckily, we just need some whitefish. Try to find whitefish and we'll want someone who can deliver it. What's that there?" she asked as Sylas came to a man standing in front of a table of fish, which were surrounded by bottles of sauce that he'd packaged in clay jars.

"What's this?" Sylas asked the fishmonger.

"That? It's a sauce for the fish. A bit tangy. It's made from garlic, egg yolk, vinegar, and oil. Plus a few ingredients I can't tell you about on the account that it is my special recipe and everyone here knows it." The man pointed a crooked finger at the other fishmongers. "They've tried before to replicate it but they can't. The bastards."

"Do you have a name for it?"

"Sure, Tartar sauce. Named after me. I'm Corlin Tartar." The fishmonger, who wore a pair of dirty overalls, grinned at Sylas, half his teeth missing. His beard, which frayed outward from his face, was bib-like in nature. There was a small cap on his head, one made of leather. This matched Corlin's vest, which had lures and other fishhooks affixed to it.

"Tartar sauce, huh?"

"That's what I call it. But I'll let the sauce do the talking." He motioned to a piece of cold fish on a plate. A bowl of the sauce sat next to the fish. "Grab a slice and dip it in." As Sylas did as instructed, he noticed that Corlin sold whitefish as well.

"Let me know how it tastes," Azor reminded Sylas. "I can't eat, but I do know the flavors your kind prefers."

Sylas took a bite of the fish with the sauce. His eyes widened immediately. It was indeed tangy, the hint of vinegar giving way to something that was creamy and unique. There was a bright, citrusy after-tang that left his mouth feeling refreshed as well. "This is amazing."

"I know it is," Corlin Tartar said.

"I'll tell you what," Sylas leaned in a bit closer, prepared to make a deal, "I'm looking for a fish supplier for my pub."

"A pub, huh?"

"In Ember Hollow, a place called The Old Lamplighter. I have a fire spirit, she's here with me now, who is an excellent chef. She's planning a recipe with—"

"Fried fish and chips," Azor told Sylas. "Fish-and-chips."

"Fish and chips, both fried. And this sauce would go perfectly with it."

"This sauce and fried fish?" Corlin Tartar puckered his lips. "That sounds like it would be fantastic."

"It would. Let's work out a delivery and we'll exclusively use this sauce." Sylas's mouth watered. "I can taste it now."

Corlin Tartar glanced down at his fish and the glass containers of his special sauce. "I think this is doable," he finally said. "Let's talk MLus."

Sylas ended up spending three hundred Mana Lumens to secure the fish delivery for this Wraithsday and next week, plus the other supplies that Azor needed. It wasn't a bad haul by any means, and he was certain they could use the

Wraithsday Feast to quickly earn back their costs. He now carried the supplies in the burlap sack and he had a few of the fish as well for Azor to fry up as tests.

"And all food sales are going to you," Sylas reminded Azor. "You really helped out last week when I was in a pinch, and I appreciate that."

"I can't take them all," she said, the fire spirit's voice now at the back of his head.

"That was our agreement."

"I'll make too much."

"Then make them and if I ever need MLus, loan me some."

"I don't want you to have to pay me back."

"That's how loans usually work," Sylas reminded her as they reached the exit of the market.

"Maybe I could be like a bank of MLus and if there's ever something we really need, like really really need, I could get it."

"And you have how many now?"

"I don't have any. Technically, I could use some of yours but I haven't had to yet. I almost did in our battle, but didn't have to. I'd use more if we were out causing trouble."

"Causing trouble? Are we not adventurous enough?" Sylas transferred the bag of supplies to his other shoulder. He looked for a sign this time and saw one that pointed to the Duskhaven portal.

"We are certainly adventurous."

"That we are," Sylas said, not wanting to mention the invasion message. If anything, the closer they got toward that ill-fated date, the more adventurous things would become.

He could sense this.

In just over two weeks, Sylas's life had changed to a point that he would hardly recognize his old self, the war-torn soldier now living a new life as the owner of a growing business, one that he loved.

Things could be radically different two and half months from now. And he needed to start thinking more about that date, whatever the invasion may be.

His jaw set as he approached the portal. Sylas was glad that Azor didn't say anything about this as he selected Ember Hollow and paid the fifty Mana Lumen fee to portal back home.

As soon as they arrived at the pub, Azor got started on some of the side dishes for a test run of the fish-and-chips. That was two days from now, which meant they had plenty of time to prepare.

Sylas left the pub and journeyed toward the forest outside of Ember Hollow, where he found the same meadow he'd trained in with Tilbud. Focusing his power, Sylas hovered up above the tree line and began to swirl around.

Flying felt different this time. He felt more used to it, like he was learning to swim and simply floating in a lake and enjoying the nice day. That was one thing he appreciated about the Underworld. The weather was always perfect.

Mira had appeared by the time Sylas arrived back at The Old Lamplighter, the apothecary seated at the bar.

"It smells good," Sylas said.

"It smells like fish," she told him. "Patches already had his share."

Sylas looked over to the windowsill to find Patches sleeping on his side, his belly distended.

"How much did he have?"

Mira laughed. "I think Azor is trying to get Patches to like her so . . . a lot. He had a lot."

"Ready?" Azor called up from the cellar.

Sylas took a seat at the bar just as the fire spirit zipped up the stairs with two plates. The plates had fried fish on them, chips, and mashed peas. Test meals. There was also a small dollop of the sauce that Corlin Tarter had given them. He would deliver more of his Tartar sauce with the rest of the fish in two days, which he explained would keep the pub from smelling.

"Let me know what you think," Azor said as she leaned forward on the bar and cradled her chin with her fireweave gloves.

Sylas took his first bite and closed his eyes.

It was perfect.

The outer layer of the fish was crispy, the inside soft and warm. The chips were cooked to perfection and flavored with salt, pepper, and a dash of paprika. The peas were perfect and the sauce brought everything together with its tang.

"I love it," Mira said, who was already working on her third bite of fish.

"Really?" Azor pressed away from the bar.

"You've outdone yourself here," Sylas told her with his mouth full. "I wish you could taste this."

"I wish I could too, but if you two are enjoying it, then I am happy."

Patches hopped up onto the bar, the cat suddenly turning visible. He took a piece of the fried fish from Sylas's plate, turned invisible, and hopped back down.

"Hey—" Sylas turned around to look for Patches and started to laugh.

"See?" Azor asked. "I told you he can turn invisible."

Mira couldn't stop laughing. "I can't believe he stole your fish."

Sylas groaned playfully. "I guess I'll have to ask the chef if there's any more left down there."

"Unfortunately, we're all out," Azor said. "But if you come to the feast on Wraithsday, I'll try to save you some."

"I'll keep that in mind," Sylas said as he returned to the food on his plate.

Patches wasn't happy later that night. The big man had barred him from sleeping in the bedroom, and he'd just found out now, *after* racing up the stairs to avoid the fire spirit.

Patches had made his rounds, at least he had done that.

He had even paced around the well and sent another hairball in to explore the tunnel he had discovered. He had yet to send a replica in, but that could wait until tomorrow.

But this? he thought as he paced in front of the door. *To come up here and find that my room has been shut tight? An insult!*

Patches pawed at the door. Maybe the big man closed it by mistake. Maybe if he just put a little force into it, Patches would be able to pry the door open. He took a few steps back and charged toward the door. Patches skidded to a halt just before collision.

Maybe there's a different way.

He began to yowl, but was immediately shushed by the fire spirit, who came blazing up the stairs. She hovered before Patches and pointed for him to go down to the main room of the pub. But Patches didn't want to go down, he wanted to go *in*.

She spoke in a soft voice. The fire spirit didn't wear her gloves, so she couldn't pet him at the moment. Even so, she got close enough for Patches to feel her heat, yet she didn't do so in an aggressive way.

Still, Patches didn't like being told what to do. So he protested. He jutted his tail into the air and paced back and forth with a scowl on his furry face.

The fire spirit spoke again and he ignored her, Patches cocking his chin in a different direction.

Let me in or I will terrorize this hallway, he told her, even though she couldn't understand him. *As protector of the Tavernly Realm, it is my duty to make sure the big man has enough power to brew more ale. Out of the way!*

Patches dropped onto his back legs, prepared to attack her. He was aware that this would hurt and hoped she would take the hint.

The fire spirit obliged.

Mumbling to herself, she headed back down the stairs leaving Patches in the hallway alone. He thought he was in the clear, Patches about to return to his yowling when she appeared again, this time wearing her metal gloves.

Before he could run away, the fire spirit swooped Patches into her arms and rushed downstairs. She placed him in the center of the pub and then returned to the top of the stairs, where she formed a wall of hovering flames.

Now at the bottom of the stairs, Patches glared at the fire spirit as he considered his options. He looked to the back door. She quickly sailed over his head, bolted it, and returned to the top of the stairs. She never scolded him, but there was a note of anger in her voice now as she spoke to him.

She's really going to force me to sleep down here, Patches thought. He offered her a soft, pleading meow, one that seemed to relax the flames on her shoulders.

He could try a sound attack, but she would likely be able to avoid it. There was also the option of sending a hairball up, but Patches was fairly certain she would burn it to a crisp.

Without any other options, Patches folded his legs beneath him and lowered. His whiskers pressed back as he continued to glower at the fire spirit.

Eventually, he drifted off to sleep, Dream Napping as he always did, but still furious.

CHAPTER TWENTY-THREE

TRIP TO DOURO

Sylas rolled to the side, his hand naturally moving to where Patches should have been. Then he remembered that they had decided to test the piebald pub cat last night, to see if he was the one refilling Sylas's Mana Lumens.

Name: Sylas Runewulf
Mana Lumens: 2026/2346
Class: Brewer
[Lumen Abilities:]
Flight
Quill

"Interesting," Sylas said as the invasion prompt appeared.

[You have 72 days until the invasion.]

He let the prompt fade away and focused again on his Mana Lumens.

Sylas looked at the numbers he had magically written in the air last night, which appeared around his bed after he thought of them. The total cost of his trip to Duskhaven and the flying he'd done later that day had come in at just under five hundred Mana Lumens.

He had sold a full cask of strong and regular ale, plus a few more pints, easily paying the cost of making two more casks. His original total was reduced by the amount he'd spent through purchases and flying, it was then augmented by his sales, and then further reduced by brewing two more casks.

"At least we know who is refilling my power," he said as he approached the door. Upon opening it, Patches burst into the room and released just about the saddest meow Sylas had ever heard.

Azor appeared, the fire spirit wearing her gloves and her apron. "Well?"

"Well?" he asked her.

"Is it the cat? Also, Mira is downstairs."

"Already?" Sylas asked. That was another thing. Mira had promised last night to take Sylas flying to a small town named Douro where he'd never been before, a place beyond the Seedlands.

"Yes, and happy Tombsday. Did I say that already?"

Sylas shook his head as Patches weaved in and out of his legs.

"That cat! He was so bad last night. Did you hear him?"

"I don't think I did."

"I had to take him away from your door and block him from going upstairs. He hates me now. He really hates me. Wait. Is it him?" she asked, shifting to the question at hand. "Is he the one refilling your MLus? You never told me."

Mira, who had heard the commotion from below, reached the top of the stairs just as Sylas answered this question.

"It's Patches."

"The cat is refilling your MLus?" Mira asked Sylas as she joined the conversation.

Sylas looked around. He was currently standing in the doorway of his bedroom with a needy cat twisting around his legs and a curious fire spirit in front of him. Then there was Mira, who had a picnic basket with her that she'd attached to her shoulder with a strap. A fashionable one, too. "Let's head downstairs."

"Good call," said the apothecary.

Once they were gathered around the bar, Sylas continued, "It has to be Patches. My powers didn't refill overnight."

"Then you need to get his MLus checked," Mira said, a hint of concern in her silver eyes. "He's a smart cat—most cats are smart, notice I didn't say all—but he might overextend himself refilling your power."

"Overextend?" Sylas asked, instantly knowing what she meant.

"Yes, he could give you all his powers and pass on to the Chasm. You don't want that."

"No, I do not," Sylas said as he watched Patches come down the stairs. As soon as the cat sensed everyone was looking at him, he puffed his tail up and started to meow again.

"You might be able find someone that can gauge his power in Battersea," Mira suggested. "At least that will give you an idea."

"But how is he doing it?"

"I don't know," she told Sylas.

"He has powers," Azor reminded the two of them. "You've seen them yourself. I thought he was going to stay out most of the night, but he came in and started howling. It was so loud. I really can't believe you didn't hear it."

Sylas grinned at her. "I sleep like a baby here in the Underworld, and I don't know why."

"Not the first time I've heard that," Mira said. "There are stresses here—"

"Like the invasion message. Seventy-two days now."

"Yes, like that. But it can be very relaxing here as well. Cozy, even."

"Tilbud called it a cozy abyss," Sylas said. "But anyway. Flying. Why do you want to take me to Douro again?" he asked, recalling the start of a conversation they'd had last night. Mira had only said they should fly there, but she hadn't given him a reason why.

"I thought you might find a new ingredient for your ale. The Wraithsday Feast is just around the corner."

"It is," Sylas said. "And a special ale to celebrate is in order. Is that what you are suggesting?"

"I don't know, you're the brewer."

Sylas trailed behind Mira, who was an excellent flier. She flew with her arms in front of her chest clutching the picnic basket she brought, which Mira assured Sylas would be worth it once they arrived in Douro.

They traveled over the Seedlands, Sylas noting that some of the farms looked much worse than the others. A herd of large bovines caught his attention, Sylas assuming they were the underoxen that Godric the fireweave tailor had mentioned. They certainly were large.

As they continued on, he thought about what Brom had said about selling his farm. Sylas didn't currently have enough MLus to buy something like that, but that was always a possibility in the future. There was also the MLR Bank, which Mira said offered mortgages.

He shook his head at the thought. He'd barely been dead for two weeks and he was already getting entrepreneurial. "A farm, really?" he said to himself as he sped ahead.

It was just Sylas and Mira. Not that Azor wasn't invited, she had preferred to stay back at the pub to cook and to keep an eye on Patches.

Sylas found the relationship between the cat and the fire spirit to be a bit comical.

Azor clearly cared for Patches, and she was always nice to the pub cat, yet the cat seemed to hold a grudge against her. It shouldn't have been funny, but it was. And it wasn't like Sylas could discipline the cat. Cats didn't take orders; Sylas had been around them long enough to know this.

"I forgot to tell you about the mice," he said as he caught up to Mira.

"The mice?"

"The other day. Patches killed a bunch of mice."

"No way." The silver-eyed apothecary glanced over at Sylas and a strand of her dark hair trailed over her face.

"It was like he killed an entire horde of them. I don't know where they would have come from."

"There's no telling. We can never forget how close we are to the Hexveil. Weird things happen in Ember Hollow. I've noticed that since taking residence there. It's not the same for other places."

"What about the cinderspiders near the volcano?"

"Well, there are the cinderspiders. How does your leg feel, by the way?"

"I forget I was bitten, that's how it feels. You really are good at what you do."

"We all have our classes."

"Not all of us," he reminded her. The only people he'd heard talk about not having a class were Henry and Mrs. Brassmere. But Sylas suspected there were others. People like Duncan and Cody, not that all the militiamen were classless. "What's so special about Douro again?"

"There are vineyards there."

"Grapes? I don't know how to make wine."

"There are berries, but that's not why I'm bringing you here. I thought you'd be interested in the roots of the Douro flamefruits. They only seem to grow in that region."

"Flamefruits? What are they like?"

"A tart berry. The Seedlands are made fertile by the Cinderpeak volcano. The Douro region is the same, and it has produced these special berries. They are the size of grapes, and they have a slight orange glow to them."

"Berries in ale?" Sylas asked, not sure of what she was getting at.

"Like I said, I was thinking you'd be more interested in the roots of the flamefruit vines. They are very smoky. People use them in fires to flavor meat. I'm not an expert when it comes to making ale, but I've seen people do all sorts of things with these roots and I figured they would interest you."

"Something smoky?" Sylas asked. Off the top of his head, Sylas wondered how something smoky would taste with a barley ale. It could make the flavor profile more complex. There could be additional properties as well. "Do the vines glow too?"

"Yes, they do," Mira said. "I thought you'd like that aspect as well. But before we reach there, let's head down now." She arced toward the ground, to a hill at the edge of the Seedlands. Mira found the place she liked to have picnics and touched down onto the ground.

This was a private place for her. Mira and Tiberius had been at odds when she had first come to the Underworld, yet his home was affixed to the deed she was given for her business.

Whatever system ruled their lives could be cruel in that way, forcing people to confront their past. Some, like Sylas, got lucky, and found it was a past that they actually enjoyed. Mira had been less lucky, especially since her betrayal had caused her uncle's death back in the real world.

The place where she had taken Sylas on the hill was where Mira visited when she needed a break from it all. Not just Tiberius, but everything. Over time, things got better for her in Ember Hollow, and she busied herself with her clients. Yet she never forgot this place.

"Not a bad spot," Sylas said as he looked out over the Seedlands. He turned to the other side, not yet able to see the town of Douro itself, but certainly able to see the vineyards. They glowed a fluorescent orange, their combined color strong enough to actually push back against the constant golden brightness from the Celestial Plains. It was almost defiant how lava-orange the berries were.

"Beautiful, right?"

"This is amazing," Sylas said as Mira opened her picnic basket. She handed Sylas a sandwich and produced a small clay container of boiled potatoes, which she set on the ground. Sylas was about to jokingly say the only thing this view was missing was a couple pints of ale, but he didn't.

Something about the look on Mira's face told him that this place meant something to her. He didn't ask why.

He simply sat back and enjoyed the view and the incredible food.

Douro was quite the town, the population rivaling Cinderpeak from what Sylas could tell, prettier too without the large volcano in the proximity. Because it wasn't forced to jut up against a volcano, there was more space here, the roads much wider and less windy. Many of the buildings had unique facades made of tile that Sylas hadn't seen in an Underworld city below.

"It is inspired by Battersea," Mira told him once he stopped to examine more of the tiles, which were arranged along the sides of the buildings and cast in blue and orange colors.

"I like it," he told her as he reached out to touch one of the textured tiles that featured a motif of orange flamefruit plants.

"You thinking about redecorating?"

"With tile? Not at the moment. I'm sure Azor would like something like this." He stroked his beard. "Tile. Where would tile even go in The Old Lamplighter?" Sylas shook his head. "It's vibrant, which is the opposite of cozy."

"I thought the opposite of cozy would be unwelcoming," she told him as they continued on toward the market in the center of town.

"It won't work for the pub," Sylas concluded, "but it could work somewhere else."

"Where else?"

"That remains to be seen," he told her with a grin.

They reached the market and headed toward the food section, where they found the flamefruit roots. Sylas brought one up to his face and sniffed it. The root certainly had a smoky scent, almost charcoal-like.

"Do you mind if I taste it?" he asked the woman who ran the shop.

"By all means. Just use that knife there to cut a little off the side."

Sylas cut a sliver of the glowing root and tasted it. It was by no means flavorful, but he could see why people would use it for a barbeque and he was certain that brewing it with the barley ale would give the ale a bit of flavor.

It was worth a shot.

Sylas purchased a pound of the root. He thought about perusing some of the other fruits and meats, but he preferred to do something like that with Azor around.

"Before we leave," Mira said as Sylas turned toward the exit of the market. She could tell by the way his eyes shifted that he had located the portal. "I thought we could enjoy one of the cafés here. My treat."

"No, my treat."

"No, Sylas, my treat. You're already down MLus because you didn't let Patches give you power. Plus, you've bought things here today and I didn't. I'm sure," she said, cutting him off before he could protest, "that you'll let me taste whatever you brew up for free. Speaking of which, you haven't let me pay for a pint in a week or longer."

"You'll never have to pay for a pint."

"Hence me treating you."

"But I owe you a favor."

"You owe me more than one favor, but don't worry about that for now. You'll like the café and you can try the flamefruit berries." She led him to the side of the market, to a place with outdoor seating. The people gathered around the small tables paid little attention to Mira and Sylas as they squeezed through and took a seat.

"This is the third time I've been to a restaurant here in the Underworld," Sylas said, which was a small revelation that didn't hit him until he sat down.

"So it's a class, the people that run the restaurant arrived in the Underworld with a particular class that allows them to do this."

"Sometimes, yes. Other times, someone classes as a chef and they partner with someone else to fix up a place and turn it into a restaurant. It really just depends. In Battersea, you'll see conglomerates of chefs, bakers, and others who have restaurant experience or something class related, like a butcher, team up. That's where the best restaurants are, but this café is nice."

The waiter came around and Mira ordered two flamefruit juices and some pastries.

"I always hear about Battersea. Are there other large cities here in the Underworld?"

"There certainly are, the farther east you head," she said. "Ember Hollow is the farthest west you can travel in the Underworld, that's why everything is east of us. If you travel toward the other side of the Hexveil, beyond Battersea, you'll find a couple other large cities."

"Larger than Duskhaven?"

"Much larger. Wraithwick is one. I've been there. Places I've heard of and have never been include Gloombra, Ghostford, Ebonshire, Sotur, and Draugr. Wait, and Geist. That's the easternmost counterpoint to Ember Hollow." She shrugged. "I keep meaning to travel, but you know how that goes."

"Easier said than done, especially if you have work."

"And I do have that. I like staying busy, though."

Their flamefruit juices came in glasses. They glowed a bright orange, one that Sylas was certain he'd be able to replicate with the ale he planned to produce later that day.

What would he call it? The ale would be a one-night-only affair, so he'd likely produce two casks to go with the Wraithsday Feast.

"Aren't you going to try the juice?" Mira asked as the waiter brought a plate of custards over, each with a berry on top.

"Right, I was thinking about brewing." Sylas sipped the juice and smacked his lips. "It's sour. No, it's sweet. It's sweet." He took another drink and smacked his lips. "How strange. It starts sour then it becomes sweet."

"It does," she said. "You like it, right?"

"It's growing on me." Sylas was glad he hadn't bought any of the berries for brewing later that day. While there may be a different way to ferment these berries, Sylas wasn't a winemaker. The roots, however, seemed like they would be perfect for his purposes.

He couldn't wait to experiment with them later.

It was slow at The Old Lamplighter that night, yet Sylas still managed to sell fifty pints total. The only problem was that most of them were regular pints, meaning he'd netted three hundred twenty Mana Lumens in total sales. He had already started the day down from where he should have been, and that was before he'd spent over two hundred Mana Lumens to travel to Douro and buy some supplies there.

At least it is enough to brew the two casks of custom ale, Sylas thought as he took a quick look at his status.

Ultimately, he would go to bed with less considering he hadn't brewed the two casks yet, which would set him back another 160 Mana Lumens. But he wasn't doing too poorly, and he knew tomorrow's Wraithsday Feast would make up for his lack of growth over the last two days.

The regulars who had visited The Old Lamplighter that night knew about it, and he'd managed to strike up a few conversations in Douro to tell people about the new pub in Ember Hollow. All Sylas needed to do tomorrow was head to Cinderpeak and spread the word there as well.

"The front and back doors are locked, cat door is open, and everything is closed for the night," Azor announced, which was her way of saying that she'd also wiped the tables. She hovered at the top of the stairs, her flames illuminating part of the cellar.

"Good." Sylas cracked his knuckles. "It's time to experiment."

"I can't wait!"

He began his brewing process and decided to add the roots after the fermentation phase. "It's a method called dry hopping," he told Azor. "A way for the flavor of the hops to be reintroduced. A sort of second fermentation, if that makes sense." He finished this process for the first batch. "It needs to steep."

"Won't that take time?" Azor asked.

"I don't know." Sylas held his hand over the pot and willed it to steep. He watched the surface of the liquid change. The flamefruit roots paled at first, but then they began to glow even brighter than they had before. The surface of the ale rippled and tiny bubbles popped, the aroma wafting into the air. Sylas took a big inhale through his nostrils. "I think that's it."

"You just modified time," Azor said, her jaw hanging open.

"I guess I did?" Sylas looked down at the orange ale. "But in a localized way." He examined his hand. Sylas placed it on the wooden table and ordered it to age. Nothing happened. "It's my brewer class. I can probably do all sorts of things if I really want to."

"Like tea?"

"Maybe. But let's just focus on this for now." Sylas grabbed a pint. He took just a little bit from the pot, made sure none of the roots were in it, and cooled the glass down to the optimum temperature. Sylas tasted it.

"Well?" Azor asked.

He took another sip.

"Well?" she asked again, the fire spirit moving closer in anticipation.

Sylas slowly nodded. "It's perfect. Just a bit smoky, robust, different from my normal strong ale. I'll strain this pot, get it casked up, and brew another. And that color." He admired the brew, which glowed a bright orange. "People are going to love that color."

"It certainly has a very Underworld appeal."

CHAPTER TWENTY-FOUR

WRAITHSDAY FEAST

Patches was certainly curious about the glowing ale he saw the big man drink earlier. He'd even hopped up onto the table and sniffed it, the piebald pub cat unfamiliar with the smell. Now, after everyone was asleep, he sat in the cellar looking at the two casks that had been brewed.

They're glowing, he thought, *the ale inside is actually making the casks glow. How peculiar.*

Patches turned to his paws, which he licked until he was certain they were clean. He focused on the sounds around him, able to hear in a way that was almost akin to echolocation. There was a precision to his power, allowing Patches to hear through the ground and into the well, where he heard a scratching sound.

Could it be another rat? Perhaps more mice? The noise was different from the mice, the instruments being used seemingly sharper. It wasn't the smoke spirit, the one whose appearance had created the recent troubles around the Tavernly Realm.

Patches headed upstairs to investigate. He turned himself invisible and passed right in front of the fire spirit, who said something to him but ultimately let him move on. Patches slipped through the cat door and quickly found a place in the dark just in case the fire spirit came looking for him.

He now noticed several sounds. The first was the fire spirit, who rested in the fireplace of the pub and was humming softly to herself. There were the general noises associated with the Underworld, a light breeze, rustling in the trees beyond.

He homed in on the activity in the well itself.

Patches hopped up to the rim and peered down into the space. He thought for a moment of sending his clone down, but the last time that he had sent something in, the mice were drawn out. He could always go down himself, and then split into his clone, but he wasn't so certain he would be able to get out.

Maybe I should try...

An internal debate started, one in which Patches ultimately surmised that he wouldn't be heading down into the well tonight. He would, however, monitor it, which to Patches meant pacing around the well until the early hours of the morning.

It was time to head inside.

Patches slipped through the cat door, invisible again, and took the stairs to the big man's room. He sat before him, happy to see that his loyal subject sleeping peacefully. Patches transferred some of his power to the big man and soon, he too found himself in a deep slumber.

[**You have 71 days until the invasion.**]

Sylas tensed up, but ultimately let the tension roll away. He checked his status and saw his Mana Lumens had been filled off.

"I can't believe you're the one that has been doing this," he told Patches. He expected Azor to burst in the room as she often did, yet she never appeared. "That's strange," Sylas said as he headed downstairs, where he found Azor moving some of the food that had been delivered into the cellar.

"The fish came," she told him.

"I can see that." Sylas grabbed a crate and headed downstairs. "Corlin didn't want to hang around?"

"He said that he had another delivery. I tried to offer him breakfast." The fire spirit placed her hands on her waist and smiled over at Sylas as he came out of the cellar.

"Happy Wraithsday," he said.

"That's supposed to be my line."

"I guess I beat you to it," Sylas said as he took another crate, this one with potatoes. Azor followed him down. "How was Patches?"

"Last night? He snuck out as always and stayed out there most of the night. I don't know what he's doing. I watched him for a moment through the window and he was just circling the well."

"The well, huh? Strange." Sylas set the crate down. "Anyway. Today."

"Today?"

"I'm going to lay low to maximize MLu gains tonight. But before I do that, I'll head to Cinderpeak to tell people about tonight's feast." He smiled at the fire spirit. "It should be a blast."

The Wraithsday Feast started slowly, just Mira and Anders at the bar, the carpenter especially excited about the meal. As it had the week prior, The Old Lamplighter filled up to the point that Mira volunteered to help deliver ale.

"You pour them up, I'll drop them off at the tables," she told Sylas over the buzz.

"I can't have you—"

Before he could get the words out, the apothecary grabbed two pints and brought them over to the farmers' table, where Brom sat, the man in the middle of a story. Mira also helped deliver food as it came, the smell of which would have made Sylas hungry had he not eaten before they opened.

Excitement was in the air.

There were the farmers, some of the militiamen, Iron Rose and a few of her friends, Mr. and Mrs. Brassmere, John, and of course the regulars like Godric. Bart the bard even started singing later that night, after most of the meals were finished.

The orange glow of what Sylas had christened flamefruit ale lit the faces of his patrons as they listened to Bart's songs, happy to see the bard taking Mana Lumen tips to perform certain numbers. He also stayed clear of any songs that would offend someone from either the Aurum Kingdom or Shadowthorne Empire. Bart was always able to walk that fine line that the best musicians and entertainers danced upon.

There were certainly free pints given away, but most of what Sylas poured that night was sold. He was especially glad to see his experimental ale was a hit and endeavored to brew more in the future. Something about the bright orange pints entertained people, and Sylas got multiple comments on how interesting the ale was, even if they should have been commenting on the taste.

"I've always thought of doing something like this," Iron Rose told him at some point, the pub owner still in the apron she wore when she painted. "There are other glowing fruits, you know. But flamefruit? It's so bitter if you cook it down. I tried. How did you do it?"

"Through the roots," Sylas told her, "and that happened to be Mira's idea." He motioned to the apothecary as she took an empty pint glass from a table.

Iron Rose giggled with delight. "She's a keeper. You're paying her, right?"

"I would if she'd let me. I suggested it earlier but she won't take MLus from me."

"You're lucky!" She lifted her pint glass to Sylas. "And cheers. Seeing you getting so motivated by the pub business has got me thinking about setting a schedule and being open on the weekends. A schedule I actually keep. Imagine that. Keeping a schedule for business."

"People like schedules. That said, I'm planning to close up on Soulsday so I can head to Battersea," Sylas told her. "Perhaps that's a good time to be open. I'm guessing I'll be gone for a couple of days. There's a lot I need to do there. Speaking of which, the Ale Alliance. Anything I need to know about them?"

"You'll find their hall in the Guild District. The building is literally shaped like a cask of ale, you can't miss it. Just tell them Iron Rose sent you and they'll set you up."

"But no bigger casks?"

"Nope. What we get is the standard Underworld size. If you try to brew up something larger and pour it into a larger cask, the rest of what you make will disappear. You also can't have more than twelve casks."

"And how is this enforced exactly?" he asked, a question he had been wondering for a while now. He understood that there were rules, but who actually was going to enforce it? Would a constable come around?

"A lumengineer set it up long ago. It keeps people like us from getting too strong. The Ale Alliance manages this all to some degree. But you can get other supplies through them. You'll also have dues too, just so you know. They fluctuate, so I don't know what they will be now."

"Right," Sylas said as he began pouring up a pint of strong ale. "I guess that's to be expected."

"It is, and it's worth it. They have access to supplies you can't get anywhere else, from pint glasses to bottles and growlers. And it's cheaper to go through them than to find a glassmaker, which you'd probably find in Douro or Duskhaven if you asked around."

"Thanks," Sylas said. "Care if I make an announcement about closing The Old Lamplighter and your pub being open?"

"By all means."

Sylas used a utensil to tap the side of an empty pint glass.

Ding, ding, ding!

"Attention everyone. First, thank you for making the Wraithsday Feast another success. Thanks to Azor, who made such a great meal." The patrons clapped for the fire spirit, which took her off guard. She turned beet red and bowed her head to all of them.

"Thank you," she finally blurted out.

Sylas continued, "And thanks to you all for enjoying my new ale. This won't always be on the menu, but I'll endeavor to have it for you next Wraithsday. Now, I have some business to attend to in Battersea. I'll leave Soulsday and in my absence, The Ugly Duckling in Cinderpeak will be open."

Iron Rose waved at the patrons.

"So be sure to visit her, and I appreciate all of you coming to The Old Lamplighter." Sylas paused and was nearly overcome by emotion. He exhaled deeply and smiled at his guests. "Anyway, back to your pints. We'll be closing up here in an hour, so be sure to get your orders in."

Patches, who had been seated in Godric's lap, hopped onto the table and mewed loudly, causing the patrons to laugh.

"Might want to get the cat a pint too," Godric joked, a bit of his ale sloshing out of his pint.

The Old Lamplighter was closed for the night, Sylas happy with their sales. He had netted 840 Mana Lumens and sold out of the special flamefruit ale. He had six casks to brew, which would cost 480 Mana Lumens, but that was all doable.

Name: Sylas Runewulf
Mana Lumens: 3164/3164
Class: Brewer

He should have had a bit more MLus, but he had expended some through his activities throughout the day, which was normal. Even so, Sylas had pushed past the three thousand mark, no small feat. If everything went well, he would be able to journey to Battersea with around four thousand Mana Lumens, depending on the next three days.

"Four thousand," he said, smiling over at Azor, who was wiping down tables. "Did you do well?"

"I did," she said. "You were right to charge fifteen MLus for food this time, especially with how big the fillets were. I netted six hundred myself!"

"I just thought it wasn't something that we should use for a special, not that we won't have specials in the future."

"Specials aren't special if there is always a special," she said.

"Heh. Something like that."

Mira came up from the cellar with a tray of clean pints, which she set on the bar. "Well, I guess I'll be going."

"I *have* to pay you," Sylas told her.

"I already—"

"Mira."

"Sylas."

"Mira."

"Mira," Azor said, jumping in on Sylas's side.

"Both of you. I ate for free, drank for free, and you're taking me to Battersea and putting me up at a hotel I like there."

"I am?" Sylas's eyebrows raised. "Sure, if that's what you want."

"It is what I want, and you'll like it. They have a great breakfast."

"I like good and bad breakfasts," he said, "as long as there's a morning meal."

"So consider that my payment. And maybe you'll take me out there. Battersea has the best restaurants in the Underworld. Competition is fierce there, so they're pretty cheap too. Anyway, I should get going." She stopped in front of the entrance to The Old Lamplighter, thought of turning back to wave at them, and ultimately decided against it.

"Wait, I should walk her—"

The door shut. Sylas exchanged glances with Azor, who started laughing. "That was great. I'll follow her to make sure she gets home. Do what you have to do here."

"Brew," Sylas said.

Patches mewed and Sylas turned to him. He opened his arms. The pub cat came bounding toward the bar top. He jumped, landed gracefully enough, and charged into Sylas's waiting arms. "I guess someone is coming downstairs with me," he told the cat as Patches mewed softly.

"I'll be back." Azor left.

Sylas headed down to the cellar with plans to brew two strong ales and four regular ales. He would definitely do the flamefruit ale again, but as Azor had said, special was special.

CHAPTER TWENTY-FIVE

BACKYARD DISCOVERY

Patches rushed through the cat door just in case the fire spirit tried to stop him. She didn't, yet he maintained his invisible form as he turned to the well and confirmed the sound he had heard earlier while he was upstairs.

Something is coming, he surmised, uncertain of what it could be.

He prepared by moving into the shadows and enlarging his form, his teeth and claws growing in size.

Patches hoped it would be enough.

Whatever was on the way sounded large. Patches expected a demonic rat or another nest of nefarious mice. What he *didn't* expect was a spider to pull itself out of the well.

The spider was the same size as Patches, with long legs, sharp fangs, and an armored black body.

Patches's sight connected with his sense of smell, and the cat instantly recognized the same scent he'd noticed on the big man a few days back.

Was this the spider that had bitten him?

If so, you die now.

Patches yowled. He pressed back, prepping to pounce.

The cinderspider veered right, its legs dancing in a complex choreography of terror.

The monstrous arachnid produced a bolt of lava from the back of its throat. The fireball would have struck Patches had it not been for the pub cat's mana-amplified speed, the cat able to lunge to the side just in time to avoid it. The stray fire hit the brick foundation of the pub, where clumps of it fell to the ground and fizzled out.

Patches hissed. Seething with anger, especially now that the spider had *dared* disturb the Tavernly Realm, Patches went on the attack.

He zipped forward and launched his furry body into the air. He twisted as the spider rose to address him and was able to claw into its side and flip it around onto its back.

Patches could tell by the way his claws felt against the spider's hardened exterior that he wasn't going to be able to cut into it the same way he could a rodent. But it had a softer underside. Patches was certain of this.

The cinderspider righted itself and surged toward Patches, who ducked beneath the spider as it tried to tear the cat's back with its fangs.

Patches twisted around and lifted onto his hind legs, fur fluffed in agitation as he came down onto the spider.

Careful of its teeth, Patches latched onto the spider's body and used his forward momentum to flip it onto its back again.

The spider's legs flailed and then curled back as Patches landed on top of it. It dug its claws into Patches's body, yet Patches was semiprotected by his fur and only received minor scrapes. The spider managed to throw him off.

Patches struck the well and hit the ground from there, pain blooming within.

Everything around him spun as the cinderspider wobbled and eventually righted itself. The spider turned to Patches. It opened its mouth and produced another fireball. Patches didn't fully get out of the way this time. While he managed to escape most of the fire, it singed the tip of his tail, which caused Patches to howl in pain.

His fur slicked back as something akin to a comet exploded out of the cat door.

The stream of fire lifted the cinderspider and slammed it down to the ground repeatedly, Patches hearing a sound similar to a shell being cracked open. The fire spirit, savage as ever, grabbed the cinderspider and soared even higher into the air before coming down again.

The impact nearly killed the spider, which now lay on its back legs mangled as the fire spirit hovered over its fallen body. To finish it off, she grabbed a shovel and bashed it a few times. Her voice went from savage to soft as she turned to Patches. She motioned for him to follow her and, for once, he listened to the fire spirit.

Once they were in the pub, she put on her gloves and placed her hand on Patches head.

The fire spirit spoke sweetly to him as she checked out Patches's tail. She pointed toward the back door and then to the stairs. Patches didn't know exactly what she was getting at, but he certainly was starting to feel tired from all the energy he had exerted in his fight against the cinderspider.

He headed up to the big man's room, but before Patches went to sleep, he transferred power as he always did.

Yet again, the Tavernly Realm was secure.

———

Sylas was woken by Patches, who scratched at the side of his leg.

"What are you doing there?" he asked the pub cat, who was sprawled out and clearly dreaming.

Patches blinked his eyes opened, yawned, licked his lips, and turned to his other side to go back to sleep.

[You have 70 days until the invasion.]

"And so I do," Sylas grumbled as the prompt faded away. He turned his focus to his status and saw that Patches had filled his Mana Lumens.

Name: Sylas Runewulf
Mana Lumens: 3164/3164
Class: Brewer
[Lumen Abilities:]
Flight
Quill

"You really are a good cat." He cupped Patches's head with a single hand and scratched the underside of the cat's chin. Patches started purring and didn't stop this time when Azor entered the bedroom.

"There's something you need to see," she said instead of her typical cheerful morning greeting.

"Happy Thornsday," Sylas said. "Did I do that right?"

The concerned look on her fiery face shifted to some degree, but it never fully formed into a smile. "You need to see this. I'll be outside."

"What did Patches get into now?" Sylas asked as the fire spirit whisked away. After he put his boots on, he headed downstairs and out the back door to find Azor hovering over the dead body of a cinderspider.

"I heard noises last night and came out here to find Patches fighting it."

"What the hell?" Sylas looked in the direction of Cinderpeak, as if he were calculating how far the volcano was from their current location. "What is that thing doing here?"

"I don't know. I killed it."

"Have there been spiders in Ember Hollow before?"

"I don't know the answer to that question either. But as we saw in the cave, when there is one, there are many."

"A nest, huh?" Sylas leaned against the well and crossed his arms over his chest. "Maybe they've got a cave in the woods outside of the village."

"Maybe."

"I'll need to ask someone who has been here a while."

"Tiberius?"

Sylas nodded reluctantly at her suggestion. "Or Henry. But let's start with Tiberius. Henry will probably tell me to ask him. I can tell Mira about it as well."

"Should I incinerate the body?" she asked.

"I would say sure, but maybe not yet. We might need proof."

"You're not planning to carry that thing over to Mira's place with you, right?"

"I could," Sylas said. "But she probably won't like that."

"If we leave it here, another animal might come get it. Or another spider."

"True." Sylas stroked his beard for a moment. "And I definitely don't want to bring it into the pub." He shuddered at the thought. The sight of a cinderspider, dead or alive, was never pleasant.

"Cover it with something?"

"Or, ahem, I hate to ask you this."

"You want me to stay here to guard the dead spider's body?"

"I do," Sylas said. "You know how Tiberius can be. He may not believe me, and if I do manage to bring him back here and the body is gone, then I'll look like an idiot."

Azor clasped her fiery hands behind her back. "Then consider me on guard duty. But you're on your own for breakfast."

"Thanks, I owe you one. And as for breakfast"—Sylas grinned at the fire spirit—"maybe Mira will have something. If not, I'll just eat a big lunch."

Sylas entered the pub with plans to head out the front door. He stopped as a set of words fizzled into existence over the bar.

Dearest Sylas and fiery Azor,

It has come to my attention that The Old Lamplighter is in desperate need of a pub quiz. I will be here tomorrow to deliver that quiz, giving you a day to promote it. May the best team win!

Yours in luminous mana,
Archlumen Octavian Tilbud

The words flickered for a few more moments and faded away. Sylas turned to the back door and peeked his head out to find Azor hovering over the spider.

"You're back already?"

"Not quite. Tilbud left a message. Pub quiz tomorrow night. Do you want to serve food as well?"

"We could do a roast or a stew? That'd be something easy to get from the Cinderpeak Market."

"Good, we'll get something today. I'll see you in a bit."

Mira was just finishing sorting some of the herbs she had picked up in Douro when she saw Sylas outside. He smiled at her, his eyebrows raising in a way that she interpreted as a request for her to come out. She motioned for him to come inside her shop instead.

"So this is the place?" he asked. "This is where all your medicinal magic happens."

Mira looked him over quickly, from his blue eyes down to his scruffy boots, which had a bit of dirt on them, dirt he had brought into her shop.

"Stop right there."

Sylas jokingly raised his hands. "I come in peace."

"Your boots are dirty."

"At least it isn't mud. It seriously never rains here?"

"Not normally, no," Mira said.

"Then how do crops grow?"

"There are mana showers in certain areas like the Seedlands. That's how they grow."

"Mana showers. Does that look like rain?"

"Sort of." Mira folded her hands together. "Is everything all right?"

"Not exactly. Last night, Patches and Azor fought and killed a cinderspider."

The color drained from her face. "At the pub? You're joking."

"At the pub. Has there ever been something like that before? Do cinderspiders normally make their way here to Ember Hollow?"

"No, they most certainly do not. Not that I've ever seen. If they did, you wouldn't find me living here. Let me guess. You're here to ask my uncle, aren't you?"

"He is a Steamed-Up Defender of Ember Hollow, or something of the sort." Sylas grinned at her.

"Stop it," Mira said. "He probably won't be able to see you right now."

"Why's that?"

"He's training with the militia out back. I'm surprised you didn't hear them. They're quite loud."

"I didn't hear anything."

"Maybe they're taking their morning break. That, or he's lecturing them. He likes to do that." Mira stood. "In that case, follow me, but don't be surprised if he sends you away."

"I'm sure he'll make time for me, especially with something like this."

"You don't know my uncle very well."

"What have I missed about him? He's curmudgeonly, hates Aurumites such as myself, and he seems to hold grudges long after he should hold them."

"Maybe you do know him better than I thought."

"But we're getting along now. I've joined him on two hunts and this is something that should concern him."

"Let's just see what he says."

Sylas followed Mira through a hallway with the walls painted in a soft purple color. It was clear that Mira was responsible for decorating this part of the home, but the next area belonged to Tiberius. There were taxidermied animals here, and everything not made of wood was made of leather.

In looking across the space, Sylas saw another room with walls that were a light paisley pattern, likely Mira's side again.

"How often do the two of you argue about the decor?"

A wry grin formed on her face. "You don't want to know."

Once they were outside, Mira led Sylas down a path that trailed around her uncle's armory into the woods. They came to an open space, the trees around it cleared away, stumps used for seats. Tiberius stood in front of a group of about a dozen men, the former lord commander lecturing them on proper engagement.

His good eye twitched when he saw Mira and Sylas.

Of course, the newcomer was going to interrupt the perfect moment he was having with his militia. Something was in the air today, and the militia seemed to truly embrace what he was saying about formations, especially after their recent encounter with the B-Rank Eldritch Horror.

Now, all that was ruined. Tiberius cursed under his breath.

Heads started turning toward Mira and Sylas, starting with Cody and Duncan. Duncan even waved at the pub owner. Waved! They were supposed to be paying attention to Tiberius, yet as he had often learned before, his militiamen, while brave, were not soldiers. Not all of them, anyway. Henry had been, but the others were easily distracted.

Rather than acknowledge them, Tiberius tried even harder to get his point across. "That is why when approaching a B-Rank demon or above, we need to flank it like so." He motioned his wooden sword in the air, Tiberius tracing the formation he'd taught them. "And when you attack it—"

"Sylas is here," Cody said, as if Tiberius didn't already know that.

"I can see that. I'm not done—"

"Uncle, something happened at the pub last night," Mira said, interrupting him.

"What? What could have possibly happened at the pub last night that is so important that you have taken it upon yourself to interrupt our training session?"

"Cinderspiders," Sylas said. "Or one cinderspider. Azor and Patches killed it behind my pub last night."

"Who?" Tiberius asked.

"The fire spirit and the pub cat," Duncan said. "There was really a cinderspider here?"

"Not possible," Henry said as he crossed his arms over his chest. Even though he carried a skeptical look on his face, his large eyebrows, which were a different color than his silver hair, made him look comical.

Sylas started to laugh. He laughed at the way Tiberius glowered at him, and Henry's skepticism. "This is ripe," he finally said. "And I'm glad I have evidence. Azor and I were going to come here together, but something told me you all wouldn't believe me, so she's back there guarding."

"I believe him," Cody said, Duncan nodding in agreement.

This only agitated Tiberius more. These were *his* militiamen, and to see them on Sylas's side was something he wasn't expecting. So he did something he'd learned to do long ago when presented with a situation like this. "Cody, go to the pub and check to see if this is indeed true."

"Yes, sir!" Cody got to his feet. He smoothed his hands over his armor and took off.

"We'll wait here," Tiberius said.

"And if it is true?" Sylas asked, his voice barely able to hide his disdain.

"Then we'll need to start patrols. Something is afoot if cinderspiders are showing up." Tiberius placed his hand on the hilt of his wooden sword.

"I have an idea," Henry told them after the group had murmured for a moment. "Something to do while we wait."

"Yes?" Tiberius asked.

Henry looked from Sylas to Tiberius. "You two were once soldiers."

"You were as well," Tiberius reminded him.

"Sure, but I think it'd be really interesting to see the two of you have a duel of it. Let's see who is the best with a wooden sword. What do you think, mates?" he asked the other militiamen, who all grunted positively at the suggestion. "While we wait for Cody to come back?"

Mira started to protest and Tiberius cut her off.

"Let him decide. What'll it be, Aurumite?" Tiberius asked Sylas.

"Do we really need to do this?"

A ripple of excitement moved through the ranks of the militiamen, one that Sylas was very familiar with. Men behaved differently in groups.

"It's ultimately up to you," Tiberius said, "But the lads would like to see it, and we've got a bit of time before Cody gets back." He nodded to Henry. "Give him your weapon."

Sylas wrapped his hands around the grip of a wooden blade. He had questions, the first one about the weapon itself. If they fought demons using maces, why were they training with wooden swords? He knew the answer instantly. Tiberius had been a lord commander of the Shadowthorne Vanguard, which came with all the pomp that one would expect from a title like that.

Of course, he had them train with wooden swords.

The next question that came to Sylas's mind was about how far they would take this. Was this a friendly demonstration or—

Tiberius charged at Sylas, his wooden blade overhead. Sylas blocked his attack, and parried Tiberius's next attempt. On the offensive, Tiberius tried again and again to get a hit in yet failed each time.

"No Lumen Abilities," Tiberius seethed. "If we were going that route, I would have knocked you off your feet before you brought your sword up."

It was only then that Sylas realized there was a faint glow around his own hands, like he had been charging for an attack. In realizing this, the glow dissipated.

Sylas brought his wooden sword to the ready. As Tiberius came in again, Sylas saw the opening he was looking for and took it. He sidestepped Tiberius's attack and struck the shorter man on the back of the heel with his weapon.

Tiberius's men gasped as their leader stumbled forward.

He was back on his feet in a matter of seconds, his blade shaky for a moment as he switched his strategy. Rather than come in rapid-fire, Tiberius tried for sweeping horizontal slashes.

Sylas had seen this maneuver before.

As he stepped back and blocked Tiberius's next attempt, he had a flashback to one of his early battles, during his years in the Royal Guard.

Sylas and his men had come upon a group of lord commanders, not unlike Tiberius. They had little protection and what happened next was something that he would never forget. There were many moments that had changed Sylas, but the slaughter of that day had always stuck with him.

He remembered how regal the lord commanders looked in their fancy black armor with its red accents and how quickly they had gone down, none of them able to fight as well as the grunts that protected them.

This memory was the spark Sylas needed to easily take the upper hand. While Tiberius had been planning wars and riding around on horses, Sylas had been on the front line. They were not the same, even if Tiberius was brave and strong in his own right.

Sylas quickly overpowered him.

Time and time again he beat Tiberius back, Sylas to the point that he was prepared to deliver a final blow when he caught a glimpse of Mira's face.

It was more than concern.

It was Mira's look that told him that whatever happened here would not only affect their relationship, but also Tiberius's relationship with the militiamen.

Sylas eased up, and Tiberius was able to swipe his sword out of his hand.

"I believe I have you," Tiberius huffed, his slick black hair in his face, a wild look in his good eye. He thrust his wooden sword at Sylas.

"I believe you do." Sylas showed Tiberius his palms.

"That was a good show, but you stood no chance."

Sylas didn't respond.

"Did you see that, lads?" Tiberius asked as he finally lowered his weapon. "That is how it's done."

The militiaman murmured.

Mira approached and placed a hand on Sylas's arm. "I believe your little demonstration is over, Uncle. And would you look at that? Cody is back." She turned with Sylas toward Cody. "Thank you," she whispered so only Sylas could hear her.

He smiled as the younger man approached holding the cinderspider by one of its legs. Mira gasped and quickly turned away.

"You actually touched that thing?" Duncan asked.

"Yeah, why not?" Cody tossed the spider onto the ground. "Apparently, we have cinderspiders in Ember Hollow."

Tiberius approached. "Yes, yes we do. We'll begin our patrols tonight. Duncan, Henry, you two are up first." The two men nodded. Tiberius turned to Sylas. "Is there anything else?"

"Actually, there is." Sylas felt Mira tighten her grip around his arm. "Tomorrow night is quiz night at The Old Lamplighter. Last week we had three teams. Maybe you all will want to come play as well? The prize is Mana Lumens and a round of strong ale."

Mira relaxed her grip on his arm and quickly dropped her hand down by her side. "Well, I believe that is everything, Uncle. I'm guessing you all will deal with the spider body."

"We can hack at it for a while," Tiberius said, "get the lads used to killing these sorts of things. The Esteemed Coalition of Ember Hollow Defenders will protect the village at all costs, isn't that right, lads?"

The men all shouted in unison.

The pub was relatively quiet that night, but Sylas was fine with this. He considered it the calm before the storm, especially with all the hype he had built around the upcoming pub quiz. Over the course of the day, he had visited Cinderpeak and Douro, spreading the word and telling people of the prize.

He had spoken to Godric and he had also stopped by the Seedlands to pass the message on to Brom and the other farmers. His conversation with the fireweave tailor had naturally shifted to the cinderspider, Godric confirming that he had never heard of one appearing as far out as Ember Hollow.

"Definitely never heard of them that far out," the fireweave tailor said. "I don't like the sound of that one bit."

Now, as Sylas cleaned a pint glass and filled it with regular ale, he thought about how the spiders could have made it to the village.

"It has to be the forest," he said as he waited for the ale to settle.

He poured another ale and Azor handed it off to a pair of militiamen still in their training armor. Sylas hadn't gotten their names, but they were soon joined by Cody and Duncan, who also ordered a round. More people came, but not enough to fill the pub.

By the end of the night, Sylas had sold around forty pints, mostly regular ale. This would cover his brewing costs of two casks and give him a small profit, which was fine because he knew that the pub quiz would likely bring in quite a bit.

Before closing up, he reminded everyone of the quiz. "We'll also be closed on Soulsday and Moonsday," he told Duncan, who was the last to leave.

"It's good to take a break," the large militiaman said. "And by the way."

"Yeah?" Sylas asked.

"I know what you did back there."

"Back where?"

"Against Tiberius. You could have beaten him. He's strong, but only because of his Lumen Abilities. That's because of his class." Duncan tapped his temple. "Lucky class. Get that class, and the powers you learn are amplified." He burped. "Apologies, mate. Yeah, as I was saying, that class. I know you would have won. Not that he isn't strong. That class. I'm saving up MLus to get my class changed to demon hunter."

"What's your current class, if you don't mind me asking?"

"No class." Duncan grinned. "Funny to say it like that, but a lot of us end up here like that. But there's time, and I'll save up enough. Then things will get interesting."

Sylas thought about this later as he finished brewing his casks. He had been gifted the brewer class. It had appeared in his status without him having to do anything for it. He knew that he was incredibly blessed in this regard.

"Good night, Azor," he called to the fire spirit as he headed up to bed.

"Night, Sylas!"

"Patches?"

The pub cat ran past Sylas and stopped at the top of the stairs. He waited for Sylas to pass and then followed him into the bedroom. "I'll leave the door open for you," he told the cat, "keep an eye out for spiders if you go out."

Patches couldn't understand what the big man had told him, but he certainly planned to keep an eye out for spiders and rodents. Later that night, long after the big man had drifted off to sleep, Patches headed downstairs, where he crept past the fire spirit and slipped through his cat door.

Noise in front of the Tavernly Realm drew his attention.

Keeping to the shadows, even though he had turned himself invisible, Patches circled around the pub to find a pair of men patrolling the cobblestone road. They reached the square at the center of the village, circled around the old tree there, and headed back toward the pub.

Patches was instantly suspicious, especially once he saw they were carrying weapons. He pressed back, his hair standing on end as they passed.

He eased up a bit when he recognized one of the men, the man's scent mixed with what he knew was the pungent smell of ale. The fellow had been in the pub earlier, Patches was sure of it.

This eased his guard to some degree. This wasn't the first time Patches had seen men like this patrolling the village.

Does it have something to do with the spider? he wondered.

Patches returned to the pub and sat in front of the well. He listened carefully, his ears quivering as he separated the low sounds of the men talking from some activity in the well below. Patches decided not to investigate further.

Eventually, he headed inside and up to the big man's bedroom, where he transferred some power and fell into a deep, recharging sleep.

The Tavernly Realm was secure for another night.

[**You have 69 days until the invasion.**]

Sylas shook his head at the prompt and turned to his status.

Name: Sylas Runewulf
Mana Lumens: 3386/3386
Class: Brewer
[Lumen Abilities:]
Flight
Quill

"Thank you," he told Patches as he scratched behind the cat's ears. "I wouldn't be able to do this without you." Patches purred in response. "Let's see if I can sneak up on Azor."

Sylas headed downstairs and noticed that the embers in the fireplace were out. He checked the cellar and found some food warming on the stove. Patches joined him.

"Azor?" Sylas called out.

"Happy Fireday!" She exploded into a flash of sparks all around Sylas, startling him.

He leaped back, his hand instinctively going to the place where the grip of his weapon should be. Patches took off, the pub cat practically flying up the stairs. Azor burst out laughing, the flames on her shoulders flickering even brighter. "I heard you tell Patches you were going to surprise me, so I surprised you instead."

"I deserved that," Sylas told her with a big grin on his face. His heart settled and he lowered his hand.

"You were reaching for a sword you don't have."

"I was. Sometimes it is still strange not to have a weapon on me. I was used to that, you know."

Azor relaxed, the fire around her dimming. "You don't speak about those times very much."

"That's because I don't want to remember them. But what you should know is that I joined when I was about fifteen, King's orders. I promised my dad I'd be back, and that never really shook out. I got word that he died." Sylas shook his head. "That's not a great story. Let me try again. I joined at fifteen, trained until I was ready, and was shipped off. I warred against the Shadowthorne Empire for about a decade, taking part campaigns like the Battle of Willcrest."

Azor nodded as if she'd heard of this fight. She hadn't, but Sylas had never really spoken about his former life, and she was interested.

"I fought archmages up there too, you know. We had a primitive form of magic. I should say, primitive to what they have here. Anyway, all that fighting kept me away from my home, which happened to be a pub. It's weird to call a pub a home, but to many, it's a place that they can most feel at home, so maybe calling it that is appropriate. I was supposed to take leave, but that never came. So I didn't get to say goodbye to my father."

"And your mother?"

"I never knew her. She died giving birth to me. She could be here too. But I'd wager that she is in the Celestial Plains based on how my dad spoke about her. Anyway, I guess that sums it up."

"Your backstory."

"Yeah, to put it simply. Yours? You never really told me yours."

Azor returned to the food she was cooking and Sylas joined her. He sat on the single stool in the cellar as she spoke. "I was born in the Chasm. We have demonic versions of archlumens there who use mana to create nefarious beings. Some of them are indeed nefarious; others, like me, turn out to be whatever normal is. So I was no use to her. She freed me from my contract, also something common in the Chasm. I took work at a restaurant until the guy running it closed up."

"Why?"

"To retire."

"In the Chasm?"

"Demons can retire too, you know," she told him. "The Chasm isn't what everyone here makes it to be. Like I've said before, less than a quarter of the demons there are bad. The rest just messed up here or in your world and are trying to manage. So there are towns, far-out places where people go to get some peace. Some of them are close to the Hexveil. It looks different from that side, you know."

"I can imagine," Sylas said.

"So our contract ended, and I wanted to get here to start a better life. Which I have."

"So elemental spirits like you want to come to the Underworld?"

"Some do. We hear about the place so much from the demons of the Chasm that we get curious. Anyone would. And it's easier for us to get through the Hexveil."

"How so?"

"We can fly over it, for one."

"Over it?" Sylas thought of the strange barrier, reminiscent of celestial tapestry unfurling from the sky itself.

"The Hexveil is made of Mana Lumens. What I did, and what others like me have done in the past, is fling myself at the barrier itself. This is risky because it can kill us."

"So you sacrificed your life to get here?" Sylas asked.

"I did. And now look at me?" Azor placed her gloved hands on a waist that didn't quite exist, yet she kept them there anyway. "I'm living happily in the Underworld with plans to serve an excellent stew tonight to people who enjoy my cooking. Sometimes, I even get to go on adventures. But not too many, which is good. I like the cozy pub life."

Sylas smiled at her. "You aren't the only one. We'll head to the market after breakfast here and then we'll wait for Tilbud. There's no telling when he's coming."

The crowd began to arrive, where they were greeted by a hearty stew made from a medley of root vegetables, lentils, a bouquet of herbs, and simmering chunks of mutton. At least that would keep patrons busy while they waited for the archlumen to appear.

"Where's the bloody quiz master?" Brom the farmer called up to Sylas at one point. He was seated at a table with the same group that had formed a team last week, already on their second round of pints.

"He's coming," Sylas said.

Mira, who sat at the bar, gave him a skeptical look. The apothecary didn't want to say it. She didn't want to remind Sylas that Tilbud wasn't exactly reliable. It was clear that Sylas and Azor had put some work into making it a memorable night, and the teams were already forming.

There was a group of militiamen—Cody, Duncan, Gary, and another fellow—already announcing they were calling themselves the Ember Maces. The farmers from the Seedlands had a proper group this time and had gone with the name the Seedlads. Godric, Bart, and two others that lived near the volcano went with Lava Boys again. There was even a group from Douro, who were going to call themselves the Flamefruits.

"Four teams so far," Mira told Sylas, rather than mention that Tilbud had yet to show.

"Wait, here comes more," he said as the door swung open. Mr. and Mrs. Brassmere were joined by John, the man who had installed Sylas's doors.

"Good to see you," Sylas told John, a bald man with eyes that were just a bit too close together. "Here for the quiz?"

"Here for the quiz and some stew," said Mrs. Brassmere, who had what looked like a new scarf tied around her neck.

"You're going to need a team name and another team member." Sylas glanced at Mira.

"Fine, fine. I'll join them. Cheers," she told them as they headed off to a free table.

"Come on, Tilbud," Sylas said as he tapped his fingers on the bar. "Where are you?"

His question was answered a few moments later as the door sprang open of its own accord. A tiny elephant made of mana stormed into the pub and fizzled out into a flash of golden sparks. Archlumen Tilbud now stood at the center of the space wearing a purple top hat that matched his silken outfit. He held several cards of notes in his hands.

"Apologies if I'm late. Azor, dear, please bring me a pint of The Old Lamplighter's finest." He turned to the crowd as if he had been in front of them all along, waiting for them to get ready. "Now, as you all know, all tables will be responsible for contributing Mana Lumens to the prize. Each table will contribute sixty." The farmers groaned. "Yes, lads, a wee bit more than last week. That will be fifteen MLus each. For being tardy, and because I am such a gracious host, I will contribute a hundred MLus. Making the prize four hundred."

"Four hundred," Brom said. "That's a hundred each if we win," he told his group.

"Correct." Tilbud was about to continue when Sylas interrupted him.

"And add *two* rounds of ale to the winning table, one round to the second-place table."

"Yes, that as well," the archlumen said. "Now, do we have names?"

"The Ember Maces," Cody said for the militiamen.

"The Lava Boys," Godric called out.

Mira exchanged glances with Mr. and Mrs. Brassmere, who were already discussing a name. The other man at the table, John, didn't seem to care one way or the other. "We'll be the Fix-Its," Mr. Brassmere said. "Unless you have a better name, Mira."

"Works for me."

"Good, and your team?" Tilbud asked the group from Douro.

"The Flamefruits," an older woman said.

"A good name. Last one," he said to the farmers.

"The Seedlads," Brom told him. The farmers gave this name a cheer.

"Wonderful. There will be three rounds. The first will be on obscure Lumen Abilities. The second, always a topic I like, will be on Battersea. And the third will be on complementary classes." He snapped his finger and sheets of parchment paper appeared on the table. "Shall we?"

The pub became a blur of activity as Sylas poured pint after pint and dealt with other things, like clearing tables and washing out some of the pint glasses below. He picked up a few things from the first round once Tilbud read the answers, namely that there were some very peculiar Lumen Abilities.

"The ability to communicate with shadows and darkness is called ... Gloom Whispering," he said as the tables graded each other's answers, which is another thing that they were doing that night.

"Would you take Gloom Talk?" Brom asked.

"No, that's not the proper name. Next. The ability to weave tangible objects out of dreams is called—"

"Dreamspinning," Mira shouted out.

"Yes. Those of you that wrote Dreamspinning get a point." Tilbud smiled at the group. "Next. The ability to manipulate droplets of water to form messages or images is called . . . Dew Conjuration. Ah, and the ability to shrink yourself should be an easy one to guess."

"It's called Shrink," Mira said.

"Correct again."

Sylas headed down to the cellar to get some fresh pints. By the time he was upstairs again, the second round on Battersea began. He heard bits and details, famous districts, the names of some of the statues, and some traveling time questions which Tilbud seemed to like.

Sylas was more interested in the answers from the first round. Knowing more about Lumen Abilities was certainly something he would have to look into in the future, but before he did that, he had a ton of other things on his mind, namely being able to see the Book of Shadows and understand the invasion message.

The teams became increasingly competitive in the last round, but no one pushed things over the line. There weren't any threats—Sylas had actually seen this before in a pub quiz, but it was directed toward the quiz master—but there certainly was tension in the air as Tilbud tallied up the final points.

"Are we ready?" he asked.

"Get on with it, then," Mrs. Brassmere shouted.

"Right. I have tallied the results of the last round, and you'll be surprised to know that the overall winner of the quiz tonight was not the winner of the last round. That can happen, you know. And yes, even with the bonus question about the Soot Alchemists and Lumen Dredgers."

Mrs. Brassmere threw her hands up in the air. "Come on, then!"

Tilbud smiled at her. Strings of sparkling mana trickled from the ceiling as he prepared his announcement. "And the winner of tonight's quiz is . . . the Flamefruits! In second place are the Fix-Its." Tilbud did a dramatic spin and bowed to all of them. "Thank you for playing, and be sure to join us next week."

Mrs. Brassmere buried her head in her hands in a comical way while her husband laughed alongside her. Mira's lips tightened for a split second and quickly relaxed once she saw Sylas looking at her.

He shrugged, she shrugged, he laughed.

Mira couldn't win them all.

CHAPTER TWENTY-SIX

SLING

Patches paced around the well, his ears twitching, his tail lifted. He could hear men outside of the pub, walking up and down the street as part of their patrol. It was good they were around, but they still didn't seem to understand the severity of the threat to the village beyond.

He hopped up to the rim of the well and looked down.

There was activity below, and he was feeling emboldened by all the power he had received from the guests at the Tavernly Realm that night. He didn't know who the magic man was, but whenever he showed up, it seemed to make people happy. Even better, that translated into even more power for Patches.

You're just going to have to go down into the well, even if you don't like water.

Patches hated to think this, he certainly didn't want to get wet, but there was a tunnel in the well and someone needed to clear it out.

The back door of the pub opened and the magic man stepped out, no hat on his head this time. He pulled the cape he wore over the front of his body, as if to protect himself from the cold.

Patches's first thought was to turn invisible. But the magic man had already spotted him, and he was suddenly standing next to Patches, as if he had been there the entire time.

The man placed his hand on Patches and petted him as he examined the well. He never said anything, but Patches got this strange sense that the man knew something.

Does he know about the smoke demon? The spiders in the well?

The magic man produced a small vial from his pocket. He slowly guided it to the air above the well. Once he was done, he corked it.

The man said something to Patches. He lifted him and brought the pub cat to his chest.

At first, Patches protested.

But then the man set him down and cast his hand over the opening of the well. Golden energy pooled in the palm of his hand and soon, the well was covered by a layer of magic.

Patches mewed at the strange hum in the air. He approached the well and stopped, the power strong enough for him to want to turn the other way.

The magic man yawned. He headed back into the pub without saying anything to Patches.

Did he just seal it? Of course, he did, Patches thought as he circled the well one last time.

He sat in the dark for a moment. The Tavernly Realm was safe, but Patches had this itching feeling that the magical barrier wouldn't hold, especially once the demon noticed it.

It was a temporary fix.

[You have 68 days until the invasion.]

Sylas placed his hands on Patches's head as he scanned his status:

Name: Sylas Runewulf
Mana Lumens: 4139/4139
Class: Brewer
[Lumen Abilities:]
Flight
Quill

"Thanks for the top off, buddy," he said quietly, not wanting to wake the cat. Sylas had sold over a hundred pints last night, netting him plenty of Mana Lumens.

Aside from the normal power he used just to exist, he hadn't spent much the previous day aside from paying Malcolm the grains dealer for a delivery. This was just to refresh his supply. As Sylas had discovered, his grains had lasted over two weeks and seemed to rejuvenate themselves in his storeroom.

Still, he figured it was smart to freshen his supply. Maybe he'd even deal with creating spirit grains in the future.

"Happy Specterday," Azor said. The cheer in her voice thinned. "You should probably come downstairs. Tilbud has something to tell you. I'd tell you myself, but I think he wants to do it."

"Will do. And if I didn't say it, good job last night. The stew was excellent. I hope you sold a lot."

"I did. And there's some left, which I'm warming now. You and Tilbud can have that for breakfast with biscuits. Did I tell you I made biscuits?"

Sylas grinned at the fire spirit. Contracting with her had been one of the best moves he had made, not for her cooking, which was great, but her companionship. Having someone around that was fighting on his side made living in the Underworld an even better experience.

"Are you coming, or are you going to lie there smiling?" she asked.

"Sorry, I'll be down in a second." Sylas was careful not to disturb Patches as he got out of bed. He wanted to pet him, but he also knew that the pub cat had given him close to five hundred Mana Lumens last night, which covered the six casks Sylas had brewed after the quiz.

Patches needed his sleep.

"Tilbud," Sylas said as he stepped down into the pub.

The archlumen, who sat at one of the booths reading an old book, closed it and stood upon seeing Sylas. "Morning. Follow me."

He led Sylas outside, Sylas's eyes immediately jumping to the well, now covered by a magical barrier. A strange, drone-like hum reached his ears. "What happened?"

"That cat of yours. He's much smarter than he looks."

"Patches did this?" Sylas asked, perplexed.

"This barrier? No. But he is clearly aware that something is happening in your well."

"Are you talking about the cinderspider?"

The archlumen turned to him. "The what now?"

Since Tilbud had appeared late last night and launched right into the quiz, he hadn't heard about the cinderspider. Sylas quickly caught him up.

"So Azor and Patches killed a cinderspider?" Tilbud adjusted his tiny hat and squinted at the well. "That's unusual."

"That's why the militiamen were patrolling last night."

"I wondered about that. I had the window open upstairs and heard them speaking. I assumed that they were worried about something that had freed itself from the Chasm. That's why I came outside, initially. Then I saw your cat closely examining the well. It looked like he wanted to go inside."

"Into the well?" Sylas rubbed the back of his head. "Azor noticed that too, about a week ago."

Tilbud took a somber tone. "There is something dark happening here, Sylas. I can sense something, but I don't know what it is. So I sealed the well. For now. I'll need a few days."

"To do what?"

"To do a little research and ask a few friends about what's going on here. Well, I may have to ask someone who isn't a friend as well, but I have captured the essence of something here. It needs to be examined. Your plans for the next few days?"

"We're planning to go to Battersea tomorrow, Azor, Mira, and me."

"And the pub will be closed?"

"At least a day or two, yes."

"That's good. That will isolate the place a bit while I get this figured out. I would advise against telling the militiamen about this. You don't want them disturbing my magical barrier here, which they may do if they learn I have sealed it. What am I missing? Water. Do you have enough water?"

"I brought some in yesterday, to the storeroom," Sylas said. "There's plenty. But if the well is sealed longer, I'll need some for brewing."

"It won't be sealed much longer. Let's plan to meet again on Moonsday eve."

"So two days from now."

"Precisely," the archlumen said as Azor arrived.

"The food is ready." The fire spirit glanced from Tilbud to Sylas and registered the looks on their faces. She knew it was bad when the archlumen had told her what happened earlier that morning, but seeing Sylas and the way his brow was furrowed made her think it was even worse than she originally thought. Her shoulders sank. "Are we in danger?"

"Not at the moment," Tilbud said. "The well is sealed. But both of you will need to keep this a secret for now."

"Perhaps I should stay here then."

"Stay here?" Sylas asked Azor. "I thought you'd go with us to Battersea."

"Someone has to be here to defend the pub, and we probably shouldn't leave Patches alone if there is danger. I don't mind staying here, Sylas. I'll keep an eye on the place."

Sylas felt a pang of guilt for leaving in the first place. Yet he had things that he needed to do in Battersea, and understanding the invasion message would be to all of their benefits. But to leave the pub? Was he making the right choice in going?

Azor interrupted his concern. "You won't be gone long, and the well is sealed. Patches and I can handle the place. Maybe he'll even start to like me again."

"The seal will hold until Tombsday, I'm certain," Tilbud said. "I will need a solution by then, but I will endeavor to have one, or I will come with someone who can make a stronger seal."

"So the dark influence you sense, the same one Patches clearly is picking up, you think this is the cinderspiders?" Sylas asked.

"I do not know. It might be something much more nefarious." Tilbud placed his hands behind his back, grave expression in his eyes. "We will have to see. But you should return ready."

"Ready for what?"

"Ready to defend the pub, if that's what it comes to."

Sylas felt his chest tighten as a flash of rage swelled within. "No one is doing anything to The Old Lamplighter," he said through gritted teeth. "No one."

"Yes, it is quite the place," Tilbud said as he tilted his chin up to examine the pub. "But not to worry. We will do our best to protect The Old Lamplighter and Ember Hollow. As I said, keep this information to yourselves. We do not want others disturbing the well, and I fear if the militia learns what I have done, they'll want to investigate. Now, I must get going. I'll see you both in a few days."

It was slow at The Old Lamplighter that night, which was fine by Sylas. He still netted 340 Mana Lumens from his sales and went ahead and brewed one strong ale and one regular ale before heading to bed.

He slept well, and awoke the next morning, ready to head to Battersea.

[**You have 67 days until the invasion.**]

"You didn't have to," he told Patches as he examined his status and saw that his Mana Lumens had been topped off. Sylas had truly laid low the previous day, no trips to other cities, no action, which meant he had barely expended Mana Lumens. This paid off, the 340 he gained the previous night added to his overall total.

"Over four thousand MLus now," he told Patches as his status menu faded away. The cat purred. "Hopefully that's enough to get some answers in Battersea and get me there in one piece. I suppose I should start with getting there in one piece. Did you see the well last night?"

The pub cat made a soft sound.

"Nice and protected, right?" Sylas continued scratching behind his ear. "You'll be here with Azor while I'm gone, okay? Protect the place."

Sylas headed downstairs to find Azor behind the bar, the fire spirit speaking to Mira, who sat on her favorite stool with a leather travel bag next to her.

Mira wore a new dress, an emerald-green one that she had picked up in Douro for this trip. Of course, Sylas didn't notice. The not-so-new-newcomer merely plopped down onto the barstool next to her and ate one of the scones Azor had made.

"Good stuff," he told the fire spirit.

"You seem to like all my cooking."

Sylas squinted at the ceiling, as if he were considering this. "I guess I do, don't I. And happy Soulsday."

"That's my line," Azor said.

"Sorry about that," Sylas told her as he finally turned his attention to Mira. "Morning. What's the plan?"

Mira swiveled around on her barstool so she faced Sylas. She knew he was playing with her, at least it felt this way, but his nonchalance still bothered the apothecary. "The plan?"

"I figured you'd be the one to know," Sylas told her. "Unless you want me to figure it out."

"Right, Battersea. You're referring to how we will get there?"

"I am. It's northeast of here, right?"

"Correct. We will start by portaling to Douro. We will take a sling from there."

"A sling?"

A wolfish grin appeared on Mira's face. She couldn't help it. "Yes, a sling. I'll let that be a surprise. And if you know what it is," she told Azor, "don't say it."

"I thought I was supposed to fly," Sylas said with another bite of his scone.

"There will be plenty of flying, don't you worry. We will reach Battersea by the afternoon and can go from there."

"And you know where the Book of Shadows is? The lumengineers that can view it?"

"I do. And they'll know who to ask about the invasion message. As for the Ale Alliance, there is a neighborhood of guilds. We can find it there."

Sylas exchanged glances with Azor. "Should we tell her?"

"About what?" the fire spirit asked, genuinely confused.

"You know what." Sylas nodded to the back door of the pub.

"About the well?" Azor slapped her gloved hands over her mouth.

"What about the well?" Mira asked.

Once they were outside, Sylas showed her the well, which remained sealed by a magic barrier. "The spider came from the well, as you know. Tilbud sealed it off, and he'll be back on Moonsday with further instructions. This gives us a day and a half or so in Battersea."

Mira sighed. "That's not enough time."

"Sure it is," Sylas told her. "We can portal back and forth, or I can, after we reach there. That's why I need to get the portal upstairs activated. We'll figure that out too. Everything will be figured out."

Mira looked him over skeptically.

"Believe me, Mira."

She turned to the well and approached, the surface of the barrier a semi-translucent golden glow.

"He didn't want the militiamen finding out," Sylas said as he joined her.

"Yes, that is probably for the best. My uncle would have men walking circles around your well. It would be comical but you wouldn't like it."

"No, I don't think I would." Sylas popped what was left of the scone in his mouth. "We have time, but we should probably get going. And if I didn't already tell you, thanks, Mira. Thanks for coming with me. Did I mention it would be just the two of us?"

"You did not, but I can see why it would be now," she said as she swept her hand toward the well. "Someone needs to stay here to keep an eye on the place."

"Exactly. And whatever hotel you want to stay in tonight, wherever you'd like to have dinner, it's on me."

Even though she already knew this to be the case, this statement cheered Mira up. "Any place?"

"Sure," Sylas said. "It's not often one visits the biggest city in the Underworld."

They portaled to Douro and Mira took the lead, the apothecary expertly guiding Sylas to the outer edge of town. The pair came to something that looked like an oversized piece of pottery, the object shaped almost like a smokestack.

A man sat out front on a wooden chair in front of it. He wore a leather vest, the front panels of which extended all the way down to his feet. The man swept these aside and motioned for Mira and Sylas to approach.

"Taking a sling, are we?" he asked.

"Toward Battersea," Mira said, who had clearly done this before. She still hadn't explained to Sylas what a sling was, but she had a feeling by the way he was looking at the cannon that he got the gist.

"You're going to shoot us there, aren't you?" he asked.

"It will get us high into the air traveling in that direction. We'll take over flying from there," Mira said. "It will use less MLus in the end."

"Good," Sylas said. "Two please," he told the man in the strange vest.

"That will be three hundred MLus."

[Transfer 300 Mana Lumens to the sling keeper? Y/N?]

Sylas glanced at Mira. "Trust me," she told him, "it will save us time in the end."

Sylas acknowledged the transfer. Once he did so, the sling operator went to work. He opened a door on the side of the ceramic cannon and motioned for Sylas and Mira to get in.

"Sit in the chair and cross your arms over your chest," he explained as he pulled on some straps that allowed him to shift the muzzle of the cannon toward the east. "You've done this before, right?"

"I have," Mira told the sling operator.

"Then you know. You'll want to let your powers take over once you start falling. When you're flying, just fly. Don't waste MLus trying to do anything else. Let the power of the sling take you as far as you can go and then take over. Also, sometimes people try to boost themselves coming out of the sling. Don't do that. That's how you explode." He tapped his knuckle against the outer wall of the contraption. "Good luck!"

Soon, Sylas was seated next to Mira, the two in a pair of chairs inside the barrel of the sling, their arms crossed over their chest.

"Fun, right?" Mira clutched her pack against the front of her body, Sylas doing the same.

"I haven't decided yet."

"Ready?" the man shouted from outside the sling. "Three, two, one—"

Whoosh!

Sylas and Mira shot forward, their movement amplified by the golden glow of mana.

Sylas felt as if his arms and legs had been cut away from his body, which made it even harder to hold his bag as the sudden jolt of acceleration vibrated through his body. The ground shrank beneath them, and for a moment, it seemed as if they would make it all the way to the Celestial Plains above.

But in traveling higher into the sky, Sylas came to understand just how out of reach heaven was. It still felt as if it were leagues away, that he could have been fired out of an even stronger sling and still wouldn't have reached it.

He glanced over to Mira, her dark hair beating in the wind, her eyes closed.

Sylas closed his eyes too, which brought an entirely different sensation. He could feel his stomach drop, his skin prickling, sweat forming as he clutched his bag even tighter. Then, there was weightlessness.

"Now," Mira told Sylas. "Fly!"

How long had they been sailing in the air? As Sylas's Flight power took over, he made the mistake of looking down to see if he could still see Douro. He could not. All that was beneath him now was an endless forest dappled with lakes. Fear instantly caused him to tense, his skin prickling.

"Focus." Mira reached out and grabbed his wrist, her hand eventually slipping into his. This calmed Sylas to some degree. He steadied out, and was soon flying alongside Mira, Mana Lumens trailing past them.

Mira continued to hold his hand even though it was clear she could let go. She only released after he shifted forward a bit, the not-so-newcomer clearly in control.

"Got it?" Mira asked just to be sure. Of course he had it, but she still felt the urge to check.

"How long do we have to fly like this?" Sylas asked.

"For the next several hours. Don't push yourself too much. Keep a steady pace. This should burn about a thousand MLus if you're doing it right."

"Do you have enough?"

Mira felt a tinge of annoyance at this question, which she quickly let fade away. He was only being concerned. "I do," she said. "Don't worry about me. Worry about keeping a steady pace and not exerting yourself too much. Otherwise, you'll reach Battersea and you will have to portal back, open the pub, sell some pints, and start saving again."

"I'll bet the portal from Battersea isn't cheap."

"It isn't," she said. "Last I was there, it was three hundred MLus per trip."

"That steep? It would cost you six hundred to go there and back."

"Correct."

"That must be why the Ale Alliance has this portal in the pub," Sylas said. "Is there anything like that for you? I mean a guild."

"An apothecary guild? There is, but I haven't joined."

"Why not?" Sylas asked.

"Guilds have their various rules and I don't have enough MLus to meet their requirements. I would if I moved to a bigger city. There would be more people to treat, but I'd also be twice as busy as I am now. Not to mention I own my shop in Ember Hollow. But mostly, it's cost. So doing things like, I don't know, flying to Battersea on a whim, would be out of the question."

"Makes sense," Sylas said, now worried about what the Ale Alliance's requirements would be. Iron Rose seemed to be part of it, and he didn't see anything at her pub that was different from his, aside from the swan paintings.

The two continued their flight toward Battersea, Mira keeping up the light chatter throughout. It was easy to talk to Sylas, and while he teased her sometimes, he was a good listener.

They passed several others flying toward the biggest city in the Underworld, which meant they were getting close.

Battersea had a nickname, the City of Seven Hills, which made it easy to spot on the horizon. Each hill was crowned with a cluster of colorful buildings, the quaint homes, businesses, and guilds painted in hues of ocher, terra-cotta, and turquoise.

The interplay of light from the Celestial Plains painted a vibrant mosaic on the undulating terrain that followed, revealing networks of cobblestone streets and alleys interwoven between the buildings of the famed city. Beyond was a lake that seemed to have no end, Sylas feeling as if he were staring out at an ocean.

"What's the name of the lake?" Sylas asked, trying to remember if someone had ever told him.

"That's Lake Seraphina. Huge, right?"

"It sure is!"

"Time to lower," Mira said as she reached out for Sylas's hand. "Let's activate the portal first and then find a lumengineer who specializes in the Book of Shadows. We can start there, and they will know who to ask about the invasion message."

"Right," Sylas said. "And what about our dinner and lodging?"

"We'll set that up later. Don't worry," Mira told him with a grin, the wind starting to rush past her, "you're still taking me out tonight."

CHAPTER TWENTY-SEVEN

THE BOOK OF SHADOWS

After activating the portal, Sylas and Mira approached a building that loomed over the others in the vicinity. It reminded Sylas of the citadel he'd seen in Duskhaven, the MLR Bank, yet there were no spires here. The building was square in nature, with a grand entrance at the top of a set of stairs made of black-veined marble.

"This way," Mira said as she grabbed Sylas's wrist. They had a lot to do in a short amount of time. He could be a tourist later. She led him up the stairs, Sylas still gawking at the size of the structure and the surrounding area.

"I wasn't expecting this," he finally told her as they got into a small queue in front of a woman standing behind a desk. There was a sign above her that read *The Distinguished Society of Lumengineers and Etheric Constructs.*

"Battersea never fails to impress," Mira told him. They waited all of ten minutes until it was their turn. "Book of Shadows," Mira said after the smartly dressed woman greeted her.

"An archlumen for the Book of Shadows," the woman said as she looked down at a ledger. "Your names?"

Mira motioned to Sylas. "We're here for him, Sylas Runewulf."

"I see." The woman looked up at them skeptically after flipping through her ledger. "I don't see an appointment here for a Sylas Runewulf."

"We didn't make an appointment. I didn't have to last time," Mira said as she minded her tone. Mira was keenly aware of this unique kind of red tape that would require navigating the services in Battersea. "We will take whoever is available."

"Whoever is available?"

Sylas stepped forward. "I'm a bit new here, and I'm just looking to reconnect with my father. I was a soldier back in our world, and I was on the front line when he died. I'm sorry, my lady, if I didn't make the appropriate appointment. I'm still learning the ropes here. It's not easy dying."

Mira turned to him, her mouth dropping open as she saw the sincere look on Sylas's face. Was he being serious or was this an act? She knew his backstory, but the way he'd just told it had tugged at her heartstrings.

Apparently, it worked on the front desk woman. She closed the ledger and smiled at him curtly. "In that case, we do have drop-in slots available. They will be with trainees, though. I should clarify—these are highly skilled lumengineers, yet they have recently shifted their focus to archives and haven't been given proper time slots or an office yet."

"But they can do the same thing as a normal lumengineer?" Mira asked.

"Of course they can. Once system access is granted, they can do anything. They're given this role so they can practice and hone their new skill set. That's all. It will be the same as visiting even the grandest lumengineer."

"And the price?" Mira asked.

The smile on the woman's face thinned. "The price was set again a few months ago. A single parent is six hundred MLus. Both parents are a thousand. We have a special this week for friends and other family members. It is buy one, get one free. One friend or other family member is a thousand MLus."

"I have parents I need to find and three friends," Sylas said. "But two of the friends are brothers."

The woman at the front desk considered this. "Then I suggest you pay the cost for parents, a thousand MLus, and the cost for one friend, another thousand MLus, and use your free slot to find one of the brothers."

"A total of two thousand," Sylas said as he checked his status.

Name: Sylas Runewulf
Mana Lumens: 3179/4479
Class: Brewer
[Lumen Abilities:]
Flight
Quill

It had cost Sylas quite a bit to get to Battersea. If he spent two thousand, he wouldn't have much left to pay any dues to the Ale Alliance or to figure out the invasion message. Then again, he could always portal back to Ember Hollow, save up for a few days, and then return.

Sylas nodded. "Works for me. Do I pay here or pay there?"

"You will pay Catia directly. Follow this." The woman motioned them to the left as a trail of golden mana formed in the air.

They climbed a set of stairs, Mira in the lead.

"Well?" Sylas asked her.

"Well, what?"

"I expected you to have something to say."

"About your little performance back there?" Mira couldn't stop the smile on her face. "It worked. I'll tell you that. I was certain she was going to send us away until you started up."

Sylas grinned. "I did what I had to do, and it's not cheap either, the cost to access this information."

"Some people will spend years saving up the Mana Lumens necessary to access this information."

"It's crazy we have to pay at all," Sylas said. "Why wouldn't they let us access this information freely?"

"That, I can't tell you." They approached a large wooden door, one illuminated by lumen lamps. Mira turned to Sylas. "The Underworld and its rules can be baffling at times."

The door opened of its own accord.

Sylas exchanged glances with Mira.

"Come in," a soft voice called from inside. They entered to find Catia seated behind a wooden desk, one in front of a large window. The only issue with her view was she didn't have one. The window looked out at a wall, Sylas not quite sure of its purpose.

Catia, who wore robes and had her orange hair braided behind her ears, saw Sylas look from her face to the window behind her.

"Yes, it's not the nicest of spaces. I've been told it is temporary and there will be some renovating in the future, but that remains to be seen." She motioned to a pair of leather chairs in front of her. Sylas took his seat first, and instantly felt as if he'd sunk a few inches into the rather plush chair. "What can I do for you?" the lumengineer asked once Mira was seated.

"I need access to the Book of Shadows," Sylas said. "My parents and a friend. We were told at the front that there's a special."

"Yes, a special. Buy one get one free. You're lucky as well because that special ends on Thornsday."

"Before we do that, however, I have a question for you."

"Oh?" Catia looked Sylas over. She assumed the bearded man with the intense blue eyes was a newcomer. Most people that wanted information from the Book of Shadows had only recently arrived in the Underworld. The woman next to him, a tall beauty with dark hair, had clearly been in the Underworld for a while.

Catia could sense things like this.

Sylas clasped his hands together. "I've been getting an invasion message. I'm wondering who I should see about that."

"A what now?" Catia leaned forward.

Mira took it from there. "He gets a message every morning telling him that an invasion is set to happen. It started with eighty-nine days. Now it's at—"

"Sixty-seven days. I don't know what the message is in reference to. I'm not provided any other information either. I simply get it every morning and then it fades away. I, ahem, *we*, live in Ember Hollow, so maybe it has something to do with the Hexveil."

"Ember Hollow? And you're a couple?"

"Us? No," Mira said, her cheeks turning red.

Catia almost laughed at this. To see the pale-faced woman go from porcelain to cherry red in a matter of seconds was certainly a sight. "So you aren't a couple?"

"She's a friend," Sylas said. "She's classed as an apothecary. I'm classed as a brewer."

"I see. In that case, you're at the wrong office. Not for the Book of Shadows," Catia said once Sylas and Mira both shifted in their seats. "This is the right place for that. But you're going to need to see someone much more powerful than me regarding the message. I know of a manaseer that could be of use for something like this."

"You're a lumengineer, right?"

"I am," Catia told Sylas.

"Sorry if I sound uninformed here, but what would be the difference between that and a manaseer again?"

Catia grinned. "Is there a difference between someone who makes ale and someone who makes wine? They are similar, but the process is different, are they not? A manaseer has access to the system in different ways than someone like us."

"What about an archlumen?"

"Those are people who have a system that allow them to assign powers. I cannot do that, but I can access the system they are able to design from and tweak it in some ways. I also can do things like access the Book of Shadows. The system I'm sure you're aware of as the owner of a pub and its limitations? That would be lumengineer."

"Alright, that makes some sense. Then what exactly does a manaseer do?"

"Divining. They are able to see and understand the Mana Lumen currents that make up our world. This gives them glimpses of the future. Consider them something like a fortune teller, but more powerful. There aren't many, and the ones that are around usually are few and far between."

"Like mendicants?"

"That's one way to look at them," Catia told him. "Mendicants with strong intuitions when it comes to the power that keeps the Underworld together. Remember, we are living in the middle of the Chasm. Lumengineers made the Hexveil, but it was through the guidance of manaseers. And the one I know would be very interested in these messages you're getting. The only problem is, he's booked solid."

"Booked?" Sylas asked.

"Like your apothecary here, he has clients. But if you're interested in meeting him, I believe you can in the morning."

"Tomorrow morning?"

"Yes. Nuno has a coffee and tea shop he likes to go to."

"Nuno?" Sylas asked. He was familiar with the name. It was common in the Shadowthorne Empire.

"Yes, Nuno Landling. The coffeehouse is in the Brenham District. It's a ways out, but you'll find him there, seated by the water having a late-morning coffee. The place is called Agatha's. Nuno may be intrigued by your issue, especially because of the ominous nature." She shrugged. "But that's up to him. I would assign you a quest contract to meet him, but doing so is up to you. Let's deal with the Book of Shadows now."

[Transfer 2000 Mana Lumens to The Distinguished Society of Lumengineers and Etheric Constructs? Y/N?]

"I'm ready," Sylas said with a nod. He wanted to comment on the name, but decided against it.

Catia guided Sylas and Mira down the hallway to a door that was twice as tall as any human Sylas had ever seen. He heard the lock click on the other side and the towering door swung open of its own accord.

The room that followed was completely bare aside from an enormous tome that sat in the center of the space. Covered in a deep, almost obsidian leather, the Book of Shadows was etched with intricate symbols and runes.

Catia stepped up to it and motioned for Sylas and Mira to sit before the pedestal on a pair of golden cushions that Sylas didn't remember seeing just moments ago.

Mana radiated off Catia as she lowered her head and placed her hand on the book. The tome remained closed, yet Sylas saw translucent pages floating into the air above the lumengineer, the pages spilling open. The almost invisible pages shifted around the room, moving to the point that they were a blur.

Catia opened her eyes and looked at Sylas. "State your name," she said, her voice amplified.

"Sylas Runewulf."

As he said these words, the nearly invisible pages rushed toward Sylas and hit him all at once like a swarm of locusts.

There was no sensation associated with this, but he did see the pages moving through him and down his arms before tornadoing into a rush of energy that struck the Book of Shadows.

"*Sylas Runewulf,*" came another voice, one that seemed to vibrate the very fabric of the air. "*Who is it you seek?*"

Sylas looked toward Catia for confirmation. She offered him a curt, almost fearful nod. He also noticed her eyes had bulged, the woman straining to concentrate.

"My parents, Luther Runewulf and Hazel Florence Runewulf."

"*Luther Runewulf was originally in the Celestial Plains with your mother, Hazel. I do not have access to either of their classes. I can tell you he is in the Chasm,*" the voice said, Mira gasping at this revelation. "*He went there of his own accord as part of a Hallowed Pursuit.*"

"A Hallowed Pursuit?"

"A crusade against demons," Mira told Sylas.

"My mother is still in the Plains?"

"*Who else do you seek?*" the voice asked instead of answering his question.

Catia cleared her throat. "I am Lumengineer Catia Almen, guide for today. Sylas Runewulf seeks two of his friends. Friends, correct?" she asked Sylas.

"Correct," Sylas told the book as the pages flipped back and forth.

"*What are their names?*"

"Kael, no Quinlan Ashdown," Sylas said, figuring he'd go with the older of the two brothers, who was more responsible.

The voice was quiet for a moment as the pages settled. "*Quinlan Ashdown is in Geist. He is classed as an adventurer.*"

"Geist?" Sylas glanced at Mira. He was certain he'd heard that name before.

"*And the other friend?*"

"Raelis Sund," Sylas said.

"*Raelis Sund is classed as a demon hunter. He is also in the Chasm.*"

"He is? So he died here?"

"*No, he went as part of a Hallowed Pursuit.*"

"With my father?"

The voice paused for a moment at his question. Finally, it spoke again, *"I do not have the answer to that question. Will there be anything else?"*

"No, there will not," Catia told the voice firmly. "Thank you for your guidance."

Sylas experienced a gnawing sense of hopelessness as the Book of Shadows slammed shut.

At least he had answers.

CHAPTER TWENTY-EIGHT

COFFEE FOR THE MANASEER

Sylas paid for a room at a hotel near the Sigur District, one that Mira had stayed in before. Rather than pay in the morning, he opted to pay that night due to the fact his Mana Lumens wouldn't be topped off later on. For paying early, he received a 10 percent discount.

[Transfer 270 Mana Lumens to the Seven Hills Inn? Y/N?]

Sylas indicated yes with a quick nod of his head. Mira had chosen a room for them, one with two small beds and plenty of seating space. It was a family room according to the innkeeper. Sylas had the notion to ask how many families traveled to Battersea but didn't.

He wasn't in the mood.

The news from Catia the lumengineer had hit him in a way he wasn't expecting. It had brought memories of both Raelis Sund and his father, memories that Sylas hadn't thought of in years.

He remembered training with Raelis and how competitive he had been; Raelis was one of the most aggressive but friendly men Sylas had ever met. He remembered his father telling him that he had always wanted to war for the Aurum Kingdom but hadn't been able to on the account of a bum knee, which was why he generally served ale from a stool, and why Sylas handled the casks as soon as he could lift them.

Raelis joining some crusade into the Chasm made sense. His father joining did not. While he had been patriotic, he'd never seemed like much of a fighter to Sylas.

Something had changed.

"You alright?" Mira asked as they turned in the direction of the Guild District.

"I guess."

"Is it your father, your friends, or your mother?"

Sylas hadn't even thought of his mother. That made him feel even guiltier. "I just didn't expect to hear my father was in the Chasm."

"It is something people do," Mira said carefully. She had heard of the excursions beyond the Hexveil. There was a time when her uncle had wanted to join one, yet she'd been able to talk him out of it. They never ended well. "What about that other friend of yours? Geist is practically our sister village. It's on the opposite side of the Underworld is what I'm saying."

"If Quinlan is there, either his brother, Kael, is there with him, or Quinlan knows where he is. They were always quite close. And that part is good news. I look forward to seeing him at some point." Sylas ran his hand over his beard, "Let's meet with the Ale Alliance and call it a night."

"Call it a night?" she asked.

"Heh. After I take you out for dinner."

The Ale Alliance's structure stood out among the other buildings on the street, the place impossible to miss. It was shaped like a cask and there was a large sign out front adorned with gilded letters and artful illustrations of hops and barley. The windows, framed with a rich dark wood, had window boxes featuring a mixture of herbs, sunburst marigolds, and trailing ivy.

Sylas spotted a streetside bar, one that was currently closed. As his eyes traced over the building one last time, he noticed the fine detailing of the wood, the knicks and grooves actually a collection of numerous sigils.

He entered alongside Mira and was greeted by a man in a gray tunic that was open at the front, his chest hair sticking out. The man stood behind a bar that looked like it doubled as a reception desk.

"May I help you?" he asked in a commanding voice.

Sylas stepped up to the bar. "I run the pub in Ember Hollow. It's called The Old Lamplighter. I'm here to join the Alliance and, um, have my portal activated."

"Join the Ale Alliance? Before you can join the Ale Alliance, you must have your pub inspected and approved. Before you have the portal activated by our sigilist, you must pay your membership fee and have your pub inspected and approved. One doesn't simply walk in and join, as nice as that would be." The man leaned forward on the bar. "It would be nice, wouldn't it? If things worked that way."

Mira could sense Sylas had tensed up, likely because of the information he had recently received. She acted on this.

"In that case," Sylas said, "I suppose I should set up an inspection. That would be first, yes?"

"Yes, and that will cost you eight hundred MLus. This is to cover the cost of transportation to Ember Hollow and the inspector's fee. You may also elect for the sigilist to come at that time and pay your full dues then, so fifteen hundred MLus total. This is, in fact, the better deal, because if you don't pay for it this way, the sigilist will have to come separately."

Sylas briefly checked his status and saw he had just over nine hundred Mana Lumens.

"Yes?" the man behind the bar asked. "Have you decided?"

Sylas thought about using Quill to run the numbers in his head, but it was pretty obvious he wouldn't have enough. "Do I have to pay it all now?"

"No, you do not. You can pay half now and half when the inspector and the sigilist come."

Sylas considered this. Half he could do depending on what day they visited. "When is the next available slot?"

"Tombsday. There isn't really a slot per se. They only approve new pubs on Tombsday."

"The day after tomorrow, huh?" Sylas said.

"How much are you short?" Mira asked.

"No," he started to say.

"Sylas, how much?"

"A couple hundred MLus for the full package."

"How much exactly?"

"Exactly?" Rather than do the math, Sylas told her how many MLus he currently had.

"So you need six hundred."

"A little less than that, but yes."

Mira motioned Sylas away from the bar so they could speak privately. "You have to be careful to go below certain amounts. If I loan you six hundred, you can surely pay me back by the end of the week."

"With interest," Sylas said.

"I don't need interest. I know this will help expand your business—"

"Mira, you don't have to do these sorts of things for me. I already owe you more than one favor, and I promised to take you out tonight."

"I want to, Sylas. I don't mind," she said, her silver eyes softening. "And the place I want to go tonight isn't expensive."

"I will pay you back double. No questions asked. Just let me get the reserves back up. I don't want Patches topping my supply off either. I don't know how much he has, and it's best not to put too much stress on his system."

"I agree with you there. You'll have to keep him out of your room. But I don't agree on paying me double."

"Mira."

"Sylas."

"It's the least I can do." He extended his hand to her. "I'll pay you back double."

"I don't want double."

"Mira."

"Stop saying my name."

"Mira."

"I said—"

"I'll stop saying your name when you shake my hand."

Mira shook Sylas's hand and a new prompt appeared.

[**Mira Ravenbane has transferred 600 Mana Lumens to you.**]

"Thank you," he told her. He approached the man behind the bar. "Tombsday is fine for an inspection. What time?"

"They usually arrive around noon."

"Good, that will work," Sylas said. "Too bad they can't come on Wraithsday. We have a feast every Wraithsday."

The man behind the counter grinned. "Hey, anything to get people into the pub, right? Especially as far out as you are. Anyway, with membership, you'll have access to unique pub items. I won't go into what you have access to now, not until you're a full member. But it is worth your while. And these items can be customized as well. What did you say the name of your pub was?"

"The Old Lamplighter."

The man behind the bar nodded. "That's a good name for a pub."

A prompt appeared, and Sylas transferred the Mana Lumens. He turned back to Mira and suddenly felt foolish. One of these days, and hopefully soon, he needed to do something really nice for her.

———

[**You have 66 days until the invasion.**]

Sylas instantly checked his status to confirm something. Mira had opted to upgrade their room to what was known as a Rejuvenation Suite, even if Sylas had protested. It was guaranteed to increase their MLus by up to 10 percent of their total. She had done this because Sylas would need three hundred MLus to portal back to Ember Hollow.

"Trust me, it's worth the upgrade," she told him at the time.

Sylas hadn't been so sure at the time, especially after he was instructed to rub a glowing algae-based substance all over his face and sleep under a window directly facing the Celestial Plains.

Now, as he glanced over his status, he was glad he had followed her instructions. Sylas now had plenty to get home. He looked over to Mira, who was already awake, the apothecary folding and rearranging some of the things in her bag.

"How did we do?" she asked.

"Happy Moonsday," came his reply.

She smiled at him. "Same to you."

"I'm at just over five hundred MLus," he said. "Enough to get back with some left over."

"You don't have any to pay this manaseer, but I suppose simply meeting him will have to do for now."

"He may take on a charity case," Sylas said with a chuckle. "Or maybe he'll be interested in trading some ale for his guidance. I have plenty of casks."

"There's no telling. Anyhoo, breakfast is in order before we set off to find this man. I just hope he's actually there having his morning coffee by the water."

"Thank you, again."

"Stop thanking me, Sylas."

"And you know I'll pay you back."

"I know, and I'll insist that you don't."

"But I will anyway."

"I know. I'm more interested in the favors you owe me, if we're being honest." She buckled something on her bag. "There are some rather rare herbs that I'm not able to get myself."

"In our area?"

"In our area indeed."

"I'm on it as soon as I can," Sylas told her.

"I appreciate that. But we can discuss herbs at another time. Let's head down to breakfast so we can get on with it."

They ate a quick meal of pastries with sausages baked into them. This was served with yogurt topped with a type of berry Sylas had never eaten before, the berry sweet and slightly tangy. Once they finished their meal, they began the long walk to the other side of Battersea.

At least that was what Sylas thought they were planning to do based on what he'd heard people saying over breakfast.

Mira had other plans.

She led Sylas up to a tall building, one with long ropes attached to its roof. She paid for them to take a skyway carriage, which brought them to the other side of the city in a matter of minutes.

"I was wondering what these were," Sylas said, recalling that he'd seen the carriages the previous day. "I suppose we could fly too," he told her as he looked out the window and saw people hovering past them.

"You're low on power. Flying isn't on the menu today, I'm afraid."

"This is just as fun," Sylas told her once they passed over a market. He wanted time to explore but could do so later. They would try to meet the manaseer and then return to the pub. Sylas hadn't forgotten that the well had been sealed off and Archlumen Tilbud was planning to visit them today to see about it.

They reached the Brenham District on the other side of Battersea. It was fairly easy to see the water from there, especially with the way the district had been cobbled together on hills that sloped toward the large expanse of water, Lake Seraphina. The seagulls in this area were quite loud. The birds squawked as they dove toward people, hoping for food.

"Aren't you glad we don't have them in Ember Hollow?" Mira asked as they grew closer to the water.

"We have demons instead."

"That we do."

"Choose your poison."

A wry smile took shape on her face. "Excuse me," Mira called to an older woman seated on a bench and gazing out at the water. "Is there a place called Agatha's around here?"

Rather than reply, the woman simply pointed them toward a dock. Sylas saw the sign for Agatha's painted on one of the buildings, the letters in a bold black. "Thank you," Mira told her. The woman nodded.

"I guess it's better than pointing us in the wrong direction," Sylas said. "Although, if we'd just turned this way, we likely would have seen the sign."

"I feel like that always happens to me."

"Happens to the best of us," he told her as they reached Agatha's. The coffeehouse was set up so they could serve patrons seated outside. Most of their chairs faced the water, but a few were tucked away in corners that would allow for more private conversations.

There were several people seated outside, none of whom looked like a Nuno. A new thought came to Sylas. "She never told us what Nuno looked like."

"No, Catia did not." Mira passed a couple and stopped in front of an older man, one with his hair combed over to the side. "Excuse me, you don't happen to be Nuno Landling, do you?"

The man gave her a funny look. "Nuno? I'm not Nuno, that's Nuno."

He gestured to a youth seated at the farthest chair away from the others. The boy couldn't have been older than fifteen. He had long hair on top, which was pulled back into a bun, and the sides of his dark hair were cut short. There were three cups in front of him, two of which were empty. The third had steam coming off it, the liquid inside a light brown.

"He's just a kid," Sylas said.

"He just looks like a kid," Mira told Sylas quietly, "but he could have been here for ages. Remember, the age you die affects how you look here in the Underworld."

"He's certainly the youngest person I've seen."

"Not the youngest I've seen, and that part doesn't matter. Speak to him as if he is an adult."

"Sure." Sylas approached the teen. "Nuno? Nuno Landling?"

Rather than answer, the teen reached for his coffee cup and took a big sip from it. He smacked his lips and finally looked up at Sylas with a pair of large hazel eyes. "Can I help you?"

"Are you Nuno Landling?"

"Yes."

Something about Nuno's eyes had Sylas wanting to press away from the teen. It was an uncanny feeling, Sylas certain now that the teenager was more powerful than he had originally anticipated. "I'm sorry to bother you."

"You've yet to bother me. If you'd like to make an appointment, I should tell you now that I'm booked for the next several weeks." Nuno took another sip from his coffee. "But we can set an appointment, if you'd like."

"Catia sent me."

Nuno's eyes flickered. "Catia? Is something the matter?"

"That's the thing. She doesn't know. I don't know either. I've been getting these messages."

"Messages?"

"Yes," Sylas said as Mira nodded beside him. "I've been getting these messages of an impending invasion every morning. The message now says that the invasion is set to happen sixty-six days from now. No one seems to know what it means."

Nuno took another long sip from his coffee. He looked out at the water and finally set his mug down. The teen stood, everyone seated gawking at him as he did so. "Come with me."

CHAPTER TWENTY-NINE

ARCANE REVELATIONS

Nuno had a flat overlooking the water, one accessible through an alley not far from the coffeehouse. The building was covered in the splattering of multi-colored tiles, some portions stripped away, others severely weather-beaten. By the looks of it, Sylas assumed that the flat wasn't where he held his practice.

Sylas also didn't know what the manaseer's practice would even look like. He really had no idea of what to expect, just along for the ride at this point.

At least Mira was there. If her face was any indication of how he should feel, Sylas should have been a little nervous.

But he wasn't.

He merely wanted answers, a confirmation that the invasion message was in relation to something breaking through the Hexveil and that he would be able to do something about it.

Sylas wanted to protect the Underworld, and this gave him something to focus on rather than the revelation about his father being in the Chasm fighting some holy crusade.

The flat was two rooms, at best, if one counted the mudroom where Nuno insisted they both leave their shoes. The walls were made of wood and the ceilings were high, not unlike the loft space Sylas called a bedroom back at The Old Lamplighter. Other than chairs on a small balcony and a small kitchenette, the space was bare.

"Welcome." The manaseer swept his hand out and the room rippled outward. Plush seating rose from the ground and the buildings outside all collapsed, giving the three a perfect view of the water.

Mira shot her hand out and grabbed Sylas's wrist. "Careful," she told him as he took a step forward. "It's not real."

"Not real?" Sylas gave her a funny look. "I can even feel the breeze."

Mira seemed hesitant.

"Please, sit," Nuno said as a chair formed for the teenage boy. It was surrounded by fauna, the plants lush and tropical, a kind that Sylas had never seen before. "Tell me about this message."

Sylas pulled his wrist away from Mira and sat. The chair felt real. What did Mira mean when she said none of this was real? He glanced at the apothecary. Why did she seem so reluctant?

"The message?" Nuno asked. "Is there anything more about it you should tell me?"

"That's all," Sylas told him. "I get the message every morning, like I said. You have eighty-nine days until the invasion. You have eighty-eight days until the invasion. You have eighty-seven days until the invasion. And so on. It's a countdown."

"And what does the message look like?"

"It looks like all the other prompts I've received here in the Underworld. Rimmed in blue, glowing letters. There's nothing different about it. The text isn't red or anything. It doesn't pulse. It doesn't do anything other than flash in the morning and fade."

"Flash in the morning and fade. Where will you be tomorrow morning? Are you planning to be here in Battersea?"

"I am not. I have an issue back at my pub that I need to see to. We'll travel back there today."

"And your pub is where again?" Nuno asked.

"The Old Lamplighter, in Ember Hollow."

"On the other side of the world."

"To you," Mira said, suddenly defensive. "To us, this is the other side of the world."

Her statement brought a subtle smile to Nuno's face. "I've been to Ember Hollow. It must have been a hundred years ago."

"A hundred years ago?" Sylas found it hard to believe this on account of Nuno's youthful appearance.

"I've certainly had a hundred deathdays since then." Nuno squinted up, and as he did stars populated the sky above them. This was what led Sylas to finally understand that this was an illusion. He hadn't seen stars in weeks. They didn't exist in the Underworld; or if they did, they were blotted out by the Celestial Plains.

"What was Ember Hollow like back then?" Mira asked the manaseer.

"It was a thriving village. An outer village, but people preferred to live there over Cinderpeak. I'm guessing that has changed."

"It has," Sylas said, Mira nodding in confirmation.

"These things do change, yet some things remain the same. Population centers like this, like Battersea, have remained the same. Only larger. But none of that matters at the moment. We can talk the history of the Underworld at another time. This message of yours alarms me."

"You aren't the only one," Sylas told Nuno. "It has to be the Chasm, right?"

"Come closer."

Sylas stood.

Nuno flashed in front of him, as if he'd been standing in front of Sylas all along. Sylas noticed there was now an auric luster radiating off Nuno's form, a threaded nature to the light.

The manaseer placed his hands on Sylas's shoulders and his eyes rolled back into his head. Sylas felt his entire body shift with it, as if he'd done a complete backflip. He landed, or felt like he landed, back in his seat across from Nuno, the youth with a look of dread on his face.

"The warning message is not about the Chasm," Nuno finally said, a bit breathless now. "I know that much. But I don't know much else. This might take me some time to decipher. And I'll need to visit another manaseer that I know, my teacher. She can be very hard to locate."

"Why's that?" Sylas asked, still dumbfounded.

"Her home is in the center of Lake Seraphina."

"In the center?" Mira asked. "How?"

Nuno didn't answer this question. "She also takes part in the excursions into the Chasm. I may have to go there to find her. But don't worry. I will do just that, and once I know more, I will meet you in Ember Hollow." The manaseer frowned. "I guess I will be canceling my appointments for the rest of the week."

"You think this message is that important?" Sylas asked.

"I think this message is of cataclysmic importance."

"But it's not the Chasm?" Mira asked.

"No, I don't believe the message has anything to do with the Chasm."

Everything on the periphery shifted. Sylas now stood in the blank space of Nuno's flat, the manaseer out on the balcony, his hands crossed behind his back like he had been there for a while gazing out at the pristine lake. "You may go," he said without looking at Sylas or Mira. "I'll be in touch."

CHAPTER THIRTY

RETURN TO EMBER HOLLOW

Sylas begrudgingly transferred three hundred Mana Lumens to the Battersea portal. Before he could grumble any more about the toll, he was portaled away alongside Mira. The two materialized into existence in Ember Hollow, Sylas glad to see the sudden quiet of the village.

It felt good to be home.

"What's that smile?" Mira asked.

"I might be starting to like it here," he said with a grin. He took a deep breath in and threw his arms out. "Pub sweet pub."

"You should have got that posted on a sign outside of The Old Lamplighter," she said as they turned to the pub.

"Yeah?" Sylas considered this. "Pub sweet pub."

"You're not serious."

"There's always room for another sign. I have *The Old Lamplighter* sign plus the *Public House* sign with my poem on it."

"How does it go again?"

"*When the lamp is lit, come in and sit. If it's dark, best to depart.*"

Mira rolled her eyes. "That's the one."

"But now I'm thinking of a pub sweet pub sign over the door."

"Stop."

"What? It's pithy. It's fun." Sylas approached the door of The Old Lamplighter.

Patches nearly knocked him over as soon as he stepped in, the cat followed by Azor.

"How did it go?" she asked, the fire spirit brimming with excitement. "Did you find out about the people you were looking for? What about the message?

Also, surprise!" She motioned toward one of the tables, which had fireweave armor draped over it. "Godric dropped this off yesterday."

"He did, did he?" Sylas asked, remembering that the tailor had said he'd make him armor.

"He didn't even ask for a pint."

"Ha. You should have given him one anyway."

The fireweave armor looked much lighter than anything Sylas had seen before, a chainmail nature to it. Sylas saw that all of it would fit quite well. He especially liked the greaves, which seemed to be woven with fireweave and a thickened leather like the bag that Godric had once given him.

After admiring the armor, Sylas set his things down on the bar and lifted Patches into his arms. He held the cat for a moment, Patches purring so loudly that Sylas's whole body shook.

"Hi, Azor," Mira said as she turned to the fire spirit. "To answer your question, Sylas did find out about the people he is looking for, but that in itself is a bit of a mystery."

"How so?"

Sylas set Patches down on the bar. "My parents went to the Celestial Plains. My mother is still up there; my father is in the Chasm as part of a Hallowed Pursuit."

"He's fighting in one of the crusades?" Azor asked him. She knew exactly what he was referring to. Azor had seen the results of these battles, the way everything was scorched afterward. Entire pockets of civilization, albeit demonic, had been torn asunder by these excursions. "And your friends?"

"One of them is there in the Chasm fighting as well, Raelis. The other is east of Battersea, Quinlan, and he'll likely know where his brother is. As for the message. We found a manaseer, and his interpretation is that the invasion isn't going to come from the Chasm."

Azor looked perplexed. "It's not?"

"But we may need a second opinion."

"Was he strong?"

"As far as I could tell he was. Nuno looked like a teenager, but he has been here for some time." Sylas shrugged. "So, Battersea. Learned a lot, didn't get to explore much, spent too many MLus, and now I have some people to find once I get things running smoothly here. My MLus are pretty much shot. It'll take a while to rejuvenate them. I don't want Patches coming near me at night until I'm back over three thousand. We don't know how many he has, but if he tried to recharge my powers now, it might kill him."

Patches mewed as Sylas continued to pet him.

"How have things been here?" Sylas asked the fire spirit.

"Right!" Azor nearly exploded up to the ceiling. "The well. You need to see the well, but I should warn you."

"Warn us?" Mira asked.

"You're going to want to stay back." Azor, who already wore her fireweave gloves, raced over to the back door and opened it.

Sylas saw the well and the magic barrier that Tilbud had cast over the rim. Once a shimmering veil of protection, the barrier had started to bubble over. Bits of golden mana fizzled in the air above it as some unseen force churned inside.

Sylas recalled a soft hum when Tilbud had cast the spell. This soft hum was gone, replaced by a whispery groan.

"It's not going to hold for much longer," Azor said.

"No, it's not." Sylas turned back to the pub so he could grab his shield, his mace, and try on his new armor. "But hopefully it'll hold until Tilbud gets here."

The magic seal remained intact. That did little to quell the apprehension Sylas felt as he waited alongside Mira, Azor, and Patches for the archlumen to come. Now in his fireweave armor, which fit perfectly, his buckler on his arm and fireweave mace in his right hand, Sylas was ready to protect the pub if need be.

"Is he always late?" Mira asked, not the first time she'd voiced her concern about Tilbud's tardiness.

"He'll come," Sylas told her. He stood near the well, Mira sat on the stoop, and Azor floated nearby. Patches also seemed keen to guard the pub from whatever was boiling up from the well, the pub cat circling every few minutes.

"Perhaps we should get some of my father's men."

"No," Sylas said, feeling stubborn and a bit annoyed that he was going to have to deal with this tonight rather than open the pub and prepare for tomorrow's inspection from the Ale Alliance. "We'll handle it."

Later, once they had been watching the well for what felt like hours, Azor headed in to make a meal. She returned with open-faced sandwiches.

"I've been thinking of a menu for next Wraithsday," she said, the fire spirit not able to stomach the tension anymore. "Not in two days, the one next week. This Wraithsday will have to be fish again with Corlin's delivery. Or, we could have fish-and-chips on Thornsday. What do you think?"

Sylas took another bite of his sandwich. It was good, but he couldn't help but feel dread in watching the mana bubble on top of the well. It had agitated further, the magical surface convulsing to the point that Sylas was certain it would blow any minute.

Yet he'd been certain of this for the last hour, and this had yet to come to pass.

"Sylas?"

"Sorry," he finally told Azor.

"Tell me what you're planning," Mira said, an attempt to help divert the fire spirit's attention away from Sylas. "I'll end up eating it, and likely serving it anyway."

Azor smiled big. "Steak and ale pie. That's what I was thinking. Sorry, it's not the right time to mention it. We have the ale, and I thought that I could marinate steak in it, put it all in a little cup, bake a crust over the top, and—"

A bubble popped on the surface of the magical seal. There had been plenty of activity like this leading up to this moment, but something was different now.

Pop! Pop! Pop!

A beam of mana pillared out of the bubble, followed by the claw of a cinderspider.

Sylas put his sandwich down, grimaced, and prepared for the inevitable as the seal officially gave way.

Cinderspiders rushed out. Mira screamed as Sylas and Azor moved into action. Patches, who had been prepared all along, leaped for one of the spiders, doubled his size midair, and latched on.

The spider released a bolt of fire, one that struck the side of the pub.

"Flip as many as you can!" Sylas called to Azor as he smashed one of the cinderspiders, full-on raging now as he tried to stop them from getting to the pub, to Mira, who had yet to stop screaming.

Mira hated insects, Sylas remembered that now. He'd made a mistake in not sending her away to get a couple of the militiamen.

Patches yowled, his voice amplified to a level that caused Sylas to push back.

He glanced at the pub cat, whose auditory attack had managed to force several of the cinderspiders onto their backs. Seizing on the opportunity, Sylas came forward with his mace, crushing them one by one.

"Sylas, watch out!" Mira shouted.

He jumped just in time to avoid another fireball, one that struck The Old Lamplighter. As Sylas got back to his feet, he finally noticed that the pub had caught fire, flames licking its side and roof.

"No . . ." he said under his breath as cinderspiders rushed past him, toward Mira, who was on the stoop trying to fire a blast of mana. The apothecary managed to release the sizzling ball of mana, but ultimately jumped to the side as several of the spiders breached the interior of the pub.

"Nasty little buggers!" Duncan came roaring past followed by Cody, both militiamen charging into the fray without hesitation.

"We heard the commotion from out front," Cody shouted to Sylas as he struck one with his mace. Duncan punted another away, the two immediately continuing the offensive as they started to push the spiders back toward the well.

The notion that backup had arrived reinvigorated Sylas. He had to stop the spiders and put out the fire. Panic rose in his chest as he crushed another spider.

The fire on the roof was spreading.

Azor had moved toward the fire, trying to force it away, but she didn't seem to have as good of control over the blaze as she would have liked.

Whoosh!

Water rushed forward, the giant wave appearing out of thin air.

It struck the pub, Azor barely able to get out of the way in time. The water twisted around all of them, Patches leaping for cover as it washed over the cinderspiders.

A new person came onto the scene, a man in purple robes with the sleeves rolled up, a funny hat on his head, his long silver hair flowing behind him.

"Sorry I'm late," Archlumen Tilbud said as swells of mana razored forward, spearing into spider bodies and flinging them to the side.

His water spirit, Horatio, cleaved through the air. Sylas was finally able to get a look at Horatio's form, that of a muscled man with tendrils of water trailing off his body and a nondescript face.

The fight was over just a few moments later, Sylas's backyard littered with spider corpses, his pub still smoldering, and all of them sopping wet.

CHAPTER THIRTY-ONE

THE WELL

Tilbud's water spirit hovered near him for a moment, silent as ever, as the archlumen surveyed the scene. The two locked eyes, smiled at each other, and Horatio vanished.

"I apologize for the dramatic entrance," he said, finally turning to Sylas. The tattoo on Tilbud's arm, which was shaped like a three-pronged ocean wave, glowed blue. "You know how these things go. One gets caught up in, oh dear, the pub."

"The pub," Sylas said, wet, angry, annoyed, and still in shock.

"Is it something you can fix?"

Sylas didn't want to turn to look at the pub, but he did so anyway. He stepped around the body of a dead spider and surveyed the damage. The roof could be repaired, and there were burn marks along the outer walls. The spiders that had made it inside were now dead. Horatio had washed them out, but that meant the interior of the pub would be wet. It would need to air out.

"Where were you?" Mira asked as she came forward, her eyes glowing with mana. She poked a finger into Tilbud's chest. "We've been here all day waiting for you. Your seal was on the verge of breaking when we arrived earlier. Had you come at a reasonable time—"

"Ah, about that." Tilbud very calmly removed her finger from his chest. "I had to be certain. I'm not classed as a demon hunter, but I sensed through a power of mine called Detection that the issue with the well was of a demon-nature, a high-level one, mind you. I know someone who is double-classed as a demon hunter and lumengineer specializing in spectral examinations. Long story, but if you must know, she was the one I had issues with when you and I first met. Actually, that's all I'll say about that for now. So let's call it a short story."

Sylas scratched the back of his head. "I've been getting water from there."

"Ah, that. I don't believe that's the issue," Tilbud told Sylas. "There is a tunnel in the well above the waterline, one that I believe our dear Patches has already uncovered. This tunnel goes two ways, like most tunnels. Imagine that! Sorry, I'm not trying to make a light of a very serious situation here, I'm trying to explain that a powerful demon has used the tunnel to connect to the Cinderpeak Volcano, hence the spiders, with plans of burrowing all the way to the Hexveil, under the barrier, and straight to the Chasm."

Mira gasped. "A tunnel to the Chasm?"

"I believe so, yes. Horatio will be able to seal off that side. The other side of the tunnel, well, that is up to us. Horatio will flood the second leg of that tunnel once we've reached the other side."

"What are you suggesting?" Sylas asked. "Are you saying we need to follow the tunnel?"

"I'm saying just that. We need to go into the well, let Horatio seal up the side heading toward the Chasm while the rest of us clear out any of the spiders left and see where it leads." Tilbud removed his hat and ran his hand through his long silver hair. "It's going to be quite a long night, isn't it?"

"Start from the beginning," Sylas said, another thought coming to him. "Did you just say we need to go into the well?"

"How would they even do that?" Azor asked the archlumen. "I could go in there for them."

"You'll come as well, but I mean exactly what I said: we go into the well."

Duncan and Cody exchanged glances. "I don't think I'm going to fit," Duncan said, the large man squinting at the well.

"No, of course you won't. Neither you, nor your counterpart, will be going on this mission anyway. I can only shrink two other people."

"I'm not going," Mira said with a shudder.

"You can shrink people?" Sylas asked.

"It was an answer in the pub quiz," Duncan said. "I got that one right!"

"It was! You remember. And that brings us to another thing," Tilbud told the group as Patches circled the well, the cat wet, irritable. "While I was able to get advice, I failed to procure the services of the previously mentioned demon hunter, who will remain nameless. Yes, if you're wondering, it's a love triangle situation that I'd rather not get into right now. Where was I? Right, sorry. There has been a load of activity here tonight and I, like you all, am still processing it. We need a demon hunter. That is what I'm trying to tell you."

"What about my uncle?" Mira asked.

"Is your uncle a demon hunter? Did you already tell me that?"

Mira nodded. "His name is Tiberius."

Tilbud rubbed his hands together. "Then that is one problem solved. We need a demon hunter. This one isn't going to give up easily."

"I don't know how he'll take this, if we're being honest."

The archlumen peered down into the well. "I'm sure he'll be interested to learn a Hellrift has escaped the Chasm. An A-Rank Hellrift, if he's looking for the technical term. That should pique his interest."

CHAPTER THIRTY-TWO

INTO THE TUNNEL

Tiberius wasn't one to dally when Ember Hollow was in danger. As soon as Mira reached their home and told him what was happening, the former lord commander of the Shadowthorne Vanguard was in his backyard armory suiting up. He barely had time to register what she'd told him, his mind spinning at her explanation of some fire, spiders, an archlumen, a water spirit, all of it.

Tiberius had only heard one word, one word that caused him momentary pause as Mira delivered the message.

Hellrift.

He'd never faced off against a Hellrift before, but he knew what they were and what they were capable of. Hellrifts were creatures from the Chasm that could possess other beings. Usually, they were C-Rank or below, and they'd do something like control a small animal. These were easy enough to kill, but Tiberius had heard from other hunters that they could possess larger creatures as well. That they could command other animals to do their bidding.

This wasn't the only thing that worried Tiberius.

Hellrifts were very difficult to kill on the account of their physical body, which resembled a mist. Tiberius could do it with one of his class skills, an ability known as Lumen Implosion Sphere. It cost a thousand fixed Mana Lumens to cast, something Tiberius was willing to part with if it meant protecting Ember Hollow.

Before stepping out of his armory, Tiberius accessed the Hunter System that he'd grown so accustomed to over the years. He mentally searched for A-Rank Hellrifts that had escaped the Chasm and didn't find any. This was odd. The Hexveil usually registered these sorts of demons as they passed its barrier.

"You said something about a tunnel?" Tiberius asked as he came into his home to find Mira standing there with, of all things, a bread roll.

"Yes, Tilbud said there is a tunnel under Ember Hollow, that one direction went toward the Hexveil, the other Cinderpeak."

Even now, as she stood before her uncle with a mana-boosting bread roll she hoped to give Sylas, Mira felt a hint of annoyance at her uncle and the way he hardly listened to her.

She also felt gratitude.

Tiberius was damn near impossible to deal with most days, but when it was time to step up, he always stepped up. And not only would he step up, he would give it his all. She knew in coming to get him that he would fight to death for Ember Hollow, that he'd do whatever it took to stop the Hellrift, the spiders, anything that was thrown at him.

Her flash of annoyance quickly shifted to worry.

This was a look that Tiberius registered, one he was used to from his niece. "This will all work out, Mira. My guess is the Hellrift came through beneath the Hexveil, that the system didn't pick it up, and the demon is using the cinderspiders to increase the size of the tunnel. We will kill them all. We will kill the demon. And there will be a rather large reward in the end."

"Only three of you can go in. I told you that."

"Go in where?"

"The well."

Tiberius blinked twice as he recalled what Mira had told him. "Right. And the archlumen can perform this feat?"

"He claims he can."

Sylas ate the bread roll that Mira gave him. He checked his status afterward and saw that his MLus had gone up by a hundred. He still didn't have a lot, but it would have to do.

"Ah, you must be the demon hunter," Tilbud was saying as he looked Tiberius over. "A pleasure."

"What do we need to do?" Tiberius asked. Sylas noted that Mira's uncle now wore his best armor, which made the former lord commander look more muscled than he normally did.

"Prepare to be shrunk. You," Tilbud said, motioning to Mira. "Once we are all small, put us on the rim of the well. We'll take it from there. And you should probably return to your tattoo," he told Azor. "You'll be the same size as you are now when Sylas summons you, so do be careful when we're in the tunnel with the miniature versions of us."

Azor pumped a fiery fist in the air. "Got it."

"You're really going to Shrink them?" Cody asked Tilbud, who stood next to Duncan, the two ready to guard the well.

"I am. We will need to be adequately small to fly down into the well and explore the tunnel from there."

"How will they get large again?" asked Duncan.

"Good question. I'll increase their size once we reach the end of the tunnel. If I die in some way, they'll need to go to an archlumen to fix them. But I won't die." Tilbud tipped his hat at Duncan. "I'm already dead. Now. Are the two of you ready?"

Sylas and Tiberius exchanged glances. Sylas swallowed. "I think?"

"That's a good enough answer for me. Come. Join me. And weapons down, my dear fellows, I don't want to be bludgeoned by mistake!" Tilbud extended both hands out.

Sylas and Tiberius hesitated.

"Well? Come on then, hold my hands. We'll all Shrink to one-tenth our normal size, clothing too. Don't worry, it's magic! As to the question of when we will return, in due time. Do not fret. And do not worry if water boils up from below. Horatio must seal these tunnels off, after all."

Sylas was the first to take the archlumen's hand. Tiberius did so second, the older man grumbling to himself.

The sensation wasn't at all what Sylas expected. He expected to feel like he was being squeezed.

What he noticed instead was the Underworld growing around him, the perspective shift met with a sensory change. Sounds were suddenly louder, the smell of the soil more intense. Before he could say anything, Mira scooped him up and deposited him on the rim of the well.

"This is insane," Sylas said as he turned to Tiberius, who was trying to make sense of his new size. Sylas's voice sounded the same, as far as he could tell, but he suspected that it sounded much different to Mira and the two militiamen. He wondered for a moment if they could even hear him. "You good, Azor?"

"I'm good," she said, the tattoo on Sylas's arm buzzing with warmth.

"Now, we fly," Tilbud said, the archlumen giving them little time to adjust. He floated over the opening of the well. "Well?" he asked Sylas. "Are you coming? Just like I taught you now, chop-chop."

Tiberius joined Tilbud and the two dropped into the well. Sylas looked back to Mira, waved, and jumped into the air, following after them.

"Fun, isn't it?" Tilbud asked as miniature Sylas caught up to him, the wind rushing past both of them.

The archlumen's long hair whipped in the air around his shoulders as he twisted forward, his hat magically staying on his head. Tiberius kept a steady pace as well, the lord commander with a look of intense focus on his face.

As the world around them grew darker, Tilbud sparked a glowing orb of golden light to illuminate their way. They reached the tunnel, which Sylas guessed was just a few feet above the waterline. It was hard to gauge the distance of things at this size.

"Horatio?" Tilbud asked. The water spirit took shape over the waterline. "Collapse the side of the tunnel that leads to the Chasm. Once we have cleared through this side, please do the same with ours as well."

Horatio nodded.

"Is he always this quiet?" Azor asked so only Sylas could hear.

Sylas shook his head. "No idea."

Tiberius turned away from the water. "Lads, shall we?"

"There are going to be spiders in here, aren't there?" Azor asked.

Sylas relayed this question to the others.

The archlumen considered it. "There might be cinderspiders in here, and yes, they will be their normal size. That should be a joy. But that's what we signed up for, right? You all signed up for this, yes?" He laughed at his own joke.

Tiberius took the lead, not at all a fan of the scatterbrained archlumen. What they were doing was serious. It was dangerous, and it was quite possibly the stupidest thing he had done yet.

It wasn't something a lord commander such as himself took lightly.

The three charged ahead, Tiberius keeping to the front. Sylas still had a hard time coming to grips with their current location in a tunnel deep beneath the ground. The fact that the three men were a fraction of their normal size made the crude tunnel seem as if it were some vast cavern.

The thought that he could die here touched the forefront of Sylas's mind.

This was different from the times he had considered dying before, when he was alive. What Sylas feared now was being sent to the Chasm, especially after all the hard work he had put in during his short time in the Underworld, and being unable to stop the impending invasion.

He had to survive this.

"We have company!" Tiberius shouted. He released a blast of mana that he'd charged into his mace. It flared ahead, revealing an enormous cinderspider which was actually a regular-sized cinderspider that was much larger now due the Shrink spell.

The spider fired a bolt of lava at them, Sylas narrowly avoiding its attack by flying to the side.

The lava hit the sidewall of the tunnel and fizzled out as an invisible force moved past. The force collided with the spider and tumbled forward, Sylas's ears met with a loud and angry yowl.

"Patches!" Azor cried. "Patches to the rescue!"

The pub cat, still full size, had made it into the tunnel. He charged ahead to defend Sylas and his companions.

"Where the bloody hell did he come from?" Tiberius asked, bewilderment on his face, his arms out wide in a panic.

"I was wondering when he'd join us," said Tilbud, who currently had spools of mana swirling around his wrists. "The cat will make traveling through the tunnel even easier. Let him finish off the spider, and we will mount up."

"Ride Patches?" Sylas shook his head, his focus returning to the fight playing out in front of them. The spider had wrapped its legs around Patches, yet the pub cat had also managed to cut into its underbelly, the spider losing its grip.

"I can help!" Azor said.

"Not yet," Sylas told her. "Let Patches do it."

It was a grim sight, especially with how close the spider's jaws were to clamping down on Patches and the fact Sylas was pretty much useless in fighting off a creature of that size. But Sylas and the others stayed back and soon, the pub cat triumphed over the spider.

"Patches." The pub cat turned to Sylas, his whiskers tensing, the cat absolutely enormous. "Patches." Sylas raised a hand and the cat dropped his forehead, allowing Sylas to pet him. "Good. We're going to need you, buddy."

Once he was ready, Sylas floated up and landed in a spot behind the back of Patches's head. He made sure the cat was fine with this before the others joined him, the other two finding a place behind his head. It was by no means comfortable, and they had to grip Patches's fur to keep steady when he moved, but Patches seemed fine with it.

"Onward!" Tilbud procured a bright node of golden mana that instantly drew Patches's attention. The cat took off toward the blip of light, the group racing ahead through the tunnel. "Ha!" the archlumen shouted. "I didn't know if that would work or not."

"Did you know if any of this would work?" asked Tiberius, flustered as always.

"Which part?"

Tiberius never had a chance to reply as they came to another spider. This time, Patches pressed back and split his form into two, his replicant charging ahead while the real Patches began licking himself.

"What is he doing?" Tiberius asked. "What is he bloody doing now?"

As his clone distracted the incoming spider, Patches coughed up a hairball.

He crouched before it and animated the hairball, which slimed forward toward the spider. It struck the spider in the face, forcing the spider backward. Patches pounced onto it, nearly bucking the three men off his back in the process.

He killed the spider and they moved on.

"What a fascinating skill," Tilbud said. "Anyhoo. Azor, dear, if you can hear me, take your form once Patches comes to a stop."

"The cinderspiders are mostly immune to my power," she said. "But I can do other things."

"She's saying the spiders are immune to her power."

"Right," Tilbud told Sylas. "But she can do something, hmmm?"

"She can flip them over."

"Exactly that. I want her to knock them over and make Patches's job easier. We will reach the end of this tunnel and likely encounter the A-Rank Hellrift from there. Can you sense it?"

Sylas shook his head.

"I can," Tiberius said. "It has been here."

"We just have to reach the end of this tunnel," Tilbud told them. "And with a fast and clever cat and a fire spirit, we have a good chance of doing so soon. Then, we get to the hard part."

"Kill the Hellrift," Tiberius said.

"And whatever it has possessed, yes."

Sylas didn't like the sound of that, but he was ready.

CHAPTER THIRTY-THREE

THE FORCES OF MANA

With Azor's help, they were able to clear through any of the cinderspiders in their path. The tunnel grew in size, which made it seem even larger considering their current heights. Eventually, they came to a space where they were certain they could take their normal sizes again.

Still, Sylas and the two men hesitated. The world was so much bigger from their current perspectives that they had to be sure. They traveled a bit farther and reached a point where steam from the volcano had begun to cloud the chamber.

"We have officially arrived. Everyone off the cat." Tilbud floated down the ground and was soon joined by Sylas and Tiberius.

"What now?" Azor asked, who hovered before them, the fire spirit practically a giant.

"Guard us while we transform. This shouldn't hurt. Too much," Tilbud said with the wink that annoyed Tiberius. "And keep the cat back."

Azor shooed Patches to the side, the cat not at all happy with the way he was being micromanaged.

"Ready, gents?" Tilbud didn't wait for a confirmation as he cast his hands out in front of him and released a swell of golden mana. Sylas saw his hand bulge three times its size and quickly closed his eyes. It didn't hurt, but it certainly felt strange returning to his normal height, and Sylas was glad once the entire process was done.

"Are you good?" he asked Tiberius, who looked down at his weapon, the lord commander still adjusting to the transformation.

Tiberius grunted a response. "Where to now?"

Tilbud checked his robes, his hat, and then summoned more Mana Lumens, which pooled in the air around him and created a halolike glow that settled over his head and shoulders. "We find the Hellrift and whatever it has possessed."

Sylas stopped dead in his tracks. "The big spider," he said under his breath. "It has to be."

"The what?" Tiberius asked him.

Azor took over from there, the fire spirit launching into a rapid-fire explanation. "Sylas and I had an active quest in this cave system, something we did for Godric the fireweave tailor back when I needed fireweave clothing so I could work at the pub. We came across this huge spider. So much bigger than the others."

"The size of a boulder," Sylas added as he used his mace to estimate its height.

"That would explain how it is able to control the mob of cinderspiders. In that case, let's look for a large spider," Tilbud said, the archlumen jutting his finger in the air. "Since there is only one way to go, I say we go this way." He forged ahead, leaving Sylas and Tiberius behind.

"Wait," Tiberius said, "I'm the hunter of the group!"

Sylas turned to Patches. He crouched before the cat and petted him. "You've done well," he told Patches, who instantly started to purr. "But you have to stay back now."

Patches mewed sadly.

"I know, I know. You want a piece of the action. But let us handle it."

"I'll keep an eye on him," Azor told Sylas. "He can't go back into the tunnel. We don't know when Horatio will collapse it."

"No we don't." Sylas checked his status to see that he had lost a bit through the battles and perhaps the size changes.

Name: Sylas Runewulf
Mana Lumens: 179/4529
Class: Brewer

"What's that face?" Azor asked.

"I just need to keep an eye on my power. I'm under two hundred MLus. Also, if and when I go to sleep tonight, Patches needs to stay out of my bedroom. I don't want him to overextend himself."

[Accept 300 Mana Lumens from Azor? Y/N]

"I can't," Sylas told her. "Those are yours."

"I'm the pub bank, remember." She smiled at him, a pair of fiery purple horns appearing on her forehead. They quickly fizzled out. "But not an evil one."

"I already owe Mira twelve hundred MLus. I can't owe you too."

"You don't have to pay me back, Sylas. Keeping you alive is more important than a few hundred MLus. Take them. And let's go kill a demon spider."

They came around a corner and Sylas saw it.

Even after seeing the cinderspiders from his shrunken size, something about the large arachnid and the way it loomed in the steam sent a bolt of fear through Sylas.

He braced himself, but then remembered that he was fighting for his pub. Cinderspiders had attacked his home and a dangerous demon was trying to free other demons like it from the Chasm. This was all Sylas needed to charge ahead with his mace drawn.

But the spider wasn't one to back down.

As it pressed back and prepared to snap forward, Sylas noticed something else about the monstrosity. Unlike its minions, this one had a golden aura, not exactly the same gold as the Mana Lumens Sylas had grown used to seeing, but certainly close.

"Careful!" Tiberius said he shot his arm out to stop Sylas from advancing.

The blast that followed, one that started at the back of the cinderspider's throat, wasn't made of lava. It was an orb of pure mana that cut into the wall of the cave, causing rocks to fall from the ceiling and debris to kick up.

Tilbud caught the rocks with a net made of Mana Lumens. "What are you waiting for?" he called to Tiberius.

"It takes a moment to charge my Lumen Implosion Sphere. It's the only way to kill a Hellrift. Hold it off for a minute! And mind its shield. That glow around its body, it's a shield. No heroics here. Just guard me until I can hit the Hellrift!"

Sylas stepped up to protect Tiberius. One of the spider's claws came right at him and he struck it to the side, Sylas focused on the task at hand and didn't look directly in the spider's face, which terrified him. The fangs alone were large enough to rip off his head.

Another leg swept Sylas's feet out from under him. It tried to drive a claw into his midsection, but Sylas's armor protected him.

Swoof!

Tilbud sent a sizzling flare of mana at the spider, which caused it to hiss. Patches, who Azor continued to hold off, began to yowl.

"Get that damn cat of yours under control!" Tiberius shouted, a vein pulsing on the side of his head now as he concentrated his power.

Sylas glanced at Tiberius to see him still working on a sphere of mana, one that looked like a glass orb filled with churning water. Rather than glowing around him, the light that Sylas normally associated with Mana Lumens seemed to be stripped from the air and Tiberius's face seemed to be without color.

Thwack!

Sylas batted away an incoming spider claw. He had the notion to rush toward their opponent and strike it directly in the face, but he knew the spider was too large to try something like that, and Tiberius had warned him of the shield.

He went for Patches instead, Sylas able to sweep the howling cat into his arms. This allowed Azor to comet forward and strike the spider, causing it to skitter backward.

The fire spirit kept up the distractions and was aided by Tilbud, who sent discs of power at the spider that prevented it from hitting them with another sizzling blast of mana.

"Now!" Tiberius said, his eyes rolling back into his head. "Everyone aside!"

Azor rushed to the left as Tiberius released the strange sphere of power.

He fell to a knee as the orb twisted forward, the dark mana around the spider sucking into it. The spider strained but was ultimately unable to stop a smoky essence from being cleaved from its body, tendrils trailing in the cavern.

Sylas only caught a brief glimpse of the A-Rank Hellrift, but he saw its sinister face, the evil in its hollow eyes, as it lurched toward them. Patches scrambled to get out of Sylas's arm, clawing and struggling as Sylas turned to the side to protect him.

But the Hellrift never reached them.

It was pulled backward into Tiberius's Lumen Implosion Sphere, where it fizzled and writhed until the orb collapsed. Mana was dispersed, all of it pouring into the lord commander.

"The spider!" Tiberius pointed at the large opponent, which was just starting to get its bearings.

A spike made of blistering Mana Lumens ripped from the ground and impaled the spider, courtesy of Tilbud. It pressed out its back, killing the beast, which lurched forward one last time as the dust began to settle.

They had done it.

Azor, who was in the process of racing toward the arachnid, shifted to the side as plumes of fire flailed all around her.

"Ah, finally I can use that skill." Tilbud wiped a bead of sweat from his brow, his voice still calm. "You know, I've been meaning to use that power, really, I have, but the Hellrift was protecting the spider's body with an invisible force, amplifying its strikes and whatnot. Also, I'd never used it before. But it worked. Cheers!" He turned to Sylas and Tiberius and smiled. "Cheers!"

Tiberius didn't seem to share the same sort of joy as Tilbud. He was experiencing something similar to Sylas, an after-battle dread in which one thanked their lucky stars at the same time they tried to recall what happened at the same time as they checked themselves for any injuries they may have sustained.

Sylas let out a haggard breath. "What now?"

"Now?" Tiberius looked around, the lord commander still down on one knee. "We lead ourselves out of this cave using an active quest. I can handle that part. I'm guessing it will come out somewhere near Cinderpeak. We portal back to Ember Hollow and go from there."

"Go from there?" Sylas asked as he thought of the damage to The Old Lamplighter. He released Patches, who moved ahead to investigate the spider's body. "I'm going to need a pint or two to do that."

Tilbud nodded. "Yes, something like that would be appropriate at a time like this."

"And something to eat?" Azor asked Tilbud.

"Certainly. I suppose I'll need to check on Horatio as well while you cook."

"I could use a good meal." Sylas approached the lord commander and offered him a hand. "What about you?"

Tiberius looked up at him. "An ale, a good meal?" He took Sylas's hand. "Yes, I believe that would be a fine way to cap a night like tonight. But before we do that, MLus. I need to transfer them to both of you. It just came in. Eight thousand MLus for an A-Rank Hellrift. I believe that is a record."

"Not just us," Sylas said. "Azor and Patches too. Come to think of it, Cody, Duncan, and Horatio. And we can't forget Mira. All of them played a role."

"Yes, yes they did," Tiberius said, a rare smile taking shape on his face. Now on his feet again, he dusted himself off. "In that case, I will distribute the MLus back at the pub. What say you, lads? Shall we leave this dreadful cave, or what?"

CHAPTER THIRTY-FOUR

NEWCOMER

Patches felt stronger. He didn't know what had happened to him, but he could tell it had changed his energy levels. As he paced around the well, the dark power he'd sensed for weeks gone, Patches scanned his status.

Mana Lumens: 1920/1920

Definitely stronger, he thought. *This means I can give more to the big man.*

Patches turned back to the pub and felt his heart sink. There was burn damage now and the air reeked from all the cinderspider carcasses that the fire spirit had incinerated. But at least the demon was gone, the Tavernly Realm safe again.

Patches knew the big man would be able to fix the place up.

He turned back to the cat door and entered the Tavernly Realm, his ears immediately flitting back. The fire spirit had formed a wall of flames in front of the stairs, blocking his passage.

Patches's hair stood on edge. She spoke to him softly and he eventually relaxed.

It had been a long night, and while he wanted to recharge the big man, there was always tomorrow. After a big yawn, Patches hopped up to his favorite windowsill and fell into a deep, restful sleep.

[**You have 65 days until the invasion.**]

Sylas stared at the prompt until it faded away. The message still alarmed him, but in the conversation he'd had with Tiberius, Tilbud, and the others over victory pints last night, it was clear that all he could do was wait for Nuno the manaseer to visit him.

So he would do that, and in the meantime, Sylas would continue to gain more Mana Lumens, new Lumen Abilities, and grow his business.

Last night had been a taste of what he knew he'd be up against in the future. Whatever was going to invade would certainly be stronger than the A-Rank Hellrift demon.

He had to be ready.

As he continued to lie there, Sylas focused on the most important part of his status at the moment.

Name: Sylas Runewulf
Mana Lumens: 1456/4529
Class: Brewer

He had welcomed his cut of the Mana Lumens Tiberius had received. It had turned out to be just under nine hundred, which Sylas knew was something that would help all of those involved in last night's proceedings.

"You're up," Azor said as she floated into the room. She was followed by Patches, who leaped onto the bed and came directly to Sylas for pets.

"Happy Tombsday," Sylas told the fire spirit. "Tilbud still asleep?"

"No. He left early. Only rested for a few hours." She hesitated. "So the pub."

Sylas felt his spirits deflate to some degree. "The pub. The inspection is today."

"It is, and I've managed to clean what I can. There's some fire damage visible inside though. And it still smells."

His nostrils flared open. "I can't smell it up here."

"You can smell it down there. There's also the well. For Horatio to flood the tunnels meant he also had to flood the well. The backyard is soaked and the water is a bit murky. We might want to wait a while for it to settle."

"How does it look?" Sylas asked.

Azor tried to stay positive, but her body language gave her true thoughts away. "Not great."

"We'll do what we can." Sylas was just getting out of bed when Patches's ears perked up.

Sylas heard the knock a few seconds later.

Azor's form shifted in horror. "They're already here? The Ale Alliance? I thought you said they'd come closer to noon!"

"They can't already be here." Sylas closed his eyes and pinched the bridge of his nose a moment. "Alright. If it's them, I'll stall them for a moment. Just to give the place time to air out. Maybe I'll show them Ember Hollow."

"Good idea," Azor said as she floated around nervously.

There was another knock.

"Yeah, I'll show them. Something. I'll show them something."

"What's there to show?" she asked, her form flaming with panic as Patches started to meow. "The abandoned market? The beautiful downtown with all the weeds and moss growing up around it. That big dead tree in the—"

"I get it, I get it," Sylas said as he slipped into his boots. "Maybe I'll take them over to Mira's. Surely they'd like to see the best apothecary in the area."

"Are you sure you're the one who doesn't want to see her?"

Sylas laughed. "Keep telling yourself that. Wish me luck."

"Good luck," Azor called after him as he headed out the door and to the stairs from there.

Sylas had just stepped into the pub when Patches raced down to join him. "Actually, good idea." He picked Patches up. "Act cute. Act really cute, okay?"

The pub cat purred.

"That's the spirit. Cute as a button."

There was one final knock, this last one a bit hesitant by the sound of it.

"Coming," Sylas called out.

He opened the door of the pub to find a wiry woman with unruly auburn hair that settled in a riot of curls around her face. She was freckled, with green eyes, the woman much shorter than Sylas, her face a mask of confusion as she stared in disbelief at Sylas.

"Are you here from the Ale Alliance?" Sylas asked her after waiting a moment for her to introduce herself.

"The what?" she asked, her voice just a bit raspy. "This is Ember Hollow, right?"

"It is."

"Good. I'm in the right place, at least. Whew."

Sylas cleared his throat. "How can I help you?"

"You're the owner of this pub?" The woman looked up at the sign. "The Old Lamplighter."

"I am," Sylas said, his skin prickling.

Was this a demon? He glanced down to Patches, who didn't seem to be alarmed by the woman. If it was a demon, Patches would have done something by now.

Sylas relaxed to some degree.

"And that's your cat?"

"He is. His name is Patches. I'm Sylas, by the way, Sylas Runewulf."

"I'm Eleanor Redgrave, but you can just call me Nelly." She crossed her arms over her chest and gave Sylas an uncertain look. "We're going to be seeing a lot of each other, I reckon."

"Why's that?" Sylas asked her. He recognized the last name. She was an Aurumite.

Nelly let out a deep, troubled breath. "I can't believe I'm saying this, but I just died. I was given the deed to the general store."

His breath caught in his throat. "The one next door?"

"The one next door."

"Wow, I wasn't expecting that." Sylas finally let Patches down. The pub cat moved over to Nelly, hesitated for a beat, and then started to purr as he wound through her legs.

"So it's safe here?" Nelly asked. "Ember Hollow."

After what had happened last night, Sylas didn't know the best way to answer this. He decided to keep it ambiguous. "Heh. Safe enough."

"I have so many questions."

"I know the feeling."

"My husband. He died just before me. Is he here somewhere?"

Sylas started to frown and stopped himself. There was plenty of time to tell her about the Book of Shadows.

"I can't answer that question, but I know someone who can. I'll explain. Are you hungry? We can have a quick meal, if you'd like, and I can catch you up. I have someone coming in the next several hours, but after that, I'd love to show you around and introduce you to some folks."

"Hungry?" Nelly bit her lip. "I don't know what I am."

"That's to be expected. Don't be alarmed, but I'm contracted with a fire spirit who loves to cook. Her name is Azor. We'll probably want to eat out here because there's a smell in the pub right now from, well—"

She leaned forward, her interest piqued. "Did you say a fire spirit?"

"I did, and it's a long story." Sylas smiled at her. "Anyhow. Welcome to the Underworld. It's not as bad as it sounds."

ABOUT THE AUTHOR

Harmon Cooper is a bestselling author of LitRPG and progression fantasy, including the Pilgrim, Cowboy Necromancer, and War Priest series. Born and raised in Austin, Texas, he lived in Asia for five years before settling in New England.

ABOUT THE AUTHOR

Harmon Cooper is a bestselling author of LitRPG and progression fantasy, including the Pilgrim, Cowboy Necromancer, and War Priest series. Born and raised in Austin, Texas, he lived in Asia for five years before settling in New England.

Podium

DISCOVER
STORIES UNBOUND

PodiumAudio.com

Milton Keynes UK
Ingram Content Group UK Ltd.
UKHW010646290124
436893UK00003B/14